THE
SEARCHER

CHRISTOPHER MORGAN JONES

PENGUIN PRESS | NEW YORK | 2016

PENGUIN PRESS
An imprint of Penguin Random House LLC
375 Hudson Street
New York, New York 10014
penguin.com

LIBRARY OF CONGRESS CATALOGING-IN-PUBLICATION DATA
Names: Morgan Jones, Chris, 1971- author.
Title: The searcher / Christopher Morgan Jones.
Description: New York : Penguin Press, 2016.
Identifiers: LCCN 2015044335 (print) | LCCN 2016001745 (ebook) | ISBN
9781594205590 (hardback) | ISBN 9781101621844 (ebook)
Subjects: LCSH: Business intelligence—Fiction. | Intelligence
officers—Fiction. | Georgia (Republic)—Foreign relations—Russia
(Federation)—Fiction. | Spy stories. | Suspense fiction. | BISAC: FICTION
/ Espionage. | FICTION / Suspense.
Classification: LCC PR6113.O7483 S43 2016 (print) | LCC PR6113.O7483 (ebook)
| DDC 823/.92—dc23
LC record available at http://lccn.loc.gov/2015044335

Printed in the United States of America
1   3   5   7   9   10   8   6   4   2

Designed by Gretchen Achilles

For Rose and Luke

PART
ONE

ONE

Hammer had seen riots before, and knew this was how they began. At the bottom of the hill, in the open square, stood a crowd of three or four thousand, not organized but with a rough air of purpose, waving banners he couldn't read and singing with patchy enthusiasm. On the placards above their heads bobbed the horned head of a balding man with the bland expression of a politician, blood dripping down his chin from a pair of painted fangs. There was a tired anger in the air, and a growing impatience that matched Hammer's own. In and out, this had to be. Find what he was looking for and go home.

The driver slowed on the broken road, muttered something to himself, and, coming to a stop in a queue of cars, sat for a moment shaking his head and blowing out air, as if at some dreary but all too familiar difficulty.

"Can you go back?" said Hammer, sitting forward.

The driver shook his head and gave a full sigh. "Nit shansi," he said, looked over his shoulder at the cars lining up behind, and shrugged.

Somehow Hammer knew what he meant: this was Georgia. They were stuck, it was bad, and there was nothing to be done but wait.

"We need to turn round," he said, but the driver merely shrugged again. Hammer drummed his fingers on his thigh and wondered why they had come this way and how much time it was going to cost. On a case like this you needed a quick start, and he was already two days late.

The sun was low but still strong, and in its stubborn heat the protesters were growing ragged and tetchy. Hammer stopped tapping out e-mails on his phone and from the cool of the car watched them for a while, took in their faces, the way they dressed, the hundred signs that made this crowd a

Georgian crowd. The faces were dark, fine, handsome, Eastern and European at once. Caucasian, Hammer thought; of course, this was what it meant. A democratic group of men and women of all ages, though the front line was mainly men now, their expressions grimmer than the rest. Banners covered in a strange, curved script billowed in the wind and a hundred flags waved alongside them—red crosses on white, and in each quadrant a further red cross, flared and ancient-looking. For a moment Hammer imagined that he had landed in the middle of some forgotten holy war.

A line of police in black carrying shields and long black truncheons contained the crowd. Hammer lowered his window and on the hot air came the sound of chanting, in this growly singsong language that he had hardly had a chance to hear. Beside him the whole front of a derelict town house had been papered with red-and-white election posters bearing another face—reasonable, impassioned, the same one that adorned half the T-shirts in the crowd.

"This the new guy?" said Hammer.

The driver twisted in his seat.

"Candidate. Politician." Hammer pointed at the posters.

"Speak Russky?"

"No." Hammer smiled. "Just American."

The driver raised his eyebrows and from the seat next to him picked up a newspaper, black with strange characters and smudged where his heavy fingers had held it. As he passed it over he jabbed at the headline on the front page.

Hammer took it and thanked him. For a moment he was distracted by movement in the square, where a young man with a shaved head had walked up to a policeman and was now theatrically tearing up a poster in front of him. When he was done he threw the last pieces at the policeman's clear plastic shield, looked him in the eye, and, with a great nod, spat down at his boots. The policeman stepped back a pace but did not respond and the young man went back to his friends with a fist in the air.

Hammer weighed the paper in his hand, felt a moment of fondness for the cheap ink that came off on his fingers, and took in the lead story, to the extent that he could. A single word in fat, round letters ran across all six columns and below it, extending beyond the fold, two photographs: one of a devastated building, its front blown off, the other of the man whose fanged face was being brandished in the square. The words were unintelligible but Hammer had an idea of their meaning.

"The president?" he said.

"President," said the driver, nodding and gesturing at the crowd. "Yes. Diakh."

"He's the guy who started all this, huh?"

The driver turned, his frowning face in profile, and shrugged. The shrug was expansive and seemed to say he didn't understand the question, but it could have meant many other things: *Who know who starts anything?* or, *Who am I to say what any of this means?*

Hammer shrugged back. He understood the gist of it, from the scant reports in English: a bomb had destroyed an apartment block in a Georgian town, killing people as they slept and sending the country into a spiraling whirl of accusation and conspiracy. It was Islamists; it was the Russians; it was the opposition. The latest story to break, and the craziest, was that to win votes the president himself had arranged the whole thing to look like a hellish Russian scheme—that to prove he was the only man capable of protecting his people against that ancient bogeyman he had sacrificed a few of them. Hence the fuss in the square. Hence the fangs.

What a case it would make. The best kind—big, delicate, visible. Dangerous, no doubt. The kind he lived for. Hammer let his instincts play with the idea, plotted its course, drew together a team and a plan in his head, imagined the cast. The president was the obvious client—he had the most to lose, or to save—but perhaps some sort of cross-party commission might be set up, to investigate independently and allow the whole painful business to close. It could be done, for the right fee, but it wasn't what he was here to do, and he had no intention of becoming involved. Besides, Karlo Toreli would have to take part, and Karlo was dead. What kind of case would it be without the man whose scoop had caused this whole mess in the first place?

Hammer put the paper down and, taking a handkerchief from his pocket, cleaned the ink from his fingers. Ahead, cars were beginning to turn round in a mess of back-and-forth; some freed themselves and came back up the hill, dusty Ladas and worn 4 x 4s, but the narrow entrance to the square was soon hopelessly clogged, and horns began to overpower the chants. Space opened up in front of them. The driver swore, pulled out fast into the path of an oncoming taxi, and braked with a jolt before the two cars met.

"Shevetsi."

An inch apart, the cars stared at each other. Hammer's driver hit the steering wheel with the palm of his hand, waved his fist at the windshield, and pointed to the side street into which he wanted to turn. Expressionless behind the dust on its windshield, the other car stayed put. The driver leaned on his horn, adding to the chorus.

"Use the sidewalk," said Hammer, but the driver merely raised a resigned hand. "Use the curb."

In the square, activity again caught Hammer's eye. Another of the protesters, an old man with his belly lazily showing through his unbuttoned denim shirt, had torn the board from his placard and was now sweeping the wooden pole in front of him like an uncertain swordsman finding his range. Others were doing the same, running skirmishes up to the line of police, who had begun to shuffle together stiffly. Before, there had seemed plenty of them; suddenly there did not.

Hammer checked his watch. His plane had landed two hours ago, and it was all of ten miles from the airport to his hotel. This was eating up time he didn't have.

The driver swore again, threw his arm over the seat beside him, and, looking over his shoulder, began to reverse at speed up the hill. Hammer kept his eyes on the crowd. Three men were now beating the clear screens of the policemen's riot shields, and it occurred to him that if everyone followed their lead they would take some holding.

"OK. Time to get out of here."

The car braked abruptly, and in the relative quiet before the driver revved the engine Hammer heard a hard crack, like a stone on glass, and though he saw no one move, nor any gun, he knew without doubt that the protester who fell had been shot.

"Shevetsi," said the driver. He let the engine surge, found his gear, and darted with a lurch down a narrow street to his left. Hammer had a last glimpse of the downed man, his friends stopped around him, and heard a new roar of fury as the moment of shock passed.

"Shevetsi," the driver said, more than once. From behind them came two more shots.

The street was lined with parked cars, each one half on the pavement, half on the pitted tarmac of the road, and though the Mercedes barely fit, the driver took it as fast as he could, the tires squealing as they touched the curb. Despite himself, Hammer started as the car clipped a wing mirror on his side.

Halfway down, an alley led back to the square. He glanced to his right and saw people running toward him, a man stumbling and another helping him up, heads turning to check behind them. A young woman, her hair tied in a flowered scarf, stopped for a moment to take a brick from a crumbled wall and hurl it in a high arc back onto the shields of the police.

This was what a riot looked like—Hammer recognized the mixture of zeal and fear in the eyes, made out in the distance the ones who were enjoying themselves, felt the panic of those running in his direction to get away. Forgotten instincts began to guide him. Best to leave the car and run with the rest, try to look as angry or as scared as everyone else. Cars got stuck in riots. Or take your camera out, make them think you're a newsman. More often than not they'd leave you alone.

But he had no camera, and in these clothes would never pass for a protester. He had packed his least conspicuous things but the truth was that he liked quality and could afford to pay for it. In every fiber he was wearing he was a world apart from the people in the square. The old instincts no longer served. They were for a young man, less respectable than he'd become. Someone without his money, and his luggage, and his briefcase, and the general air of comfort.

"Fast as you can," he said, and shifted in his seat to watch the road behind.

The first protesters appeared and, without stopping, turned in his direction. First came a group running, keen to be gone, but the mass of people emerged into the street in confusion, stumbling ahead, shouting behind them, raising fists, picking up whatever they could find and turning to throw it. Wooden poles swayed like pikes. They were a frantic, angry troop, and Hammer was happy enough to be leaving them behind.

The car braked sharply and the driver let out some grand Georgian oath. Ahead of them an ancient red Nissan, unconscious of what was closing on it, had pushed out into the road, discovered that it hadn't enough room to get its nose past the car in front, and was now inching serenely backward before making another attempt. Hammer's driver pummeled his horn. The first protesters were now level with them, and as Hammer looked back the street was full of people churning in his direction, smashing the windows of the parked cars with bricks and poles. He raised the window but the yelling and the chanting seemed to remain inside the car.

"You need to go round, OK?" shouted Hammer, leaning forward to touch the driver's shoulder and point at the curb. "Go round!"

The driver understood, began to roll the car onto the high curb, and was blocked by the Nissan, which juddered into the road again, taking its time.

"We need to fucking go," said Hammer, locking his door and doing the same on the other side of the car. The noise dulled, for an instant; then the small space filled with a crash of sound. Hammer recoiled, his hands behind his head, forearms tight against his ears. Another crash. He stole a glance. Two men were beating the back windshield, which splintered and sagged.

"Go!" he screamed, but there were people all around now, rocking the car, banging on the windows, pressing their faces up to the glass. Through them he saw the Nissan driving off ahead, and a rock bouncing off its bumper. His driver had shrunk into his seat, arms up round his head.

Ben, I'm going to wring your fucking neck when I find you, thought Hammer and braced himself.

TWO

The man sitting across the table had come on his own, with no sign of an entourage, and had requested that Hammer do the same. That was surprising, and so was his appearance. His suit, though expensive, was too big and sat clumsily on his shoulders, which were lightly scattered with dandruff, and his glasses looked as if they hadn't been cleaned for days. He was mousy in coloring—a little mousy generally, in fact—and somewhat stiff in his greeting, so that if Hammer hadn't seen his photograph and read the headlines he would have found it hard to imagine what was generally held to be true, that this was the richest man in Poland. The head of the risk department of a provincial manufacturing firm, perhaps, or a tax partner in some calcified City law firm, but no ruthless entrepreneur or clear-eyed oligarch.

Still, he had to have something. Such people didn't rise by chance.

From a cheap-looking metal case the man produced a card, slid it across the table, and, while Hammer inspected it, looked down at London, bright and jumbled below them. The view was quite something from up here, or so Hammer had been told, but he took it in calmly, almost blankly, as one might a menu or an invoice. Milek Rapp. Just the name on the card—no company, no phone number.

Hammer passed him his own card in return.

"Welcome, Mr. Rapp. Beautiful day."

"My lawyer says I can trust you."

His voice was deeper than Hammer had expected, and more commanding, like the sound of a tuba coming from a penny whistle. When you heard it, it was easy enough to imagine it being obeyed.

"Then you're well advised."

"This is a sensitive matter."

"I don't doubt it. Most are."

So there would be no small talk, which was a shame; as a rule it was rather more revealing than the big talk. Rapp took a moment to consider the man in front of him, seemed to approve of what he saw, and continued. Behind the smeary lenses of his glasses his eyes were wary and quick. In the main he kept them on Hammer, but he was also checking out the details, just as Hammer was: the cut of his clothes, the lines in his face, the clues in his manner.

"How many leaks have you had, in your time?"

"From my organization? None. In twenty years. From my clients, their lawyers, hangers-on? A few."

"This matter, no one knows about it but me."

"Then we should be fine."

Rapp took his glasses off, inspected the lenses, and, satisfied, put them back on his nose.

"Do you have a family, Mr. Hammer?"

"I don't."

"A wife?"

Hammer knew from his reading that Rapp was on his second. He shook his head. "I came close. But no."

Rapp studied him some more, without hurry, before committing. Hammer knew this tactic: dictate the pace of a meeting and you dictated the meeting itself.

"You control your risk. This is clever."

That wasn't my intention, Hammer wanted to say, but he left it. Across the table Rapp clasped his hands together and Hammer saw the muscles in his forearms flex as he squeezed, hard. The dusty exterior masked a passion or two, it seemed. His fingernails were cut so close that no white showed.

"I am good with risk," said Rapp, his tone matter-of-fact, as if the subject were cooking or some other manual skill. "I make it work for me. There is advantage in it. But not always. Not now."

Hammer thought he knew where this was heading, and wondered whether he should save the man his discomfort and tell him that Ikertu didn't do matrimonial work, no matter who the client. Too grubby, and too messy. But Rapp interested him, and he wanted to see how he would come at it. With a nod he encouraged him to continue.

"In one corner of my life there is currently too much risk. It is dangerous for my interests. I am hoping that you can restore the balance."

"I'm an investigator, Mr. Rapp. I work best with specifics."

Rapp nodded, twice. A resolution made. His hands tensed again and his eyes stayed locked on Hammer's, transmitting a certain expectation of power.

"My wife is sleeping with a man. A young man, Russian."

Hammer nodded in sympathy, and confirmation. He raised a hand.

"Mr. Rapp, we don't do that kind of work. Never have."

"You don't know what I want you to do."

"I can imagine. You want us to prove it's happening. Get some evidence, get rid of the guy."

Rapp shook his head. A brisk shake, impatient, as if Hammer might yet disappoint him.

"I have all that. No. Something else. I want you to study him, this man. Where he goes, who he calls, his e-mails, bank accounts, everything, going back as far as you can."

"You planning on ruining him?"

"I can do that on my own. And I will. No. She gives him money. I know this. An allowance, she will say, but it is blackmail, in another form. I want to show he has done this before, with other women. That it will get worse. That as I was a business proposition to her, so she is to him."

"You know he's done this?"

"I have reason to believe."

"And then what?"

Rapp's eyes screwed a little tighter and he shook his head again, not understanding.

"What does that accomplish?" said Hammer. "Where does it get you?"

"She stops entertaining thoughts of freedom." Rapp's hands relaxed and separated, his voice chill. "It restores the contract. And then I can stop worrying."

Hammer was glad he had allowed Rapp to come this far. This was a species of craziness that in all his years he hadn't seen before, not quite in this form. One for the collection. Before he let him down he had one more question.

"Why us, Mr. Rapp? You clearly have resources."

"Because if this comes from you she will be forced to believe it. From Isaac Hammer."

Hammer raised an eyebrow to acknowledge the compliment.

"Well, peace of mind is important, Mr. Rapp. But I'm not sure we're the right people, and I'm not sure you've thought this through. First thing, we don't eavesdrop. Not on phones, not on e-mails. We can't, and we won't."

Rapp cocked his head a fraction, as if to suggest that between men of the world there need be no pretense about such things.

"It's a practical objection, Mr. Rapp. A lot of people would love me to put a foot wrong, and so for your benefit, and all my clients, and the couple hundred people on this floor whose livelihoods depend on me not screwing things up I try very hard not to. OK? Apart from anything else, we do things properly, I get to charge you more money."

Hammer smiled, a little curtly.

"And we could. We could do things properly. But I don't want to, is the thing. This kind of work I leave alone, because I don't like it, and neither do you. Even if I do a great job, you're never going to think fondly of me again. You're not going to send me a Christmas card. I'm like the guy who comes to do your drains. You forget the sweet smell I leave behind and remember the stench that brought you here in the first place. Some of the stench stays on me. Now, I hate to send you to the competition, which ordinarily is what I do in these situations, because I'm a helpful guy and you have a problem that needs some help. Ordinarily, that's what I'd do. But in this instance, I have to say I don't agree with your strategy."

"I didn't come here for strategy advice, Mr. Hammer."

Hammer smiled again, beginning to mean it. A stubborn client brought out the contrary in him. "Well, with respect, that may be your loss, Mr. Rapp."

The quick eyes were considering again, and Hammer could tell that the conversation had reached a crisis. Even money he would leave, but if he did he wasn't the right sort of client in any case.

Rapp didn't do what most men would have done in such a situation. He didn't narrow his eyes, or stroke his chin, or cross his arms, or try to establish his dominance by staring Hammer out. He just sat, and looked at Hammer, and thought. After perhaps half a minute he gave a little nod; Hammer reciprocated and went on, after a brief ceremonial pause to acknowledge the new footing of their relationship.

"Good. OK. Twenty years ago, this company was maybe a year old, I took on a case for this well-known guy, a very successful guy in entertainment. You'd know him. A big name. And he says to me, 'I think my wife is cheating on me, and I want you to follow her and find out.'"

Rapp cocked his head again, but this time it meant something different. Is this relevant? We may have an understanding but my time is important.

"Bear with me, Mr. Rapp. I don't enjoy this story but I think it's something you need to hear. I tell this guy everything I've just told you, but I made a mistake, which was to tell him that in any case I'd have to charge him a million pounds. This was when million-pound cases weren't so common. I shouldn't have said it, but I thought it would end the conversation. And of course he says, fine, make it two, whatever it takes. So I have nowhere to go, and part of me is thinking, OK, this is good money, and also he's this big guy and back then maybe I'm a little wowed by that, so we do the case. For two months we followed that poor woman everywhere she went. Team of God knows how many people. We did everything. Wired the house, the cars. We knew every step she took. No terrorist has ever been as closely watched, and I hated every minute. I have never liked a case less. And after everything, this huge operation? There was nothing going on. Not a thing. She went to the shops, she played with her kids, she had drinks with her friends. That was it. Didn't so much as smile at another man all that time."

Hammer paused, took a breath, nodded to himself. Rapp was still paying attention.

"I had the guy just pay me my costs, because I didn't like myself very much by this point and didn't want to make a profit. And a year later, less, they divorced. She met someone else and left him."

"She knew what you had been doing?"

"No. We were spotless. Maybe he told her, but I doubt it. No. He wanted it to happen, is my guess, somewhere deep down. Or he made it impossible for it not to. Anyway, point is, some situations, you don't need information. Information's my business, and I believe in it, and I can see you do, too. But this guy, everything he needed to know was in his head, and in hers. He didn't need surveillance, he needed a conversation."

"This is what you're saying? I should talk to my wife?"

Hammer grinned, held his arms up. "That's what pays for all this, Mr. Rapp, advice of that caliber. Of course you should talk to your wife, but that's not what I'm saying. What I'm saying is, take the route you're planning and where does it get you? It doesn't change the situation. She breaks it off with this guy, but what about the next one? Maybe he's not a gold digger, and what then? You've got the same risk and no defense."

"It is always about money."

"Maybe the next guy's rich."

"He will not be as rich as me."

That was true. Hammer had to admire the singularity of the man's perspective.

Rapp's brow tensed a little into a frown. He had the look of someone encountering something foreign for the first time.

"Why do you tell me this?"

"Because it's true, and one day you might remember that. Man like you has other problems, I imagine, and advisers everywhere telling him what he wants to hear."

Rapp pushed his glasses up his nose. Hammer felt the urge to clean them for him.

"So you do not want my business?"

Hammer smiled. "I've told you. It's not business."

Against expectation, and all the odds, Rapp smiled back. It was dry, and quick, but a smile nevertheless. Putting both hands palm down on the table, he gave Hammer one last, significant look, and stood.

"I think you are right to concentrate on your work."

"Keeps things simple."

"Perhaps we will talk again."

Any time, Hammer was going to say, but he was interrupted by the phone on the table.

"Excuse me," said Hammer.

It was Katerina, one of Hammer's directors. "We need you in reception."

"I'm just finishing with someone."

"Well, finish quickly. It's the police."

"What do they want?"

"You. There are fifteen of them."

He put the phone down. If there were fifteen they had come to talk about Ben. No question. Not for the first time Hammer cursed the man and his deceptions.

"My next meeting's here," he said, and ushered his new friend toward the door.

THREE

Once, in Algeria, working for *The Times*, Hammer had watched as two men were pulled from their car by a mob and dragged away to be stoned. His photographer had caught it, and now, watching people bang on the window and pull at the doors, it was that image he remembered: the first man's eyes closed against the sun and the dust and the thought of what was to be done to them as the rioters hauled his friend from the backseat. A Frenchman and a Dane, whose driver had taken a wrong turn on the way to the airport, as innocent of the politics of the place as the children who sat on walls and at windows to watch. They had probably known as much about the Islamists as he knew about Georgian bombs. Hammer hadn't seen them die, the crowd around them was so dense.

His car slowly rocked. The crush of people was now too great for him to tell whether they were being driven on by the police behind. He positioned himself in the middle of the seat, sitting forward, an eye on each door and slipped his wallet and phone from his pockets, stuffing them down the gap between the seat cushions. An urge to flee began to give way to pure fear; two dozen times a year he made a journey like this: car to the airport, comfortable plane, car to the hotel, cosseted all the way and spared contact with anything like real life. Well, here it was. It had been waiting for him.

Above the din he became aware of one voice louder than the rest, and looking up saw a young man, his face pressed against the driver's window and alight with power. He was skinny and gaunt and his eyes were full of the righteousness of his cause. He wore a cap down low on his brow. Shouting the same words over and over and each time pounding the glass with the flat of one hand, he pointed with the other at Hammer in the backseat. The driver shook his head and held his arms up, but the man just repeated his question, jabbing his finger into the back of the car and staring right at Hammer. The driver turned to look at him.

"US," he said, pointing. "American."

From the man's expression and the new fervor of the crowd he guessed being American wasn't good. A friend of the president, on the wrong side of this thawing cold war.

These were his thoughts as the window to his left frosted and with a dead sound became a sheet of ice, a thousand crystals bound together; it held for a moment, sagging heavily, and fell in; after it came hands blindly searching for a handle. In an instant the door was open, and Hammer was sliding across the seat and into the reeling chaos of the crowd. He felt the heat of people's bodies as he was jostled and passed among them. He didn't resist. Curiously, now that he was out of the car he was less afraid. It was happening.

Spun round, this way then that, he was pushed forward until he faced the man with the question. Someone strong locked his arms behind him while the young man spoke.

"Vy Amerikansky. Vy yobaniy Amerikansky," he shouted, one hand screwing into Hammer's collar. His head was tilted in a leer, and flecks of spittle struck Hammer as he talked.

This was Russian. "Niet," Hammer shouted over the noise, shaking his head emphatically. "No." He held the man's gaze, kept his expression open. Match his craziness with as much calm as you can manage. Their eyes were level. "English. UK. London."

"Passport. Pokazhi mne passport."

Hammer struggled against the hold on his arms and shook his head. "I don't have it." He shouted again above the noise all around. "I don't have it."

The young man cocked his head, considering. He was a bony specimen, all of a hundred and forty pounds at most, with staring wide pupils and a sprinkling of mustache that ran across his upper lip and pointed down round his oddly fleshy mouth. His cheeks were pocked from old acne and on his sleeveless white T-shirt was a bad drawing of an AK-47. A revolutionary in his own mind, running on the energy of his convictions and the wildness of the crowd. Hammer understood him, but wanted very much to send an uppercut into that delicate-looking jaw.

Cocking his head the other way the Georgian fished inside Hammer's jacket with his free hand, first one side then the next. After that, the breast pocket and the two side pockets, coming up empty each time. Finally he ran his hands round Hammer's midriff, looked him in the eye, grinned, and ripped his shirt apart to expose a money belt secured around his waist. Unzipping it, he pulled out a passport and a sheaf of dollar bills, and briefly there was an almost innocent pleasure in his face as he felt the notes and registered their value. Folding them, he pushed them into the pocket of his jeans and began to leaf through the passport, rotating it to check the photograph against the face of the birdlike man in front of him, staring hard at both. He shook his head and let out a long, low whistle.

"American. American not good."

"This American's here on vacation. Holiday. Understand? Holiday."

As Hammer said it he felt his right arm being twisted up into its socket. He yelled in pain and protest but could hardly hear himself above the shouting and singing and screaming.

"Tell them to get the fuck off."

"Vacation." The man looked him up and down, releasing his hold on the tie and rubbing the fabric between his fingers. "Amerikansky bullshit."

Glancing back, Hammer saw two men taking his bag and his briefcase from the trunk of the car. The driver looked on with his hands raised.

"There's more money in that case, OK? More dollars. It's locked. Bring it to me."

The young man continued to leaf slowly through the pages of the passport, studying each, as if somehow he had secured a pocket of silence and time, while the strong hand on Hammer's arm continued to twist. The pain built until, unable to bear it, Hammer stamped on his captor's foot, hard, with the sharp edge of his heel, and in the instant that the grip loosened wrenched away and pulled himself clear.

The revolutionary was still grinning at him. Guided by some old instinct that he hadn't drawn on for a long time Hammer sent his fist in a neat up-percut into his jaw, watched the grin slip, and followed with a left to his sharp little nose—felt it give, and the hardness of bone underneath. The guy reeled into the crowd, brought a hand up to the blood on his lip, a look of bewilderment and hurt in his eyes, and Hammer grabbed for the passport that was still in his hand. But he was pulled back; the man who had held him cursed, turned him, and brought an elbow round into his face.

Hammer's sight went and, stumbling backward, he fell into passing bod-ies, which pushed him away. For a moment he swayed in a small space of his own making, black and red pulsing behind his eyes. He tried to compre-hend the pain that cut up through his skull; he'd never been hit like that without gloves. When he opened his eyes, still staggering, his interrogator was there, his bloodied face a foot away, the leering turned to viciousness. Hammer felt first one arm then the other twisted up behind him and winced at the fresh pain.

The punk spat at him, the spittle red, and brought his face so close that Hammer could smell the beer on his breath and something else, something rank and crazed.

"Shevetsi. What is this?"

The punk held the passport up to Hammer's face, jabbing a finger at the page.

"Israel stamps."

Hammer looked down at himself. There was blood on his tie, down his white shirt, dripping onto his jacket. People crowded past, barely aware of him.

"You are fucking Jew. You work for president. You come to kill Georgians."

"Yeah, that's right. I'm going to start with you."

The young man leaned back to grin at his friends and opened his eyes wide and punched Hammer in the stomach, not a great punch but enough to double him up. Then he closed the passport and handed it to someone by him. Hammer's eyes followed it.

"Give me that."

The passport was passed on again. Around them the crowd continued to rush, began to thin.

"Give me the fucking passport."

"You are enemy of Georgia." The young man leered into Hammer's face and pushed his hand up into his throat, straightening up. Hammer felt his breathing tighten. The lock on his arms was total.

"I'm a fucking tourist, you idiot."

Hammer fought for breath. He felt the blood pulsing round his skull.

"Why you here?"

"To drink the waters."

"Why you here?"

The punk was shouting now and showing no signs of backing down. The leer had gone. Hammer was getting no air, and his body was beginning to panic.

There was no way he was going out at the hands of this schmuck. He tried to kick, to bring his knee up into his crotch, but the little fucker was standing to the side of him now and nothing found its target. He jerked his head back but for a runt he had strong hands and he kept an iron hold.

"Why you here?"

Hammer could barely talk and his lungs felt full of acid. The time for wisecracks had gone.

"To find a friend," he said, with the last breath he could find.

The revolutionary looked into his eyes.

"Bullshit."

From somewhere down the street came three shots, and Hammer felt the hold on him relax, just a degree. Then two more shots, from the same gun. The young man looked beyond him down the street, released his grip, and nodded at his friend, who with a glance backward let go of Hammer's arms and moved off, at one again with the scattering crowd. Hammer bent over, sucking in air, and felt himself being pulled upright by the young man, who patted the breast of Hammer's jacket and gave him a look, somewhere between mischief and mania.

"Next time, American," he shouted, and slipped into the tide.

The last stragglers hurried by, throwing some final taunts behind them, until Hammer was alone with his driver and the beaten Mercedes, all its windows smashed and one door hanging from its hinges. Placards lay broken at his feet, and papers spilled from the car onto the ground. He felt in his trouser pocket for his handkerchief and brought it up to his nose, bending over to catch the drips, watching them spread crimson onto the smudged white cotton.

His hand shaking, the driver walked toward him, holding out an open cigarette packet.

"You OK?" said Hammer, twisting his head to look up.

The driver nodded, but his face was white. He offered the pack to Hammer, pushing up a single cigarette.

"Hell yes," said Hammer, and took one. His own hand shook as he reached for it. If his memory was good it had been twenty years since his last.

Before he lit it from the driver's trembling lighter, he sensed movement behind him and a new voice shouted something he didn't understand. The driver let the flame die, raising his hands once more in submission, and as Hammer straightened he saw six policemen rounding the corner, guns up and pointing at him.

FOUR

An investigator, Hammer liked to call himself. Not a private detective, which sounded a little seedy, and anyway, who detected? That wasn't what he did, at any rate. He talked to people, and he scoured documents, and then he sat back and figured out some part of the problem, and then he did some more talking. He liked to talk, in part because he was good at it but mainly because people told you things when they talked back—consciously or unconsciously. Information was to be found in documents or in people's heads, and Hammer had always thought that the heads held the best stuff.

No, he didn't detect. He investigated. It was a better word—it meant something. It suggested you might be interested in getting to the truth.

The fifteen visitors in the Ikertu lobby were detectives, come to do some detecting, he supposed. Some were in uniform, some weren't, but even those in plain clothes were plainly police; they had an air of prerogative that most people coming into this office did not. Hammer resented the deliberate aggression they had shown by turning up in force—five could have done the job, which meant the remainder were here to scare him and unsettle his staff. Katerina was with them, and his two receptionists looked on in confusion.

A woman in a suit had turned to meet him. She was forty, Hammer guessed, a little gaunt, the face tired but the brown eyes keen and sharp and resolutely on his. A band of freckles ran across her cheekbones under pronounced bags. She looked wary but belligerent, as if she spent her days in fluorescent-lit rooms, as she probably did, listening to people lie to her; there was a suppressed fervor about her, a tension that suggested she was trying to appear calmer than she was.

"Isaac Hammer?"

"I'm Ike Hammer."

"Detective Inspector Sander. I have a warrant to search this office for documents and computer equipment."

She handed him a piece of paper. He had seen its like before but this one had the name of his company at the top. Ikertu Limited. Then Isaac Hammer and Ben Webster. Their names still joined together. The wording was stark, familiar, and in order.

For a second he felt unsteady, a sort of swaying in the stomach, like a man feels on land after weeks at sea. Used to calmly advising clients in the worst of crises, now he reeled briefly, buffeted by the thought of confronting his own: advising was easy; living it would not be. But he was quickly in charge of himself again, and with a facility perfected on others' behalf began to rank the dozen questions competing for attention. What was at stake. How to defend himself. What to tell his people.

"Ben Webster no longer works here, Inspector."

"I'm aware of that. It's his computer I want."

Sander pressed her mouth into a line, the opposite of a smile. Better for you if we just start, it said.

"OK, Inspector. This all looks fine. But I'd appreciate it if you could give me two minutes. I have a guest to take care of. He was just leaving."

Hammer turned to gesture toward Rapp, who had come through the glass door into the lobby and was frowning mildly at the crowd he found there. He looked at Hammer in search of an explanation.

"No one leaves," said Sander.

"An hour ago I'd never seen him, nor him me. He has nothing to do with this."

Sander held his eye, establishing control. She was his height, more or less, and her stare was level. Her eyebrows had been plucked into thin arches that gave her a look of fixed surprise.

"Until the search is complete no one leaves."

"He has a plane to catch."

"There'll be other planes."

"You have discretion, no?"

"I do. And I'm exercising it." The eyebrows lifted a little further. "You know your rights, do you, Mr. Hammer?"

"I've had clients in this situation."

"I bet you have. Then you'll know you're not in charge. Your guest stays."

Their audience seemed to sense that this was growing into a contest. Probably it wasn't a fight worth winning; Sander was here to do a job and nothing Hammer might do could stop her. Nor was there any clear benefit in making her like him even less than she seemed to already. But her manner, and the prickling hostility he detected in it, were unnecessary. Raid my offices, by all means, but don't try to humiliate me.

Rapp was watching the business calmly, confident that he occupied a different universe.

"Can we talk for a moment, Inspector? Privately."

Sander shook her head.

"Mr. Hammer, this is a simple process. I ask you for things, you give them to me. There's no negotiation."

If it had been wise, Hammer would have sighed. In his experience, the people who found it so difficult to behave appropriately had some lack in them, a need to inconvenience others to feel good about themselves. He had respect for the police but expected some in return. So be it.

"Inspector, I wasn't going to make a deal. I was going to make a plan, see this all goes smoothly. Get the material ready, go over the computers and the servers and everything, because this can be a complicated process and if I can help make it easy for both of us then I will. We can do it like that. Or we can all just sit here and wait for my lawyer, which may take a while because he'll need to get a big team together to keep an eye on your hundreds of people, and when we get started I can drag the whole thing out with ten questions to your every one. I'm happy either way. No doubt you have all the time in the world. But my friend here, he has a plane to catch, and until just now no connection with this company, and I'd appreciate it greatly if you let him leave. OK? I shouldn't think he'd mind if you checked him for pieces of evidence."

Throughout his speech Hammer kept his eyes on Sander and smiled a cool, hard smile that he didn't mean. Anger tended to show itself as frost in him. But given the chance he'd have marched her out of the building.

Sander looked from Hammer to Rapp and then back to Hammer, calcu-lating, he imagined, the price and value of a compromise.

"What have you been discussing?"

"An e-mail breach in Poland. Nothing that concerns you."

"Who is he?"

Hammer fished inside the top pocket of his jacket, pulled out a card, and passed it to her.

"He's a Polish businessman. He owns a television company." He didn't think it necessary to mention all the others.

"Parker," Sander said, with a nod, and one of the plainclothes officers walked over to Rapp, who held out his briefcase to be searched. Hammer went to shake his hand.

"My apologies."

For the second time, Rapp surprised him by smiling.

"All the best people get raided from time to time, Mr. Hammer. Let me know if you need help with your strategy."

Hammer saw him into the elevator and watched the doors close.

Webster's old office, still unfilled, was designated the hub (their jargon), an irony that may or may not have escaped Sander. Hammer felt it keenly enough as he watched officer after officer tramping across the floor with arms full of folders, papers, binders, taking them to be bagged and numbered as evidence. All those secrets. All that work.

Without Ben, none of this would be happening. Without his obsessions, his crusading, his perpetual fucking moral crisis, this would just be an or-dinary day, with reports to be written and clients to see and money to be made. If Hammer had only acted sooner, on instinct rather than evidence, this less than ordinary day wouldn't be happening. Know someone for ten years and you get used to their nonsense. Your defenses drop. And your standards. If Ben had pulled that shit in his first week he would've been out, straightaway, without so much as a discussion.

Each time Hammer was asked a question—where the servers were kept, what the archiving procedures were, dozens of pointed, dreary questions—

his frustration grew. Who were these people, anyway, to be going through his things? Over this nonsense, this fad of an offense. How had they earned the right? No one had died. If there was a problem here he should be investigating it himself. This was his territory. His jurisdiction.

But not his world. The world was hysterical about small things these days, and heedless of the big ones. That was a change he had seen. It was like a man careering toward a cliff edge straightening his tie. So much energy consumed in the pursuit of empty rectitude.

For a start, he would be forced to defend himself. Better than most he knew how tedious that would be—the countless statements, the endless meetings with solicitors and barristers, the narrowing of one's life to a tiny set of disputed facts. Then he'd have to explain himself. Tomorrow or the next day news would leak and there'd be headlines reporting that the great detective had come unstuck, and sometime after that it would emerge that every e-mail to and from every client, on every imaginable sensitive subject, was now with the police. To each of those clients he would have to give an explanation, and some of them would leave, and he would watch them taking their problems and their confidences elsewhere. That was OK. Fuck 'em. He'd find out who his friends were.

Seven floors below, the world was doing what it always did, oblivious. Through the trees he could see groups of office workers eating their lunch on the grass of Lincoln's Inn Fields, while his own staff stayed inside, unable to leave. Traffic sat clogged on Fleet Street. It was a clear blue day, a late echo of summer. He entertained the childish notion of rappelling down the building and simply running away. Buying a dodgy passport. Spending his fortune somewhere remote where nothing ever happened.

But that was not his way. He had fought to create this company and he would fight to save it.

Sander, it seemed, would cause him as much pain as she could. He'd met her type before, and thought he recognized that particular brand of zeal. There would be no reasoning with her. In her mind, every private investigator was the same: a stalker, a phone tapper, a rummager in other people's rubbish. An unnecessary form of lowlife that lived in the dark spaces left unlit by the shining light of the law. He hated that crap. He'd heard it ever since he came to London, when everyone he met was surprised not to find him trailing spouses in a grimy trench coat and a worn trilby.

There were nearly two hundred people on this floor—his people—and more than anything Hammer wanted them to go home this evening knowing that they had no reason to be nervous about their jobs, or ashamed of them. They did good work, and the Sanders of this world would never see that. As soon as the police had gone he would talk to them. Sitting down at his desk again, flushed with a sort of righteousness of his own, he took a notebook from his pocket and began to sketch out a speech. A short, powerful speech.

It was good to do something, however modest; the first step to restoring control. After the speech he would talk to Hibbert, get the PR people in. Make a plan. But before he could finish writing, Sander appeared in the doorway, Hibbert at her shoulder looking grave and excited. He was a good man, Hibbert, but he did enjoy a crisis.

"Inspector. I hope you found everything you needed."

"We have enough." Sander came a yard into the room, looking pleased with herself. Not triumphal, but expecting triumph.

Hammer looked at Hibbert. "You're staying, yes?"

"You can talk later." Sander moved past Hibbert and up to Hammer's desk. "Isaac Hammer, I am placing you under arrest on suspicion of breaching the Computer Misuse Act 1990. You do not have to say anything, but it may harm your defense if you do not mention when questioned something which you later rely on in court. Anything you do say may be given in evidence."

Hammer had been arrested before but never had his rights been read to him. In Nicaragua they hadn't troubled themselves with the niceties. Nor in Iraq. The words had an unreal quality, as if they hadn't been written to be read aloud.

He looked at Sander and barely heard her. Everything else he had been prepared for, he realized. This, he was not.

FIVE

The police station in Tbilisi was a green glass cube, and it glowed above the river like a jewel in the dusk. There are no secrets here, it said; watch us work for your protection; we are accountable to you. Hammer had been expecting something as dusty and established as his first glimpses of the city, but this was modern, new, even shiny. It might have been the headquarters of a minor insurance company somewhere quiet and European, Berne or Bonn. But tonight it was full of chaos, and even as he was led toward it, wrists cuffed in front of him, Hammer could tell from all the commotion and the running about that the Georgian police were having a bad night.

Inside, all was noise and hurry. Officers in and out of uniform marched new prisoners to the cells, ignoring their colleagues leaving the building to fetch more. The police were focused, their charges angry, drunk, shouting. The place had the strained air of a crisis not yet quite out of control. With his hands cuffed in front of him Hammer was pushed through a chaotic press of people waiting to be booked and into a room at the heart of the building, without windows, where he was left alone.

Two police stations in two days. Good going for a respectable citizen.

It was hot and airless but with his handcuffs on he couldn't take off his jacket or the sweater underneath it. Every so often he gently checked that the bleeding from his nose had stopped. It had, but God it still hurt, and the cartilage slipped around queasily as he examined it. He looked down at himself. The stitching on the cuff of his jacket had come loose, and there was grime on his lapels and on his sleeves where he had been held. Most of the blood was on his shirt, as far as he could tell. When he closed his eyes he heard the crowd's thick roar.

Perhaps a younger man would have sidestepped all that trouble: caught a bus from the airport, run from the car, taken out that little fuck who'd stolen his passport. A wiser one might have sidestepped this whole business a long time ago. In either case, it was time to sharpen up. This wasn't the kind of job that could be done behind one's desk or in meetings, and an adjustment would have to be made. Well, if he needed a jolt, this qualified.

The room was completely blank. White walls, no mirrors, no cameras, no tricks that he could see. After five minutes he tried the door and found it locked.

No one came, and in the bare stillness of the room he waited. Hammer was never truly at rest. In quiet moments, in meetings, in conversations that didn't demand his full attention he tapped out rhythms, twirled pens, doodled on documents. His fingers kept pace with his thoughts. Now they beat an impatient, quickening tattoo on the desk.

His clothes were replaceable, his computer well protected—it would take a government to get inside. If they returned his wallet, which they'd graciously let him recover and then instantly taken, at least he'd have access to money. And medication he guessed he could replace. Presumably Georgians got depressed—God knows they had reason to. All he had lost was his passport, and time the one thing he couldn't control. Six days he had, and the first one, at least, lost to poor planning and bad luck. How long could one go missing in the bureaucracy of Georgia? Weeks perhaps, being processed, interviewed, forgotten.

Still no one came. Without any hope of a response he banged on the door and shouted, in English, Georgian, and Russian. Hello. Gamarjobat. Pazhalsta. Outside he could hear rushing footsteps and doors slamming and distant shouting, and somehow knew that in here he wasn't a priority.

Six o'clock in London. The office would be beginning to wind down. Ordinarily he'd be watching them leave, waving the occasional good night from his office, thinking about his run home, wondering what Mary had left for his supper. Except not tonight, of course. Tonight he'd have been adjusting his tie and checking his shoulders for dandruff, maybe brushing his teeth clean of coffee and the residue of the day's talking before heading out to meet the perfectly nice Barbara Reynolds—a drink at the Connaught and then dinner at that overpriced place round the corner where you paid to watch the preening and the strutting. Not quite a blind date, because they had met once, at the Goulds', but as good as. An interesting woman, a good woman, but a little earnest. Not quick with the jokes, at least not that evening. Even without the whole jail sentence thing on his mind it would have taken him a while to warm the evening up, and he had been relieved to have a good reason to cancel, but God, how good it looked now, sitting in a cell without so much as a window or a glass of water. He'd have settled for warm beer and a conversation about the growing incidence of death among one's friends.

At the two-and-a-half-hour mark the door opened and a man in a bad gray suit came in. He had a bouncing walk and a slight frame at odds with a round, young, heavy face. Skinny pudgy, thought Hammer; office-bound but gym-fit, like that sidekick of Sander's. His thin lips and jutting chin made him look as if he was clenching his teeth, and Hammer wondered whether it was an affectation intended to make him look mean. His eyes helped. They were small and animal and a little too close, and they looked at Hammer from the first as if it was important to stare him into compliance. He was the kind who strove too hard for effect.

Hammer stood and offered his cuffed hand. Thrown by the courtesy, the man looked at it for a moment, then sat down without shaking it.

"Sit," he said.

"Thank you," said Hammer, smiling his most winning smile. This was a tactic, built on an inclination. It made sense to treat people with respect, if only to disarm the ones who weren't expecting it.

The man crossed his legs, made sure that Hammer knew he was comfortable, and gave him a long, appraising look, continuing to establish who was in charge. His suit was beginning to shine at the knees. Hammer kept his smile even.

For a moment the detective, if that's what he was, studied the top sheet of a sheaf of papers, reading it and rereading it and imagining, no doubt, that he was making Hammer uneasy. Hammer suppressed a sigh. At least Sander knew what she was doing.

"No passport?"

"No passport. It was taken from me. In the riot."

"In what?" The detective frowned in annoyance, as if the fault were Hammer's for using a word he didn't know.

"The riot. The march. The big fight, where you found me."

Another stare, and a grunt.

"Why in Georgia?" His voice was a clear tenor, probably a fraction higher than he would have liked.

Hammer had thought about how to answer this. To keep his purpose secret made no sense.

"I'm here to find a friend of mine."

"What friend?"

"He's an Englishman. He used to work for me."

"Name?"

"My name is Isaac Hammer. His is Ben Webster. He came here for the funeral of a friend and no one's seen him since."

The policeman frowned and stared, grimly unbelieving.

"Why are you here?"

"To find my friend."

"Who you work for?"

"No one. I'm here for myself."

The policeman turned the corners of his thin mouth down, shook his head.

"Who you work for?"

"Myself."

"You will tell me."

"I have told you." Hammer maintained his smile. Obstinacy in an investigator was a good thing but should have its limits. "You don't seem to have heard me."

For a moment they looked at each other, until the policeman spoke again.

"No passport, no papers. You are in social demonstration against Republic of Georgia. Two weeks now there is election. This is bad. If you are spy, for Russia, for enemy of Georgia, this is crime. Very bad crime."

"I'm not a spy. I'm a businessman."

"Who you work for?"

Oh Jesus, thought Hammer. They really are going to lock me up.

He leaned forward on his chair, friendly and confidential, hiding all signs of exasperation, his senses working hard to find the essence of this man. He was rigid, that was for sure, unimaginative, leaning on process in the absence of ideas, but he was serious, too, and not corrupt. There was no point offering him money—if that had been his game he would have signaled it by now. An appeal to logic was the only thing that might work. Hammer's hands were usually busy when he talked but it was difficult to be expressive in handcuffs, so he clasped them frankly.

"Can you tell me, are you a policeman, or a spy yourself? I'm guessing you're a policeman."

"Tbilisi police."

"I thought so. You have that straightforward air. Look. I understand you're having a tough evening, and things here aren't easy. Right? You've got a police station full of angry people for the third night running, and things could get a whole lot worse real quick. But I'm not a problem. You've talked to my driver. You know what happened. But in case you didn't, let me tell you. This is my first visit to your fine country. Half an hour from the airport I had my things stolen and my nose broken. I've had better welcomes but I'm prepared to believe it wasn't personal."

He smiled again and went on.

"There wasn't so much spying I could do in that half hour. OK? All I spied was one little punk taking my passport and another big one cracking my face open. I spied his elbow real close, and if you like I can tell you about that. He stole my bags and I'd love you to find them for me. But right now, all I really want is a bed, and some dinner, and in the morning I'll go to the embassy and sort out my passport, and you can get on with the riots, which don't concern me and look like they do need you." He smiled frankly. "How does that sound?"

It was possible, of course, that the policeman had caught barely a word. Throughout, his pinched little eyes had been on Hammer's, but now they looked down to his papers. He slid a single sheet across the table, without comment.

Hammer looked at it.

"This is my company, yes."

"You own company."

"I own the company."

"Here, it says intelligence company."

Hammer gave a reassuring shake of his head. "If I was a spy I wouldn't advertise the fact on my website. I'm an adviser. I help companies. If anything, I'm more of an investigator, like you."

"OK. What you investigate in Tbilisi?"

"Where my friend is. That's all. Ben Webster. Maybe you know what's happened to him. Would you check?"

The policeman continued to stare. There was an ill-defined dimple in his chin that Hammer was beginning to find annoying. He took the piece of paper back from Hammer and placed it carefully in the pile. "Karlo Toreli," he said, watching his fingers thrumming on the table, nonchalant now. "Journalist." Joornaleest. "You know him?"

"I met him once."

"Your company," he tapped the papers firmly with a finger and looked up at Hammer's face, "it gives him money. Why?"

So he wasn't completely stupid.

"He did some work for me. Once or twice."

"Karlo Toreli is dead."

"I know."

"Karlo Toreli is bad person to know."

"Was."

The policeman did his best to stare Hammer down and then stood.

"Worst thing, we find you are spy, you stay here long time. Long time. I talk to my officer."

Hammer raised a palm in protest and started to respond, but the policeman cut him off.

"Best thing, we put you to airport, you go home."

Then Hammer understood. This wasn't a proper interrogation. It was just the prelude to being deported.

SIX

I n a tiny, shabby room in the heavy stone headquarters of the City of
London police Sander had been joined by one of her officers from the
raid, a flushed young man in a gray suit who looked no more at home
here than he had in Ikertu's offices. He was awkward; he couldn't look
Hammer in the eye for longer than a moment. Perhaps he felt the absurdity
of the charge. His shirt was a fraction too small, and he had the tree-trunk
neck of someone who lifted weights, but next to Sander his manner was
meek, making notes and saying little. She had confidence enough for both
of them.

Since the raid, the look of fanaticism in her eyes had calmed to a sort of
excited certainty—the eagerness of a fisherman who has landed a catch
and is looking forward to gutting it. Hammer understood what she was
feeling: the faintly sadistic thrill of knowing. You interrogated someone
to catch them out, not to gather information, and he wouldn't be here if
she wasn't sure she already had enough to make him squirm. Or worse. She
could see her cards; his hadn't yet been dealt. It was possible that he would
spend the night in this place, perhaps many nights. And while he talked,
outside he would have no voice. Days might pass before he could explain
himself, and tonight everyone in his office would go home without the
least idea of what had just happened to them. The thought sat in his head
like a canker.

Sander started the tape, gave the time, announced the people in the
room. Her colleague was called Gibbons, apparently, but a gibbon was a
quick, elegant creature and the name didn't suit him. From a folder of loose
papers he took the first document and handed it to Sander, who slid it across

the table to Hammer, describing the action and the document number for the recording. Hibbert leaned in to look.

"Have you seen that document before, Mr. Hammer?"

Hammer glanced at Hibbert, who nodded.

"I have."

"Would you describe it?"

"It's an invoice from Saber Risk Management to my company, Ikertu Limited."

Risk management. The idea was laughable.

"In the amount of?"

"In the amount of ten thousand pounds."

What an absurd English phrase that was.

"Is there any description on the invoice?"

"'Payment for information services.' That's all it says."

"And the date?"

"June the thirteenth."

"Of this year?"

"Of this year."

"Is there a reference on there?"

There was. And there really needn't have been. How could these idiots be so clever about some things and so stupid about others?

"Project Pearl."

"Tell me about Project Pearl."

If there were two cases Hammer would rather had never existed, this was one of them; the other was the marital surveillance he'd described to Rapp. His mistake had been different in each case, however. The first he shouldn't have taken. Project Pearl he should never have given to Ben.

He checked with Hibbert, and went ahead.

"Project Pearl was a dispute between Canadian Gold, our client, and a mining company called Mistral. Nasty outfit. They were having a fight."

"A fight?"

"A lawsuit. Over a mine near Tashkent."

"What was your job?"

"To understand Mistral. Put pressure on them."

"To dig dirt."

"No." Hammer was firm. "More subtle than that. To see what they'd done before, if there was a pattern. Work out what would make them negotiate."

"To dig dirt."

Hammer knew she was trying to rile him, and that he shouldn't react. But at the same time it would be quicker and simpler for everyone if she stopped.

"Ms. Sander, if someone took something from you, would you just let them?"

"I'd leave it to the law."

"This was Uzbekistan. There is no law."

"Of course. You must like it there."

He paused, watched her carefully, trying to work out where this animus was coming from. Chances were it was one of two things: she knew of colleagues who passed information to private eyes for cash, something Hammer liked as much as she did, or she resented the money to be made doing what he did. Or perhaps she was simply taking out a bad day on a reasonably substantial, reasonably rich suspect—a decent scalp. Probably he would have done the same.

"And Saber? What were these information services?"

"I don't know. I didn't engage them."

Sander took a deep breath, eyebrow raised.

"Really? Who did?"

"I don't know."

"Did you run the case?"

"Ben was the case manager."

"Ben Webster?"

"Yes."

"Who has left the company?"

"Yes."

"But this was your case."

"It's normal for me to delegate projects."

"Is it normal for you to delegate responsibility as well?"

Hammer didn't answer, and for a moment he and Sander simply looked at each other. He could feel pride rising in him, and outrage, and enclosing everything a keen frustration. She had him, and it was his fault.

"Why don't I tell you what Saber does, Mr. Hammer? Seeing as you don't know what your company's been paying them for."

Sander sat back, crossed her legs, jutted her chin in readiness, eyes on his all the time.

"Saber Risk Management, Mr. Hammer, is two former Special Branch officers, one of whom specializes in computer crime. He used to investigate it, and now he commits it. What Saber did for you was hack into Mistral's network and suck out of it every e-mail they could find. Information from which ended up in the lawsuit your client filed a month later in a Toronto court. That's the kind of work Saber does. That's what they did for you."

"My client can't be expected to comment on work done by another company," said Hibbert.

"He can comment on what his company asked them to do." Sander smiled her non-smile. "Mr. Hammer, if you help me now, maybe I'll feel more inclined to help you later on. If you decide to be clever, it makes it marginally harder for me and a lot harder for you. Do you understand?"

Hammer nodded, more in recognition than anything else. He had been waiting for the line. Sander went on.

"Your lawyer will tell you to say as little as possible. Not to give us anything to work with . . ."

"But at some point I have to cooperate and it might as well be now. I'll be helping myself. It always ends up in the same place. I know how it goes, Inspector. I've sat on that side of the desk. And you're right. It never does anyone any good to hold out. So I won't."

Sander, registering the change in tone with the smallest of nods, pressed on.

"Ben Webster. Why did he leave?"

She was good, he had to concede. Hammer breathed deeply, thrummed his fingers on his leg. He'd been in his suit for far too long, and in this windowless, featureless room it felt as if the air was running out. With no hurry he took off his tie, rolled it neatly, placed it on the table, and undid the first button on his shirt. A small act of control.

"He'd run his course. Have you spoken to him?"

"You're telling me you wouldn't know?"

"We no longer speak. And for all I know he might be in the next cell."

"This isn't a cell. Why don't you speak?"

"We agreed about less and less. He left to set up his own company, do his own thing."

"So you didn't get rid of him when you discovered the hacking he'd been doing behind your back?"

Hibbert started to speak but Hammer raised his arm to check him.

"He resigned, all on his own."

"Had he been with you long?"

"Ten years, give or take."

"Really? He's here and happy for ten years and then this happens," she laid a hand on the documents on the table, "and within a couple of months he's gone?"

Hammer smiled, shook his head. Sander watched him, her eyes wide open and waiting for an explanation.

"Ben doesn't really do happy. Not consistently."

"No?"

"He's a complicated guy."

"You mean he's a liability."

"I don't employ liabilities. I've worked with a lot of good people and he's one of the best."

"Then it must have been a blow to lose him. You didn't fight for him to stay?"

Sander was beginning to piss him off. What was all this about, anyway? Why the fuss, the sham gravity? Somebody had hacked some people who were, any sane person would agree, scum. Polluters, corrupters, chiselers away at anything good. Whoever had done this work had made the world a little healthier, and to treat it as a more terrible crime than the ones it had exposed was absurd. A very modern neurosis, wrongheaded, hysterical, trivial. And here he was, caught squarely by it.

"You need to understand something, Inspector—people don't pay me to go round the law. Or Ben. They pay me to supplement it. If you spent a week in my company you'd know I take that very seriously."

Throughout the conversation Sander had been enjoying herself; now she turned stern.

"This isn't a conversation about your ethics, Mr. Hammer. You're a big man, you have money, you have friends. Things have gone your way for a long time. Trouble's new to you. But understand, this is trouble. You of all people ought to recognize it. We know that hacking happened here. That's five years, straightaway. Your case. Your name on the engagement letter, your client, your company. Five for starters, let's say. And that's just the hacking. Then there's the other work Saber was doing for you. That information about the FBI investigation into Mistral? There was nothing about that in the e-mails. It comes out Saber bribed someone for that, your trouble just got a whole lot worse, because your countrymen are going to want to be involved. They're already interested. Bribing a public official, you can say good-bye to another decade. At least. I have it down here you're fifty-eight. Is that correct, Mr. Hammer?"

"That's correct."

"Seventy-three. There's not much living to be done after that. Is that how you imagined your last good years playing out?"

She's trying to make you scared, he told himself. First she makes you uncomfortable, now she makes you scared. It's all just technique.

Fight them as he might, though, no logic was equal to the thoughts that started pressing into his head. For a moment, he saw himself in rooms like this for the rest of his life, without color, without humanity, where living was suspended. No more being in the world. No more Ikertu. No more variety, influence, control. Five years was unimaginable; fifteen a black pit with no bottom. The person sitting across the table from him, he realized—as she wanted him to—had the power to end his life.

Sander had leaned forward again, her hands clasped on the table.

"This is the thing. You're a clever man and no doubt you understood this the moment I arrived in your office, but let's spell it out. Unlike half the people I interview in here you have a lot to lose. If you built that up by sailing close to the wind, then you deserve a fall, a long one, and I'll make it happen. But if you took your eye off the ball for a minute, trusted someone too much, made a mistake, then it makes no sense to throw everything away just to cover that up. In short, Mr. Hammer, you have options. I don't like what you do but if you're more or less blameless in this you should say so."

Hibbert was saying some words that Hammer heard but didn't catch. His mind had settled on a single, determined point.

It wasn't his place to give anyone up. Ben would have to do that himself.

SEVEN

A Georgian policeman in a peaked cap took Hammer from the interview room down to the cells, which were clean enough—white walls, bright under two rows of untiring bluish lights—but decidedly solid, and full of men whose evenings, like his, had been brought firmly to an end. There were perhaps thirty of them in a cell the size of the smallest meeting room in his office back in London. A few looked round when he was pushed through the door; three or four continued to stare at him as he looked about for some space to occupy between all the bodies. As a matter of policy, Hammer returned the stares, just enough, and tried to communicate that he wasn't as small or as puny as he might look. At least his hands were free now, should he need them.

The best places were on the four low bunks, the next best against the wall, and in every inch someone lay slumped. Most had their legs pulled up to allow others to sit cross-legged in the middle, but some stretched out in comfort, and Hammer approached the smallest of these and gestured for him to make room. He was a scrawny man, with sparse hair and one eye half closed and a wispy, uneven growth of beard, and he looked up at Hammer with idle contempt, holding all the power. As if to confirm it, he crossed his legs at the ankles, and then his arms. Others watched the impasse.

Tired, and in no mood for games, Hammer thought. There was a certain purity to this. There was nowhere else to sit. He needed something, and this ratty character didn't want him to have it. A neat conflict with no obvious solution, not least because he was missing his usual tools. He couldn't talk to the man, to reason with him or threaten him or humiliate him, as you might a cocky schoolboy in front of his friends. He had no money to buy him off, and no leverage: he didn't know him, what he wanted, what secrets he needed to keep. An expert opponent in his own world, Hammer found himself in a different arena. And if he didn't find a way round, others would sense his weakness.

Force seemed disproportionate. It was only somewhere to sit, after all. Then his memory jogged him with an idea, and from his shirt pocket he took the driver's cigarette.

"Here," he said, offering it to the man with a friendly hint of a smile. "Something to save face."

The rat considered it, then reached out a hand. Hammer looked down, and when he finally drew up his legs, gave him the cigarette.

"Obliged to you," said Hammer, and sat carefully down in the space.

The air was warm with the smell of old alcohol and tobacco smoke and sweat accumulated over days. Some men slept; some talked and smoked; some stared ahead. Over everyone there was a settled lethargy, as if no one expected anything to happen for a good while yet.

In among them, Hammer's thoughts raced. If the Georgians weren't about to deport him they might leave him in here for a few days while they dealt with more pressing problems. How to get out? Feign illness? Surely that didn't actually work? Bribe a guard. That was more like it. Except without actual cash he had no means of explaining his offer. There wasn't a prison guard anywhere who'd free a prisoner at the sight of him grinning meaningfully and rubbing his fingers together. His watch might do it. But that would be a gross overpayment, and chances were would only see him out of this cell.

Hammer looked around at all his new companions—impassive, contained, unknowably Georgian—and wondered how in the world he was ever going to make himself understood.

It was late now, air was in short supply, and despite the bright lights most slept, heads bobbing on their chests. No one took any notice of Hammer, except for a new arrival who perched on the end of a bunk next to him. He had a shaved head and a dry trickle of blood from a gash on his temple, and every so often he lazily switched his gaze to Hammer, kept it on him for a while, then turned his head again. He had forced someone further down the natural order from his precious spot. Hammer did his best to ignore him.

It wasn't the best environment in which to think. Apart from the heat, and the stale air, all the shifting and sighing, his neighbor was making him feel conspicuous. It didn't take a detective to see that Hammer stood out. Ten years since he had last been in the field, fourteen since his last stay in a cell, and in that time he had become respectable. And rich, by anyone's standards, least of all those of a Tbilisi police station. The fine leather shoes said it, and the linen jacket, bloodied though it was, and the neatly rounded nails that hadn't ever seen manual work. He wasn't so much from a foreign country as from a foreign world. Fourteen years ago he had felt, if not at home, then at least as if he and the jail occupied the same universe. Not now.

Now he had money, and a reputation, and people he hadn't met knew his name. A hundred and ninety-three people relied on him for work. Private bankers competed in vain to look after his fortune, invited him to days of golf in the countryside, persisted in the face of his increasingly impolite refusals. As he had once called important men, journalists now called him for comments and tips and leads, some of which he was happy to give. People listened to him. And though he never spoke of it, nor really thought of it, the money he gave away—to his faith, to protect journalists, to the boxing gym that he wouldn't allow to bear his name—was enough to accomplish good things. He was a big man. A "big macher," his mother would have said, with pride, though she hadn't lived to see him become it.

That was at home. And there not for much longer, perhaps. Here, all she would have seen was a Jew without papers, in a police cell somewhere very close to Russia, doing his best not to catch the eye of a thug who looked like a neo-Nazi and seemed to want for entertainment. I predicted this, she would have said. You court this sort of thing, always have. This once, she would have been right.

The staring had become continuous, he could feel it. Maybe this man had been put here to scare him, or worse. A thought that he should have had long before came and rattled him: if neither Ben nor I make it back, who will look after Elsa?

So absurd, this situation. To be arrested for being beaten up, on a quest to avoid prison.

A strong hand gripped his upper arm. Hammer looked down at it and then up into the eyes of the man with the shaved head. The whites were a filmy red in a face of deadened gray that looked as if it hadn't seen the light in months; a waxen scar stretching back an inch from the corner of his mouth was the only relief. He seemed at once barely alive and animated by some terrible energy. Strengthening his grip, he reached for Hammer's wrist with his free hand and roughly pulled at the cuff, revealing the gold watch underneath. In this place it seemed pointedly flawless. He said something slowly in Georgian, a question, looking into Hammer's eyes.

It was important not to show fear, no matter how much he might feel it. This just wasn't in the normal realm of his experience. Other people fought with their fists; Hammer did his fighting from behind a desk, and until recently on others' behalf. This guy could do him some damage, no question, and if he had a knife in his pocket it could be worse than that. But he didn't want to give up his watch. It was a nice watch, fancy by the standards of a Georgian jail, pretty modest for a man of Hammer's wealth, that he had bought for himself twenty years before at the conclusion of a favorite case, which had also been his first and only real murder investigation. And the thought of this punk pawning it for a few lari and spending the proceeds on junk just didn't sit with him.

With the hand of his free arm he took the man's little finger and firmly bent it up and back, until he felt the tendons tighten and the resistance grow. Hammer was strong, under his jacket, and fit; every day he exercised hard to allow his body to take all the running he put it through. Small he might be, but he was not without power. Sinewy is the word a lazy journalist would use.

He kept the finger just on the edge of pain and held his cell mate's eye.

"I'd like you to let go of my arm," he said, glancing down at the hand on his sleeve.

Confusion and then anger registered in the man's face. He kept his hand where it was and with the other reached for Hammer's neck, driving his thumb up into the soft flesh under the jaw. Hammer felt his throat tighten and his breath weaken, and in among the pain was aware that his opponent had the advantage not only of size but of position: he was a foot above him on the bunk, and his weight pressed down. Calmly and swiftly Hammer wrenched the little finger back as far as it would go; felt something give inside. The man roared and jerked backward, releasing Hammer and clutching his hand.

"Shevetsi!" he shouted. "Shevetsi!"

Hammer was up instantly, his feet set like a boxer in among the bodies and his hands in fists, prepared for a knife or a piece of broken glass.

Wrong-footed, in pain and in shock, Hammer's opponent looked up at him, his expression curiously empty, as if he had no idea what to do next. He scanned the room, saw the drowsy faces taking in his humiliation, brought his eyes back to Hammer, and arranged his brow into an exaggerated frown, continuing to cradle his bad hand. Hammer saw a broader fear in him, and wondered whether it had afflicted him his whole life. The man turned his shoulder to Hammer and brought his fists up, purpose returning to his eyes.

A key clattered in the lock and two police officers, roused no doubt by the noise, stood in the doorway and took in the scene. Then one of them addressed Hammer.

"You. American. Here."

Blood coursing, every sense alert, Hammer unclenched his fists, smoothed down his hair at the sides, and went, with a final look at his adversary that was not without a strange sympathy.

EIGHT

For Hammer, running was thinking. Once a day, sometimes twice: down the hill from Hampstead in the mornings, an easy freewheel to arrive at the office with some momentum, and then back home after work with a problem that wouldn't crack, carrying it up to the top of the city until he had it broken down into pieces.

Not today. However hard he went at the hills he couldn't so much as chip it. He'd read a story once, he forgot where, about a group of Italian resistance fighters who needed to move a massive boulder to build a shelter. It was too big whole, and for hours they hammered at it, big strong men, but it just looked back at them. Then out of the woods came an old man, the last of their party and a mason, and all the others stepped back. He walked all round the rock, ran his hands over it, found his point, and with great precision gave it a distinct but not forceful tap with a sledgehammer. Obediently the boulder fell in two. Today Hammer felt like the first group, hopelessly beating away, his own name a dim ironic taunt.

Sander had released him at seven, after four hours of dogged questioning. No charge, not yet, but he was to return to the station a week from Friday, by which time she would have gone through the haul she'd made that afternoon. No traveling abroad in the meantime. And no talking to anyone about their conversation, unless he wanted to add perverting the course of justice to her list. That included Webster.

The day had been humid and now as he ran the rain started, big soft drops that he barely noticed. Barely noticed the road ahead, or the route that he knew so well, or the people and cars that he threaded in between. Ignored the hamstring that had been tight for days; ran through it, fast on the flat and faster up the hills. What the fuck had Ben done? The question repeated itself like a mantra. What had he done? How great was his talent for creating so much trouble to so little purpose?

Isaac Hammer sent down; the great detective behind bars. A bunch of people would like the idea. The crooks who had come his way, a handful of other investigators, at least half a dozen lawyers whose noses he had put out of joint over the years. The newspapers would have a blast. Spies, corruption, a fall—it was a good story. He'd have been happy to write it in his day. The shame he could endure, but what he couldn't contemplate, and yet knew was certain, was that there was no way Ikertu would survive. Who wants an investigator whose boss isn't even at liberty? Clients would desert him, and his people would rightly follow. He couldn't sell the company, because without him there was nothing to sell, and even if there had been, he wasn't sure he could bring himself to do it. It was his. He had brought it into the world.

No. If this had been his doing, fine, he'd take the rap. But stand by and watch while someone else destroyed his world? Ben had to stand up. There was no other way. He'd made the decision, he'd done the work. And the least he could fucking do, after the risks he'd so blithely taken, would be to come clean for once, without that slippery evasion he wrapped up so neatly in superiority.

What had he said, when he left? You sell hypocrisy, and value nothing but profit.

For days after their final meeting, Hammer had raged over the words, but recently all he had felt was a great sadness—that their friendship had ended, and that Ben had contrived so skillfully to screw up his life.

Now there came fresh fury at the man's own cant. For what had he endangered everything Hammer had made? For a scrap of pride.

Beyond Hampstead the streets flattened out and the houses grew less moneyed and soon Hammer was on Hiley Road, wet through and steaming, walking the last few hundred yards to relax his legs and try to cool his thoughts.

He rang the bell, conscious for the first time of just how wet he was. The rain fell cold on the back of his neck and he counseled himself to be calm. Don't hit the fucker. An unexpected nervousness mingled with his fury, light in his throat, and with it a dull memory of relationships, and rows, and the anxious hope that came with trying to make up.

Elsa opened the door, harassed, as if the last thing she wanted was a caller. Her dark hair fell across one eye, and she pushed it back distractedly.

"Christ, Ike." She seemed concerned more than surprised. "I thought you were a salesman."

So absorbed had he been that he hadn't thought for a moment that he might see her. The question that only now struck him, and for which he had no answer, was what she would do if Ben was no longer around.

"I'm sorry. I was passing, on my way home, and there's something I need to talk to him about. I thought I'd stop by."

Her frown grew puzzled. Elsa was the last person in the world to be convinced by a bad lie.

"He's not here. He's away."

Of course. He would be.

"When's he back?"

"I don't know. Tomorrow maybe. He went to Karlo's funeral."

"Karlo?"

"The journalist."

"Jesus. Karlo?"

Karlo Toreli. He had more life in him than ten men.

"I thought you might have known."

"I'm the last to know things these days. That's kind of unimaginable. Karlo?"

"I'm sorry."

"Listen, I barely knew the guy. But I liked him." He shook his head. "Ben's in Georgia?"

He said it with disbelief but there was no reason to be surprised. It was a miracle he wasn't at one of the poles.

"Ike, you're sodden. Do you want to come in?"

He did, of course. This was the only place that offered him noise and laughter and the healthy purpose of family life—in short spells, maybe, and not regularly, but he loved it here nonetheless. In his mind it was always full of talk and warm light. His own house was old, quiet, beautiful, and in it he felt like a passing tenant; this was a home, and to be a part of it from time to time had given him a glimpse of a sort of happiness from which he feared being completely separated. Elsa it was, he was fairly sure, who had been acute enough to spot this lack in him and kind enough to try to fill it.

"No. Really. Better that I keep running." He smiled. Tried his best, absurdly, to sound breezy. "I like the rain this time of year."

"You're sure? Is everything OK?"

"Everything's fine. Just an old case that's come alive again."

No, he wanted to say. Everything is listing pretty badly and for once, after half a lifetime of being paid to be clever and decisive, I don't really know what to do. I thought I did, but standing here I'm losing certainty.

"How are the kids?"

"They're fine. I was reading to Nancy."

"I'm sorry. You go."

She gave him that reserved, searching look that meant she wasn't fully persuaded.

"You look terrible. Come in. Really. You read to her. She'd love it."

It seemed a scarcely imaginable pleasure, after the day he had had, to be in Nancy's room, reading to his goddaughter from a story that had no mention of policemen or mining companies or hacking or prisons. And yet he couldn't. To come and go and not tell Elsa why he was here was one thing; to be in her house and read to her daughter—to draw comfort from her family even as he prepared to fracture it—that was as repugnant to him as it would be to her.

Regret filling him, Hammer forced a final smile. Another thing Ben had fucked up.

"I'll go. He won't want me here when he gets back. Send her all my love."

"If you're sure."

"It was good to see you."

"You, too."

"Tomorrow?"

"Should be."

"Have him call me. First thing."

There was regret in her smile, too, he thought, as he turned away to make the short run home.

NINE

Hammer was expecting to be marched from the cells into the nearest police car and driven directly to the airport, but instead he was taken back to the first room and left to wait. No cuffs, and an open door: a test, perhaps, or a trap. Much later he would wonder whether it had been a show.

A minute or two passed. He got up, stuck his head out of the door, smiled at the uniformed policeman standing guard. So he wasn't free to leave.

"You speak English?"

The guard turned his head, uncomprehending.

"You fancy a nice watch?" Hammer pulled his cuff up, showed him the watch. "It's a Rolex. Real. Worth real money." He rubbed the fingers of one hand together then began to unbuckle the strap. The guard frowned but leaned in a little. Maybe, if this all worked out, he could come back and buy it back off the bastard.

Above the shouting and the doors opening and closing and the general hubbub he became aware of voices raised outside—a single voice, in fact, a woman's, strong and keen. The guard stiffened and gruffly turned Hammer back toward the room he had just left, pushing him inside.

It was the first time Hammer had heard Georgian spoken by a woman and it took on a different quality, musical but piercing. Someone was getting a dressing-down, and between her controlled, angry questions Hammer heard a man grunting short apologies in reply.

After a minute or two of this, the policeman who had questioned him earlier appeared in the doorway, pushed forward by a woman in a black suit who was slight and full of fury.

"Mr. Hammer," she said, "please listen."

Hammer looked from her rigid face to the policeman, whose head was bowed, all the petty menace gone from his little black eyes.

"Sorry," said the policeman, closing his eyes as the words came out.

The woman stiffened. "Look up," she said, emphasis on each word. "Again."

"Sorry," he said, just meeting Hammer's eye.

"That's OK," said Hammer, not sure what he was witnessing.

"Go," said the woman.

Still stooping, the policeman left.

The woman came round to the side of the desk and offered Hammer her hand. Hammer rose to shake it.

"Mr. Hammer. It is an honor."

The anger in her face had slipped into a smile as easily as snow melting in the sun.

"It is?"

"I am Elene Vekua. I work for the Foreign Ministry. I am sorry for all that has happened here." She handed him his wallet and his phone. "These are yours, I think."

At first sight her face had seemed angled and pointed, as if ruled rather than drawn: a sharp chin and precise cheekbones and an even brow, black hair pulled back from it and tied sleekly behind, thin lips pinched in so that they seemed to disappear. A handsome, unforgiving, symmetrical face, with something regal about it, and something wintry. Watching her force an apology from the policeman, Hammer found it easy to imagine her judging her subjects, and harshly at that.

With the smile everything changed. Austere became welcoming, warmth seemed to fill her pale gray eyes, and the creases of a frown across her brow were smoothed away. Hammer felt himself not judged but studied, as an ornithologist might appraise a rare bird.

"Our police are not so bad, but they are not international people. They have no idea who you are."

"I'd be amazed if they did."

"If they ever looked beyond Georgia they would. Your work is important. Come."

She stood back and ushered him toward the door.

"We're done?"

"I will take you to your hotel."

"How do you know who I am?" said Hammer.

Whoever Elene Vekua was, she warranted a driver, and a Mercedes—not flash, but a Mercedes nevertheless. She sat down in the back with Hammer, turned slightly to him with her back straight, smoothed her skirt, and held her hands clasped in her lap. No jewelry, he noticed, no polish on her nails, no makeup at all, so that in every detail she suggested sufficiency, a great confidence in what she had. The cut of her suit was elegant, her posture correct, her whole manner that of someone who didn't need to embellish to be understood, to speak loud to be heard.

Hammer was a careful watcher of people's devices and tics. From the hard long stares, he had the policeman pinned as ambitious but incompetent; Ben, always circumspect with those he didn't know, had a habit of absently buttoning and unbuttoning his cuffs. Hammer's own custom was to place a hand on a person's upper arm as he went to shake their hand, because it gave the impression that he really was pleased to see them. Most of the time he was.

Vekua was an engager. She held Hammer's eye as if everything he said was wise and new, smiled just the right amount, asked questions that didn't flatter him but required answers that did. After his hours in the cell—for which she apologized many times—he felt himself beginning to revive.

It was past one now, and the city was largely quiet, but further along the river they saw groups of police running after the last stubborn protesters, and fires still burned by the grand buildings on the opposite bank. Every so often the driver swerved to avoid pieces of wood and bits of destroyed bus stop and car bumper in the road.

"It always like this?" said Hammer.

"It can seem that way."

"Looks like my friend picked a good time to come."

"We are accustomed to it. You are not, I think."

Hammer had underestimated the tension. Probably Ben had, too. Strange, how hard it was to see a situation until you were in it. He felt his nose, which moved uncertainly under his touch, and shrugged.

"I used to be."

"The riots are not dangerous. What lies behind is dangerous."

Hammer waited for her to explain.

"For ten years Georgia has been drunk on her freedom, like a wife who runs from her husband. Russia watches her dance and waits for her to come close enough to snatch back. This is that time. Quietly, through an election. The modern way. And the president knows this."

"And the other guy? His opponent?"

"He is a friend of Russia. His money comes from men who owe their fortunes to Russia."

"OK. I get it. So when the bomb goes off, everyone thinks it's the Russians, because who else would do such a thing, and the president says how terrible, don't vote for the other guy, he's a Russian in disguise."

"Except it went wrong. So now the president is finished."

"You're kidding me. That's how things work around here? Really?"

"Logic gets twisted in Georgia. In the pursuit of survival." She shook her head with a sort of thoughtful regret. "You more than anyone know that it is difficult to find the truth. In Georgia it is impossible. To be an investigator here you must be happy with half an answer. Or two answers. You must be happy with doubt."

"What's your half answer?"

She hesitated, thinking. "Most probably the president did not know. He is a vain man, he thinks he is the center of all things, but he would not do this. He is not evil. And not so crazy."

"So who did it?"

"In my service there are evil men."

"Your service?"

"I am a spy, Mr. Hammer. I work for our intelligence agency."

"You're very direct."

"You would find out. Perhaps you know already." She smiled. "A small group did this for the president. Many of my colleagues, they still hate the Russians."

The car had slowed to let a convoy of police vans pass, sirens going.

"And Karlo Toreli?" he said.

Vekua held his eye.

"That is a very direct question. And sensitive."

"I'm like you. I like things direct."

She continued to watch him, making up her mind.

"You told the police that you have no client."

"Just me. No oligarchs, no Russians, nothing sinister. On my word."

"Why are you here, Mr. Hammer? Really?"

To save my hide, he thought. Had she spoken to London?

"To fulfill an obligation."

With a brisk nod she decided.

"I want to suggest a deal. But it is also my best advice."

"Please."

"I will tell you what I know. But then you must leave it alone. Just find your friend. If you investigate the bomb, or Toreli, I cannot protect you."

"I'm no spy."

"I know this. I am not an idiot. But these people. They think you have been brought here to save the president before the election. Some think this. Others think you are here to destroy him. How? I asked them." An incredulous smile. "What would he do? He is one man. But he is a spy, they tell me. There is a plot. The American. He works for the oligarchs who oppose democracy in our country." She paused and held his eyes with hers. There was fire somewhere behind their level gray, he was sure. "This is a joke. They care nothing for democracy."

"So I'm famous, huh?"

"At times like this everything has a meaning. Your arrival. Your departure." Even in the dark of the car her eyes seemed to glow icily. "Do you accept my terms?"

"Go ahead."

Vekua clasped her hands, utterly serious. This was more like the face he had seen berating the policeman.

"The bomb exploded in Gori, an hour from here. A normal town. Immediately people think of Russia because Gori is close to the border. The target was a normal apartment building, nothing special to it. People were sleeping. A large part of the building was destroyed."

She paused to let Hammer consider the words. He did; it was hard not to.

"The bomb killed seventeen Georgians and two men who were running from the building. They were rebels, from Dagestan. They set the bomb. We knew them. Their group claimed responsibility."

"Did they screw up? Or did someone blow it early?"

"The bomb was meant to kill them. Someone wanted them to be found."

"They were set up."

"Of course. Whoever was responsible, this is certain. They were running to their car, which was not destroyed. Inside the car were two telephones. Untraceable, clean. One of these phones had received calls from only one other number. We know from network data that all of these calls were made from inside my building. My headquarters. Inside, or near."

"You've got a mole."

Vekua didn't respond.

"Do you know who it is?"

"I cannot say."

She gave him a look that told him this track was closed.

"So this is how it went. Bear with me. Someone in your organization, some renegade group, they get these guys from Dagestan to do the dirty work, and then they send the journalists looking in the wrong direction, and everyone thinks it's the Russians, because who else would pull a stunt like that. Yes? And then Karlo spills the beans that actually, it's not your age-old enemy, it's your government. So what did he find out? What gave the game away?"

"Probably he had a source."

"No shit."

Vekua shrugged and held his eye. That's all I'm giving you. The car had crossed a bridge and turned onto cobbles that shone with the rain that had begun to fall. From inside her jacket she took a business card. The streets were narrow now and dark, but the sparsely set lamps gave just enough light. Colonel Elene Vekua. A colonel; he was flattered.

"This is not an easy country. Not today, certainly. If you need help you can call me."

"Do you know where my friend is?"

"He has not been arrested. I have checked. There is nothing on our computers."

The car slowed to a stop in a small courtyard of jumbled old buildings.

"How many hospitals are there in Tbilisi?"

"Not so many. But we would know if he was there."

"I'm sure you would." Hammer opened his door. "Why are you helping me?"

Here was the smile at its most deliberate.

"Because I want you to find your friend and leave, as soon as you can. Understand, you are an interesting person. Myself, I am pleased you are here. Georgia is not."

TEN

One final run hard up the hill to Hampstead and then home. Wednesday was one of Mary's nights off, and as Hammer turned the key in the lock he found himself hoping that she had decided to stay in, as she sometimes did. No. Even before he saw the oven light on and the usual note on the kitchen table he knew the house was empty.

Good evening, the note said. Will you ever get in at a reasonable hour? I'll be at my sister's tonight and will see you tomorrow. Hammer sat down at the kitchen table to read it, then simply sat for a while, gazing at the last light of the day over London, not thinking, until his wet clothes grew cold and clung to him.

When the kitchen grew dark he got up, showered, changed, ate. Sat by the unlit fire in his sitting room with a bottle of decent whiskey and tried one book after another, failing to settle on any.

It was after midnight when the phone rang. The landline, which no one ever used; his sister, it might be. Or the police.

"Hello."

"Ike."

"Elsa. Hey."

"Were you asleep?"

"Not even close. This is early. You OK?"

"Ike, I'm worried about him."

Worried how? Hammer wanted to ask. Worried because he's on the other side of the world causing trouble, as usual, or worried because when he gets back he won't be allowed near any trouble for a long time? It was possible that the police had been to see her. He didn't enjoy the thought, but for his own sake he rather hoped that they had.

"Why? What's up?"

"It might be nothing."

"Tell me."

"He's not answering his phone. I don't know where he is."

"I thought you said he was in Georgia."

"He was. He is. He was coming home yesterday, but he phoned me in the morning and told me he was staying an extra day, maybe two."

Oh boy, thought Hammer. This was like him.

"I didn't . . . We argued about it. He shouldn't have been there at all, the way things are going for him. For us. I haven't heard from him since."

Hammer put his book down, closed his eyes, and leaned back in the chair.

"OK. It's not even two days. And you know how he is."

"Ike, he always calls. Or lets me know. Even when things aren't good. We've never gone a day without speaking to each other."

"Really?"

"Really. He hates having things on his precious conscience."

Hammer shook his head and finished what was left in his glass. Elsa was not a woman who worried easily, and it would be like the bastard to get himself killed this week.

"You want me to come over?"

"Really?"

"Sure. You know where he was staying?"

The man's capacity for chaos was phenomenal. First he destroys my company and now he's doing his best to finish his family.

Elsa hadn't been harassed earlier, he realized, so much as anxious. When she opened the door to him now she was smiling, but the shine had gone from her eyes, and the familiar sense of cool command was missing. He kissed her on the cheek and held her arms.

"You OK?"

"Ike. Thank you."

"Hey. I haven't done anything yet."

He followed her through to the kitchen at the back of the house. Everything was as neat as it always was.

"I'm drinking whiskey."

"Then so am I."

Elsa brought her glass from the table, took another down from the shelf, uncorked a bottle standing on the side, and poured a generous slug into each. It was a supermarket brand, not their usual. He nodded yes to water and when she was done she handed one to him and by way of a toast raised hers an inch.

"Nancy was sorry you didn't come up."

"I couldn't, really."

"Just because you and Ben aren't speaking doesn't mean we can't see you."

It wasn't that, exactly, Hammer wanted to say, but instead he only smiled.

He had never seen Elsa like this—her gray eyes were tired and she was wearing makeup to mask the bags underneath. She never wore makeup. It occurred to him that she hadn't slept.

"So I called the hotel," he said. "He checked out yesterday. Booked it last week, arrived Saturday, left yesterday as planned. Used his Visa card, three nights. No calls on the hotel's phones. The person I spoke to didn't know exactly when he went."

"What does that tell us?"

"Not much. How does he manage his money?"

Elsa frowned.

"Joint account, or does he have his own?"

"He has his own."

"Manages it online?"

"No. He doesn't trust the security."

"He calls them?" She nodded. "You know his code? His password?"

"No. Should I?"

"It would help, but no. What did he say when he called?"

"He said he had something to check out, and probably it would just be one more day, no more than two."

"Check what out?"

"Christ, Ike, I don't know. Whatever you people check out."

Elsa took a good swallow of whiskey, and her near-black hair fell over one eye as she drank. There was a settled, quiet fear on her face and something else that Hammer couldn't interpret.

"Fuck was he doing, going to the other side of the world for a funeral?"

Elsa shook her head. "Don't. We had that discussion."

"Long way to go."

"Long way to go. He could have sent a wreath like a normal person. Do you know anyone there?"

Hammer blew out a sigh. "It's not my part of the world. Just Karlo."

"Did you ever meet him?"

"A couple of times. When he was seeing Ben. One night we had dinner."

"Were there toasts?"

"Endless. I couldn't keep up."

Elsa smiled. "It's sad."

"It sure is. How did he go?"

"He killed himself. Apparently."

"You're kidding me. Karlo?"

"That's what Ben said."

"My God. I can't imagine Karlo keeping quiet long enough to kill himself."

Hammer sat back and folded his arms. Now it was beginning to make sense.

"So he went to investigate."

"No. Ben? He went for the museums. The history."

She set her glass down on the table, her eyes red with anger, Hammer realized, as much as worry.

"It hasn't been easy, Ike. Since he left you." She toyed with her glass for a moment, turning it round and round. "Why do you want to speak to him?"

He looked her in the eye and hoped he looked honest. "There's a problem with an old case. I need to sort it out. One of those things—important and not important."

He might have hesitated for the merest instant before replying. Now she watched him coolly, as he imagined she watched her patients as they recounted their problems, and not for the first time it struck him that her profession and his own were not so different.

"You might as well tell me."

How had he not anticipated this? His plan had been to say nothing, in part because he shouldn't be saying anything but mainly because he had no desire to make her more worried than she had to be. He hadn't imagined for a moment that she would be on to him so quickly. Well, shame on him for underestimating her.

"It's nothing. Someone who worked on it—an outside guy—let's just say he isn't honoring his confidentiality agreement."

"Ike, you came to the house. Unannounced, in the pissing rain, to talk to a man who last time you saw him pretty much called you a worthless piece of shit. Also, you're tapping and fidgeting even more than you usually do. So tell me what it is, because I have a feeling I need to know."

Hammer took a drink of his Scotch, but only to delay. She had him.

"You're the one I should've hired."

He told her almost everything, stopping short of explaining why he needed Ben, and when he was done she kept her eyes on his for what felt like a full thirty seconds. She didn't look tired anymore.

"Has he heard from them?" he asked when he was done. At the back of his mind was a growing notion that Ben's absence was way too convenient.

"From the police? Like I'd know." She relented. "No, I don't think so."

"This is the first you've heard?"

"Should you be warning him? Isn't that tipping off?"

"No." Guilt crept up on him. Not for his sake but for hers. He should have been straight from the start.

"It's not a warning, is it?"

Hammer said nothing.

"Christ, Ike. What, you want to interrogate him, is that it? Get him to confess?"

"I need to know what he's done."

"He's dug you a hole, and you need him to fill it."

Abashed, he held her gaze, and quickly righted himself. That was it, in its essence. He had no reason to feel bad about it.

"This thing could kill the firm."

"Oh, Jesus, the firm. So you need a sacrifice?"

"No. I need to make sure he realizes his responsibility."

Her face opened up, incredulous.

"That's why you want to find him? I don't believe this, Ike. I thought you were helping me."

"You think I like this? I keep quiet, they send me down. I say something, they go after Ben. It's a shit choice, but it's not a choice. I shouldn't have let him get out of control in the first place. That one's on me. But everything else is his doing."

Elsa pushed her glass away and gazed into the blackness of the kitchen window. Hammer in turn watched her, and examined his position. What was he meant to do, help Ben out? Take the blame himself? Let him hide out in Georgia for a while until it was all too late?

If he was hiding. More likely he was in one of three places: a hospital, a cell, or somewhere worse than either. None was good.

With a sigh, Elsa returned to him.

"What Ben said to you when he left was terrible. It must have hurt. But it's no reason to punish him. Can't you work on this together?"

"We're past that."

"You two. My God. You're a pair of fucking mules."

"I'm going to go and find him."

"Excuse me?"

"What can I do? I'd say the odds of him just forgetting to phone home are what, ten to one? He's not cavalier, he's obsessed. Something's happened out there, and if I leave it we're both fucked. You and I. Never mind him for a moment. Let's just pretend that he doesn't get to dictate events, for once,

OK? So, which is better? We let him rot in Georgia, or he comes back to face the music he's written for himself? You tell me."

The fight that had flared up in her had died, and when she looked at him now her eyes were resigned, and simply sad.

"All right. Find him. And then forgive him. It's eating you up."

ELEVEN

W hy are you here? Vekua's question, like everything about her, was astute. Why are you here, really?

The cause of all this, the whole business, Hammer could trace back years, to the day he had hired Ben on the suggestion of a client who'd been the target of his best work; and through the hundred cases he had handled since, each one a shade harder to control than the last. But the most prominent moment, the one that wouldn't leave his thoughts, was an evening at the Websters' all of three months before. It had happened on a Sunday, and Hammer hadn't been ready for it, even though he had known it was coming.

The three of them had been sitting at the kitchen table, Elsa, Ben, and Hammer. Elsa had poured wine, and when each glass was full Hammer had raised his to make a toast. Rain was beating steadily on a skylight above their heads.

"To your fine children, especially my delightful goddaughter. And to their parents, who seem to be doing a nice job."

Elsa smiled at Webster and the three touched glasses.

"Thanks, Ike."

Hammer nodded with a touch of gravity and drank. A toast was a serious thing to him.

"It was a fun party."

"Thank you for coming."

He smiled. "You know how busy my weekends are."

"And for her present," said Webster. "That was generous."

"Not at all." He drank. "That was a lot of kids. I never saw so many."

"She'll be writing thank-yous for days."

"She can leave mine till last. Listen, you must be beat. I'm going to call a cab."

"Don't be silly," said Elsa. "We need adult company. When Daniel's in bed I'll make some supper. Stay."

"I'll take him up," said Webster.

"I'm fine. You two talk."

She gave the impression there was something for them to talk about, and in that moment Hammer imagined Webster sharing his troubles in recent weeks—the old narrative that circled round and couldn't quite resolve itself: Ben the idealistic taker of risks, tamped down by his conservative boss. Really, Elsa should be mediating. They needed a professional. Still smiling, but meaning it less than he had, he half stood as she left the table, an old habit that somehow felt natural enough in New York but stiff in London. Nevertheless he did it. It was a question of form.

For a moment he and Webster looked at each other, the comfortable, wary look of men who know each other thoroughly but just short of understanding. They were friends, and their friendship extended far beyond the office, so that when Elsa told him he was now a part of the family Hammer knew that was almost true; but its basis was still work, and work was always between them. Particularly now.

Webster drank his glass down, topped up Hammer's, then filled his own.

"Long day."

"I bet."

"I may be in a little late tomorrow. I have to talk to Nancy's teacher about something."

"Take your time. Everything OK?"

"One of the girls in her class is throwing her weight around. I'm glad I wasn't a little girl. The politics are vicious."

"You want me to have a word?"

"With Nancy?"

"With the girl."

Webster smiled. "Dig some dirt?"

"Something like that."

"If it comes to that I'll let you know." Webster took another sip of wine, his eyes on the table, as if searching there for the right way to say something until now unsaid. Without looking up he said, "That was some present."

"Too much?"

"Not for her, no."

"I talked to Elsa about it."

"I wish she'd talked to me."

"It was something for her future."

"I know. But we try to keep it moderate. Their friends get such ridiculous things."

"If it was excessive I'm sorry."

"And I need to think about Daniel, keeping things fair."

"I'd be happy to do the same for Daniel."

"That's not really the point."

What's eating you? Hammer wanted to say; what is it you really want to discuss? But he held the thought. This was not the place for that conversation. These dark moods that came on Webster were best given a wide berth and dispelled at the start of a new day, with a sort of blithe energy.

"Look, sleep on it. I'm happy to scale it back if it's too much."

Webster drank a good draft of wine. "OK."

"OK." Hammer held his eye and tried to let him know that he meant no offense and wanted no conflict. He pushed his chair back. "I'm going to go. I think I'll walk."

"It's pissing down."

"I have a coat. Don't worry." He stood and held out his hand. "That was a lovely day. Thank you."

Webster stood but didn't shake. "You in tomorrow?"

"In but busy. I've got the auditors in the morning and the Italians in the afternoon."

"Can we talk about Pearl?"

"Find me. We'll squeeze it in."

"The client's here on Tuesday. We need to talk about it properly."

"And we will."

"I'm not sure you understand what's going on."

"I'm pretty sure I do."

Webster cocked his head, just a half inch. "What does that mean?"

"Ben, not here. When I'm done with the auditors I'll look for you. OK?"

"You'll look for me and you'll give me just enough time to brush me off. I know. Listen. I'm serious about this. The case is a joke. We're not being anything like aggressive enough. They're as dirty as the coal they dig out of the ground, and we're treating them like they're saints."

"What's aggressive?"

"Fight fire with fire. Do some proper work."

Hammer sighed. Here it came. If it had to be now he could do it now.

"OK. We've been through this. We do anything out of line on this case and nothing good happens. Even assuming we find something, we can't use it because it'll be obvious how we got it, and then we're in trouble, and so is the client. OK? You get paid to be clever about it. Be clever."

"Clever's getting us nowhere."

"So you thought you'd be stupid, is that it?"

"Practical."

"Is that right? Why don't you tell me what those sleazeballs at Saber have been doing on this case?"

"You've been spying on me."

"I told Karen I wanted to see any invoices from them or anyone else who does what they do. That's not spying, it's self-preservation."

"Does that mean we haven't paid him?"

"What's he been doing?"

"Some proper work. All legal."

"You need to tell me."

"You're the detective."

Hammer shook his head. If he didn't love Ben he wouldn't have put up with him as long as he had. No talent was worth this.

"When you give those idiots work, you're an officer of the company. Right? OK? You're not Ben Webster, agent of truth. You're Ben Webster, employee. Sharer of responsibility. Understand? Secrets are not acceptable."

"I do what I think is best for the client."

"No, you don't. You do whatever you think is necessary for this crusade you're on. I don't pay you to crusade."

"Then don't pay me."

"Excuse me?"

"Don't pay me. I quit."

Hammer looked steadily in his eyes and saw that he meant it.

"This is it?"

Webster's voice had been quiet but now it rose, as if some long-held conviction could finally be aired.

"This is it. Listen to you. You don't care about nailing these fuckers. You don't care if the client wins or loses. It's all about the company. Keeping it safe and keeping it fed. Everything else, it's flexible. You want a certificate saying it's OK to do business with that crook? Fine. We'll find a way. Thirty grand. You want to take down those Russians who've been stealing from you? Pay us a hundred grand a month and we'll see how many months we can rack up. You're the Russian who's been doing the stealing? I'm sure there's a gloss we can put on that. You call it your philosophy but it's whatever the company needs. When you were a reporter you cared about the truth, the one you can't forge. Now, you make a big thing of selling the truth but actually it's all profit, and growth, and running the machine. The machine has to keep running, and it's corrupted you. That's what it does, turns everyone into a hypocrite. Hypocrisy is what you sell. Which is a shame. A fucking shame. Because you should have made a difference, and if I'm saying too much it's because when I joined up I expected so much more. And you know what, I think you did, too. Something died in you, Ike. That's why you get depressed. That's why you run. To keep a bit of you alive."

He stopped for a moment, surprised by how far he had gone. Or just to let the words do their work.

"I thought we were going to do great things, but apparently I'm just an employee. Just someone you pay like your clients pay you. And that's fine. You paid me, and now you don't. You bought me, but now it's over. I'm setting myself free. So I don't ever have to suck up to some entitled fuck of a banker or fawn over some minor-league oligarch who's made a fortune from chiseling and pimping and wants me to make him even more money or protect the rotten heap of shit he's already got. I've had it with them, and I've had it with you. Tomorrow I'm going to take my children to school and talk to Nancy's teacher and then I'm going to find myself a job that doesn't involve me selling my fucking soul every day of the fucking week."

Hammer heard the words as Webster jabbed them at him, and though he'd known for a while they were coming, still each one pierced him. Blood coursed through him but he kept his voice cold and level.

"I'll get someone to clear up your things. I don't want to see you in the office again."

Webster frowned, almost recoiled.

"That it? You've got nothing to say?"

"Plenty. But you wouldn't hear it." Hammer looked around the kitchen, as if taking his farewell. "I'm going to leave you with all your certainty, in the house my company paid for, and tomorrow I'll get someone to replace you, and Ikertu will carry on as before. OK? And when you find this world where everything's correct and no one ever had to make a compromise, and money doesn't matter and people don't need jobs, you let us know, OK, and see how many follow. Because we would all like to go there, no question. You let me know."

With a last look at Ben he turned to go, and saw Elsa standing in the doorway.

"What's going on?"

"Ike's leaving."

Hammer held her by the arms and kissed her on each cheek. "Thank you. It was a lovely party."

"Ike, what's he said?"

"Something he should have said a long time ago."

PART
TWO

ONE

===

H ammer believed in enduring what came his way, and while he might not look like much, he could put up with a lot. Cold, hunger, boredom, all glanced off him; before he had settled into comfort, for two decades he had reported the world's deepest injustices and darkest horrors as if they left no mark (though the reverse was often true). It was important to him not to burden others with his weaknesses.

Sleep, though, he had always needed. Seven hours was the right number; six and a half was livable; less than six, he was not himself. His brain clouded, and when there was thinking to be done, as there almost always was, he resented the handicap. To clear his head, he had taken up running. Now he ran almost every day, so that to miss it was as bad as missing his night's rest, and for all that it kept him fit, he recognized in his bondage to it something of the rigidity of an old man's routine. But this morning there would be no running, because his shoes and his kit were in the same bush as his clothes and his razor and his books.

Dogs barking woke him at first light. He was dreaming of home, which even after twenty years in London was still New York; of running up an endless set of steps in Central Park toward a policeman sitting reading a newspaper in a chair.

Outside, Tbilisi was finally quiet, bar a drunk or two on the bridge and the pack of strays gathered at the base of the cliff beneath his balcony. This morning it seemed utterly benign. Lined with plane trees, the river rolled silently by and above it, dotted over a great ridge of land, twenty squat churches with identical cone-topped towers glowed like torches above yellow floodlights. A castle sat on top of the ridge, with a heavy keep and a snaking wall, and from it galleried, pink-roofed houses tumbled down the hill as if they had been dropped there and left to settle where they might. The place was old and stubborn and ageless, waiting patiently for the next invasion that would fail to altogether destroy it.

Calm and beautiful it looked, with the sun slowly bringing the dawn. He might be tired, dried out, hungry, still sore, a little jet-lagged (it was barely two in London), but it was hard to resent this place that had done its best to reject him the evening before. For an instant he imagined being in his own bed, ahead of him a regular day of running and talking and thinking, and felt the uneasy satisfaction of knowing that here he would have no choice but to extend himself.

He showered, checked the progress of the bruises on his arms and chest and the dark crescent under his eye, adjusted the bandage on his nose, and dressed in yesterday's battered clothes. What a sight he was; like a hobo, or a ghoul. Sander might enjoy seeing him this reduced.

Without dwelling on the thought he left his room and wandered without purpose into this strange, raging, enchanted place that didn't seem to want him. He couldn't blame it for the rejection; it was a wonder it allowed strangers in at all. In the scant ten pages of history he had read on the plane there had appeared so many invasions, sackings, and razings that even he, a student of conflict, began first to marvel and then simply to lose count. For hundreds of years the Persians and the Turks and the Mongols and the Armenians had taken turns to savage Georgia, drawn by its fertility and its place at the heart of the world, forcing its people to retreat into the mountains in the north and leaving its history an endless seesawing of raid and counterraid. Being destroyed and rebuilt had become the pattern of Tbilisi's existence. And then, only two centuries ago, the Russians had arrived, finally crossing the Caucasus range, to offer protection and deliver the rawest betrayal.

This, he imagined, was why its people rioted. He would have built a wall around the city and let no one in.

In the brightening morning he went down to the river, giving the dogs plenty of room, across the bridge and up into the old town, past elegant, sagging buildings, old plane trees, courtyards shaded by vines, walls collapsed into heaps of brick and laths and plaster, rusted pipes crossing above his head, glazed balconies with not a pane of glass intact.

Tbilisi looked as if it had been sacked again last night, but there had been no rioting here. It was decay that had done all this, the long, slow violence of poverty and time. Hammer, revived by the beauty of it, walked at a slowing pace, up through steepening streets toward the castle. This early, with no one in sight, everything felt ancient and unused, like some ruined citadel abandoned long before, but people still lived here, and as the sun rose his eye began to pick out the signs: clothes hung on washing lines, flowers growing in tubs on sills, fresh graffiti inside houses whose outer walls had fallen away.

In his torn jacket and bloodstained shirt, hungrier than he had been in years—going through his own process of revival—he seemed to belong, and he began to feel a faint and forgotten sense of freedom. The trials of the day before were over, and here he was in this stirring, seductive, illogical place, so distant from London, without papers or possessions, without a client, with no authority or support; with nothing to return to except trouble; with nothing, in fact, but a purpose, and much work to do. Today was Friday. By Tuesday he had to be on the way home with his bounty. Anything else was too little or too late.

As he reached this conclusion he stopped, and found himself by one of the churches whose conical towers rose up all over the old city like the tips of lances. Backing up against the hill under the castle, it seemed like the last forgotten building in a forgotten city; its pinkish brick was crumbling and its windows were dark. The only sign of use was a yellow notice taped to the carved and blackened door setting out a crude code of conduct in a series of symbols crossed through with thick red lines. No sundresses, it said; no shorts, no smoking, no guns.

Early that morning he had discovered from the wan young girl in reception that Ben had left the hotel on Tuesday, three days before, and that while room 27 was not available, an identical one above it was free. No,

Mr. Webster had left nothing behind, and because she hadn't worked on the weekend, she hadn't really noticed him during his stay. But she could see from her screen that he had paid in full for three nights and had checked out in person.

She was there again when Hammer came back from his walk, and at the sight of him still in his ripped clothes gave him the same look of pity and alarm.

"Gamarjobat," he said, cheerfully, compensating for his appearance. He had mastered three Georgian words on the plane. "You work a long shift."

"Gamarjobat." She tried a weary smile that made her look a little paler than she had last night. Hammer waited for her to volunteer what he wanted, but it didn't come.

"Will you be here after breakfast? I need to know where to buy some new clothes. I'm frightening people."

This time the smile was real. "I leave now. My colleague, he will help you."

"You get some sleep. Although it looks like a lovely day."

He was the first at breakfast, but by his second plate of eggs the small room had begun to fill up. A pair of Russian businessmen, an Indian family, an elegant German woman with her teenage daughter. He was a figure of some interest: as they came in each would look at him, then look away, not wanting to engage with whatever trouble had driven him here. Even without him, he sensed the atmosphere would have been tense. From the cliff on which the hotel sat they could see the river cutting through the city and by it various signs of last night's trouble: broken placards, a car turned on its roof. Conversation was sparse.

As he ate, he flicked through the pages of his notebook and tried to get a purchase on the day. There was so little in there. Elsa hadn't known Ben's e-mail password, or his credit card number, both of which would have helped. He had Karlo's cell phone number, for what it was worth now, and through Facebook a name and place of work for his wife, which some bright spark in the Ikertu research department had managed to convert into a home address and landline number. And he knew where Karlo had worked, of course. That was about it. On the plane he had read through each of the reports Karlo had written for Ikertu but none had contained anything relevant.

Otherwise there was the standard stuff. Call the hospitals, check with the police. If he could trust Vekua there was nothing there, but he had Katerina back in London go through the motions to be sure. She was to try all the hotels in Tbilisi as well, and through her Russian sources to keep an eye on the border, because it would be like the bastard to have crossed into Russia; it drew him. Elsa and Katerina were the only people who knew where Hammer was.

As for his own job, it was simple, to the point of being slender: try to pick up Ben's trail, as quickly as he could.

A man and a woman in neat travelers' clothes, the kind that don't crease, sat at the next table to him. Pushing his plate away, Hammer nodded a good morning and made to leave.

"Anything in there about last night?"

The man nodded at Hammer's paper lying on his table. If he'd been more observant he'd have noticed that it was still perfectly folded. The voice was American; Northwest, if Hammer had it right.

"To tell you the truth I haven't looked. Probably a bit soon for the *Tribune*."

"I guess."

Hammer smiled at the man and pushed his chair back.

"Arnold Witt."

Witt held out his hand and Hammer took it. The grip was self-consciously strong.

"Ike Hammer."

"This is Mary." Mary half smiled. "Looks like you had some trouble of your own."

"I took a wrong turn on the way from the airport."

Pressed up against the little table, Arnold Witt was big, broad across the shoulders, and he had a thick gray mustache that entirely hid his upper lip. His wife—somehow she could only be his wife—smiled tightly in a way that suggested that she had sat through many conversations at breakfast with strangers. Witt shook his head and smoothed the corners of his mustache.

"You got caught up in it? Heavens!"

"I've had smoother welcomes."

"They take your stuff? You need to borrow a shirt or something?"

Hammer imagined himself for a moment with a huge checked shirt hanging off him like a boy in his father's clothes.

"That's good of you. Thank you. But I'm going shopping. I'll be fine."

"You think the shops'll be open?"

"Something will. I'll be fine."

"Anything you need, you let us know. That's awful. Really. We nearly didn't come after the bomb but then we figured no, lightning won't strike twice. And we'd paid for those tickets. Guess we got that wrong. They hurt you?"

"More than I hurt them."

"Well, that's terrible. Awful. I guess most of it happened a ways upriver but we could see it from our room. You wouldn't want to be down in that."

"No, you wouldn't."

"Jeez, I'm sorry. Clumsy of me."

"Don't worry." Hammer stood, nodded a good-bye. "I should be going."

"I guess I'm a little rattled. This your first time here? We've traveled all over but this is our first time out here. May be our last, too. Shame. It's so quaint. It's like there's a war on in Fairyland. You staying on?"

"I've got business here."

"You need to get out of here. No business is worth getting caught up in something like this. I've spent the last hour trying to find a flight out but everything's all messed up." He looked at his wife. "Our guide, he told us we could get a bus to Yerevan, fly out from there, but it's twelve whole hours and you should see the bus. It's not what I'd call a bus. We're going out to the airport this morning, see what we can get."

"Good luck." Hammer backed away.

Witt shook his head and whistled a low note. "Got to watch these things. Remember the riots in LA? Broad daylight, everything's calm, next minute there's dead people on the corner. And that's Los Angeles. California, for heaven's sake. The civilized world. This place may be pretty but these things escalate. That's what they do."

TWO

Downstairs at reception the wan girl had gone, and in her place was a young man with heavy black glasses and a bowl of thick hair. Hammer greeted him cheerily, and explained that his wife would be arriving later, around six, and they would go straight for dinner, he imagined, and afterward she, being tired, would probably come straight back to the room but he had plans to see some friends, although they weren't yet set in stone. The plans, that was. The upshot being that it would be good, to be on the safe side, to have an extra key card for the room.

Charmed or baffled, the young man was sweetly, incuriously eager to help, and to practice his English, and in a minute or two Hammer had a key to room 27. That was easy, at least: had he been asked his name he would have had to go down the messier route of tricking or bribing the cleaners.

"Gmadlobt," he said, trying out his second Georgian word, which was odder even than the first. The "g" was silent. "You're most kind. This is for you." And he handed him a twenty-lari note. "What's your name?"

"Rostom."

"I'm Isaac. Pleased to meet you, Rostom."

By leaning out from the balcony of his room and peering down, Hammer could see that the doors leading onto the terrace of number 27 were open and could make out no movement inside. Chances were they'd have shut the doors before leaving for the day, which meant they were either still asleep, or showering, or at breakfast.

His room and theirs were set apart from the main body of the hotel and occupied an annex with its own staircase. He propped his door open so that he might hear any noise from the little stairwell, sat on the bed, and looked at his phone. The police, or whoever Vekua worked for, had had ample time to clone it while he was in the cell, and in any case he should assume that any calls he made would be intercepted. His e-mail was encrypted and secure enough. The hotel phone was no better, because they knew where he was staying and by now in which room. He needed a local cell phone.

From downstairs he heard people coming back from breakfast and the click of a door closing. He'd give it till nine for them to leave.

For twenty minutes Hammer sat on his bed and answered e-mails with the absent attention of someone whose mind is occupied by more important things. Responses to clients he liked and clients he didn't, letters of instruction to his bankers, polite refusals to unlooked-for invitations, and a late reply to his sister in Connecticut about his next trip to New York, now very much on hold. He wondered when he would see the city again. He missed it, especially this time of year when the leaves were turning. He wrote a note to Dr. Levin postponing their next session and finally one to Hibbert, who had sent two of his own since last night: one trying to confirm a time for their meeting and another wondering whether Hammer was taking this whole business seriously. As seriously as it's possible to take it, thought Hammer, in my own way, and stalled him with a scarcely believable tale of a trip to see clients in Glasgow that wouldn't keep him quiet for long.

When all this was done he sent a text to Elsa telling her that he'd arrived and was starting work, and a final message to his personal solicitor—so many lawyers in his life—asking to change his will to include an annuity to be paid to Mrs. Elsa Webster of Hiley Road, London NW10, the sum to be taken from the charitable trust he had arranged to be set up on the occasion of his death. This settlement to be put in place immediately and to remain until you hear from me again, and this e-mail to serve in lieu of a signature, which will not be possible.

A practical measure, by and large, and the right thing to do; one night in Georgia had told him that he should prepare for the worst, for Ben and himself. But it was also a challenge, a side bet, something else to focus his mind on finding what he had come for and getting out as cleanly and as quickly as possible, and there might have been superstition in it, too. Set this up for Elsa and she wouldn't need it, like taking an umbrella to discourage the rain.

From outside came the sound of a door opening, then voices. American voices, faintly irritated. Have you got the key? I have the key. What about the passports? Of course I've got the passports.

Hammer crept out of the room and onto the landing. Through the banisters he could see the running shoes and khaki trousers of his friend from breakfast, who stopped to let his wife go first and then followed her along the corridor that linked the annex to the lobby. They were both wheeling large suitcases. Hammer waited. From here he could see the small square at the back of the hotel where taxis congregated, and in a minute or two the Americans appeared, looking around for their driver. In a minute more they were in the car and away.

On the door handle of room 27 hung a sign asking the maid to make up the room. Hammer turned it round so that it read "do not disturb" and went in.

The room was identical in plan to his own, with a sitting room and a small bedroom that both gave out onto the terrace, but where his was rather brown this was painted white and more cheerful. Trying to remember when he had last searched a room, he set to it, peering under the mattress, checking the wardrobe, squashing the spare pillows, unfolding blankets, feeling under every piece of furniture. Twenty to one there was nothing here but it had to be done, and he knew from traveling with him Ben's habit of leaving things hidden in hotel rooms. Passports, sensitive documents—he preferred not to have such things on his person, especially in a place like this.

Hotel rooms at least were blank spaces, and easy enough to search. He tried the bathroom, feeling along the edges of the mirror, prying a panel away from the side of the bath; lay at full stretch on the floor to grope under the heavy sofa in the sitting room, leafed through the phone book, shuffled the little fridge out of its space, ran a hand behind the tops of the curtains. He was on the terrace, turning the little wicker table upside down, when he heard the click of a card in the lock, and the opening of the door.

He was in plain sight, and there was nowhere to go.

"Hi there," he said to the man in the doorway, whose face in the dark room he couldn't yet see. Hammer let the table down and walked inside with his hand held out. "Mr. Witt. So it's you under me. I'm sorry. This is embarrassing."

Witt just looked at him, no longer so talkative, and shook.

"The maid let me in. I was out on my terrace going through the few papers I have in my wallet—they left me my wallet, thank heaven—and my social security card slipped out and fell down onto yours. Your terrace. See how yours is a little bigger than mine? Because—sorry, this is all back to front—I have to go to the embassy and get an emergency passport this morning, because they took mine last night, and I'm going to have to prove I'm me. So the maid let me in, but I guess the wind must have taken it because it sure as hell isn't there now."

Shocked and polite, as Hammer had hoped he would be, Witt still didn't know what to say.

"That's tough luck," he managed at last.

"I promise you, I'm no cat burglar." He laughed at the absurdity of the thought. "Not at my age. I went straight in and I'm coming straight out. You get on with your day. Mine just got a little harder."

Standing, Witt was a head taller than Hammer, and a big presence in the doorway. Soon he would start to think, and that wouldn't do, so Hammer grinned, put a friendly hand on his arm, apologized again, and skirted round him through the open door, past the "do not disturb" sign, his heart beating a little faster than when he went in.

With the Witts finally gone and probably discussing the strange little man at breakfast from the safety of their car, Hammer went back downstairs and explained to Rostom that he didn't want to pay the hotel rates for a local call he had to make and would it be OK if he gave him a few lari to borrow his cell phone? That would be no trouble, not for Isaac, who thanked his new friend and wandered outside into the square, where the sun was already hot and the wind seemed to blow in from all the surrounding streets.

He took a piece of paper from his pocket and dialed. The phone rang and rang, and he began to think that she must have already left for work.

"Gamarjobat." A woman's voice, low and hoarse.

"Gamarjobat. Mrs. Toreli?"

There was a pause. "Who are you?"

"My name is Hammer, Mrs. Toreli. Isaac Hammer." He heard the click of a lighter's wheel and the crackle of paper and tobacco. "I knew Karlo. Your husband. I'm a friend of Ben Webster."

A long, deliberate exhalation.

"I have no husband."

"I have something for you. I wanted to know when I might deliver it."

"I do not understand."

"A letter. I have a letter for you."

"I do not want it."

"My friend has disappeared, Mrs. Toreli. Did you talk to him?"

"Your friend is not here."

The line went dead.

THREE

As his taxi pulled out of the square Hammer thought he saw the tail; after a mile he was certain. Two men in an old burgundy Toyota sedan, doing quite a nice job two cars back but inclined to panic a little at junctions. As far as he could tell they were alone, which meant that he only warranted a two-man team, which told him something, even if he wasn't sure what. He didn't envy them, trying to do their job in this chaotic traffic.

It was a while since he'd been followed. He wondered whether this was routine for prominent foreigners or whether he really was a special case. Had the same men tailed Ben?

He checked his watch. Nine twenty-five. This would add half an hour to his schedule.

Whoever they were they kept close during the drive to the embassy, where it took him an hour to secure a temporary passport, and then to the newer part of the city, where Rostom had assured him he would be able to find clothes, shoes, a toothbrush. Everywhere he went his appearance prompted stares, but much of the city looked just as he did: broken, assaulted, a mess.

Some shops were open, but many weren't. As he walked, Hammer saw shopkeepers boarding up windows, sweeping up debris from the pavement, going through what remained of looted stock with the unhurried air of people who had had to do such things before. This was the smart part of the city, where those with money came to spend it. The streets were wide and lined with fine old plane trees and flower beds that had somehow survived the night untouched; the buildings, solid and European, housed banks and hotels. None of this was what Hammer had expected. Turkey lay one way, Azerbaijan the other. This was meant to be the Middle East, but Tbilisi felt like a part of Europe that had drifted loose across the Black Sea.

Every fifth shop, maybe, had had trouble, but around them the life of the city went on, oblivious or resigned, and soon he had reconstructed himself completely: canvas trousers, sneakers, a sports shirt, a plain navy sweater, and a light zip-up jacket. Decent clothes, not his style, but apart from their newness anonymous enough. A little more youthful than he was used to, not to mention more casual, so that in his reflection he saw himself in costume: a younger character, less moneyed and more relaxed. Hammer was precise about how he looked, as he was about most things, and this enforced slackening felt a little like an escape. For the first time in a long while he had a sense of how others might see him. He threw his old clothes away, but kept the shoes.

It took him a while to find a pharmacy and when he finally did he left it empty-handed. Mirtazapine, he told them: Avanza, Mirtaz, Remeron, to give it its other names. At first he thought he was failing to make himself understood, and then that he needed a prescription from a doctor, but no, they simply didn't have any. They had Prozac, and Seroxat, and for a moment he wondered whether he should be taking something, at least, to take the edge off. God knew there were enough unknowns in this without having to worry about what his brain was going to be doing.

Forget it. He was on the other side of the earth, in the middle of an insurrection, under surveillance, and fighting for his freedom. And what, he had time to be depressed? Old patterns didn't apply, he resolutely told himself, even if the thought scared him. How long had it been since he last went a day free of the stuff? For years now, it had done its job; kept the encroaching blackness at the edges of his thoughts, where he could feel it waiting now. He resolved, as he always did, to fight it.

At the Kopala, once Hammer had dropped off his bags, the driver turned to him and asked where next.

"The Hilton hotel, gmadlobt," Hammer said, sliding into the backseat.

The driver frowned. He was an old man, with a white shirt and a white mustache, and from the deep creases of his forehead it seemed that he had frowned a good deal during the course of his life. He said something in Georgian, but when it became clear that Hammer hadn't understood he shook his head all the way from one shoulder to the other and said, "Hilton, niet. Niet Hilton."

"No problem. The Marriott? That's OK? Great. Gmadlobt."

Letting Hammer know, with a succinct puff of his cheeks, that he thought all foreigners were crazy, the old man shrugged and pulled out of the square.

Hammer couldn't see the Toyota, but as they turned onto the first main road there it was, making a one-eighty turn across traffic. Not subtle, and a foolhardy move on a busy Georgian road. Cars charged chaotically past, braked abruptly, swung across lanes, without warning pulled out from the curb. Hammer had seen it all morning but was not yet used to it.

The tail stayed close, and in ten minutes they were at the Marriott, a drab cream block of a building on the other side of the river.

"Marriott," said the driver, who seemed inexplicably put out by the last leg of their journey.

"Thank you, my friend," he said, and giving him a good tip told him as best he could that that would be all. As he got out of the car, the Toyota drove past and pulled in fifty yards ahead.

The Marriott was a shinier, less Georgian affair than the hotel Webster had chosen. At reception there was no queue, and the young man in the company suit was happy to tell him that there were just a few rooms left, all in the higher price brackets.

"How much is higher?" said Hammer.

"The cheapest room we have is three hundred lari, sir."

"And how many rooms do you have empty?"

"I couldn't say, sir."

"You told me you had only a few left."

"That's right, sir."

"But too many to count?"

"I'm not allowed to say."

Hammer nodded, sympathetic. "Look," he said, leaning in a little over the counter and keeping his voice low. "You have your policies, and I understand that. Also, you're not the boss. Not yet. But it's two o'clock on a Friday afternoon. Lots of people leave town on a Friday. But even if Friday's a real busy day in Tbilisi I wouldn't mind betting a bunch of people saw the riots and aren't coming to town today, and maybe a few more decided to cut their trips short and are now at the airport. If you're half full I'd be amazed. Now, I don't want to pressure you but do you think you could give me one of those three-hundred-lari rooms for a hundred and fifty lari? I think that's a fairer price."

The young man looked a little thrown but saw that Hammer was serious and picked up the phone, saying that he would see what he could do.

"Yes, sir," he said a moment later, the conversation complete. "That will be fine."

"Thank you," said Hammer, looking out through the lobby's great glass walls onto the street. "Most accommodating." He handed over his credit card and his new passport, waited patiently for them to copy it and return it with his key, and, declining the offer of being shown upstairs, took the first elevator, to the fifth floor.

The room was modern, square, identical to ten he'd slept in that year alone. It looked onto the street, and from his window he could see the Toyota, which had now turned round so that it was on the opposite side of the street and facing the hotel. It was empty, though, and there was no sign of the two men; probably they were downstairs, finding the manager or the security guy they knew and asking what the little American had wanted. Once they found out, they would wonder who he was meeting upstairs, or when he would reappear, and might begin to investigate taking a room next door to his.

Hammer turned on the television, tuned it to CNN, set the volume high, and left. The elevators were in the center of the building, and on each floor corridors lined with doors ran from them along its entire length, marked at either end with green fire escape signs. He walked back past the elevators to the far fire escape and took the stairs down to the ground floor, where one door gave onto the public rooms and another led outside. Pushing the bar that released the lock, he found himself in a narrow service alleyway behind the hotel, just wide enough for the two trucks to his right that were unloading food and huge bags of linen.

Feeling the thrill of the truant, he peered carefully round the edge of the building and walked briskly away from the main road, taking the first side street he could find and checking behind him at every turn he made.

FOUR

Natela Toreli's office was in an annex of the Ministry of Education, a worn modern building four stories tall that crouched humbly next to its grander sibling. It didn't invite attention or, Hammer imagined, many visitors. Taking one of the battered metal doors, he found himself in a bare lobby, whose oddly fine marble floor was interrupted by a single desk and a single chair, on which sat a man wearing a nondescript uniform and a magnificent gray mustache. Shaded by the peak of his cap, his eyes followed Hammer without expression.

"Gamarjobat," said Hammer. What a lovely word it was. Not just to say, with its improbable sequence of consonants, but because it warmed things up. Georgians seemed to doubt that any foreigner would take the trouble to get through it. "Gamarjobat," he said again, laying it on thick, smiling. "I have a letter—here." He fished an envelope out of his jacket pocket. "For Mrs. Toreli. Mrs. Natela Toreli. I think she works here."

The security guard held Hammer's eye with his own, implacable. He didn't look altogether like Stalin, but the elements were there: the coarse nose and the low brow and the black look. His gaze fell on the letter. He picked it up and weighed it in his hand before putting it down and smoothing it out with his palm.

"It's a letter," said Hammer. "Just paper."

The guard said something in Georgian, and pointing with the letter up the stairs behind him nodded gravely, as if to say he understood and would make sure the letter found its destination.

"No. I need to give it to her." Hammer gestured at the floor. "Here. I," he put his hand on his chest, "need to see her," he raised his eyes, "here. Right here." The guard was doing his best but wasn't quite there yet. "Call her," said Hammer, his eyes on the single phone on the desk. "Natela Toreli. Gmadlobt."

The guard raised his ample eyebrows, shook his head to himself, and before dialing ran a finger down a frayed piece of paper taped to the desk. When he was done he sat back, crossed his arms, and nodded with great purpose. Hammer thanked him and waited. In time, the illuminated indicator on one of the elevators began to count down.

The first thing that Hammer learned about Natela, from just a glance, was that she didn't dissemble. She approached with her arms crossed and her lips set, the lower pushing out a little, and Hammer knew that she knew exactly who he was and why he had come. Her eyes were down, not from shyness so much as ill-contained rage, but he couldn't look away from her face. There was a power in her presence that held him just as it unnerved him.

"How do you find me here?"

Hammer had considered all manner of approaches to this meeting: looking at Natela now, he ditched them all.

"I'm an investigator. It's my job to find things out."

Now she looked right at him, and Hammer had to resist an impulse to take a step back, so strong was the set of her face and the fury behind her stare. She had the worn skin of a smoker. Flecks of orange and silver moved in her green eyes, which were tired and alive.

He did his best to show her that she had nothing to fear from him but Natela only closed her eyes and sighed.

"I want you to leave. You cannot be here."

"Five minutes, Mrs. Toreli."

"No. Go." Her eyes wished him away. "I am leaving."

"I'm a very persistent person. I can wait."

By now the guard was sitting upright in his chair. He said something to Natela in Georgian and she raised a hand as if to say, don't worry, not yet.

"I can just wait outside," said Hammer.

"I will bring police."

"The police are kind of busy at the moment. You may have noticed."

He watched her making up her mind. "I wouldn't be here if it wasn't important."

She closed her eyes again. "Outside. Two minutes."

She led the way, her shoes clicking briskly on the floor.

Two hulking Soviet trucks hammered past on the street, and she waited for the noise to die before speaking, pulling strands of dry black hair back behind her ear. In the light she was beautiful, suddenly, clutching her arms to her, furious and defensive.

"Two minutes. What do you want?"

"To find my friend. And to give you this." He held out the envelope.

"What is?"

"A check. Karlo did a lot of good work for my company. When the people who work for my firm die or retire I like to make a contribution. It's not much."

She looked away and shook her head.

"Everyone, they think they can buy us."

"I'd do this for anyone, Mrs. Toreli. It's a token of respect."

Natela gave an abrupt laugh. "To give money is not respect."

"Take it. Please."

"And then I answer your questions?"

Hammer didn't have an answer to that.

"Your name is Hammer, yes?" He nodded. "American? Yes. I thought. An American man. For you it is easy to give money. Easy to take money. Easy to answer questions." She shook her head, tensed her bottom lip. "Nothing here is easy now."

"All I want . . ."

She jabbed a finger at him, and her voice was harsh. "No. I want. I want no more husband. I want forget him and me." She paused. "Since three years he was not my husband. I leave him. He refuse divorce but I go, yes? And now, he leave me. He leave us, all of us. And you know, you know who give money to put him in ground? I do. All money. Because his idiot family? No money. No lari. Understand? And my children, still they love their father. So now I have no money, and my children do not know if he is traitor, or hero, or how you say, a man of fear."

"A coward."

She jabbed her finger again, just below Hammer's shoulder.

"I know he is not any of these things. He is a man. A Georgian man. Is all. Full of words and drink and bullshit. And when he dies, does he go? No. He is here now. You bring him here. To my work. Understand, please. There is no money. No money in Georgia. They see you here, my work? They find reason, I go. Out. So I want quiet, peace. But you come here, you make noise. Just like him. Bang, bang, bang. Always. You are just like him."

"No one saw me come here."

"This you think."

Hammer couldn't hold her eye any longer, and looked away.

"I'm sorry."

"You are sorry. He is sorry, probably, where he is. You are all sorry, always."

Shaking her head, she looked past Hammer up the street.

"I never met your friend. He was at funeral. That was all."

"You saw him?"

"There were not so many foreign people there."

With a last glance at him she turned and walked back toward the building.

The wind flapped the envelope in Hammer's hand. "Maybe I'll give this to his idiot family," he called after her, loud enough to be sure that she heard.

FIVE

She was a tough proposition, Mrs. Toreli, and he had played her all wrong. The offer of money had been genuine, but he should have thought harder about how it would look. As he walked to his next unmade appointment, he toyed with various ideas to win her over, and none seemed good.

The *Sakartvelos Tribuna* occupied the second and third floors of a grand, shabby building not far from the parliament. A single arch led from the street to a courtyard lined with cars and weeds, and from there steps rose up to a grand lobby, all art-nouveau moldings and finely wrought balustrades, where an old laminate table and plastic chair suggested that sometimes there might be a guard, or a janitor, or some person of authority to negotiate. Today there was no one.

Nor was it obvious who to speak to in the office itself, where desks and papers and screens started abruptly and sprawled across the entire floor, and between them journalists sat shouting into phones or at each other. It was a familiar and comforting sight to Hammer: somehow newsrooms and journalists everywhere had the same air of beleaguered concentration. The place rattled with the noise of a big story. He approached the first desk, asked for the editor, and, receiving only confusion in response, tried the next. This time he was understood, and directed irritably to a screened-off glass box in the corner of the room.

For some reason Hammer had been expecting a seasoned old hack, but this one was young, with a neat suit and a technocratic air; he gave the impression of having recently finished a course of some kind. There was an empty desk by his door that Hammer imagined was usually policed by his secretary. Taking the opportunity, he knocked on the glass and the editor looked up frowning, annoyed at the interruption.

"Diakh?"

"Mr. Jeladze? My name's Isaac Hammer." Hammer came into the room and offered his hand. It takes a lot to refuse a handshake, and Jeladze didn't have it. While he shook, his eyes went to Hammer's nose.

Hammer brought his hand up to it. "I got on the wrong end of some Georgian hospitality."

Jeladze stayed seated and took the card that Hammer now gave him. "We are busy, Mr. Hammer."

"Of course you are. Shouldn't think you've ever been busier. You don't know me but I just wanted to say you run a great newspaper. Really, first-rate. Great stories, great journalists." Hammer sat down, unasked. "I wanted to speak to you about one of them. Karlo Toreli."

Jeladze stiffened, looked down, then turned over the papers he had been reading and slid them to one side of the desk. His movements were neat and disciplined, his expression conscientious. He had the soft face of a boy; Hammer guessed that he needed to shave only every third day.

"I don't have anything to say."

"Really?"

"It is only ten days since he died."

"All the more reason to talk," smiled Hammer. "While it's fresh."

Jeladze looked up and watched him warily, wondering what he had done to deserve this irritation, perhaps, and what he might do to get rid of it. He pushed his chair back, so that Hammer thought he was about to stand and leave; but for a moment he just sat, and thought, and looked again at Hammer's business card.

"You are a spy, Mr. Hammer?"

Hammer laughed, determined after his last encounter to keep this light. "I get that a lot here. No. I'm an investigator."

"Someone pays you to investigate a suicide?"

"That's not my interest."

"No?"

"No. A friend of mine has disappeared, in your fine country. I've come to find him."

"But you want to talk to me about Karlo."

"I do. And because I know I'm imposing here, and you have no reason to help me, if you have a minute I'll explain."

"I don't have a minute."

"Mr. Jeladze, I was never an editor but I was a journalist. For many years. And I always had a minute to hear a story."

Jeladze nodded faintly, without enthusiasm.

"My friend, he's not the kind to disappear. A family man, very responsible. Too responsible. Something, if I'm honest, of a pain in the ass in that respect. The last thing he would do is cause his dear wife concern, and right now she's very concerned. He went missing a few days ago, and I'm here on her behalf trying to find out what's happened. And at the moment, in the absence of any information at all, I'm entertaining two theories. One is he got unlucky and someone robbed him of his winnings on his way home from the casino, or slipped him a pill and harvested his kidneys, or some such business that might happen to anyone anywhere. But I did a little checking on Georgia and this is a nice country you have here and not so much of that nonsense seems to take place. Riots, yes; killing tourists, not your thing. So—and because I don't believe in chance—I wonder if his falling off the face of the earth has something to do with why he came to Georgia. Which was to pay his respects to your friend. To Karlo."

Hammer paused and took in a deep breath, giving the editor a look that said: I'm giving you everything here; we're together on this.

"Look. No one has more respect for what you do. Really. Especially in a place like this, where it isn't easy to write a story that people don't want to see written. Especially the bomb story. They don't get bigger than that. So the question I was asking myself, is there something going on here that my friend has blundered into? Because he has some form in that area as well, by the way. He blunders into things." His smile was sympathetic, and he paused to let it take effect. "People like this can be difficult to control, no?"

Jeladze nodded again, without engaging. "I don't know what you're asking me."

"Ah. Forgive me." Hammer leaned forward, and lowered his voice. "Two questions. That's all. Where did Karlo get the story, and who benefited from his death? He publishes the most incendiary article in the history of your country and then kills himself? No journalist I've ever known would do that. They'd be high for months."

Jeladze nodded slowly as if now, finally, he got the point. All the while he held Hammer's eye, but it didn't come naturally. He was willing himself to do it. After a moment of this he spoke.

"I don't know you. That story . . . I can't talk to you about that story."

"I understand. Really, I do. But first, you should know I'm a good guy to know. I get a lot of stories and I know a lot of things and, if I can, I'm always ready to talk. Plus, I'm grateful. I'm a grateful guy, OK? I employ a lot of former journalists, and count many among my friends. Anything you share with me, I'll remember it. I have a good memory for good people." He gave a little ceremonial nod to show that he had made a solemn promise. "As for the story? One of your best journalists died on you. You've got to have theories."

Jeladze breathed deeply, steeling himself, and Hammer could tell from this little act of preparation that any theories he might have would remain private.

"Mr. Hammer. Karlo was a good man, and once he was a great journalist. But he was . . . How do you say this? He had big passions. For stories, for women, for drink. For gambling. He was full of life and then next minute in a black place. Always one to the other. But recently it was all black. This is why he killed himself."

Hammer tried to read the editor's face. There was something callow about it, something untested, something too young for his position. He hadn't lived enough to make judgments about a man like Karlo, and his certainty was either mistaken or feigned. Perhaps the latter: behind the smooth presentation Hammer thought he glimpsed a wavering thread of fear.

Nodding, Hammer considered. "So you have no doubt?"

The editor shook his head.

"Had you published everything? Was there more to come?"

"On the bomb story? Everything." He shrugged. "Think about it. That was his greatest achievement, and then nothing. It makes sense."

"So not all black, then."

Jeladze took in a sharp, executive breath.

"Mr. Hammer, I must work now. This is a busy time."

"Did you go to his funeral?"

"Of course."

"Did you happen to see my friend? English, tall, short gray hair?"

"There were many people there. Karlo was still loved."

"But many foreigners?"

Jeladze picked up a sheet of paper from his desk, looked at it, and moved it to another pile. He was beginning to fidget. "I wasn't . . . I wasn't there to report, Mr. Hammer."

"I know. You're not a reporter. You're an editor. But you notice things, of course. You'd have noticed if he'd been here, for instance? Ben Webster. Another fellow journalist."

Jeladze stood, like a man who has finally made up his mind. "Mr. Hammer, I have to ask you to leave now."

"It's important that I find him, Mr. Jeladze. It's worth a great deal to me." It felt strange, trying to corrupt a man with a statement of such truth.

"I can't help."

"What if I was to make a donation to your retired journalists' fund?"

Jeladze seemed genuinely confused. "What fund?"

"Never mind," said Hammer. The man wasn't about to be corrupted. At least not by him.

SIX

Outside, with the sun high and strong, the wind blew dust along the street, and in the doorway of the building whirled a little eddy of leaves and dead cigarettes.

Hammer crossed the street to a corner café, took a seat under its black awning, and ordered coffee and something to eat. It was early for lunch but he might be here for a while. To be a good investigator you had to know when to press and when to wait. And when to persevere, especially when your two primary sources had rejected you.

Further up the pavement men in fluorescent jackets were taking away the scattered pieces of a bus stop that looked as if it had been destroyed the night before. Two of them flung metal and glass onto the back of a flat-bed truck while another swept. He watched them at their work, keeping an eye on the door of the newspaper building and trying to imagine what the editor knew and why he wouldn't part with it.

That too was interesting. Instinct told him that Jeladze had only let him talk to find out what he might have to fear from this bold stranger who had marched straight into his office to discuss the most delicate subject in the land. And there was fear there, no question. Had he refused to talk about Ben because he knew something, or from a general unwillingness to stray into dangerous territory? Hammer couldn't tell, but if Ben had been here—and it was an obvious place for him to start—others would have seen him, no question.

On the flight over, reading a little about Georgia and imagining where Ben might be, Hammer had thought it a one-in-ten chance that he had been knocked down by a car or robbed and left in a ditch, but after seeing Natela and this Jeladze character he put it at one percent, no better. Their eyes were strained with fear. It was in the air, at the rally, in the police station, all over the city. Ben would have been aware of it the moment he came here, and from that point unstoppably drawn to it, as he always was. And somehow, whatever was going on, he was involved.

Once, Hammer would have been the same—no less reckless, and wholly susceptible to the thrill of it. At a certain point, though, he had pulled back, like a drinker who comes to understand that the hangover isn't worth it, for himself or the people around him, and over the last twenty years he had lived his life by his own careful calculus of risk and benefit. Ikertu had been his way of controlling the variables. But here he had no control whatever, and no choice but to follow his former friend into the fire.

After half an hour, two men and a woman came down the three steps to the street and huddled together under the arch to light cigarettes off a single lighter. Hammer recognized the woman and one of the men from the newsroom. Slipping a banknote under his cup, he left the café and waited on the pavement to cross the busy street. Cars rushed endlessly by.

A hand on his shoulder caused him to turn and look up into the unshaven face of a great block of a man, with an unbreakable jaw and a powerful air of invulnerability. The muscles in his arms strained against the fabric of his cheap suit. He was more than a head taller than Hammer and his hand rested idly but with purpose, like a threat.

Without saying a word he passed Hammer a phone, and Hammer, barely thinking, put it to his ear, shrugging off the man's hand. "Yes?"

"Isaac Hammer." A statement, not a question, in a dark, heavy voice that took its time.

"This is Ike Hammer."

In vain Hammer looked up and down the street for some sort of explanation. He had been sure. He had lost the tail; known that sweet, unmistakable feeling of no longer being watched.

"My name is Iosava. I must speak with you."

"You are speaking to me."

"Face-to-face."

"Then come and see me."

"Now. You go in car."

"Mr. Iosava, I'm too old for orders. You seem to know where I am. Come and find me. I'll be happy to talk."

Hammer handed the phone back to the man in the suit and stepped again to the curb, scanning the street in each direction to see whether his latest new friend had friends. It was busy enough for them not to try anything, and there were no obvious goons in sight. With a glance back at the big man he willed the cars to clear so that he might cross.

From the mess of traffic a dark gray Audi separated and pulled up smartly in front of him. In a single moment he felt an arm wrap round him from behind and another pull him up from under the knees and together carry him forward like a child. The rear door opened and he was thrown inside. The engine revved and the door shut and the car drove off. Only an instant had passed.

Beside him on the seat was a second man the size of the first. He, too, wore a suit, and a tie that in the absence of a button kept the collar of his white shirt tight to his neck, and before Hammer could collect himself he was patting the pockets of his jacket and pulling out his phone.

"What the fuck was that? Who are you?" said Hammer, but neither the driver nor the man searching him said anything. "Give me that."

He snatched at the phone but the man held it out of reach, calmly slid the casing off the back, removed the battery, and slid it into his top pocket. Then he handed Hammer the dead case.

"That's great. Thank you. You have nice manners."

The car drove the way cars like this did in such places, with misjudged confidence and great surges of speed. These two men were special forces of some kind, almost certainly; they had that air of calm efficiency that might at any moment turn to violence. They were not the sort to listen, even when they understood, and for once Hammer didn't make the effort to talk.

At the first set of traffic lights Hammer tried the door, more from curiosity than any real desire to escape, found it locked, and for the rest of the journey sat back and didn't speak, fingers tapping angrily on his knee. For a full minute he breathed slowly and forced himself to calm down. This escapade might lead somewhere; in the absence of good leads it was at least a lead. And they would hardly have returned his phone, even without its battery, if they were planning to kill him right away.

Every journey in Tbilisi seemed to cross or follow the river, but after running beside it for a short stretch they headed upward through the old town toward the castle, through a neighborhood that Hammer began to recognize. After ten minutes the car slowed in a triangle of sloping streets, where every other house was falling into itself, and the moment it stopped, Hammer's door opened. No one said anything, and as he got out he felt a hand on his upper arm start guiding him toward three well-kept houses in a row, pushed up against the hill directly under the castle. The last houses in Tbilisi.

SEVEN

Otar Iosava had a monstrous look. Some of it was in his eyes, which were black, as far as you could see them, and quick with a sort of bruised cunning. Some was in the stoop of his back when he stood. But mostly it was his skin, bubbled and pockmarked and a dead yellow-gray, like clay molded onto the face and left in the heat to shrink and crack.

"Mr. Hammer. Sit, we talk."

When he spoke, his gray lips barely moved, so that to Hammer it seemed that he was addressing a mask whose occupant was somewhere far within. He rose stiffly an inch or two out of his chair and offered his hand, its skin in contrast pale and smooth. Hammer looked at it for a moment, arms crossed.

"You want to tell me why I should?"

"You are grown man. You understand world, how it works."

His voice came from some deep gurgling place in his throat.

"Not this world," said Hammer, and meant it.

He was solid, thick around the neck, clearly strong under his bulk, like a boxer in comfortable retirement, and he dressed as his henchmen did in clothes a fraction too small—a T-shirt and a zipped black cardigan and trousers with a light shine in them. Everything expensive and apparently new. A gold cross on a simple gold Georgian chain swung clear of his neck when he leaned forward. He sat back down, withdrew the hand.

"This is not respectful business, but OK, is not surprise. Americans not so polite."

"You're serious." Hammer laughed and shook his head. "Who the hell are you?"

"You do not know me?"

"No. I don't know you. I don't know your country and I'm beginning to wonder if I want to. But I'm sure you're a big deal. No doubt that's my loss, and if we'd met under other circumstances I'd be just dying to spend time in your company. Now—no, listen—you tell me why I'm here and what you want and I'll decide if I'm going to stay. Yes?"

Iosava's black eyes looked at him, too recessed to be read.

"OK. You play, I play. Is OK." Abruptly he stood. "Come."

They were in a huge, bright room, the width of the three old houses that had been knocked together. Through the long galleried window, over the cracked and crooked rooftops of old Tbilisi, Hammer could see the river, the president's residence, his hotel, the whole city. He felt like a duke taking stock from his palace. Old beams lined the ceiling, warped wooden boards the floor, and everywhere there was modern furniture in a sleek, bland style. It was an elegant room, at odds with its owner. Maybe somewhere there was a wife with taste.

At the far end of the long wall was a vast pair of doors on black iron hinges. Iosava walked to them and turned.

"Come."

Hammer crossed his arms. "I guess you're used to being in command. But no, thanks. I'll stay here and you can tell me what you want."

"You are big detective. But you do not want to know things."

He had a point. The wise thing now was to leave here having learned more than he'd given away. Hammer breathed deeply, put his anger to one side, and relented.

With some ceremony Iosava opened first one door then the next, throwing both wide and revealing another large room, light, bare of furniture, with a concrete floor. Two yards in, metal bars ran across the width of it and up to the ceiling, and half of the outside wall was also railed and otherwise open to the air. Beyond were the woods that rose up to the castle, but Hammer barely registered them because his eye was fixed on the room's one occupant—a brown bear, huge and unmoving, lying on its front against the back wall. One eye watched him back.

The cage was maybe thirty feet square, and empty but for two troughs, one for water and another for food. It smelled deeply of old fish and the wild. Iosava said nothing, enjoying the effect as he must have done many times before.

"What's it supposed to do all day?" asked Hammer. On his list of all the disgusting things in the world, caging vulnerable creatures came somewhere near the top.

"Eats, sleeps. Shits. What we do."

"Why are you showing me this?"

From a bucket by the bars Iosava took a fish and threw it to within a yard of the bear, who eyed it lazily, adjusted its weight, and reached out a paw to slide it under his snout. Holding it there, it began without urgency to tear at the flesh. The fur on the top of its head had come out in clumps and exposed the starkly white skin beneath.

"See this bear?"

"I can see the bear."

"Was police bear. Lived in cell, like this."

"A police bear?"

"Sure. The police want you scared, they put you in cell."

"With the bear."

"With bear. But I feed bear. And they do not."

Iosava waited for a reaction, but Hammer had no intention of giving him what he wanted. He looked from this man's dying face to the poor faded creature in the corner and wondered which had seen the greater horrors. He had a good idea.

"I saved it," said Iosava. "In civil war, they wanted kill it, I saved it. My enemies say I am bad man. But in my way I do good."

"That's why you showed me this? That's the lesson?"

"Come. We have things to talk."

As he left, Iosava threw another fish, which slapped across the floor and came to rest a foot from the bear's paw. The bear glanced at it and slowly closed its eyes.

Back in the grand room Iosava settled into his armchair and Hammer perched less than comfortably on the front edge of a sofa. He didn't want to accept anything from this man, not even a seat. The guard who had led him up the stairs remained by the door, hands crossed in front.

Iosava leaned forward to take a cigar from a lacquered box on the coffee table and held it out to Hammer, who raised a hand to refuse. He clipped and lit it, taking his time, smoke obscuring his face.

"Only pleasure for me," he said at last, watching smoke spiral from the tip. "Everything else . . ." he shrugged. "OK. Webster. Ben Webster. Tell me where is he."

Hammer hadn't expected that.

"I have no idea."

Iosava exhaled, laughing through the smoke.

"OK. This is good. You don't know where is he. OK."

"No. I don't. Do you?"

"Mr. Hammer. You give job, you expect job be done, yes? How business works."

"You hired Ben?"

Iosava laughed again, a phlegmy chuckle, and shook his head.

"I hired him, I hired you. What fuck I care, so long job is done?"

This was a misunderstanding, surely. A miscommunication. Iosava was staring hard at him with those black pits he had for eyes.

"Ben left my company three months ago."

Iosava watched him for a few moments, smoking, the eyes calculating, wary.

"He told me you were together. That you work on my case."

"We are not together."

That was the limit. In London he blackens my name, here he pimps it out. So Ben had come here looking for work, trading on the Ikertu name, his high-minded plans shot—this was where his morals had brought him, to the palace of this monster. Despite everything, Hammer didn't want to believe it—and why believe anything this piece of work said?—but it had the air of being true. It fit.

"He doesn't represent me. You need to tell me what he told you."

Though his face barely moved—could barely move—somehow Iosava let Hammer know that the fun part of their conversation was over. The ash on his cigar had formed a brittle gray plug and he knocked it off into an ashtray.

"I paid you money," he said, his eyes dead on Hammer's.

"You paid him. How much?"

"One hundred thousand dollars. Retainer."

A hundred grand. That was a proper piece of work for one man.

"I don't have your money. I don't need it. What was it for?"

"I think you know what I ask him."

"Let's just pretend I don't know. Can you do that? You play, I play."

The look in Iosava's eyes shifted as he considered this strange person who wouldn't bend to his will. Then he nodded, the calculation made.

"This?" He brought both hands up to his face and pressed them to his cheeks, where they made no impression on the cracked flesh. "President do this. Since two years. He thinks I wish to be president. To push him out. Who vote for this face, yes? Is smart move for him. But I do not want to be president, never. I have different businesses, very important, everything complicated. I like better to be power behind power, understand? There is control."

He reached forward, took a glass of water from the table, brought it up to his lips, and tilted his head to pour the water into his mouth. A little ran out from the corner onto his chin and he wiped it with the back of his other hand.

"Very simple. Simple operation. I drive, two policemen they stop me. They say I drink, I say no, they take car and some of my blood. Two weeks after, this. Dioxin. Enough to kill but it does not."

This was said with a kind of pride: clearly it would have killed lesser men. He put the glass back on the table, eyes on Hammer throughout. "Who else has power to do this? No one. Only president. Now I am dark part of his soul that he must always see. I look like this outside. But president, he look like this in here." He struck his chest with a clenched fist. "And Georgia must know."

"So that's what Ben's doing for you? Investigating what happened to you?"

Iosava's laugh was black and from somewhere deep inside him.

"No. Georgians not care who does this to me. They think I deserve. Maybe I deserve. Who knows?"

His stare grew more intense. Hammer got the impression that if he'd been sitting any nearer Iosava would have reached out and grabbed him by the lapels. He prepared himself for a harangue.

"Poison is in me, is in Georgia. Soon it will die. No one has money, no one has job. Is no respect. Respect for church, for how you say, rules of life. Georgia is old. Oldest country, enemies everywhere. But even oldest tree can die. Everyone, they fear Russia, but Russia is not enemy. Enemy is inside." He held his fist against his breast. "Russia story is bullshit. Politics. President uses to win election. But he is poison. Understand? He is inside tree. He kills Georgia."

Iosava stared at Hammer and let the words take effect. His face was like a mask of dried mud, and Hammer found himself disturbed by the contrast between the dead exterior and all that fire within.

"So. I ask your friend, show who made explosion in Gori. Find proof was president."

Now that was a case that would get you disappeared.

"I thought Karlo already did that."

"Karlo was good man but he could not say president signed order. Not hundred percent. President knew, for sure he knew. I need proof. Strong proof, no doubt. So he will be in prison. For thousand years."

Iosava held his hands out, appealing to Hammer to see the sturdy logic of his case.

"Game is over. Opposition will win. My money, good candidate. No question. Is over. Over. But president, still he fight. To death." He leaned forward, confidential, threatening. "So. I need your friend. Where is your friend?"

"He's not my friend."

"Then why you look?"

"I need him to do something for me. Just like you."

Iosava watched him for signs of deceit but appeared to find none.

"Probably he is dead. Like Karlo." He leaned forward and slowly ground the end of his cigar into the ashtray, releasing a final acrid stink.

Probably he was, if this was what he had taken on. Hammer imagined a series of scenes: calling Elsa with the news, flying back from Georgia with a body, his awkward presence at the funeral. Trying to convince Sander that the hacking and everything else had been done by his former colleague, now conveniently dead.

"So now you do work for me," said Iosava.

Hammer kept his eyes on him, with difficulty. Of all the foul people who have come my way, he thought, this one may be the foulest.

"Mr. . . . What is your name?"

Iosava eyed him for his impertinence. "Iosava. Yoss-av-a."

"Mr. Iosava. Tell me something. How did you find me? There was no tail."

"Newspaper is mine."

Of course. Jeladze. Oh, to know how this country worked.

"Television is mine. Banks mine. Water mine."

"The water, huh? Anything else? Don't you own any investigators?"

"You. And your friend. If he lives."

Hammer held his brow, closed his eyes for a moment, and let his thoughts settle. God, this was a mess, but in it there had to be opportunity. Everyone is a source.

"Tell me what you said to Ben."

"You take job. Good."

"I don't take any job. I don't work for people like you. Here's how it's going to work. I'm going to look for my friend, OK? You tell me what you know. When I find something that's good for you, I'll tell you. That's it. The hundred thousand I'm going to pay you back."

Iosava sat back, crossed his legs, and clasped his hands together tight until the knuckles whitened. He looked at Hammer for a good ten seconds without saying a word, his eyes shining black in their deep clay sockets.

"Your friend is dead, I think. By end you will be also."

"I'm kind of immune to threats."

"No threat. Statement. Without my protection."

"I'll be fine."

"The police," he said it with a short i—polliss, "they do not have bear, but they are same. Always same. Put drugs on your clothes. Pay drunk man to cut you with knife." Abruptly he sat forward again and mimed the action, a stabbing and then an upward rip. "They do not want you here. They will find way."

"I can look after myself," said Hammer, wishing that he believed it. "Tell me what you know."

EIGHT

Probably your friend is dead. As he walked back through the narrow streets into the city the words knocked around in Hammer's head. There was a good chance Iosava was right; he hadn't allowed himself to entertain the thought, and it lay on his unformed hopes like ice. Your friend, who is not your friend, may be dead, and your quest already over.

For a moment Hammer felt the anger that had brought him here fade, and in its place an old, familiar sense of slipping under layers of blackness, of a forced retreat to a place where thought was reduced to a series of indistinct, unmanageable fears. Something about Iosava had sparked it in him. His mouth was dry and his hands wet with sweat and he found himself unable to tell whether these were the first signs of withdrawal from his medication or the normal reaction to a reasonable dread.

He had come to see it as a loss of faith. Not in God, but in the unseen fabric of life: in the taste of food, in the possibility of friendship, in next week. In every healthy breath there was an assumption that the next was worth taking—an assumption that otherwise you never so much as noticed. Depression assumed nothing. It broke the tacit contract with the world, until everything in it was just an empty form.

Today Hammer did his best to banish it to the edges again. Concentrated on his work.

Iosava had told him little that he didn't know beyond a few more details. The men from Dagestan who had set off the bomb belonged to a group called the Islamic Army of the Caucasus, rebels who wanted to establish a Sharia state across the region. The Russians, the Georgians—everyone had relationships with these groups, who loved nothing more than to play them off against each other. The two men had come through the mountains, picking up a 4 x 4 just this side of the border and driving it to Tbilisi only the day before the bombing, which suggested that someone else had prepared the ground.

Otherwise, all Hammer learned was that Iosava was at the center of all things. Without him, very little of note would happen in Georgia, and nothing without his noticing. The president had been his creation from the start, of course, something that was now a source of regret to him. Karlo had been a brilliant journalist, and in his pay. His relations with the Russians were excellent—if Hammer ever needed help in Moscow, he should say. Georgia needed Russia like a dog needed its master. The dog did not understand that it could not survive on its own.

If he wasn't the most important man in the country he was a world-class fantasist, and in either case a bully. Hammer hated him. It was a good, clean emotion and he nourished it.

The goon had returned his battery but his first task now was to buy some Georgian phones, which was easier than he'd imagined: some cash, a few smiles, and a false US address. He bought three—one for now, one for someone else, as the need arose, and one for emergencies or the unforeseen.

A mile or more from his hotel he saw what he had been looking for: an Internet café, its door open and its fluorescent tubes fixing the rows of screens with a cold, dead light. Hammer went in, offered some lari, and took a seat in the furthest corner, having been told by the manager in a brusque gesture that he could pay at the end of his session. The room was cheap and tatty, the computers four or five years old, and there were no cameras in sight. One other customer, an untidy man in a thick black coat, sat peering at a screen.

There was a single e-mail waiting for him in the account he had set up for the purpose, and though it wasn't artfully written it contained a great deal that was of interest. It had been sent by Wesley London, who did not exist, but was in fact Dean Oliver, who did, more or less. From a blank office somewhere north of King's Cross Oliver delved discreetly into people's lives: into their bank accounts, their telephone bills, their health records, and sometimes the rubbish they left outside their houses. He was a slightly more refined version of the people Ben had used to do his hacking, but hardly refined.

The hypocrisy and the risk were unavoidable. Elsa hadn't known the passwords to her husband's various accounts, and the official route would have been too slow.

One of the paradoxes of Oliver was that for someone who did such aggressive work he was scrupulously polite (as he had to be, of course, to win the confidence of those he tricked), and his e-mail began with his hopes that Hammer was well and that Webster, whom he knew and respected greatly, would shortly be found. After that it was raw and technical, as Hammer wanted it.

Webster's current account had seen no outgoing activity, as Oliver put it, since he had left for Georgia almost a week earlier, the last payment being by direct debit to a building society. The balance of the savings account had diminished steadily over the previous three months, but just three days earlier a sum of sixty-four thousand, six hundred and seventy-eight pounds had been received from a Cyprus company called Swift Holdings Ltd.

Since Webster had landed in Georgia, only six calls had been made from his mobile: five to Webster's own home and one to a mobile number registered to Elsa Webster, who, in Oliver's ponderous prose, cohabited with Webster at a north London address. This told Hammer that if he had made other calls in Georgia, as he surely had, Webster had bought a local phone for the purpose, and his mind began to turn to how on earth one might find the number. But just before he had left England, Webster had made a number of calls in a short burst: to Lufthansa, to the Hotel Kopala, to his bank, to two Georgian numbers, and to one Moscow number, which Hammer thought he half recognized. One of the Georgian numbers was Natela's; the other he didn't know. It might be Iosava's, or it might not.

He moved on to the credit card statement, much of which was predictable. Five hundred lari to the hotel on the morning he checked out, a cash withdrawal from the airport the night he arrived, some money for meals. An hour after paying the Kopala—on the day he was supposed to be going home—he had given two hundred and seventy lari to a car-rental company in Tbilisi, and half an hour after that two hundred and forty to what appeared to be a Gulf gas station.

Unless rental companies had started sending their cars out empty this was odd. He looked up the price of fuel in Georgia, and worked out that Webster must have bought about thirty-two gallons, roughly another two full tanks. For a few minutes he wandered round the rental company's website, trying to work out which car Webster had rented and for how long, but it was impossible.

Two more people had now arrived and were quietly tapping at keyboards; neither paid him any notice. From his pocket he took one of his new phones and made his first call.

"Hertz Rental." A young, male voice, Georgian.

"Good morning. This is Bob Hopper from the central fraud department at the head office in the UK. You speak English, by any chance?"

"Of course, Mr. Hopper."

"That's great. Can I have your name, please?"

"Ilya. Ilya Muladze."

"That's great, Ilya. Thanks for helping me this morning. This won't take long. I'm looking at a job here, opened on Tuesday, name of Benedict Webster. Let me give you the credit card number."

Ilya listened, taking it down.

"Now, Ilya, we have that card on a list of stolen cards, and I'm not sure how it got through the system, but it's been flagged and I'm a little worried that maybe the guy who rented the vehicle isn't what he seems." Hammer could hear Ilya's concern on the other end of the line. "I need you to give me some details about the booking, because I can't see everything you can on my end."

"Of course."

"That'd be a great help. OK. What vehicle type was that?"

"A Mitsubishi. Pajero."

"That's great. You have the color?"

"Silver."

"A silver Pajero. That's great. Registration?

Ilya obliged.

"And what's the transaction time on that, Ilya? When did he pick up the vehicle?"

"It says here . . . sorry, OK, here it is. Eight twenty, in the morning."

"Very useful. Did you serve the gentleman?"

"I did not, sorry."

"That's OK, no problem. Can you tell me who did?"

"My colleague, Mariam. She is not here right now."

"And when will she be in, Ilya?"

"I do not know. Perhaps Monday now."

"OK. No problem. Just a couple more things. The vehicle hasn't been returned yet?"

"No, sir. Return date on the order was yesterday but it was not returned."

"OK. That makes sense. And one last thing, Ilya, before I let you get on. That would have gone out with a full tank of gas, yes? There a reason why it wouldn't?"

"Of course. Is there a problem?"

"No, no. Not in the least. Thank you, Ilya. That's been very helpful. I may call again on Monday, speak to Mariam."

Hammer hung up and returned to his computer, where he found out that the Pajero could travel roughly four hundred miles on a single tank. Georgia wasn't a large country, and it seemed to have a reasonable number of gas stations. Where had he planned to go?

From the evidence left by his credit card Ben had headed west, stopping in Gori, where the bomb had gone off, to buy lunch. That night, he had spent two hundred lari at somewhere called the Restaurant Tamar, which a quick search found to be in Batumi on the Black Sea coast, and a smaller sum at a bar nearby. Two hundred lari was a big dinner. The following day there were payments to the Batumi Sheraton, Turkish Airlines, and the Istanbul Café inside Batumi airport. After that, nothing. That was Tuesday, three days ago. If he had spent money on that card since, Oliver would have known about it.

In each place he had eaten well. Enough for two, in fact—Hammer was almost sure he hadn't traveled alone. At the Sheraton, which wasn't cheap, his room had cost three hundred bucks a night.

Maybe the bastard wasn't dead. Maybe he was altogether too alive.

NINE

Batumi. The seaside. Casinos and promenades and nightclubs, to judge by a quick search. Palm trees and bright colors and couples strolling arm in arm on the beach at sunset. It had seen no bombs, no dead journalists, no riots. There was no link to Karlo or Iosava or anything that had brought Ben here, no obvious thread.

This much was clear. The day after he had last called Elsa, Ben had rented a car and driven to Batumi, via Gori, traveling in some comfort. If he was following a lead, why not call Elsa? And if he wasn't alone—if he was traveling with a woman—why stop in Gori? There was a final possibility, of course, that someone had stolen his credit card, but any sensible thief would spend as much as he could within a few hours and then dump it. He wouldn't have it fund his holiday.

Life was a good deal simpler last week, thought Hammer. He had imagined himself finding a clear trail but everywhere there were only indistinct tracks in the mud. Still, he must make a decision. Leave Tbilisi, the heart of the whole business, at the heart of the country, and risk losing time; or stay, and try Natela again, God knows how.

In the end there was no question: the card was his best lead.

The next train left the following morning, but the journey was only two hundred miles, and the roads seemed fine. He called another car-rental company and told them that he'd be there in an hour to pick up a nice, solid, unremarkable car. That was no problem. They shut at six. He could be in Batumi by ten.

This settled, he headed back to the Kopala, walking fast now through the old town and across Metekhi Bridge, where a young boy with a crutch, running alongside him to keep up, begged him for money, the crutch going comically under his arm like a broken piston.

"Mister, mister. Lari, mister. Lari."

Hammer kept walking, and the boy went faster until he was a little ahead and skipping backward.

"Mister. USA. Lari." His face sank into a practiced frown. "Very bad." He patted his thigh, the wrong leg. "Mister. Very bad."

Hammer stopped. The boy had chutzpah. He was skinny and dusty and wore odd shoes.

"Bad leg, huh?" he said.

The boy grinned, then remembered that he was in pain and grimaced once more. He clutched his thigh. "Very bad."

"You want to get that seen to."

Looking around for any quick-fingered friends the boy might have, Hammer took his wallet from his back pocket, found a five-lari note, and held it out to the child, who after a moment's hesitation, as if this was too good to be true, snatched it and ran off to boast to his friends about the tourist he'd just fleeced.

From this point of the bridge, near the northern end, Hammer could clearly see his room, two stories up from the top of the cliff on which the hotel perched, and looking up now he thought he could see movement inside, a brush of shadow across the door that led onto the balcony. He stopped for a minute and watched, but saw nothing, and made to move on. But his eye was caught by something else, on the floor below: a rectangle of what seemed to be black plastic on the outer lip of the wooden balcony. Of Webster's old room. As he walked closer he kept his focus on it. It was hard to tell from this distance what it was: it might be some sort of electrical housing, but there were no wires coming from it, and that was a strange place for it to be.

To reach the hotel he had to climb the road to the side of the cliff and double back, and by the time he got to his room everything appeared to be as he had left it—but then there wasn't very much. His new clothes were still wrapped in their bags; the things from the pharmacy lay undisturbed on the sink. If someone had been here, chances were they'd come not to take anything but to leave something behind, which was fine. He was leaving now in any case. Once he had made a second trip downstairs.

The wind had calmed, and the late sun, glaring past the shaded hills and churches opposite, was caught on the brick terrace of the balcony. Hammer had showered and put on a fresh shirt, and stood now for a moment with his hands on the railings letting the heat sink into him, drinking deeply from a cold bottle of water and encouraging his thoughts to settle. A path to follow. That was good; it felt like progress. The dread that had settled on him after seeing Iosava began to lift.

When the water was finished he set the bottle down and leaned out over the edge to make sure there was no one on the balcony below. Two sun lounge chairs were angled toward the sun, towels rumpled on each.

A moment later he was downstairs outside the door to number 27. Before trying his key card Hammer knocked, and was surprised to hear steps inside, and a few words, and a door closing, before he was greeted by Mrs. Witt in a bathrobe. Her wet hair was a dark gray and her glasses, the kind without rims, held drops of water. Behind them her eyes registered an instant suspicion.

This was excruciating but there was no way round it. There was simply no time for anything else.

"Mrs. Witt. You didn't make it out?"

"We have a flight tomorrow."

She was a less helpful sort than her husband, but Hammer persevered.

"That's great. Thank heaven for that. Mrs. Witt, Arnold may have told you that this morning I managed to lose the one document I need to get my emergency passport and get out of this country. I'm only supposed to be here until tomorrow and then I fly to Istanbul, but if I can't find my social security card I'm going to be here until Monday at the earliest."

"That's too bad."

"Mrs. Witt, it is a holy pain in the rear end, is what it is. Now I'm ninety-nine percent certain it isn't there, but could you stand for me to just check your balcony one last time? I'd feel such a fool if it was there all along."

It was plain on Mrs. Witt's face that whatever charitable construction her husband had put on the morning's events, she didn't share it. But the request was hard to refuse. There was, after all, no harm in it.

"Come on in." As invitations went, it was reluctant.

Hammer moved past her into the room and made straight for the balcony, turning only to say that she shouldn't worry, he'd be done in a moment and she should get on with whatever she was doing. As the bathroom door opened he heard Witt's voice inside.

Though he couldn't see it, he found the package straightaway, fishing through the railings and feeling along its edges. It was held on with tape, and irritatingly secure, but his fingernails finally found a loose corner and in a minute he had it. Slipping it into his trouser pocket he stood and turned to find Witt in the doorway, his head on one side, his expression aggressively blank. He wore a white Kopala towel around his waist and another over his shoulder, and there were smears of shaving foam on his neck.

"D'you find what you're looking for?"

"Arnold. Hi. I'm here again." Hammer grinned, and pulled out his social security card from his pocket, where he had put it earlier. "There's a little gutter down there, like a little lip. Quite a relief." He made to leave. "Arnold, I've been a real pain in the butt. I'm sorry. This is the last time you'll see me."

"What about the other thing you got in there?"

"Excuse me?"

"Whatever you just put in your pants. I'd like you to tell me about that."

"My wallet?" Hammer's hand went to his back pocket.

"Uh-uh. Not that. If that's drugs or some other nonsense in my room I want to know about it."

"You sure about that?"

Witt didn't have an answer.

"OK," said Hammer. "You're right. I didn't want this but it's my mistake. Arnold, would you get Mary out here?"

Witt hesitated, unsure. "I think we should leave her out of this."

"What I have to say, I have to say to both of you. It's nothing bad."

Witt held Hammer's eye and made up his mind. "Good thing you got a good face." He turned to the room and shouted to his wife. "Mary. Mary, come on out here."

Mrs. Witt had put on a dress and wrapped a towel round her head. She looked warily at Hammer and went to stand by her husband.

"Please," said Hammer. "Have a seat." He sat down on one of the lounge chairs. "Please. I can't shout about this."

The Witts sat opposite him, as upright as anyone has ever sat on a lounge chair, and Hammer dropped his voice low so that they were forced to lean in.

"Tell me. Have you noticed any strange activity in this room?"

They both looked at him, half suspicious, half intent.

"Your things being moved around? Housekeeping coming in at strange times of day? Any beeps or clicks on the phone?"

The Witts had gone from looking lost to looking nervous.

"No. I mean I don't think so. Why would—"

"That's good, but then you might not notice. OK. Here it is." He dropped his voice a further notch. "This business in Georgia? There's a US dimension to it."

He let the words take effect before going on.

"The president loses the next election and Russia's hold on the Caucasus is complete. Yes?"

"Sure," said Witt, relieved by the relative sanity of the statement, but sounding less sure than he might.

"That's a nightmare for us. It's probably going to happen and we're going to have to get used to it. But these riots? We suspect foul play."

He raised a meaningful eyebrow, made sure the Witts grasped the severity of the implications, and went on.

"Up until three days ago, a colleague of mine was staying in this room. He chose it because from up here, with the right equipment, you get a great view of a certain house across the river. I can't tell you what goes on there but let's just say that there are some interesting comings and goings. Yes? Now this colleague, he's gone missing. These papers," he patted his pocket, "he left for me to find. Until this evening, I didn't know where."

Hammer paused, and looked steadily at one then the other.

"OK. You know what I'm going to say now, yes?"

Mr. and Mrs. Witt were lost.

"What I've told you can't leave this room. That's very important."

"Of course."

"Also, I'm going to give you a number." He stood, went inside, and came back with pen and Kopala paper. "Anything unusual happens in here I want you to call me. Don't use the hotel phone. You have a cell?"

"I got a cell," said Arnold Witt.

"That should be OK. Here, Arnold. Keep this safe."

Witt took it and made to stand.

"Don't get up. Please accept my apologies for bringing this into your holiday."

"Is there anything we could do to help?" said Witt. His wife blinked slowly, not seconding the offer.

"Do you know, Arnold, there is. Just a small thing. I'm going out now. You happen to be here, you hear footsteps in my room in the next two hours, you let me know. If I can, I'll see you at breakfast tomorrow."

"We're not going anywhere," said Witt. "Not tonight. We'll leave that to guys like you."

"That's probably best. And one last thing. Never put the clean-my-room sign on your door. It's an open invitation for thieves."

It was a neat packet, constructed with care. Inside, once he had torn through the many layers of plastic, Hammer found a sheaf of documents that had been carefully folded in half and then in half again. There were several pages torn from a ring-bound notebook and covered in Webster's swift, expansive handwriting, which Hammer had always had trouble reading. But the final document was a fax of two paragraphs, all information about its origins removed, in typed Russian—which he couldn't read at all.

Batumi would have to wait until morning.

TEN

L ast night's riot had started in Freedom Square, by the city hall, and according to Rostom a few thousand people were already there again. Police had been drafted in from Rustavi and Kutaisi and all over, and a huge number were now stationed around the city. The only good advice was to stay in the hotel, but if Mr. Hammer insisted on going out he should stay in the old town, and at all costs well away from the square.

Hammer thanked him, walked down to the bridge, crossed the river, and turned right onto the busy road that led to the new town.

It was another warm evening, the day's heat caught hanging in the air and close on his skin. He passed police slowly patrolling the streets, machine guns slung casually across their chests, and watched police vans racing ahead of him with their lights flashing. Every face he saw looked Georgian. The tourists had already left or were staying inside.

The tail was there again, as he knew it would be. Two men on foot, one of whom he recognized from earlier, and a car, a blue Toyota this time. A proper team. He was gaining in importance. He kept his pace steady and stayed on wide streets where his pursuers were unlikely to worry about losing him.

Soon he was part of a flow of people that slowed and thickened the nearer it came to the square. Songs broke out and fists punched the air. Red T-shirts were everywhere. This was a different crowd from the night before—there were old women, mothers with their children—but the anger was a constant. Hammer could hear it in the shouting, see it in the jaws set all around him. A heavy-headed man in a denim shirt walking by him clasped his shoulder and asked him something in Georgian. Hammer smiled up at him and shrugged, and the man seemed content with the reply. Soon they weren't walking but marching, all at a uniform rate.

Ahead, he heard a speech being made over loudspeakers, loud cheers punctuating it. The flow became a mass, which slowed as they reached the square itself and patiently shuffled into the standing crowd that already filled the space. Thousands of bodies, a different sort of heat coming off them, all intently facing a platform fifty yards away where a tiny figure was pacing and gesticulating, his words booming at them and drawing huge cheers in return. Hammer kept moving onward through the hot air and the smell of fresh sweat, threading his way through the press of people, not stopping but occasionally looking over his shoulder to see whether he could see movement behind him. A long way back there was some jostling, and through the heads of the crowd he glimpsed one of his tails pushing people out of his way. He became more conscious than ever of the documents folded in his back pocket.

He went faster, trying to slip between people and leave as little trace of his direction as possible. Most ignored him; some scowled at the disturbance. "Gmadlobt," he said often, and tried his best smile. Behind him he could hear a single voice shouting commands over the tinny drone of the speech, and a rumble of discontent in response. The crowd was thicker here in the center of the square, and he had to use his arms in front of him to pry open space between the bodies. He was beginning to get on people's nerves.

A hand grabbed the collar of his shirt, twisting, and brought him to an abrupt stop. Hammer looked round into the full beard and gray eyes of a solid man who was regarding him with curious contempt, a sneer on his lip. He wore the red T-shirt of the opposition, and in his free hand held an unlit cigarette.

"Sorry," said Hammer, wishing he knew the Georgian word. His captor brought him closer, until they were only a foot apart, and bending down said something slow and threatening whose gist Hammer thought he understood. He was close enough to see a small patch of bare skin in the man's beard and smell old coffee on his breath.

"I'm sorry," he said, reaching up to his neck to try and loosen the man's grip and wondering whether to bring his knee up into his groin. "I have to go." The Georgian said something else and twisted Hammer's shirt a little harder. Over the man's shoulder he could see the policeman gaining, now only a few arm's lengths away. "Police," he said to the man, pointing the way he had come. "Polis. Polizei. They're chasing me."

The man turned to look and saw the policeman approaching, the only person in the crowd in a suit. His sunglasses weren't helping; he looked every bit the secret service agent. Hammer felt the grip relax, and without saying anything the bearded man let him go with a push in the right direction. As he set off he saw his new friend square up to the policeman, with his arms out, and draw some of his neighbors into the cause. The policeman pulled out a badge, but as Hammer disappeared finally into the crowd the last thing he saw when he looked back was the bearded man pushing his new prey hard in the chest with the flat of his hand.

Despite his maneuvers, he was first to arrive. She had named somewhere at the edge of the old town as it backed up against thickly wooded hills, in a hidden square where people on benches talked intently and old men played bowls on a broad track of sand. Hammer could hear amplified voices in the far distance but no one here seemed conscious of them. They might have been in a different country altogether.

The restaurant was called Pascal and inside, with its bare brick walls and wooden floor, it reminded him of cafés in Greenwich Village from many years ago. No two pieces of furniture were the same, and every old table, lamp, and chairback was covered in a different fabric, a calming mess of floral prints and faded stripes. A high, pretty room, conscious of its sense of romance, like the city around it. It was almost empty: three couples, a group of what looked like foreign students arguing earnestly across a table. A wooden record player played old European folk songs, and the reedy violin was a sound directly from his childhood. Someone might have designed all this to make him at once relaxed and unsure of himself. After that intense, seesawing day he finally felt comfortable, for the moment, at his corner table, and out of place. Somehow out of time. They had rye whiskey here, to his surprise, and he ordered one with ice.

A second day over, almost. His crop of information whirled around his head, refusing to be reconciled. Ben was investigating false bombs and fake suicides. He had come here to take a gangster's money; he had come to bury his friend. He was in Turkey, living the high life, or more likely in a makeshift grave. He sent a text to Elsa that hinted at progress and mentioned none of this.

Nothing was fixed in this country, Hammer realized. Certainties had deserted him. In their place was a set of rotating hunches and assumptions and half-truths whose probabilities he could only guess at. It was like playing poker with an unknown number of unseen opponents. Vekua was right: logic was twisted here, into a shape that he couldn't yet make out, but given long enough he might begin to see its outline. Already he had some dim, instinctive sense of it. If you were weak and ringed by enemies a hundred times more powerful, your national bearing would be a mixture of pride and steeliness and cunning. That he understood. What he didn't understand was the charm. In a little over a day he'd been beaten up, arrested, followed, briefly kidnapped, and threatened with being savaged by a bear, a first in his experience, but Tbilisi was nevertheless beginning to take hold of him. It had the precarious beauty of some delicate treasure that against all odds had survived repeated attempts to destroy it. The flaws were testament to the achievement.

Natela, when she came, seemed intent on piercing the mood. She walked stiffly to the table, her back straight, and held out a rigid hand to Hammer as he rose. Her gaze said: you're still on trial; I can leave at any time. She was wearing the gray suit she had worn at work that morning, and around her was the fresh, dank smell of a cigarette just smoked.

"Thank you for coming," said Hammer, smiling but serious.

Natela sat, without replying, and looked around the room, from table to table, checking the faces, not looking at his.

"This is a nice place," he said.

She was trying to find something in her handbag on her lap. Without looking up she said, "It is Georgian but not Georgian. I come here when I want to escape."

"I'm amazed it's open."

She didn't respond but continued to root around in the large bag, which seemed full and unfathomable.

"With the demonstrations going on, I thought everything would be closed."

"Why? There is no demonstration here."

Finally, she gave up on the bag, put it on the floor, and fixed Hammer with a straight look, which he met. She did not return his smile.

"You say you have work. For me."

"I do," he said. "What will you drink?"

"Whiskey. With ice."

He attracted a waiter's attention and ordered two more.

"So you live in the city?"

"That does not matter."

"Actually, I know you do. At 23 Gudauri Street. Half an hour from here."

Natela sat even straighter in her chair. "How do you know this?"

"I'm an investigator. It's what I do." He drank the last of his drink and challenged her with a frank look. "It's in here." He pushed some folded papers across the table to her. "They're my friend's notes. Yours is one of a bunch of addresses and telephone numbers he needed." He separated out the sheets. "I can't read half of it, but they mention K a lot, and I think that's your husband."

"My husband, for all time."

"I'm sorry. Your ex-husband. I'm showing you this because I want you to see I'm keeping nothing from you. In my job you're taught to trust no one, but in fact that's never practical. Comes a point where you have to share, and you're the only person in Georgia I can begin to trust." He gave her a frank look. "You're also the only person in Georgia I know."

Her eyes relented and he thought she might smile, but she held it.

"So these are in English. But this," he brought the final sheet to the top, "is clear enough, but it's in Russian. And I don't speak Russian."

Natela scanned the document and frowned. "This is work?"

"Yes."

"It is nothing. How much you pay?"

"This much." From his jacket he produced the envelope.

Natela closed her eyes in frustration and shook her head. "No. No. I do not like tricks."

She pulled her chair out and Hammer reached across the table to touch her arm.

"Sit down, will you? You sure have powerful principles. Listen. I need to know what this says. I can't send it back to London because I can't do that safely. OK? I can't take it to a translator because God knows who they are or where it'll end up. You're the only answer I've got. That makes you valuable."

Staying where she was, her chair pushed back, Natela looked from the document to the envelope.

"I am here for work. Not gifts."

Hammer grinned, incredulous. "Natela, would you just take the money? Please? You need it, I need what you can give me. It's a transaction. A deal. I'm an American. This is what we do."

"In America money makes everything simple."

Their drinks came. Hammer took his, and the waiter set Natela's down on the table. She looked at it for a moment, shrugged, and tucked in her chair.

"Your nose. What is wrong?"

Hammer smoothed the bandage out across the bridge.

"I got in the way of someone's elbow. Careless of me."

"Does it hurt?"

"Just enough."

Apparently satisfied, she took the Russian fax and started studying it.

"You have pen?"

Hammer took a pencil from his pocket and pushed it across the table toward her. "Will you have something to eat?"

"Sure. Why not." She drank half an inch of whiskey and set the glass down. "But I pay."

Hammer laughed. "Is this a Georgian thing? Are you all like this?"

She glanced up from the document. "Why should we trust strangers? I do not know why you trust me."

Hammer watched her as she worked: in silence, concentrating, taking large sips from her glass. When it was empty he ordered her another. She wore no jewelry, he noticed, unless you counted the enamel clip that held her hair, nor any makeup. Freckles clustered at the bridge of her nose.

She was dark, her skin olive and tired around the eyes, which in this light were close to black. Her black hair was tied tightly back. Had her lips been fuller and her skin less dry she would have been beautiful in the way that men instantly prize, but Hammer saw something much greater there, in the lines on her brow, in the sorrow and humor of her eyes: a great seriousness, a deep engagement with life. This was someone who had never turned from reality, even when there had been rather too much of it. Beside her he had the odd sense, not usual with him, of feeling frivolous. Insubstantial.

"OK," she said at last with another shrug. "You want to know what is here?"

"Please."

"It says this. Thank you for your question. I have asked my normal—I do not know this word."

"Sources?"

"Sources. I have asked my normal sources the question and I have met a wall. In Russian, it is stena, literally wall. The wall cannot be climbed. I asked very high sources, and they all stated they did not know the subject, or any information. Nothing. So. Second . . ." she pointed with the pen.

"Paragraph."

"There are two possibilities, it says. One is subject not known in Russia. Two is subject who is special and no one can talk. Result is same."

She looked at Hammer, who smiled, alone, and nodded for her to go on.

"Then here, last one, it says this. I received strong feeling that subject was person sources were not happy to discuss. Person was . . . how you say . . . made safe . . ."

"Protected."

"Protected. This happens when person holds money for administrators or when person is spy."

She ringed the two Russian words, put down her pen, and started her second whiskey.

"'For administrators'?"

"For government. For politicians."

Hammer had suspected before but now was almost certain. The fax was from Mr. V, former KGB, former FSB, an old spy who was Webster's first resource for all matters Russian. Mr. V knew everyone in Moscow: from the men in the archive rooms who would quietly pull a file for a hundred dollars, to his old colleagues, the colonels and generals who had quietly taken back so much of the country.

"Are there any names? Of people?"

"No. Only this."

"Nothing else?"

Natela raised her eyebrows, as if to say that she didn't intend to repeat herself, and pushed the paper back to him.

"So, you are detective or spy?"

"I'm an investigator. I don't really trust spies."

She touched the paper.

"This is about Karlo?"

"Maybe. Ben sent a request to Russia. To find out about a person. This was what came back. I have no idea where it fits."

She nodded, considering.

"He is good friend, your friend?"

"He was."

"Not now?"

"We don't speak."

"Then why do you look for him?"

"It's complicated. I need him."

Natela nodded slowly, and then finished her drink all at once.

"The people who go away, they never go."

"What do you mean?"

"Your friend. Karlo. My apartment, they search it, I am sure. Sometimes they are waiting outside and they follow me to work, to supermarket. I want to scream at them that he is dead, it is over, I know nothing, but I cannot."

He shouldn't have called her. He hadn't thought.

"Did they follow you here?"

"I don't know; no, I did not see." She reached down for her bag. "Do you have family?"

"No. Passed me by."

"That is good. You can be a detective by yourself. Run around, investigate. No one will suffer. I need cigarette." She felt around in the bag. "I'm sorry. I should not have said."

"It's fine."

"Do you smoke?"

"No. That's another thing I left behind."

Natela surveyed the table, shook her head, and stood up.

"I have to go. I'm sorry."

He stood with her. "Stay. Let's order some food."

"I want to forget all this things."

They looked at each other for a moment, and he thought, perhaps fondly, that there was a trace of regret in her eyes.

"Would you take this?" said Hammer, picking up the envelope and holding it out for her. Natela eyed it, for the first time not sure.

"You did your part," he said.

She closed her eyes, as if making some accommodation with her conscience, and took it.

"Thank you."

"And take this. Call me if you need to."

He handed her a business card, and she took it with a nod.

"Good luck with your friend," she said, and went.

Hammer watched her leave, her steps quick, her bearing correct. At the door she stopped, took a moment to find something in her bag, and came back to the table.

"For my drinks," she said, dropping a twenty-lari note on the table and turning again.

It was too much, but Hammer knew better than to say anything, and with his own regret gathered his papers, put the twenty in his pocket, and picked up the menu.

ELEVEN

Hammer slept in pajamas, not for formality's sake but because he found that they kept his body evenly warm and encouraged an even sleep. As with most things, he had thought closely about it, to a point just short of fussiness. Now, sitting up in bed with his notebook open before him, the pajamas made him feel old. An old man gone to bed early while the city outside went inexorably about the business of living. The door onto the balcony was open and through it he could hear shouting and the yowling of sirens and dogs and the occasional crack of a distant gun.

These pajamas were Turkish, cotton, and had a scratchy label at the back of the neck. They could do with a few washes. He put his tired thoughts away and continued to fail to write anything coherent; after two whiskeys and some red wine and that long quick day, he could do little but catch fragments of his thoughts as they bounced about. Images of Ben, tied up or holed up or dead. Scattered bits of information with little to connect them. And one recurring memory, of Natela drinking whiskey as she worked, and of the pang of responsibility he had felt when he had realized that they would be listening to her phone.

Putting the book aside, he switched off his light and tried to concentrate on sleep. No matter what everything meant, he had to be up and at the car rental office by eight.

When there was a knock at the door five minutes later he was awake enough to hear it but not to register it as real. But it came again, a firm double knock, and switching on the light he swung himself slowly out of bed and went to answer it.

On the landing, backlit by the bright light on the stair, was Colonel Vekua, rigid and correct.

"Mr. Hammer. I am sorry to wake you."

"You didn't."

"Of course."

"Not quite."

Hammer blinked, growing used to the light.

"Can I come in?"

She was smiling her winning smile. No, he wanted to say. It's late, by my standards, and I've had better days, and the last thing I can stomach is sitting in my pajamas being charmed or warned or whatever you have in mind by yet another policeman or spy or whatever the hell you are. I would like to be left alone to do what really ought to be a simple enough if difficult job.

"Of course. Please."

He grabbed a robe from the bathroom.

"I get you anything?"

"What do you have?"

"Scotch. And that bizarre stuff you call water."

"Borjomi?"

"I don't know what it is. It tastes of plumbing."

"It is good for you. Your digestion."

"Like I said, plumbing."

Vekua smiled and pointed to the tiny bottle of Scotch he was holding. He poured it into the one clean glass, took another miniature for himself, and sat on the bed.

"Shouldn't you be out on the streets?"

She was in black again, a different suit but precisely cut and immaculate, even now, at the end of a hot day. She sat upright on the room's one chair with her hands clasped on her lap, still the same, strange combination of strict and engaged.

"I told you, I am not a policeman."

"But you must be busy."

"And you are important. Some people think."

"Really? You have big stuff going on here tonight."

She drank a little whiskey, considering.

"To you it looks big. To me it looks the same. Occasionally there is a little war that no one cares about. A bomb goes off. There are riots. The president changes. This will be the same, always. Georgia is a constant."

"That's cheery."

Vekua smiled. "You are American. You can believe in progress, because sometimes in your country there is progress. We have been the same for thousands of years. We are different animals."

Hammer drank, the whiskey jarring with the taste of toothpaste. This woman unsettled him.

"Forgive me for being direct, Elene, but what brings you here? I have an early start tomorrow."

Vekua smiled and put her drink down.

"I have been asked to tell you that you are embarrassing our police force."

"How am I doing that?"

"Do you always rent two hotel rooms in the same city?"

Hammer smiled back.

"OK. I get a little edgy when people are tailing me. Especially when they're not so good and I can see them all the time. No offense to your colleagues but they . . ."

"They are not my colleagues."

"Whoever they are, they're not the best."

"Was it necessary to lose them twice?"

"I lost them twice?"

"Mr. Hammer."

"I had no idea. I haven't seen a tail since the Marriott."

Vekua raised an eyebrow.

"They are not the best. But they do not have resources. It is difficult work, as you know."

Hammer acknowledged the point.

"If you continue, you will have to leave. I will not be able to argue for you again."

"If it makes things any easier, tomorrow I'm going to Batumi, follow a lead. Ben's wife just got a postcard from him. Tell them where I'm going, by all means."

"You have found him?"

Hammer shook his head. "We'll see."

"They may not follow you to Batumi. I will tell them."

"Thank you. Appreciated."

Finishing her whiskey, Vekua stood and held out her hand.

"This morning I looked in our files, about your friend."

"You did?"

This was curious. Hammer longed to ask her what she wanted in return.

"He was monitored, when he came to Tbilisi."

"I wondered."

"This is normal, at a time like this."

"You mean I'm not that special?"

"He was watched for two days. While he was in Tbilisi. Then the surveillance stopped."

"Why?"

"Because it was clear that he was no threat to our security."

Hammer waited for her to explain.

"He went to Karlo Toreli's funeral. Afterward he went to a bar, by himself. Then he went to a restaurant, with a woman. After that to another bar, and then back here, to this hotel. With the woman. On Tuesday we followed them to Gori and then we turned back."

"I guess you don't do marital work either, huh?"

"Excuse me?"

"Never mind."

Vekua opened the door and stepped out into the hall.

"Thank you for the drink. I am sorry to give this information."

"Hey, no problem. I'm not his keeper. Who was the girl?"

"We do not know. Russian, I think. Blonde. Not Georgian." She attempted a sympathetic look. "You will still go to Batumi?"

"I still need to find him."

Hammer slept, and dreamed deep, irretrievable dreams full of unnamed and fearful things churning about.

At their deepest point something like a great crash broke in, and when he opened his eyes the room was bright and voices not unlike those he had dreamed were shouting something he couldn't understand. Groggy, instantly registering anxiety, he twisted and raised himself on his elbows, and found two men standing over his bed. They looked like brothers—squat, heavy, heads shaved above recessed eyes, arms bulging—and at least one of them smelled strongly of cheap, soapy aftershave. One wore a shiny sky blue tracksuit, open a little at the neck to show knots of black hair and three or four gold chains, the other a leather jacket. The first one pulled the duvet off Hammer and flung it into a corner of the room.

"Polis," he shouted. "Passport."

Hammer felt small and exposed, like a bullied child. And old. He was fit enough, and strong enough, but not against people like this. These were expert frighteners. Career men. He made to stand and was pushed back onto the bed. Properly awake, he felt rage and fear starting up in him.

"Don't touch me, and tell me who you are." He kept his voice level.

"Passport."

"Tell me who you are."

The first man blinked dully, looked at his partner, and gave him the merest of nods. The second man moved toward Hammer, grabbed him by the arm, pulled him off the bed, and pushed him toward his partner. His chubby fingers dug in.

"You get the fuck off me."

Unhurried, the first man looked Hammer up and down and then stared at him hard. His eyes were dark and bloodshot. Without looking away he said something in Georgian, and his friend let go of Hammer's arm and started to search the room, opening cupboards and drawers and throwing what he found there behind him.

"It was stolen from me. I don't have it."

They didn't seem to understand. Hammer stayed where he was and watched, wondering who these men were and who had sent them. How many others they had intimidated and terrorized in their time. They looked nothing like police, and cruder than Iosava's mob—they were gangsters, plain as day, but then gangsters in places like this could work for anyone. The thought scared him: why involve such people if not to do the dirtiest of jobs? Last night, in the police station, he had felt ill equipped. Now, he felt acutely alone.

"I have money. There's money in my pants." No reaction from the man in front of him, who continued tirelessly staring. "Dollars. Lari."

Eventually the man gave up his search, throwing his hands up in a shrug. At some further instruction from his friend, he picked up Hammer's clothes from the chair where they had been neatly folded and thrust them at him.

"Uh-uh," said Hammer, shaking his head. "I'm not going anywhere."

The first man nodded, slow and deliberate.

"Forget it," said Hammer.

Reaching behind him and under his tracksuit top, the man produced a pistol—black, automatic, efficient—and holding it by his side nodded again.

TWELVE

There was no one in reception, and barely anybody on the streets. He had no idea what time it was, but the city had finally gone to sleep. He had no one to call to, and no words to call.

Hands bound with a plastic tie, Hammer sat in the back of the car next to the man with the gun, who held it casually in his lap. The air was a dull stink of cigarette smoke and bitter sweat. His neck squashing out under his massive bald head, the thug in the leather jacket was driving, too fast, along the empty road alongside the river and then off into a part of the city Hammer hadn't been to before, where the buildings grew less solid, the road more uneven. Houses gave way to warehouses and scrappy undeveloped lots studded with rusting machinery and overgrown with grass and weeds.

Now he was scared. Everything else had been negotiable, but this—this was looking final. His last trip. The fear was different, too—consuming, but somehow healthy. If he had ever worried that life had no meaning, now he knew without doubt that it did.

At a red signal Hammer quietly moved his hands across to try his door, ready to spring as quickly as he could into the dark side streets, but found it locked.

"Where are you taking me?"

The man with the gun seemed not to hear. Hammer patted the pocket of his trousers.

"There's money here. Lari. How much do you want? I'm a rich man. Ten thousand dollars."

The car continued to drive.

"No one's paying you anything like ten thousand dollars. You want to be rich?" Nothing. "A hundred thousand."

But neither man answered, and their silence felt like the end.

Finally, they stopped at what seemed to be the edge of the city, a black wasteland of dead buildings and abandoned things. Nothing happened here; no one came here. That was why he had been brought.

Hammer felt his heart quicken and his breath go short. This was the kind of fate he'd imagined for Ben, but it seemed it had been his own all along. He cursed his preparations, or the lack of them. He should have found a bodyguard of his own. What would that have taken, a couple of calls and a hundred bucks a day? Never underestimate your opponent. How many times had he said it? Even if you had no idea who they might be.

The first man pulled him from the car and marched him with the gun at his back toward a compound of low prefabricated buildings surrounded by a high metal fence and sparsely lit by two dim lights in dirty housings. In among them stood a larger concrete block, windowless, with a stubby chimney rising above it. Three ancient vans stood by the gate. A waste management plant, Hammer thought. The mob were the same the world over. In the air there was the sound of howling and an acrid stench of ammonia and shit that went deep inside and made it impossible to think. His captors seemed not to notice and pushed him on. He forced himself to think.

Four concrete blocks marked the end of the road and beyond them, perhaps half a mile away through the darkness, he could see a highway with the odd car and truck on it. The ground in between he couldn't see, but whatever was there couldn't be worse than being shot in the head without any kind of struggle. Probably they'd simply shoot him in the back instead, but it was dark, and he was still quick, and neither of these lunks was a runner. Poor odds, but at least they were odds.

Hammer ran. Got a good start on the loose dirt underfoot and, leaning forward as far as he could with his hands tied together, set off, half a dozen determined strides, aiming for a gap in the concrete blocks and waiting every moment for a shot to crack the air and tear into his back. Voices shouted and footsteps followed, clumsy and heavy, and still he ran. Then with an abrupt clap a shot came, and he felt the muscles in his back tense in expectation, but the bullet flew past him—where, he couldn't tell. A second, then a third; he was off the road now and forced himself to concentrate on staying upright on the sand and stone that stretched ahead of him. The light to see by was going and a single stumble would end it. Ignoring the shouting and the shots he propelled himself forward, foot after foot, until, coming down a bank, he saw the darkness in front of him take on a different quality and only by sliding onto his backside stopped himself from pitching into the lights from the road reflected in a broad channel of water.

"Fuck," said Hammer, and pushing himself up on his elbow got upright again. The water ran across his path, a canal of some sort; it must have been twenty yards to the other side. He ran to his right but found the driver scrabbling down the bank; turned to see the other man standing above him with his gun faintly silhouetted against the night sky.

"Sakmarisi," said the man, and gestured to his partner, who walked calmly toward Hammer and with the back of his clenched hand struck him across the face. Hammer cried out with pain and felt himself being pushed up the slope, back toward his fate.

While the driver held Hammer tightly by the arm his friend shot the padlock off the railings that ran round the compound. The first bullet didn't do it, and he fired another, relaxed in the knowledge that there was no one nearby to hear or care. Breathing hard from the exertion, Hammer turned away, his head resounding with the noise and the fresh pain, but he couldn't escape the smell—an unholy caustic dying reek that seemed to occupy the whole of him. Like sulfur and burning tires and month-old fish. Somehow it scared him more than the two men who had such total power over him. He brought his sleeve up to his newly broken nose in a hopeless attempt to filter it.

As the ringing of the shot died and he was pushed through the gate a frenzy of barking began, and over it the howling Hammer had heard earlier, high and ghostly. There were dogs here. Many of them—dozens, it sounded like, fear in all their voices. Hammer recognized it as his own.

He was pushed past the low buildings to the side of the enclosure and rounding the corner saw in the scant light two rows of pens made of chain-link fencing about six feet high. There were maybe ten in all, and in each one there were ten or fifteen dogs, some lying down, some prowling madly, some with their muzzles pressed to the wire and their teeth bared, angrily barking, crazed at the sight of the three men. The straw in their cages was matted with feces and slick with urine. Hammer halted, gagging at the smell, and was pushed ahead once more. This was where the strays were brought to be destroyed. This was where he had been brought for the same purpose. He looked at the dogs and wondered who was better off, the ones who didn't understand or the ones who had given up hope. With panic starting up in him he struggled against the grip on his arm but it was unyielding, and too strong.

The man with the gun walked down the corridor between the two pens and, stopping by the last one on the right, took a flashlight from his pocket and shone it inside. A large black dog was by the door; Hammer could see its ribs under molting fur and a red sore that ran from its neck down its foreleg. As the light flashed in its eye it bared its teeth and gave a long, low growl. A smaller dog, tan and wire-haired, yapped behind it, alternately inching toward and backing away from the fence.

The man aimed the gun at the smaller dog and shot it. The bullet struck it in the flank, halfway along, and Hammer shouted out as he watched it topple from the force. Something about the casualness of the act and its innocent victim appalled him, even here. The black dog whimpered and turned, and as it backed away the man tucked the gun in the back of his trousers, opened the door to the cage, took the dying dog by the scruff of its neck, and pulled it out, shutting the door behind him. He held the dog by his side, its blood streaking his tracksuit.

With a jerk of his head he told his friend to follow, and set off toward the biggest of the buildings, three stories tall and now looming over them in the night. In the light of the flashlight, Hammer saw the dog's blood dripping onto the ground and by some old, futile instinct stepped around it. The butt of the pistol was visible under the man's tracksuit and he began to imagine how he might reach it, but his guard seemed wise to the possibility, and hung back while his friend opened the heavy metal doors.

The stench outside was of animal decay; in here it was chemical, like a blast of bleach with fire in it. It hit Hammer in the face, burning his eyes and the back of his throat and causing a new terror to rush through him. He fought again to get free, stamped his feet on the man's shoes, tried to wrestle his arm away, but the man tightened his hold and then brought the point of his elbow sharply onto the base of Hammer's neck. His knees went and he sank back, powerless, into the man's arms.

The lights were on. He was being dragged through a vestibule into a larger space, perhaps twenty feet wide, that was gloomily lit by two fluorescent strips. The walls and ceiling were concrete and filthy with muck and blood; but for a tiled strip running round the outside, the floor was a pool of liquid.

Hammer knew what it was the moment he saw it. It was thick, like loose mud, and an uneven brown made up of blacks and dull reds, and though it was still it seemed to seethe, as if it had purpose of some kind. There was a pure horror in it. He turned away, but that did nothing to dull the sense of it, the dark presence that filled his head. His chest had tightened and his lungs seemed to contract.

One of the men shouted, and Hammer felt his head being lifted by the hair above his ears.

"Please," he said. This was how he would die. Pleading for life to men who had never known the value of it. "Please."

He hadn't thought he would beg. He would go out nobly, even if there was no one to see his dignity. But that was a vain thought; of course you begged. Every cell in him was straining in terror from the end that seethed and swirled beside him, and his tongue was no different.

"Don't." If he could see the man's eyes, find some forgotten scrap of good in them. But his head was being twisted away.

His time hadn't come. He was just required to watch.

The leader was squatting down halfway round the side of the pool, holding the dog out with a straight arm above the sludge. The dog seemed to be moving, but Hammer couldn't tell whether it was alive or just swinging in the man's grip.

He let go, and the dog dropped onto the surface of the liquid, sank an inch and stayed there, its legs out awkwardly beside it.

It was still, thank God; already dead. A terrier: short-haired and black-eyed, a chunk gone from its uppermost ear. Nothing happened for several seconds, and then Hammer heard a faint fizzing noise as the fur began to burn. He looked away but the man in the blue shell suit was by him now, gripping his chin and forcing him to watch.

After thirty seconds the fur was slipping off; after a minute the flesh on the creature's legs began to dissolve, melting into the ooze around it. A minute later, bone showed on its front leg. Through the acid fumes Hammer could smell burning meat. Time slowed to a stop.

Revulsion and fear filled him; he had had enough. He wrenched his head from the man's hand and looked him full in the eye.

"Fuck it. If you're going to do it, do it."

The man glanced at his partner, nodded, a mere jerk of the chin, and grabbed Hammer's shirt around the neck, twisting it until he had a firm grip. Then he turned so that Hammer's back was to the pool and his shoes at its edge, and began to lower him toward the surface. Hammer grabbed instinctively at the man's jacket and let his feet slip between his legs, but still he went down, the fumes growing stronger, until his head was six inches away.

The man's face above him was fat and solid and certain. He didn't blink. Sweat beaded at his hairline; half his teeth were yellow-black. On his neck a tattooed spider crawled up toward his face. Tightening his fist he let Hammer down.

Hammer could sense the acid beneath him as surely as if it had been a flame and its heat playing over his skin. His bravery was all external. All he knew was his fear. He closed his eyes and when he did he saw Ben, and Elsa. Saw Natela, at dinner, pen in hand.

"You. Go."

Hammer opened his eyes and the man repeated what he had said.

"You. Go."

With that he swung Hammer round and flung him hard against the wall. For a moment he stood over his broken form, letting his prey appreciate the quality of his mercy, then nodded to his partner.

"You go. Georgia. Now," he said, and together they left, calmly, their work done.

Hammer stayed where he was, on one elbow, pressed awkwardly against the wall, tears of fear and exhaustion and pure release starting in his eyes. The dog was almost gone.

The palm of his hand was tingling sharply, beginning to burn. Some acid had splashed onto the tiles and was now eating into his trousers and the sleeve of his sweater. He stood quickly and left the gruesome place, staggering out into the air and breathing the dogs' stench with something like relief. Hardly hearing the barking all around him, he watched the car drive away, throwing up dirt behind it.

By the pens was a pile of buckets and a freestanding tap. He rubbed the water between his hands and let it run over his clothes, and when he was done brought some up to his face in his palms, again and again, the cold vital and pure and finally familiar.

Still the dogs barked. As quickly as he could, Hammer made his way between the two sets of pens, shooting back the bolts as he went.

THIRTEEN

The first thing he did when he got back to the hotel was to tidy his room. As long as his things were strewn all over the floor those men would still be here, and it was important that he forget their existence. They had to cease to exist. This was logical: nothing could happen while they remained in his head, so he set about forcing them out. Put his clothes away, made the bed, restored order. Checked his passport, taped inside the gathered tops of the curtain. Showered, with his head bent under the jet, until his skin was red from the heat and the stench had begun to leave his nostrils. Removed all the traces.

The aftershave was still there, though, when he came back into the room, hanging in the air like a memory he could neither confront nor banish, and for a moment he stood in the doorway and contemplated the knowledge that those men and that place would always remain. They had made themselves a part of him. This was what such people did, the world over, every day. They got inside and didn't leave.

It was five now, and the day had begun. Hammer dressed in his new shorts and T-shirt and pulled on his new sneakers and left the hotel to run, over the bridge, into the old town, through the waking streets, bidding "gamarjobat" to the few Georgians he saw, reconstituting himself. Being Isaac David Hammer. Who had not gone so soft in his comfortable middle age that he couldn't absorb some hardship, or overcome a trial. That was all this was. A trial.

He found the steep road to the castle and attacked it as fast as he could manage until the air was deep in his lungs, expelling the acid fumes collected there. At the top he turned and flew down the hill and at the bottom turned again to make the climb. God, how alive everything was. Every tree, every face, every leaf of every vine, every crack in the wall, sharply defined as itself, lit from within. He felt the fear begin to leave him.

On the fourth repetition the roar in his head was beginning to fade and he found himself able to think. Those men could have been working for anyone—for the police, who couldn't be seen to terrorize him, or for Iosava, who didn't like being scorned. For someone else, whose motives he couldn't possibly know. Who they were didn't matter, not yet.

All that mattered was that they didn't want him here, and he could think of only two reasons for that. Because he was Ike Hammer, and there was an election, and someone thought he was up to no good. Or because he was looking for Ben, and Ben had stuck his meddling nose into some delicate business neither of them could do more than guess at.

But then, if Vekua was to be believed, it wasn't Ben's nose that was leading him west.

There were so many possibilities. This woman, the Russian, was helping Ben; he was investigating her; Vekua was lying to get him out of Tbilisi; Iosava was lying, and Ben was here for other reasons altogether. For a while Hammer's mind flitted from one to the next, until he realized that he should be looking not for the answer, but only the next step. And that was to Batumi.

Almost the moment he stopped running, the doubt set in. You. Go. The words were imprinted on him. When he closed his eyes, he saw them, and the man who had said them, saw his blackened teeth and the spider forever stamped on his neck. Smelled the sweet soapy smell of his aftershave.

In three or four hours he could be on a plane, in business class, safely cosseted in a world he understood. By this evening he and Hibbert could be working out a solution to his problems that didn't involve Ben. And Hibbert was good—at the very least he'd minimize the damage, and maybe better than that. Maybe there was a route out of this Hammer hadn't even considered.

It was crazy to come here. Fear drove me, and the need to do something in the face of it. If I was a wiser man, I'd have stayed and toughed it out. Following Ben was the sort of idiocy Ben indulged, and like all his follies, just another form of running away.

And then a voice that until now he hadn't chosen to heed told him why he had really come. He wasn't here to protect himself from Detective Inspector Sander and the worst that she could do, or to save the company that had become his life, though he wanted both those things. He was here to prove Ben wrong—to show that this gross hypocrite could still do something selfless and plainly good. And to rub the bastard's superior nose in it.

By eight he was packed and ready and waiting by the car-rental office for the door to open—tired, pale, but something approaching himself. The second day without his medication. Only when he thought of it did he miss it.

They had his booking, and his paperwork was all in order. All they needed was a credit card, which he gave them, and a driver's license, which he could not. Usually it sat in its own pocket in his wallet, behind the credit cards and the library card and the coffee shop loyalty card, but now it was gone, no matter how many times he looked. He was certain it had been there after the riot and less certain that it had survived the police station or the search of his room.

Plead as he might, Hammer couldn't persuade the charming man behind the counter to make an exception in his case, even with the offer of more money, perhaps in cash. With great reluctance he left, and surveyed his options. A car was out; chances were that no rental company in Tbilisi would take him. He had dismissed the taxi driver who had brought him here and who in any case drove like a lunatic and spoke no English. And that day's one train to Batumi had just left.

Scanning the traffic for cabs, he phoned the Kopala. Rostom answered, and from him Hammer learned that his driver was still off work but they had other drivers they could provide, a good one came to mind, an older man, experienced, knew Georgia very well. Rostom would call him and see if he was free.

FOURTEEN

Across the plain west of Tbilisi the wind gusted, strong enough to shunt the car out of its lane and into the wayward traffic ahead. Hammer's new driver, twitching the wheel, didn't seem to mind—the lanes were a loose guide, and overtaking a lazy drift across and a lazier drifting back. They spent half their time on the white line. But Hammer saw no point in protesting. As a taxi driver in Istanbul had once explained to him, it was all in God's hands.

Koba was genial, at least, knew where he was going, and clearly wanted the work; he had been at the Kopala within twenty minutes, helping Hammer with his bags, promising to take him to all the most ancient sites in Georgia, and generally behaving with great hustle and verve. Hammer was grateful to be distracted.

"Ha!" Koba had said, on meeting his client, "We are brothers, yes?"—making great show of the discovery that they were the same height and roughly the same age and had less hair than had once been the case. Hammer was five years his junior, probably, but in every other respect they would have made strange brothers indeed. Where Hammer was slight, Koba—he volunteered no surname—was broad across the shoulders and round through the middle, filling out all the contours of a white linen shirt that was thin with wear; and where Hammer, though he cared little about it, was always careful with his appearance, Koba seemed rather more relaxed. Three or four days' growth of graying beard sat by his white mustache, and a distinctive smell of sweat and cigarettes and last night's garlic followed him around.

All this was fine with Hammer, who was pleased with the way things had worked out; for a hundred bucks a day he was getting a driver, a guide, a half-decent translator, and someone to talk to. And this morning he needed to talk.

The sun shone and the wind blew at them and they quickly left Tbilisi behind.

"You live in a crazy city," said Hammer as they headed into open country.

"Ya," said Koba. "Everyone crazy." He tapped his temple with a stubby finger.

Hammer learned that no, Koba had not always been a driver; he had lost his job as a building inspector five years earlier and, jobs in Georgia being scarce for normal people, had been forced to take whatever work came his way ever since; he had his 4 x 4, a good car, thanks God, and he drove for people when he could—mainly tourists, taking them up into the mountains or to the seaside, but also some local businessmen, friends of his, who did their best to keep him busy. When there was no driving he did whatever else came his way. His wife had work as a cleaner in a government building, and their children had all left home, thanks God, and when there was time he and Lela went to their little house up near the mountains—a tiny house, but Hammer must come, of course, there was a bed for him; after Batumi they would go. There he kept bees and grew some grapes and made chacha, very good chacha, they would drink some later, because since this president came to power it was no longer as easy to drink and then drive. Hammer should have some now. Two fingers, for the journey. With persistence, Hammer persuaded him that he would wait.

Koba was an easy talker, and with the help of some sweeping sign language made himself well understood. He had a slow, thick voice that Hammer liked, stretching all the vowels until they were halfway to song. Ten miles outside Tbilisi he pointed to his right, where miles of flat hot fields reached up to a low range of mountains that ran across the horizon. They passed a sign: Ankara, 995.

"Beautiful, yes?"

"Very beautiful."

"There is story, all Georgians know. You believe in God, Isaac?"

"Less than I should."

Koba looked across, puzzled.

"I don't think about it so much."

Koba replied with a deep, tolerant nod, as if he were a big enough man to accept all positions.

"Is OK. Is normal. Story is about God. He has finished world, has made all things, and He says to all peoples, come, I will give your land. Yes?" He looked across for seconds at a time as he talked, so that Hammer, still on edge, was torn between meeting his eye and watching the road. "So Chechens come and God gives mountains to them. Armenians, they have desert. And on and on. All peoples wait, in big line. But Georgians, they are at big party. Much wine, much chacha. And when they come, line has gone. Yes?" Koba glanced back to the road and twitched the car back into its lane. "God says to them, is no more land, land is all gone. You are late. Why you are late? And Georgians, they, how you say?" Koba dipped his head emphatically toward the steering wheel, twice.

"Bow," said Hammer, promptly.

"Bow. They bow, and say we were drinking to Your name, oh good God. And God, He is so happy He says OK, I give you land I keep for myself."

Koba grinned, and clapped Hammer on the shoulder with a thick, strong hand.

"Georgia is paradise. This is good. So everyone wants it. Not so good." Laughing, he jabbed a finger at the windshield toward the mountains in the distance. "Here is where I come to fight. Russians came here." He tapped his watch. "It was five years. Tanks and how you say? Army cars?"

"Jeeps."

"Ya, jeeps. Bombed Gori. In Tbilisi, we think we are next. Me, my friends, everyone, we take guns, stick, everything, come here. To fight Russians." He waved one belligerent hand at the mountains.

"Did you fight?"

"They run! How you say in American? They fuck their mothers."

"Motherfuckers," said Hammer.

"Ya, motherfuckers. They run. Or they stop. This, here, nearest they go to Tbilisi. It's good for them. Motherfuckers!" He laughed a grand laugh, his head so far back he could no longer see the road. Hammer was getting used to seeing him in profile: the squat forehead, the still muscular, sturdy neck, the flat drinker's nose, the old man's broken veins across his cheekbone.

"Smoke?" Koba pulled a packet of cigarettes from his pocket, thumbing the lid and offering him one.

Hammer shook his head. "No. Thank you. Not anymore."

"Is OK?"

"It's fine."

Leaning across, one eye occasionally on the road, Koba opened the glove box, scrabbled around in a mess of stuff, and after what seemed an age, as the car wandered toward the shoulder, produced a lighter.

"You have fight?" he said, lighting the cigarette.

"Excuse me?"

"This." He touched his nose.

"Oh, OK. Yes. I got into a fight."

"You hurt them more, yes, Isaac?"

He beamed at Hammer, the cigarette hanging from his lips.

"Something like that."

"Of course. We are brothers." He took a deep drag. "You want go to Gori, yes? Stalin museum."

Hammer tried to explain that no, he didn't want to see the Stalin museum. He needed to go to the apartment building that had been bombed.

Koba's smile flattened out until his lips were a dry line.

"Apartment? Why?" he said.

"To pay my respects," said Hammer.

The driver shook his head. "I not understand."

"I want to give respect to the dead." He put his right hand across his breast, as if swearing allegiance. "It's the right thing to do, a visitor in your country."

The driver nodded intently and clasped Hammer's shoulder, so that the car began a new drift. "You are good man," he said. "Good here."

He mimicked Hammer's action, with a fist on his heart. "We go to Gori."

Koba headed into the town with great confidence, conceding only after twenty minutes of circling and stopping and doubling back that he didn't know the place so well, but though Hammer would have preferred no delay he was pleased to be off the main road, and content enough to watch Gori passing by: avenues of pine trees, pavements overhung with vines, old low streets lined with terraces of sandy houses that reminded him of Brooklyn. It was dusty and quiet, and the few people he saw seemed to be slowly going about some important but not urgent business.

After Koba had asked directions from an old man who wore nothing but shoes and dungarees, thanked him curtly for his long, complicated answer, and taken another wrong turn or two, they finally arrived. Away from the center the roads ran between colorless apartment blocks in leisurely rows, and one of them had been blocked off halfway with a makeshift barrier of netting and oil drums and planks of wood. Two policemen or soldiers in green fatigues stood one at each end and beyond them, like a dead tree in a healthy row, was the splintered stump of what had once been a building. Koba parked up on the pavement fifty yards short and Hammer started to walk toward it.

The far corner had collapsed entirely in a grim, twisting fall of concrete and rubble and rusted steel rods. The whole ground floor was gone, and the roof sagged down, but in between, behind the mess of plasterboard and cable and pipework that hung off the face of them like dead moss, many apartments could still be seen, open to inspection and curiously intimate, as if someone had wrenched off the front of the building to inspect the lives within. Blue wallpaper in one room, pink in another, patterns in a third, a patchwork effect. Most had been stripped, but objects remained to suggest the lives that had been lived and ended inside: a grimy mattress on its end against a wall, an upright chair, a mirror oddly unbroken. Hammer wondered whether the blast had taken everything with it and deposited it in the pile of debris that still lay before the building, or whether looters had made off with anything that hadn't been destroyed. Wondered, too, where the dead had been sleeping when the bomb had gone off, and how anyone had survived. No one beyond the second stairwell, where the whole structure had caved in, could possibly have made it out. Weeds had already begun to grow through the broken stuff on the ground, but even now the air smelled of woodsmoke, and ash spun in the wind.

This, too, was a first for Hammer. In Iraq he had seen buildings shelled and bombed, but never in peacetime, and never in a place that was otherwise so calm. There, it was the mess of war, and expected. Here, it was all too possible to see the blinding instant in which this community, these homes, once pristine like their neighbors, had ceased to exist. All along the wire fence that separated the building from the road, flowers and banners were tied.

For a moment he simply stood and looked. Koba was standing by his side.

"Very bad," Koba said.

"Very bad."

"Women here, children."

The soldiers had been watching them with a sort of casual care, and now one of them addressed Koba.

"He want to know who we are. I tell him we . . ." Koba finished his sentence by beating his chest twice with his fist. "I tell him you friend of Georgia."

"Ask him what he thinks happened," said Hammer, breaking from his thoughts. Koba looked at him to make sure he was serious, and at Hammer's nod shrugged and said something in Georgian.

"He says, Muslims come here and kill our families. From Dagestan. Like Shamil."

"Who is Shamil?"

"Shamil?" Koba shook his head and made a low groaning sound. "Motherfucker. Real motherfucker. He come to Georgia, kill women and children. Over and over."

"He did this?"

"No." Koba frowned and laughed at once. "No. Since two hundred years. Long time."

Hammer nodded, beginning to realize that time here had a different consistency. "Do you agree? With him?" He gestured at the soldier.

"With him? No. He is army. President's guy. After election, he change his mind."

"So you think the president did this?"

"Of course," said Koba. "Is normal."

FIFTEEN

They had coffee at the café where Ben had bought lunch, and when Hammer showed Ben's photograph to the old woman who ran the place she remembered him instantly because he had spoken Russian to her in an accent that was not quite Russian, and they had talked for a while about her nephew who had gone to study, not in London but in Bristol, which she thought was nearby. He had ordered khachapuri and coffee, and no one else was with him. She was certain about that. Hammer thanked her, left a tip good enough to draw a look from Koba, and then they set off for Batumi.

Once Hammer had politely explained that he didn't want to see the country's most beautiful national park, much as he would have liked to, or the splendid old church, or the even older church, or any of the other places that Koba suggested they visit along the way, it took only another three hours or so to reach the city. The more of these offers Hammer declined, the quieter Koba became, and the faster his driving, until it became important for Hammer to give him an explanation.

Though he might look like one, Hammer told him, he was not a tourist. He was in Georgia to find a friend of his, who had come here on holiday and had gone missing several days ago, and whose wife was beginning to be concerned. Sticking to an old maxim that the best lie was as close to the truth as you could make it, Hammer obscured a fair amount and embellished only a little, so that by the end of the journey Koba was alternately cursing Webster for abandoning his wife and children for the fleshpots of the East, and forgiving him for what was by all accounts an unusual lapse of character. All men must be allowed some time to themselves, he explained, to let off steam. This, too, was normal.

"Is good friend?"

"He was once."

"He do this for you?"

Hammer considered it. There was no doubt. "Yes. Yes, he would."

Half an hour short of the city Hammer's phone rang. His UK phone, a withheld number. It might be Hibbert, or Elsa. He hoped Elsa.

"Ike Hammer."

The line was poor and the road loud and he struggled to hear what the voice said, but something in it jogged an indistinct memory.

"I can't hear you. Tell me again."

The voice repeated what it had said, and in the mess of sounds he made out four words:

"We have your case."

Concentrating now, his ear pressed to the phone, Hammer gestured to Koba to wind up his window.

"You have what?"

"Case. With computer. And paper."

"You found these things?" But he knew the answer to that; this was the voice of the rioter who had pulled him from the taxi.

"Yes. We find. We give back. Tonight, you come, we give."

"I can't do tonight."

"Tonight. Only tonight."

"And you're just going to give them to me."

"We need reward."

"I thought so. OK. Listen closely. You want to give me my things today, you take them to the US embassy and I'll pick them up when I get back to Tbilisi. OK? How does that sound?"

The line was quiet.

"Two days ago you were a revolutionary hero, now you're just a thief. OK. Listen closely again. Those things aren't worth anything to anybody else, so I'm the only game in town for you. Right? You phone me again to-morrow and we'll fix a time and a place."

"Ten thousand dollars."

Hammer laughed. "You guys are hopeless. Call me tomorrow. Not before."

He hung up. Koba wound down the window, looked over at him.

"You have trouble, Isaac?"

"Motherfuckers, Koba. Just some motherfuckers."

It was a little after one when they arrived, and Hammer was keen to go straight to the restaurant where Webster had eaten, despite Koba's insistence that they eat at his friend's place a little out of town that served the best khinkali in Georgia, whatever they might be. This looked like it might cement his disappointment, but Hammer reminded him that their search was urgent, and that there was always dinner, and at last he rallied.

Batumi was all color and light. They drove along the seafront past grand old pink hotels and shining new casinos and neat municipal gardens full of red and yellow flowers. Couples strolled in the sun, and the wind inland had become a breeze. The whole city had a restful, end-of-season air. After the night he had had, Hammer felt a strange comfort in being able to smell the sea.

Restaurant Tamar, when they finally got there, turned out to occupy its own short pier that jutted thirty yards out into the water. A few tanned bodies splashed in the waves on either side. Hammer and Koba crunched over the stony beach, Koba complaining that this place would be no good, too touristic, bad khinkali. If they were quick with their questions, though, they might still make his friend's in time. He brightened instantly when they tried the door and found it locked.

"End of season," said Koba, studying a sign in the window. "Dinner only." He checked his watch. "This is good."

"Let's go to the Sheraton."

Koba was indignant. "No, Isaac. Sheraton very bad. We must eat."

"Koba, I don't have time." He put a finger on his watch. "Every minute is important."

"My friend, he is good guy, knows everyone in Batumi. Is good for you. He help, I help, your friend OK."

"Is it close?"

"Ya, very close."

Hammer sighed inside at the needless delay and set off back up the beach.

Koba's friend's place didn't look like a restaurant. And it wasn't close: it sat about three miles outside the city, set back from the road in what appeared to be a private house. There were no signs anywhere, nor any entrance: they simply drove into a courtyard, parked, and took one of the plastic tables that sat on a square of grass under an apricot tree. They were the only ones there.

A woman appeared, with two menus, and set a jug of water down in front of them. Koba consulted his menu for all of thirty seconds before closing it and making his order, with the confident air of a man who has made up his mind long before. An apricot fell from the tree onto the ground by Hammer's feet.

"I decide for us," he said, pouring himself a glass of water. "This for me. For you, you have wine from Kakheti. Very good. Just one liter."

One liter. That should be enough. Hammer thanked him, and with an apology called Mr. V.

It rang and rang.

"Allo."

"Vladimir?"

"Who is this?"

"Isaac Hammer, Vladimir. From Ikertu."

"Ah, Isaac! The great detective. It has been too many years. How is life? You are saving the world, I hope?"

"Not right now, no. I'm trying to save a friend of yours."

"Of mine?"

"I'm in Georgia. Ben's gone missing. You were the last person he called before he left."

"That is not good."

"So he called you?"

"He called me, yes. I told him and I tell you. I know nothing more. Whole thing is above my level, Isaac, you understand?"

"I understand. Did he tell you why he was asking?"

"Isaac, this is not a safe line."

"Whatever you can tell me."

There was a pause. "He sent me a fax. I sent him a fax. Then he called me, a week ago. Friday. He wanted to know what more I could tell him. Nothing. I ask him why he is interested, he told me that a friend had given him the name, and now it was very serious. That was all he said. That is all I know."

"What was the name?"

"I cannot tell you."

"If I came to Moscow?"

"I would say the same. Isaac, find Ben. He is a good friend. But it is better you do not call me again."

He hung up. Koba had leaned across the table to pour, a cigarette in his mouth.

"Delicious wine. From Kakheti. We go there, too. After Batumi. Drink."

Hammer took the little beaker and drank. It was good, resinous.

"That's got some punch."

"Ah, best wine. Thousands years old. Drink."

Koba topped up Hammer's glass with a look of pride and childlike regret.

"Ah, you lucky. First Kakheti wine."

Hammer smiled and sipped again, his thoughts still elsewhere.

The waitress brought plates of food—salads and bread and grilled meat and ghostly white dumplings—and in his hurry to clear a space Koba knocked over the jug of wine. Hammer watched it drip onto the grass with relief.

"Dedamotknuli!" he shouted. "Shevetsi. Now we must toast. In Georgia, you spill wine, you must toast the dead." He gestured for Hammer to finish what he had left.

"To the dead of Gori," said Hammer, raising his glass to Koba.

Koba looked grave, but pleased.

"You are good Georgian," he said.

SIXTEEN

Hotels held no pleasure for Hammer anymore, he had stayed in so many, but as an investigator he loved them: so much information, and no real determination to keep it private. There was a reason why Philip Marlowe and Sam Spade were forever finding themselves in hotels, talking to the house dick.

Now he was called the head of security, and at the Sheraton he was most obliging, once he and Hammer had agreed on terms (a hundred dollars, taken without shame). He hadn't noticed Webster, no, but then he wouldn't have. There were two hundred rooms and guests coming and going, and he tended only to pay attention to the high rollers, and they got quite a few of those. Mr. Webster had stayed in an executive double, facing the sea. Just the one night, with a bottle of champagne on room service, ordered at around six o'clock, and two glasses of cognac at one in the morning. Koba, who had been translating, remarked that it looked like Isaac's friend had had a good time.

And yes, it had definitely been him, because they had taken a copy of his passport. It was his, for sure, even in the poor photocopy they produced. So either Ben really had been here, or whoever had stolen his card had stolen his passport, too. Hammer asked if he could speak to the receptionists who had checked Webster in and out. One person had done both, it turned out, but she was off duty today. How about the maid? Who had turned down the bed that night?

The security chief found the maid, a Turkish woman with poor Georgian called Irem, who looked at the photograph on Hammer's phone and shook her head and then decided that maybe she had seen the man. She would start turning down the beds at seven, and one night recently, she couldn't be sure of the night, she had knocked as always and gone into one of the suites only to be shouted at by a man in a dressing gown who had emerged from the bathroom. He might have been that man. Was she sure? She wasn't sure. How many people did she think might have been in the room, Hammer asked her. Were there two suitcases or one? That, she couldn't remember.

No one remembered much more at the bar where Webster had drunk that night, or at the café at the airport, which was a couple of miles out of town. The bar owner thought the man in the photograph looked familiar. The short gray hair, almost silver, was distinctive. But perhaps not. It was the end of the season but still, so many people. The bureau de change showed no inclination to help. But Hammer did manage to charm the young woman at the ticket desk of Turkish Airlines into telling him that Webster had bought two tickets, one for himself and one for a woman called Galina Umov, a Russian, and that they had sat next to each other on the flight to Istanbul three days earlier. Again, Webster's passport number matched. For what it was worth, he called Katerina and gave her the new name.

Hammer returned to the city in low spirits. Ben was closer, but it gave him no pleasure. Was it possible? That he'd come all this way to catch a paltry cheat?

He owed Elsa a call, but couldn't bring himself to make it.

God, Ben didn't seem the type. He wasn't the type. Hammer had worked with him for eight years, traveled with him, been to his home, played with the children he so obviously adored. It was unimaginable, but then these things were. Men did this. They harbored some fantastic notion that there was a better future elsewhere, and invariably that future came in the form of a woman. It was a powerful and treacherous thought. He had known its power himself.

The skeptic in him resisted this conclusion, in spite of the plainness of the facts. There were other, hopeful interpretations, however tenuous: the woman was helping him, she was part of the plot, he was leaving a deliberate trail of some kind. Why else use his credit card?

But the balance had shifted, and now it looked as if this would be Hammer's last night in Georgia. Some people would be pleased.

Hammer felt like he had been chasing a man in a crowd, only to tap him on the shoulder finally and see the face of a stranger as he turned. The urgency went from him, and tiredness took hold. The last flight to Istanbul had left; the next was at eight the next day. All he could do was call one of his people in Turkey, a private detective called Talat, and ask him to check all the hotels in Istanbul for a Benedict Webster, who would have arrived three days earlier and might already have moved on. After that, he booked two rooms at the Sheraton, showered, changed, and waited outside the hotel for Koba, who was late.

When he arrived, Koba again argued the case of the six or seven restaurants in the city that were better than the place on the beach, and though Hammer was tempted to hang everything and have a decent dinner, to forget this sorry episode and start planning the next leg of his journey, he was too stubborn not to check this final lead. Promising Koba that from this point on he would bow to him on all matters of food, he insisted on Restaurant Tamar.

They were among the first, and were shown to a table at the end of the little pier. The sun was warm and low, and beneath their feet, through the boards, they could see waves breaking and dragging on the beach. Koba inspected the menu sternly.

"Let's have some fish," said Hammer.

Continuing to read, Koba shook his head.

"No fish?"

"Not good. Not so good. You ask questions, we go to other place. Good place."

"Koba, we're here now. Let's have a drink."

"I will get car."

"Koba."

"OK, OK," said Koba, with an air of frustrated martyrdom.

A waiter came and Koba ordered, bearishly asking questions and pushing out his bottom lip.

"And a bottle of their best wine," said Hammer.

"Is not so good," said Koba.

"Get it anyway. I want them to like us. And tell him I'd like to talk to the manager."

After five minutes a tall man in a black shirt and trousers came to the table carrying a bottle of wine and a corkscrew. He had the even, deliberate tan of someone who spends his spare afternoons lying in the sun. Koba, with an ill grace and a jerk of his chin, indicated that Hammer was the man to talk to.

"Gamarjobat," said Hammer, half standing from his seat to shake the manager's hand. "Gamarjobat. Do you speak any English?"

With a look of regret the manager shook his head.

"Then my friend will translate." Koba raised his eyebrows and nodded, and Hammer began. "You have a lovely place here." Koba delivered the compliment flatly, and the manager acknowledged it with a little bow. "Listen. I'm a detective. A private detective." He made sure Koba knew what he meant. "I'm here to find a man who has run away from his wife. OK? He was here four nights ago. This man." He unlocked his phone and showed him the picture of Webster. "Do you remember him?"

The manager shrugged. He thought so. He saw so many customers.

"Koba. Explain to him that I know exactly how much he spent. A hundred and seventy-three lari exactly. I need to find that bill, and speak to the person who served him."

Koba translated, and the manager laughed as he uncorked the wine.

"He says impossible," said Koba.

"Ask him if it's still impossible if I leave him a hundred-lari tip."

Koba frowned. "Is too much."

"It's fine."

Koba translated and the manager, pouring Hammer's wine, considered the offer before responding. Koba looked affronted, and they argued for a moment.

"I said fifty. He wants two hundred," said Koba, as if it was the most ridiculous notion, and took a deep drink.

"Tell him one fifty."

"Wine is terrible."

Finally a price was agreed on, and the manager went inside to see what he could do.

Food came, and Hammer was pleased to find that very little of it was meat, and that most of it was pretty good.

"This is OK," he told Koba, who made a face that didn't quite concede the point.

When the manager returned he had with him two small pieces of paper and a young waitress, whose pale, serious face was tense with worry.

"This is bill," said Koba, passing the papers to Hammer. One was the credit card slip, with a signature on it. At a glance it looked like Ben's. The bill was in Georgian, but the script was roman, and it seemed to show that two people had eaten.

"What's this?"

"Beer."

"And this?"

"Champagne. Two bottles."

"You don't remember two bottles of champagne?"

The manager shrugged.

"And this is her name? The waitress?"

Koba nodded.

"Tell him thank you very much. That's all for now."

The manager hesitated for a moment, but Koba repeated himself and he left. The waitress shifted on her feet.

"Nino. Thank you for talking to me. I won't be long." Hammer smiled. "Do you remember, a few nights ago, Tuesday, there was a man here, a foreigner, young but with gray hair. This was his bill. Do you remember him?"

Nino said that she thought she did.

"Where did they sit?"

She pointed to a table in the corner.

"Was he alone?"

No. He was with a woman.

"What did she look like?"

Koba translated as best he could. The woman was blond, young, pretty. Russian.

"They spoke Russian?"

Nino nodded.

"Only Russian?"

And some English, she thought.

Hammer asked her what the couple had eaten, how long they had stayed, whether they seemed to know each other well, and to each question Nino gave nervous answers that smacked of the truth. The couple had come late and seemed, in Koba's word, close. They hadn't seemed that interested in their food. They had held hands across the table. No, neither had smoked.

His questions almost at an end, Hammer thanked her and held up his phone for her to see. He had saved four photographs there, corporate mug shots downloaded from the websites of lawyers and consultants, all of men in their thirties with short gray hair. Webster's was in among them.

"Is this the man?"

Nino peered at the phone from a distance, as if she didn't want to come too close to it. She shook her head. Hammer swiped across the screen and showed her the next.

"This one?"

"Ah-rah." She shook her head again.

She said no to the third, and to Webster's, and to the last. Hammer went through them again, encouraging her to make sure of each. She was. None of these men had been to the restaurant that night.

Shyly, she began to say something in English, and then hesitated.

"What is it, Nino? Tell my friend."

The man she had seen was handsome, very handsome. But his hair was different. She had noticed it when she had stood by him to pour his wine, a bald patch at the back of his head. She remembered thinking that he was unlucky, to be losing his hair so young.

"Happens to the best of us, Nino. You're certain about this?"

"Diakh."

Hammer quizzed her a little more, but Nino was sure.

"Gmadlobt. You've been very helpful."

His mouth open, Koba watched Hammer hand her a hundred-lari note.

"You are crazy, Isaac. Is too much."

"We need to leave."

Koba put his glass down, triumph on his face.

"I tell you. Place no good."

"We need to leave Batumi. I have to be back in Tbilisi tonight." Standing up, Hammer pulled some more notes out of his wallet to cover the bill. "Let's go."

"But, Isaac. I cannot drive." Koba turned his empty wineglass upside down.

"You've had one glass. Come on."

But Koba shook his great head. "In Georgia, is same as ten glasses."

"I'll drive."

"You drink also. No, Isaac. Tonight we must stay."

SEVENTEEN

As they left the restaurant the sun was a red line on the horizon and the air had grown humid and thick, and together they trudged up the heavy beach like an old couple, Hammer impatient and ahead.

"I not understand," said Koba. "Where is your friend?"

"Not here."

"In Turkey now, yes?"

"If he wasn't here, he isn't there."

Koba put his hand on Hammer's shoulder, in part to steady himself.

"I not understand, Isaac."

Hammer stopped. "Someone wants me to think my friend was here. But he wasn't."

"What someone?"

"I don't know."

"Perhaps someone steal his card."

"Perhaps."

They started up the promenade at the top of the beach, Hammer brisk and always a few steps before Koba, thinking hard. The stalls were shut, the cafés quiet. Cars streamed past.

Whoever had been at the Sheraton, and at the restaurant, and everywhere else, it wasn't Ben. And if the impostor was a mere thief, he wouldn't have booked a flight out of the country on someone else's passport, or spoken Russian and English at dinner. No. This was a sham, a masquerade. A trail had been set for him and he'd followed it. He had been gulled.

In the past three days he had imagined so many fates for his friend: mugged for his money in the wrong part of town, kidnapped for ransom, knocked down by one of these crazy drivers, working out some personal torment in the wilderness. Drifting down the Kura River to the sea. He could discount all those. Whoever had done this had power, and resources, and a purpose.

Gori was the key. It had sat squarely in Hammer's imagination all day. He needed to know what had happened there: who had done this, and why, and by what dark means. Ben, of course, had wanted the same thing; he couldn't have seen what Hammer had seen and not felt compelled to investigate it. That was Ben. He had to know. And while he was a self-righteous bastard about it, he was right. To stand there and see that much pain and simply pass by, knowing you might help, was a betrayal, of oneself and the people who had died. There was no great difference between that and walking past a murder with your head turned.

His own mission had been feeling less and less righteous; now it felt wrong. Who was he here to help but himself? That unease, the dread that had been following him around, this was the cause of it. A herald of his hypocrisy.

In the trees bordering the wide pavement ahead some unexpected movement caught his eye, and above the noise of the traffic he could hear a sort of roaring that he couldn't identify. He slowed for a moment and was scanning the trees when from them, twenty yards away, staggered a drunk, his silhouette made strange by an overlong coat that swept its skirts across the ground. Howling at the night, he reeled and lurched toward the road, in his hand a glass bottle held high and oddly steady above his head. He looked set to pitch straight into the cars rushing along the street.

"Hey!" shouted Hammer, as loud as he could.

The drunk caught himself, just, swaying this way and that and looking round to see who had challenged him, the bottle now tucked into his chest. Bent almost double, he screamed something at Hammer and started moving toward him, muttering in Georgian as he came.

"Oh, great," said Hammer.

"Bozis shvilo," said Koba behind him.

"Gamarjobat," said Hammer, keeping a straight line. "Lovely evening."

As Hammer passed, the drunk reached out and grabbed his arm, slurring a string of words. The deep stink of filth and old booze radiated from him. He was young, as far as it was possible to tell, no older than forty, but had the dismal air of someone whose time was almost up. One glazed eye tried to stay on Hammer's face.

"No, thank you," said Hammer, jerking his hand away and shrinking from the smell.

Under all his clothes the man was slight but his grip was strong. He was leaning on Hammer now, still talking and making his points, whatever they were, by repeatedly shoving his bottle into Hammer's chest. Through the alcohol his breath had an empty metallic tang.

Puffed up, his big chest out, Koba came forward, screwed his hand into the clothes over the drunk's chest, and in one movement pulled him off Hammer and shoved him backward, hard, so that he fell to the ground in a sprawl. His bottle skittered over the pavement but didn't smash. Before Hammer could register what had happened, Koba stood over the man and kicked him hard in the thigh with the accomplished air of someone who has done such things before.

"No," shouted Hammer, dragging him back.

"Motherfucker," said Koba, shrugging Hammer's arm away and glaring back at the drunk, who was stirring on the ground. "He hurt you?"

Hammer had turned from him to tend to the drunk.

"No. I'm fine."

He squatted down and touched the man's shoulder. His eyes were closed, and the smell of ammonia rose up off him. Koba was still tensed, ready to continue.

"He needs a doctor. Where's the hospital?"

Koba made a low, disdainful noise, took a step back, and lit a cigarette. "Fuck him. Not need."

"Koba, he's a mess. Get the car."

"No way. My car?" Koba laughed. "No way in my car."

As Hammer stood to remonstrate, the drunk raised himself on his elbow, looked stupidly around him, and sat up.

"Are you all right?" said Hammer.

There was no recognition in his eyes, and it seemed likely that he remembered neither Hammer nor what had happened. He blinked a couple of times with his good eye and started to stand, Hammer instinctively supporting him.

"You need to see a doctor," said Hammer, but his drunken charge was up now, and moving. Without looking back, he stooped to pick up his bottle, all but empty, and stumped back through the trees.

"You see? He is fine. Motherfucker."

Hammer watched the man walking away and took a deep breath. The smell of him was still on his clothes and in the air.

"Isaac, you are too good. Such people do not deserve."

Before going to bed, Hammer picked a pair of tiny whiskey bottles from the fridge in his room, poured them into a glass, and sat on the bed. He had one more duty, and it would be the hardest part of the day.

Elsa picked up on the first ring.

"Ike."

"Hey. How you doing?"

"I'm OK."

"Good."

"Thanks for your texts."

She sounded cautious, as if she didn't know how things stood between them.

"I wish there'd been more to say."

"Are you . . . do you have anything?"

He took a drink, uncertain where to begin.

"I'm getting there. He did go to the funeral. He was in Tbilisi and then he went to a place called Gori. That's as far as I can see."

"You said you had a good lead."

"I did, but it's like all leads, it only gets you so far."

Elsa didn't respond.

"Hey. It's progress. Progress is good."

She was quiet for a moment longer, and Hammer knew she wasn't convinced.

"Ike, please. I can't get more worried. Tell me."

Oh boy, he thought, and told her about Iosava, and Gori, and the trail to Batumi that had turned out to be a fiction. He left out the men in his room and their visit to the dogs.

"So he was never there?"

"Never."

"Why? What does that mean?"

"Stop anyone coming to look. Listen, if I'd had a half-decent man in Georgia I'd have sent him, and chances are he'd have been happy with the story. They did a pretty good job, and anyone not looking really closely would have believed it. Or I might have done it all from London, on the phone, checking Ben's cards. Either way we'd think he was in Turkey now, with some woman, and this call would be very different. So whoever did it wants us to look the wrong way."

"Because something's happened to him."

That was the conclusion Hammer hadn't wanted to reach. Not with Elsa, at least.

"I can't think what else it means."

"God, Ike. What's he done?"

What had he done? What had he been thinking? For two days Hammer had been in Webster's world, but now he was jolted back to that other reality, of children and home and simple, immediate responsibilities. See the devastation in Gori and it became your duty to expose what had happened; speak to Elsa for a moment and you knew that was impossible. Both were essential and could not coexist.

This was the same paradox that had colored Ben's every moment at Ikertu. He loved it, he had loved Hammer, but his inability to ignore the tiniest promptings of his conscience had led him to try to destroy it. This Hammer at once understood and didn't understand. Understood the impulse but not the absence of any mechanism to control it. He had loved Ben for it, his seriousness, his sense of justice. But controlling impulses was what it was all about; learning to do so is life.

"Got himself involved. Like he always does."

Elsa said nothing for a moment.

"I don't think I can take much more of it, Ike."

"Hey, I may be wrong."

"No. You're not. Find him, would you? The mess he's made. For you and us. You were right. He needs to clear it up."

EIGHTEEN

In the rain you couldn't see what was coming, and that was almost a comfort. Whether he was disappointed about Borjomi, which again Hammer refused to visit, or ashamed of his treatment of the drunk the night before, Koba drove as hard as the rain fell, overtaking everyone they met, sliding round corners without slowing, playing chicken with any car bold enough to occupy the middle of the road. Hammer didn't protest; it was probably impossible to reconcile Koba's protectiveness with his desire to kill them both on the roads, or to curb either. It had been a long time since he'd met anyone whose energies ran in so many conflicting directions.

He was smoking more than usual, and if it hadn't been for Hammer would have been happy to do so with the windows closed. Hammer had opened his but the car was thick with smoke, and eventually he had to deal with it.

"Koba. Would you open your window a little, please?"

Koba looked across at him, drew on his cigarette, and opened the window an inch as he exhaled.

"I did bad last night. You think."

"No. I don't. I just need to get to Tbilisi."

But Koba, determined to be petulant, only raised his eyebrows.

"That man, he is fine. He is fine today."

"I know."

"I no stop him, he hurt you, that motherfucker."

"Koba. I was grateful. Really. Thank you."

Koba held his fingers up to the open window and let the wind take his cigarette.

"We will be quick, to Tbilisi."

"That's great."

The quicker the better. Hammer's anger with Ben was going; in its place arose a steadily swelling fear. For days now he had pictured himself victorious in the act of saving his former friend, refusing to crow but knowing that his own methods had been proved superior, and justified. He might tell himself that he took no pleasure in the notion, that he was a bigger man than that, but his own quest was selfish, a chance to save not just his creation and his name but his idea of himself.

After his discovery in Batumi, and his last conversation with Elsa, that vain little fantasy had collapsed. If he could simply find Ben alive he would give thanks to the God he hadn't addressed directly for the last fifty years. And besides, he wasn't sure that his idea of himself was worth saving. Ben ignored his responsibilities to chase some notion of justice. That was his problem. Hammer's was the reverse. He had no responsibilities, not really, no one who couldn't survive without him. And with this freedom, what had he done? Less than he should. He should have been the one out here investigating Karlo's death and the bombing of Gori. He should be making a difference, in Ben's trite, true words.

At least now he had made a start. The central question had changed from a what to a who. Ben had been in Gori. Gori was an hour from Tbilisi, but he had gone there with enough gas to last him a thousand miles. He was on his way somewhere, and it wasn't Batumi; even if he'd been aiming for the Black Sea, down to Turkey or up into Russia, the coastal road was lined with resorts. With that much fuel he had to be heading for the wilderness. Who benefited from stopping him?

If Iosava was telling the truth, the president was responsible, and therefore stood to benefit the most. He certainly had the resources and the instincts to mount the deception that followed. But Iosava wasn't a truth teller, Hammer guessed, by habit or inclination. At best he was a braggart, and at worst? At worst he could be running the whole thing: the bomb, Karlo's death, the lot. He had the money, the people, the links to Russia. A motive for encouraging Hammer on a false errand. What better way to finish the president for good? What better revenge?

Hammer would have paid a handsome fee to anyone who could tell him how this place was constructed: who was in hock to whom, who controlled the information, who had the real power. The nearest he had to a friend was Vekua, but he was as suspicious of her friendliness as he was of Iosava's bullying.

A plan began to form. Whoever had set the false trail for him wanted him to leave Georgia—probably had hoped it would deter him from ever coming. That much was plain. So on his return he'd see Iosava and Vekua, tell them that he'd failed and was going home, and watch their reaction. That was a start, at least.

At precisely nine o'clock, with odd punctuality, Hammer's phone rang, and as deep as he was in thought he knew right away who it was.

"Ah, the jokers. Good morning. You decided to return my things?"

"Things, thousand dollars. E-mails, fifty thousand." It was the same voice, and through the accent Hammer thought he could hear courage being worked up.

"That's cute, but you don't have my e-mails. So a thousand for the computer and the other stuff. OK? The five hundred in my briefcase you can keep. For a couple of days' work that's not so bad."

The voice said something in Georgian, and then came back to Hammer.

"We clone hard drive."

Koba, sensing a change in mood, looked over.

"You OK, Isaac?"

Well, that would really do it, he thought. The head of the firm behind bars, and every former client awaiting a call from a blackmailer. On that computer were the secrets of a thousand clients, not to mention his own, and though it might be protected, in time clever people would find their way in. If he didn't get it back he might seriously consider disappearing altogether from the world.

"OK. Seems like you're smarter than I thought. Which means you'll understand I can't just get that sort of money and hand it over. I'm going to need a bank account from you. Also, we need to find a way to come to some trust over what happens next. Far as I know, you've made two copies of the disk and you're going to ask me for more next month and every month.

Understand? So we need to meet. I'll give you a thousand now, show some goodwill, and we can discuss. OK?"

"Freedom Park, tonight, eighteen hours."

"No. We meet at the Marriott hotel. In the lobby."

"Freedom Park, under statue."

Hammer took the phone from his ear, closed his eyes, and shook his head.

"OK, Isaac? Problem?"

"Small problem. Koba, how good are you at following people?"

"Follow?"

"Track. See where someone goes."

"Ya," said Koba, in his deep growl, with a great affirmative frown. "Is no problem."

I n a normal country, under normal conditions, he would report the theft to the police and have them wait with him in the park for the thieves. Here, that wouldn't do: even if they were competent he had no idea of their motives, and little confidence that they wouldn't take the opportunity to have a go through his files themselves, finding material for heaven knew what fresh fantasies. He was alone in this, as he was in his search for Ben, and though he regretted not having the help that he was used to—oh, for a surveillance team and a Georgian Dean Oliver—there was something about the simplicity of his position that he relished. It was like the first year or two of Ikertu, or all his days as a journalist, trading entirely on his wits. But he had Koba, of course. He had recruited less likely and far less useful people than Koba.

Besides, it was simple enough. There wasn't much one could do except follow the bastards from the rendezvous and then the money from bank to bank once it had been transferred. He could expect help with that when he got home. Compared to finding Ben, it was a neat enough proposition.

Koba's driving became less spiky the closer they came to Tbilisi, but the rain showed no sign of calming. The roads ran with it, the windows streamed; the lights of the cars were the only relief from the settled gray. It might be Sunday but it seemed everyone was out; half an hour outside the city the traffic slowed to a stop and then began to nudge testily forward. Hammer's watch told him it was noon, and though he had nothing to be late for he was taken by a frustrated sense of urgency. He wanted to go. He wanted to make progress.

"What is it?" he asked Koba.

Koba shrugged and lit another cigarette, opening the window a crack.

In a little while they passed the obstruction: a hatchback had left the road at a bend and was now nose down in a ditch. Other cars had stopped—to help, Hammer presumed—but their occupants were just standing watching, with no activity apparent.

"Should we stop?"

Koba laughed and drew on his cigarette, accelerating away on the newly clear road. "Isaac. You not learn."

"They might be hurt."

"They are fine."

"Maybe we should slow down."

"Isaac. We will be fine. And if not, we will not. You have fear, here, I think." He tapped his temple hard with his forefinger.

Hammer couldn't argue on either point.

NINETEEN

By guesswork, and by keeping the castle in sight wherever possible, and with a deal of Georgian cursing and reversing out of dead ends, they finally found the uneven square that Iosava had made his own. It wasn't yet noon; almost a full day ahead. As the Toyota approached, rocking through the countless puddles, two sentries left their station under the long balcony of the house and came toward them, opening their raincoats over the guns at their hips.

"Nice friends, Isaac."

The guards separated and went to each side of the car, standing straight in defiance of the rain. Koba lowered his window, and his guard shouted something at him in Georgian. What do you want? Get the fuck out of here.

"Gamarjobat," said Hammer, leaning across Koba. "I'm here to see Iosava. Isaac Hammer. He'll want to see me."

Koba looked at Hammer with a frown.

"This is Iosava? Otar? You know him?"

"Not well."

"Nice friends, Isaac. Very nice." Koba shook his head.

"I know. Just tell him."

Raising his eyebrows in resignation Koba translated, and the guard replied with some more Georgian and a jerk of his thumb over his shoulder back toward town.

"This guy is gangster, Isaac. Real motherfucker. We go."

"We're not going anywhere. Tell him I have something important to tell his boss and if he doesn't let him know I'm here chances are he won't be in his job for long."

Koba enjoyed that. He translated with relish, and after a little more posturing and a final mean look the guard gestured to his friend to go into the house and deliver the message. The three men waited, the guard with his arms crossed, wet through and staring at Koba, until the second guard reappeared and beckoned to them.

"Stay here," said Hammer. "Play nicely."

"You will be careful, Isaac. Rich men in Georgia, they think they own all of us."

Iosava was at the far end of the great balconied room, at a glass table, hunched over what appeared to be a bowl of soup. Sitting beside him, facing away from Hammer, was a woman in a scarlet dress with a deep V cut out of the back. Through the windows the city was misty and sodden.

Iosava looked up and rested his spoon in the bowl.

"You have news?"

"Something like that."

"Sit. Here, sit."

"I need to speak alone."

"She speak no English."

"Alone. No company."

Iosava glanced at the woman and back to Hammer.

"More brain in this." He lifted his spoon from the bowl and let some of the soup slop back in from a height.

Hammer told himself that he wasn't here to like the man, and taking a moment to overcome his acute repugnance moved round the table, sitting opposite the woman and at Iosava's left hand. She was young, and beautiful, Hammer supposed, in an unreal way that he had seldom encountered and struck him as somehow strange. Blond, for a Georgian, and pale-skinned, and red-lipped, and pushed tightly into her dress, which had a rubbery shine to it and was a little overwhelming for lunch. She smiled as he sat, but didn't speak. The perplexing thing was that she had no flaws. No blemish, no irregularity, nothing to disrupt the perfect symmetry. She seemed to have come from somewhere else, somewhere he had never been and was unlikely ever to be invited.

Iosava raised a hand to summon a servant and muttered something to him in Georgian. He was dressed more casually than before, in a pale blue sweater whose soft perfection only served to emphasize the pits and cracks of his face.

"You will eat."

"I don't have time to eat."

Iosava looked at him with his black eyes. "You are rude, Americans, always. You eat this, with her," he said, gesturing with his spoon over the table, which was spread with dishes of smoked salmon, mushrooms, salads, potatoes, bread. "I eat this." He rapped his spoon against the bowl. "All I can. And even this I cannot."

He went back to his soup, dabbing at the corners of his mouth with a napkin when some of the liquid trickled back out.

"My cook, he make best soup in Georgia. He must."

This was a joke, or at least Hammer thought so. Without the usual signs there was no way of telling what Iosava really meant. Even the slightest turn of the mouth, the smallest narrowing of the eye was denied him, and the effect, curiously, was to give him a sort of power. It wasn't his job to communicate; you had to make the effort to understand him.

A plate came for Hammer, and the servant piled it with food that, despite his hunger, Hammer didn't want. Then he took a bottle of wine and made to pour it, stopping as Hammer put a hand over his glass.

"No, thank you."

"You drink with me," said Iosava. He took the bottle from the servant's hand and filled Hammer's glass. This, apparently, was Iosava in a good mood.

"It is good. Khaketi. Only good thing I can have. And cigars. And her."

Iosava raised his glass and drank, tipping his head back to let the wine pour safely down his throat. With an effort, for the good of the case, Hammer took a sip. Let this man think he had submitted; his best hope lay not in confronting him but in catching him out. The woman smiled at him, a practiced, distant, empty smile.

"After tonight, she go. New one come," said Iosava. Had he been able to, thought Hammer, he would have grinned. "Russian import."

He drank his wine down, wiped his mouth, and pushed back his chair.

"So. Tell me. What information?"

"I'm going home."

Iosava leaned forward to put his glass on the table, waiting for an explanation.

"I'm getting out of here. Leaving. Tell me where to pay the hundred grand."

"Bullshit. This is not job."

Hammer shook his head. "There never was a job. OK? Our agreement was, I find information you need, I share it. What I found you don't need."

"Tell me."

"It's personal. It doesn't concern you. Turns out Ben's got some problems in his life."

"I pay for job, job is done. Where is he?"

"He's not even in Georgia anymore. He's gone." He glanced at Iosava's Russian friend. "He's happy enough."

The black eyes stayed on him. Hammer would have given another hundred thousand to know what was going on inside that brutish head. Whether somewhere he was registering relief.

"Then job is yours now."

"I'm going home."

Iosava took the wine bottle, filled his glass, and drained it, this time wiping his mouth on his sleeve. Hammer waited to see which way he would go, and when he spoke, his voice was like acid.

"Your friend, he steal from me. Understand? My money. He come here, he lie, he steal. In my home. Like he put his hand here and take it." He slapped his chest and left his hand on his heart in a gesture of pride and rage. "You want save your friend, you must save him from me. You finish job. Or bad for you."

"He never even started your job. There's nothing to investigate."

"Bullshit. He talk to people. He talk to Jeladze, he talk to Karlo's wife."

Hammer breathed deeply and tried in vain to read the shell of a face.

"He talked to her?"

"Of course."

"You're sure?"

"He called me, first day."

"She never said."

"She lies. That woman, all she say is poison. Like poison that gave me this face."

Hammer stood to leave, suppressing the urge to belt the guy.

"Mr. Iosava, you have the face you deserve, and I think you know it."

He took his wallet from his back pocket and from it handed Iosava one of his business cards.

"E-mail me your bank details. Otherwise I'll pay the hundred to charity. Any event, we're all square. Yes? This thing is over."

TWENTY

Natela's apartment was in an old Soviet block on Gudauri Street, a quiet street near the university. Hammer had Koba drive him to within a few streets, and after much resistance persuaded him to go and eat while he walked and thought. They would meet later when he'd figured a few things out. Vekua could wait.

"But you will be wet," said Koba. "Too wet."

"I'll be fine," said Hammer.

"Take this." Koba reached behind him and scrabbling around in the footwell produced a ragged red umbrella, hanging open.

"Thanks, Koba."

"Where you go?"

"I just need some time."

"Why you see Otar Iosava? He is bad man. Bad, bad."

"It's OK. I'm done with him."

"What are you not saying to me, Isaac?"

"Koba, if I could explain it to you, I would."

A confidant would be no bad thing—someone to share his theories with, and some of his growing loathing of Iosava—but Koba wasn't the man. He ran too hot.

In the rain it was impossible to tell whether anyone had followed them from Iosava's, and probably as difficult to be doing the following. But Hammer had to be sure, because Natela must know that no one had seen him come. So when Koba dropped him he took the most tangled route, doubling back several times as if lost, until he was certain he was clear.

The sky had darkened further, and thunder now rolled lazily somewhere in the distance. Her building was painted a tired pink, five stories high, six windows across, and on its own small block, bounded on each side by narrower streets. Four apartments on each floor, Hammer guessed, with a central stairwell. Half the third floor, where Natela lived, was lit up behind half-closed blinds.

He walked past just once, under the trees across the road, keeping the umbrella low over his head and checking each of the two rows of parked cars. They were all empty, but thirty yards beyond her door, facing Hammer, was a blue Toyota with a solid-looking man sitting in the driver's seat. The end of a cigarette glowed through the windshield, and as Hammer drew level the man flicked his ash through the small gap he had left at the top of the window. Hammer kept his pace even and carried on to the end of the street.

Turning left three times he approached the building from the back, hoping to find another entrance and looking for anyone who might be watching it. He saw neither.

Out of the line of sight of the sentry, if that's what he was, looking up at this unlikely stronghold, Hammer stopped to weigh his options. The most direct, sadly, were the worst. He could simply ring Natela's buzzer and hope to be invited up, and if he had better Georgian he could buzz someone else and try the old forgot-my-keys trick. But there was a light above the doorway and in both cases the guy in the car might sit up and take greater notice. At least if he was any good.

No, the front door was out. Nor could he call her and ask her to meet him somewhere because he had to assume now that her phone wasn't safe, and that she'd be followed. Also, she'd say no. Somehow he needed to get in there without being seen.

There was always a distraction, something to get that guy out of his car. As he discounted various unconvincing ideas Hammer paid closer attention to the building itself. At the back a narrow strip, perhaps three feet wide and too unintentional to be called an alleyway, separated it from the building behind. Closing his umbrella and hunching his shoulders against the rain, Hammer walked along it, treading down the high weeds. He was now a prowler, and his heart beat a little faster. The windows began at chest height for him, but all were shut. Some were lit up, and through net curtains he made out a bathroom, a bedroom full of boxes. Directly above the bathroom, perhaps twelve feet above the ground, a window was open an inch or two.

He stopped and thought. He was just beyond the midpoint of the building and so long as he was quiet, no one who passed by the narrow gap would think to look his way. Anyone foolish enough to be out in this weather would be walking fast with their eyes down.

The window was hung on vertical hinges and held open by a metal arm. It looked wide enough for him. Koba might have struggled but he would fit. If every floor was laid out the same way, it would lead into a bathroom, and if the light was off, as it was, there was almost certainly no one in it. The windows next to it were all dark, too.

All this was good, but the window remained frustratingly high, the walls sheer, and there was nothing to grasp to help. A leg up from Koba would probably have done it.

The two buildings were close enough, though, for him to brace his back against the one and with his legs straight out slowly walk, or shuffle, up the other. He had seen it done. Presumably it could be done. He failed on his first two attempts to lock himself into position, but soon enough started moving, his feet by the window on the ground floor and walking slowly up to the next. Someone walked by in the street and he stopped, rigid, with his head down, as if that would make any difference, making a note to himself to buy Koba a new umbrella when this was done. His coat was wet through against his back. After a moment, listening to the rain and his own breathing and wondering how he might explain himself to Vekua, he started again.

In another minute more he was there, with his feet alongside the sill and no notion at all how to get himself through the window. It wasn't obvious. The room beyond was wholly dark, and below him the ground a surprisingly long way away. A fall would break something. He leaned forward and unhooked the arm that held the window open; shuffled down a little and then across, so that his toes were touching the frame; and with a lunge grabbed the two uprights with his hands, loosening the lock in his legs as he did so. In that instant he felt his weight again, and the balance getting away from him. His hands slid on the wet frame, and the fall began, but as he went he clawed at the sill and caught it, scraping his forearms against the wood.

"Fuck," he said, as he hung in space. Using the frame of the window below, he gained some purchase with his feet and dragged himself up and through, slithering headfirst onto the floor with his hands stretched out in front of him. His legs noisily followed.

Lying with his face next to what seemed to be the porcelain bowl of a toilet, conscious of his wet clothes, Hammer stayed still and listened. The floor was tiled and cold on his cheek. In a room nearby, voices and laughter were coming from a television or a radio, and to his left a warm light showed along the frame of the door.

Moving lightly and with care, he stood up and walked across the room and listened once more. Music started playing, but he sensed no movement. If he was right about the layout of the apartments, the stairwell was now on his left, and if he was lucky he would find the front door right there. He turned the handle and opened the door a crack. The music continued playing, a Georgian song. If someone came he had no idea what he would say.

Outside the bathroom was a short dark corridor, at the end of which were two other rooms, the light on in one and not the other. But the noise came from the far end, where the corridor turned toward what he hoped was the front door. He slipped off his shoes and inched forward until he could look around the corner with one eye. There was the door, past a row of hooks hung with coats and a mess of shoes on the wooden floor, and just before it, on the right, was the room from which the music came, its own door open. Hammer heard a man's voice over the singing, and knew that it wasn't from any television. Some of the shoes were children's shoes, he noticed, looking closely, boys' and girls'.

Keeping close to the wall, he moved ahead and stopped by the open door. The music turned to talking. He considered the odds. They were watching some show or other. Chances were the television was in a far corner, because most televisions were. And if anyone was facing this way he was done for in any case.

He crossed the gap in one swift, silent movement and stopped on the other side, not breathing. On the television the song finished, and there was applause. He took the five steps to the front door, turned the latch, and slowly opened it an inch, wincing at the harsh creak it gave. But still no one stirred behind him, and after listening for footsteps outside with his ear to the crack he slipped out.

He was in a fluorescent-lit stairwell, roughly painted in a drab blue, its steps worn concrete. On the landing there were three other doors. With his hand on the handle, he closed the door as softly as he could and in a few long strides was on the floor above, waiting motionless. He heard the click of a handle below and a man's voice saying something indistinct, and then a final click. Putting on his shoes, he went up one more flight.

Natela was in 3C. Taking a moment to compose himself, brushing water off his coat, Hammer knocked. Now that he had come to a stop he realized that his heart was beating hard, from exertion and nerves.

For half a minute there was silence, and he thought with a sinking sense that his elaborate entrance had been for nothing. But then there were footsteps inside, and a hand on the handle, and Natela opened the door the four inches that the chain would allow.

Her eyes showed not surprise but a sort of weary expectation, and the first thing she said was in Georgian, to herself. But she kept the door open.

"You saw Ben."

Hammer watched her closely, looking for signs of admission and seeing nothing but resolve. Dark rings underscored her eyes, and he smelled tobacco and alcohol on her breath.

"You cannot be here."

"No one saw me. There's a guy in a car outside, but I came in the back door."

"There is no back door," she said, meeting his look for the first time.

"I found one," he said, smiling. "It's OK."

But the smile was wrong, and her eyes hardened on him.

"I have no time, for this. For you. I have appointment now."

"Natela, I need to know what you said. This is serious."

"You must go. Now you must go."

"It's OK."

"It is not OK. It is not OK to come to this, my house, like it was public place. And you bring them. Understand, I want them to forget me. I want you to forget me."

"They were here already."

Hammer reached out but the door was already shut.

He would have done well to see more clearly the fear behind her anger. He knew it was there, so why badger the poor woman? Because you have to, he told himself; you've been careful, and no one else knows what she knows. If it wasn't necessary you wouldn't be here.

No answer came when he knocked on the door. He tried again, and a third time, but inside was silence, not even the footsteps he had expected to hear. Carpet, perhaps—or perhaps she was standing by the door, torn about closing it in his face or simply waiting to know that he had gone.

Leaning against the door, he spoke as loudly as he dared, his voice echoing brightly round the stairwell.

"I think Ben has been kidnapped. If he hasn't been killed. I don't know how much time I have."

Still no answer came.

"Natela, please. He was a good friend to Karlo. A good friend to me."

Possibly that was a mistake. The silence continued, and with a shake of his head Hammer started down the stairs. On the third step he stopped, shook his head again, and went back up to Natela's door, knocking a final time.

"Natela, I need a hat. Or an umbrella. The only way out is out the front and the guy in the car may get a look at me."

For a moment he stood by the door, not knowing if she'd heard.

"Something I can hide behind."

As he knocked again, the door opened on the chain for only a moment and Natela pushed something purple at him. Then he was on the landing again, holding a woman's raincoat in a vivid shade of mauve. It was too big for Natela, and for him, but it had a hood and did the job. And it would keep out the rain.

TWENTY-ONE

Hood up, sleeves rolled at the cuffs, and feeling more conspicuous than he probably looked, Hammer turned right out of the building, away from the guy in the car, sparing him not so much as a glance—even though he'd have to be really good to recognize anyone in that coat at that distance in the rain and the stubborn gloom—and once off Natela's street half walked, half ran in a large rectangle that brought him up again behind the sentry.

He was still there, still smoking, one arm rested across the back of the seat beside him. Hammer wondered whether his brief was to watch the building or to follow Natela, and hoped that he was about to find out. With luck, her appointment was real.

It was a miserable day to be conducting surveillance without a car. The rain had pooled across the uneven pavement and as Hammer took up his post behind a tree he began to realize that his new shoes weren't quite equal to the job—slowly, they were growing damp. At least there were few people about, and those that passed didn't linger long enough to notice his vigil. Not for the first time in this city, he wished that he still smoked.

For more than solely professional reasons he would have liked to know where she was going—to have some glimpse of the life that he had so glancingly strayed into. It was Sunday; probably she was going to see her children, or friends, or a new man. Questions like this he was used to asking to some fixed end, but now they pressed themselves on him with more urgency than the situation seemed to demand. It didn't matter where she was going, and yet it mattered very much. More, almost, than everything else.

His instinct was protective, he told himself, even guilty—a natural result of his rekindling the danger in her life. But he was honest enough and far too logical to believe it. She had taken a hold on him, and when he asked himself why, he found no clear answer. In his fastidious later years he had become fussy about people smoking, but in her he liked it. He knew nothing of her life, her country, the language that she spoke, and yet these were not obstacles but opportunities. Her black eyes did their best to keep him out but succeeded only in drawing him in. In London, roughly every six months or so, his friends would make an introduction, suggest a blind date, and he had gone through with enough to think that the lack he felt each time was something that now sat permanently in him. Well, it didn't, and the realization left him giddy and faintly fearful, as if someone had whirled him up to a great height.

For an hour he stood, under his tree, whose leaves had begun to fall in the wind, until he began to think that the appointment was a fiction, a way of telling him in shorthand that her life extended beyond his clumsy attempts at drawing information from her. In another hour he would have to leave for his rendezvous with the idiots, curse them. And if she came out, would he know her? Of course. Her brisk, clipped walk was already familiar.

There she was. In a navy coat and carrying an umbrella that obscured her face, but he was right, he would know her anywhere. She headed up the street toward him, on the other side of the road, and, keeping one eye on the other surveillance team, he moved round the tree as she passed. This coat was going to be a liability if he had to keep up the tail for long.

He let her get thirty yards ahead, and so did the guy in the car, who now opened his door and headed off after her, beeping the lock behind him and talking softly into a radio or a phone. Hammer slid back to the other side of the tree. This was going to be hard.

One of the strange effects of following someone was that it inured you to the idea that you were being followed—you tended to concentrate on what was in front. That's what the Georgian did now, and after half a mile or so of walking in a spread-out chain of three, Hammer had been reassured of a couple of things: he wasn't going to look round, and wherever she was heading Natela wasn't taking the bus, which would have made the whole thing more or less impossible. Surveillance was luck at the best of times, and without a team of five it was a lottery.

He was finding a wary rhythm when it happened. Natela was walking away from the center of the city, through blank streets of apartment blocks made blanker by the rain, leaning a little into the wind, with the policeman or whatever he was thirty yards behind on the other pavement and Hammer another thirty further back behind him. They were alone on the street, which was narrower than most and had at its far end a cluster of shops and what looked like a café in a small square, its chairs tilted against the tables for the rain. The odd car drove by, but it was quiet here; it felt like a Sunday. It was just occurring to Hammer that Natela might only be going for food, or cigarettes, when a figure by the café started moving quickly in her direction. A man, in what looked like a white shirt. Right away there was something about him Hammer didn't like—that he had no coat, or the way he moved, which was swift but stuttering. Purposeful but not in control. Natela seemed not to have noticed him and kept the same pace.

In front of Hammer the policeman slowed and stopped by a side street, still watching Natela, and Hammer pulled himself into a doorway. Natela went on, and so did the man in the white shirt. As he came nearer Hammer could see that the shirt was unbuttoned almost to the waist and filthy round the cuffs. Matted beard ran up into patchy black hair that looked like he'd cut it himself. He was wrong, out of place. He shouldn't be here. Every instinct told Hammer to break cover, or to shout, but he hung back, waiting for the policeman to resume or to walk away. And why had he stopped? He seemed expectant, which was a strange thing for a man doing his job to be.

When he was ten yards from Natela, the man in white reached his hand into his pocket and came out with something that he held down close by his side. Hammer couldn't make it out but knew instantly what it was.

"No!" he shouted, as loud as he could make it, and breaking cover ran to her, past the policeman, dodging a car in the middle of the street. "Natela!"

He was still so far away. Natela stopped and looked back at him, but the man in front of her didn't falter. He had the knife up now, and its long blade looked savage in his hand. His eyes were far apart, like a prey animal.

In the same moment, Natela turned and he jabbed the knife at her; as she recoiled, the blade seemed to disappear inside the folds of her coat. Hammer shouted again, shouted at the policeman to fucking help, saw Natela stagger back silently and look down while the man, unsatisfied, tried to set himself again. But he was unsteady, and it took him a second to find his balance, and in that time Hammer was on him. With all his weight he barged him, shoulder to shoulder, keeping his head down and away from the blade.

The man hadn't seen him, and he went over easily; together they fell against a wall and down onto the pavement. Hammer landed on his elbow and rolled instinctively onto his back, pushing the other body away from him and looking for the knife. He couldn't see it. The man held on to him, stopping him from getting up, and his grip in his left hand was strong despite the stale sweet smell of drink that came from him. Hammer tried to get enough room between them to land a decent punch but he was too close and his efforts had no force.

Then the knife appeared. A kitchen knife, probably nine inches, incongruously new—pristine in the filthy hand. The man was on his side; he was heavier than Hammer and was trying to get on top of him. Succeeding, in fact. Hammer grappled and kicked but could not get free, his blows slipping off in the wet, and the only thought in his head was that he needed to win this fight for Natela's sake. If she was injured he was the only thing stopping this madman from finishing his job. He couldn't see her. It was possible she had managed to go, to crawl away.

The drunk had his full weight on Hammer now, astride him. He brought the blade up and at the top of its arc Hammer imagined its extreme sharpness, the softness of his flesh, its unerring passage into him. As it came down toward his heart he wrenched his body to the right and reached up one last time to pull the man off balance; felt his weight shift, and the knife slice cleanly into his upper arm, so sharp that he felt not pain but just the clinical intrusion of the blade.

Electrified, his mind and body coursing with the need to survive, Hammer grabbed the man's leg with his good arm and heaved, trying to unbalance him, as the man drew the blade back again. But then Natela was by him, and in one powerful motion kicked the man squarely in the face.

Hammer saw her boot connect with his scraggy jaw—saw his skin pressed into his skull like a face against glass—and watched him topple backward, cracking his head on the wall, slumping into a heap, his expression half stupor, half surprise. He was done. Natela kicked at his hand and the knife fell from it, and only as it clattered onto the pavement did Hammer register that the blade was clean.

"You're all right?" he said, as Natela reached down to help him up, her face pale but resolute. She looked down at her attacker with something like disgust.

"Who is he?"

"I have no idea."

The policeman had gone from the corner opposite, and was nowhere to be seen on the street. Hammer's legs were shaking as he stood and he was breathing hard. Almost instinctively he touched her coat, expecting to find a wound there, but there was nothing, not even a mark on the fabric.

"You're OK." His tone had changed from concern to a sort of wonder.

"He did not touch me. You?"

"I'm fine. I'm fine. We should go."

Shaking her head, Natela gently raised his arm to inspect his wound. He hadn't looked at it, but now he saw that blood was streaming down the sleeve, pooling at the bend of his elbow, some of it washing away in the rain.

"It's nothing. We have to get you somewhere safe," he said.

Where, he didn't know. Maybe Koba knew somewhere. A cheap hotel, pay cash, somewhere they didn't insist on passports.

Hammer squatted down to look at the man in the white shirt. He wasn't unconscious, but his head twitched from side to side erratically and his eyes saw nothing. From a few yards along the pavement Hammer picked up the knife. It was evidence, but he didn't trust anyone to read it correctly.

"We go to my brother. He is doctor, for your arm," said Natela. Her face was pale and fixed.

"That won't be safe."

She shook her head with a weary frustration.

"Where then? Where is safe now?"

"Somewhere they don't associate with either of us."

"Jesus. This mess."

From her bag Natela took her cigarettes and pinched one out of the soft pack. After some rummaging she found a lighter, lit the cigarette, and took a deep drag.

"Can I have one, please?"

Frowning, she held out the pack. "You smoke?"

"I do now."

Pain had begun to spread out from his arm. He clicked the lighter, touched the flame to the cigarette, and inhaled, the smoke familiar and foreign, harsh and comforting at once. Suppressing a cough, he drew again. The comfort was in the companionship.

"Karlo's brother. He is not my friend but he is good man."

"You're sure?"

"Last time we speak was five years. Last time Karlo speak was ten."

He had nothing better.

"Let's go."

TWENTY-TWO

I t took twenty minutes to walk to Luka Toreli's and by the time they arrived Hammer was dizzy and nauseous. The cut wasn't so bad—no blood vessels, just muscle an inch or two below his shoulder—but either the pain or the shock of it was making him weak.

How conspicuous they were. Or how conspicuous he felt, with his bloody arm rigid at his side, and his mauve coat shining in the dull afternoon. If he had been careful about being followed before, now he was obsessed by the idea that they weren't alone. Everyone behind them was a threat; everyone passing in the other direction would turn after them as soon as it was safe to do so. The streets were just a grid for the game to be played on, a place for them to be caught.

But they made it, and even in his paranoid state he was almost certain they hadn't been followed. Twice he made them turn abruptly, to Natela's consternation, to expose anyone who might be there, and twice he found the street behind them empty. The rain had drenched the city into quiet— they saw no protesters, no police. But by the end, his uppermost thought, to protect Natela, had become laughable. She was the one who knew where they were going, and she was the one leading the way. She was now protecting him. This was wrong, because he had got her into this mess; but as they walked he reflected that the blame was not perhaps all his, and that without Karlo and his obsessions neither of them would be here. Or without Ben and his.

Luka was half the girth of his brother and a quieter proposition altogether. Behind small metal-rimmed glasses his expression was wary but studious, and as he was introduced to Hammer at the door he looked him up and down as a doctor might an infectious patient—carefully, with an eye on what was to be done, but keeping his distance all the same. He was Hammer's height, wiry, and had only a few sparse hairs neatly combed on the top of his head; if Hammer had a brother in Georgia it was this man, not Koba. He wore an old blue jumper with holes at the elbow and white hairs and dandruff on the shoulders. An academic, Hammer thought, or a librarian, or a registrar of some kind. Rather than shake Hammer's hand he gave a single slow nod of his head.

He showed more irritation than surprise at being disturbed. Natela talked for a minute, and when she was done Luka looked at her, unblinking, for what felt like a minute more. There seemed no animosity between them, only distance. Finally, with a small nod that signaled his thinking was done, he headed into his apartment and they followed.

From the narrow hall he turned into a bare, functional kitchen, brightly lit by the two fluorescent lights that he now switched on. Formica counters and cupboards, a table with two wooden chairs, every surface clear and noticeably clean, a net curtain across the bottom half of the single narrow window. Natela raised an eyebrow at Hammer and gestured to him to sit, while Luka busied himself with supplies—from one cupboard a roll of bandage, a roll of tape, and some sort of ointment, from another a new dishcloth, from a drawer a pair of scissors. He placed them with slightly fussy care on the table.

He said something short and curt to Natela and left the room.

"Take off your coat," said Natela. "And everything."

Two coats he was wearing—he had forgotten. Still dazed, he peeled them off one shoulder and Natela helped him with the other, and it was a relief to get rid of them. As he unbuttoned his shirt she went to the sink and ran the tap for a minute before wetting the cloth.

"He OK?"

"He does not like people. They are in his way. He writes. All the time he writes."

The last time Hammer had sat with his shirt off while someone cleaned a wound he was six years old and he'd fallen onto a rusted iron rod while playing on a building site with his friends. The scar was on his other arm, a little lower down. His mother had washed it and dressed it and put him to bed only to wake him an hour later and take him to the hospital for stitches. This was like her: independent but ultimately careful. Natela had a similar manner, gentle and stern at once, and it calmed him. He worked hard not to wince.

"It hurts?"

"You shouldn't be doing this. You've had a shock. You need sweet tea."

"Why?" She was squatting by him, dabbing at the cut.

"It's what mothers give their children when they've been in an accident. It relaxes you."

Natela took the cloth away from Hammer's arm and looked up at him.

"I do not need tea." She turned her head toward the door and shouted, "Luka!" and a string of Georgian words. His reply was gruff.

Standing, she opened one cupboard, then another, and pulled from a third an old water bottle full of golden brown liquid. It looked like the bottle rolling around in Koba's car. She found two odd glasses, and poured a couple of inches into each.

"Drink," she told him, handing him one. "Like this."

Throwing back her head she downed it all, shuddered, set the glass on the table, and watched Hammer, who didn't need prompting to do the same. He flinched at the fire of it. It was like a blow to the back of the throat.

"Chacha," said Natela. "Brandy. His father makes it. He has vines."

"Some vines," said Hammer, feeling the heat spread through him, almost inch by inch. Better than Mirtazapine, no question. Natela resumed her work. That was the first thought he'd given to his medication all day.

"What does he write, Karlo's brother?"

"Poems. He is poet."

"Any good?"

"No one knows. He does not show."

"You're kidding?"

"He is taxi driver, at night. In day he writes. For thirty years, but no one sees."

"You sure they were brothers?"

Natela gave him a weary look. "Same here." She tapped her temple three times. "Do what they like."

It wasn't a subject he should have brought up, and he changed it.

"You OK?"

"I am fine." She went to the sink, washed out the cloth, wrung it dry, and went over the wound one last time. It was deep but narrow. With a good bandage it wouldn't need stitches.

"Really? That kind of thing's normal in Georgia? You're used to it?"

Ignoring him, concentrating on the job, she smeared pink ointment from the tube onto Hammer's arm.

"Natela, that guy was going to kill you. And he wasn't some random lunatic. He wanted you."

"Bullshit. He never saw me before."

"Exactly. You want someone whacked, the easiest way is find a drunk who can just about stand up and pay him a couple hundred bucks. There's no comeback."

She cut off a length of bandage from the roll "You live in dream world."

"I wish I did. Where were you going? You often go that way?"

"To my brother. His family. Today, he cooks, people come."

Hammer didn't say anything, waiting for her to look up. When she did, her eyes had relented, as if finally acknowledging something she'd been trying hard to ignore.

"I know nothing. Nothing."

"Doesn't matter. They think you do."

Shaking her head with a sort of frustrated fury, she finished taping the bandage, pressed the edges in place more firmly than she needed to, and then stood abruptly to pour herself another glass of chacha. Hammer put his shirt back on and with clumsy fingers did up the buttons. His arm was stiffening up and he felt cold.

She poured the chacha and drank it down in one swig without so much as a shiver. She seemed to glow when she was done.

"You want?" she said, once she had drunk it down. He didn't. "Cigarette. I need cigarette."

"Natela, would you sit? Please. Sit down."

When she had the cigarette lit she drew angrily on it, pacing the tiny room. She opened the window and fanned smoke toward it, with little effect.

"You. You bring this here."

"Maybe. But I think it was Ben."

"Excuse me?"

"He came to your apartment, and they saw him is my guess. They think he knows something, and now maybe you do, too."

"I didn't see him."

"I think you did."

With her free hand Natela rubbed one eye, wrinkling her forehead, as if refusing to wake from a heavy sleep. Hammer watched her and waited, knowing he had said enough.

"He came to me," she said at last, flicking ash out of the window and looking down into the street. "Day after funeral."

"What did he want?"

"He said someone killed Karlo. That he didn't kill himself." She paused. "He said Karlo had asked him a question. A week before he died. It was important."

"What was the question?"

"I do not know."

"You didn't ask?"

She looked right at him, a reproach. "I do not want to know."

"What did he ask you?"

Holding his eye, stubbornly holding on, she took another drag. Each question was a new opportunity to decide she'd had enough. "If I knew Karlo's work. If he said something to me."

"Did he?"

She gave him a look that suggested he couldn't possibly be serious.

"Karlo called me for the children. Or for money. That is all. Sometimes to say he was better." Crossing to the sink, she took a plate from the drainer and tapped ash onto it. "He never was."

Hammer waited a decent interval before he spoke again.

"Was that all?"

Natela shrugged. "Yes, I think. I told him nothing."

"You mean there was something you didn't tell him."

Natela's eyes held his for a moment, then resumed their vigil beyond the window.

"Karlo came to my apartment, first time in many months, the day before he died. He was crazy-crazy. Like there was a devil in him."

"What kind of crazy?"

"Like a boy before his birthday. His big story, it had been in paper, but he told me it was wrong, that the new story was bigger, more impossible. He told me he would be famous all through world."

"Did he say what it was?"

"No. I did not ask. I did not want. He said he would write, then go away. London, somewhere."

"Why go away?"

"Because it was too dangerous here."

It took effort for her to say it in a level voice, and Hammer stopped pressing.

"I'm sorry."

"It's OK. You did not kill him."

No. He hadn't. It wasn't in his nature to do things. Other men did them, and he arrived later to investigate what they had done. He hadn't thought of himself in these terms before, but now he doubted that he had earned the right to cause a woman like this anguish. While she was dressing his wound, he was scratching away at a scar that had barely formed over her own, and somehow his having so little to do with any of it made it worse.

Enough scratching. Enough questions. In any case, he believed her—she may not be giving him much but it was more than she'd given Ben. It was four now. Soon he would have to leave for his showdown with the motherfuckers, but no part of him wanted to leave.

Hang the motherfuckers. Hang his clients and their paltry secrets. Hang the bankers and the lawyers and the fund managers and the chief executives, all marching with such certainty to an end they couldn't see. What did Ben call it? The Project. The unexamined faith that all this work would somehow save the world—that money would prevail. For years he had marched with them, but in this moment he felt himself pulling up and watching them march on. A deserter discovering his conscience—or perhaps his consciousness. Waking up to the plain truth that there was more for him in this blank little room than in all the offices in the world.

Hang the march.

The mood had changed. Natela seemed to sense his unwillingness to go on. She stubbed her cigarette out on the plate, and Hammer found himself amused by the thought of Luka's reaction when he saw it.

She pulled the other chair out from under the table and sat down. There was a new connection in her eyes.

"Your friend. Who is he?"

"We worked together for years."

"He must be good friend."

"He was."

If she noticed his evasion she didn't show it.

"You are not like him. I know him. He is like Karlo."

"He's a good man. And a fool, like many good men."

"You are fool maybe, to follow him."

"He drives me nuts. But somehow that's the point."

"Sounds like son," said Natela. "Or husband. You want more chacha?"

Natela topped off their glasses. The little room had grown darker and thunder rolled around them. He should have been keeping a straight head but all that nonsense seemed so distant. And in any event, how hard could it be? Hand some money over, tell the little bastards what was what and get out of there with his things. Compared to everything else it was simple, and when it was over he could turn his mind to the more difficult and important business of keeping Natela safe. After consulting her, he sent a text to Koba telling him to be waiting outside a pharmacy four streets away in half an hour.

They sipped their drinks now, in silence. Natela lit another cigarette and as an afterthought offered him one. There was no reason not to. Natela got up to shut the door, as far as he could tell to prevent the smoke from reaching Luka, though it was too late for that.

"Why do you come here?" she said at last, watching his slightly awkward handling of the cigarette. She was a natural; he felt like a teenager trying to look as if he'd been smoking his whole life.

"To ask you about Ben."

"No, no. To Georgia."

"To find my friend."

"This is not whole reason. Why must you find him?"

It was like being with Elsa. No secrets. Only Natela's bedside manner was a deal more brusque.

"I've been asking myself that."

She frowned, not understanding, and Hammer sighed. He didn't want to explain himself—not, as he might have told himself once, because it was complicated and hard to translate into words she would know, but because he wasn't proud of what he was doing. That was another difference between the two women. With Elsa, he wouldn't have felt that.

"I came because something he did got me into trouble and I need him to get me out."

"You look like this is bad."

"There's not a lot of glory in it."

"I know this people. They make big explosion," she threw her hands out, "you get hit. But you feel like mess is your mess. Why do you feel bad?"

"Because I think his trouble may be a whole lot worse than mine. And every night I call his wife and that puts it in perspective."

Natela didn't know the word, and gave a short shake of her head to say as much.

"I'm scared she's not going to see him again."

Natela nodded, and Hammer knew he didn't have to say more. When she understood, she understood.

"Who waits to see you?" she said, after a moment. "This is dangerous for you also."

Hammer smiled and took a slug of chacha.

"A housekeeper. A bunch of people who work for me. The police."

"No wife?"

"No. No wife."

"Is she dead?"

"No. I've never had a wife."

"You are not gay because you like me. I can see. What is wrong, you are scared?" She was frowning, as if genuinely interested in the answer.

Hammer laughed. "Maybe."

"But you break in my apartment. You attack that man."

"I didn't break into your apartment."

She waved his objection away. "You are not quiet man. You are not Luka."

Hammer blew out smoke, nodding, and tapped his cigarette against the plate, watching the ash drop.

"I had some disappointments on that score."

"What does this mean? Disappointments."

To his surprise he found it easy to look at her as he told her.

"I loved someone, and she died."

"When she die?"

Hammer laughed again.

"You're meant to say, Jesus, I'm sorry. My God. How terrible."

"You know is terrible. When?"

"I was twenty-eight."

"OK. OK to be scared up to forty. Are you forty?"

"I'm fifty-eight."

"Too long to be scared."

Now she looked at him with a new intensity, as if she wanted to heal him right there. Hammer looked back, and wished she could.

"You've never been scared?" he said.

"Not like you. To me Karlo died slowly, since many years."

"Not for your children?"

"Ah, OK. Children is different. Always I am scared for them. Is my work. But they are big, grown." She reached up to show him. "Gone."

"You see them?"

"Of course. One in Moscow, one in Kutaisi. They are good." She smiled. "Now they are scared for me."

"Maybe they should be."

"Bullshit."

"We need to get you out of here. Out of Tbilisi. Out of Georgia, just a few days."

"This people do not make me run."

Hammer felt a strange surge of something like pride in his chest. Nothing would make this woman run. She was immovable, and it thrilled him just as it troubled him.

"When I'm done I'll come back. We'll figure it out."

She gave him a look of forbearance, as if she'd consider tolerating his odd foreign ways.

His cigarette was finished and it was time to go. With great reluctance he stubbed it out and looked again at his watch, calculating to the last second how long he might leave it. It really was time.

"You stay here," he said, standing. "Don't make any calls, don't go out. Don't let Luka tell anyone you're here."

"He never speaks to anyone."

"OK. Take this." He took one of the spare phones from his pocket and handed it to her. "You need to call me, there are two numbers in the contacts. The first one is better but both are OK. You still have the number I gave you in the restaurant?"

She nodded.

"Don't use that unless the other two don't work. OK?"

Natela took the phone, turned it over in her hand as if it was some strange device she'd never come across before, and put it on the table.

"I'll be an hour, maybe two. What's the address here? Case I can't find it later with your crazy writing."

Without answering, Natela went out into the hall and came back with a pen and a piece of paper, which she wrote on and handed to Hammer.

"So you want me to come back."

"Is better." She smiled. It was the first time he'd seen her smile.

From the back of the chair he picked up his own jacket and put it on. It was damp, and blood had dyed the navy black along the arm.

"These people, they know where is your friend?"

"I wish. No. These people are just a distraction."

"You know where he is?" said Natela.

"I know where he isn't."

"What you mean?"

"All I know is this. He's not by the seaside, but someone wants me to think he is. He's not in Tbilisi, because he rented a car and filled it up with enough gas to get him to Moscow."

"The mountains."

"I guess."

"No. He asked me, about the mountains."

"Asked you what?"

"He wanted to know did Georgians speak Russian there."

"Is that it?"

"Yes. Before he left."

"Did he say why?"

"That was all he said."

"What did you tell him?"

"I said where—which mountains. He said Tusheti."

"What's Tusheti?"

"It's a place. Chechnya here." She pointed at intervals on the table. "Dagestan here. This is Tusheti." She drew a circle. "Very quiet. Quiet in middle of much war. I said yes, people speak Russian a little because always there was buying and selling."

"What did he say?"

"Nothing. Thank you. He left."

"How far is it?"

"A day."

"They have gas stations in Tusheti?"

"I do not know. Is nothing there."

Hammer bent down and kissed her, an emphatic one on the cheek. She looked back at him perplexed.

"Thank you. That's what we call a lead."

TWENTY-THREE

Koba knew Freedom Park, of course he did, and he knew the statue, too, the biggest you could imagine. Bigger than ten men. It was a good place for them, at the top of a hill, trees and bushes everywhere, good for hiding and tracking. He had tracked boar and wolves—two motherfuckers would be no problem.

"There might be more than two."

"OK, Isaac."

He and Hammer arrived at the park an hour before five and made their way to the statue, two hundred yards away and even in this rain dominating the hillside. It was immense, black, perhaps a hundred feet tall, and held both its arms aloft at the top of a grand flight of steps.

"Lady of Victory."

"You had a victory? I thought the Georgians always lost."

"Russian victory. Soviet," said Koba, with no further explanation, and headed for the long set of broad steps that led up to her.

"Is there a back route?" said Hammer. "Through the woods?"

Koba touched his nose conspiratorially. "Of course," he said, and led the way into the trees that lined the avenue.

They passed only half a dozen people who had defied the weather to walk, and on the climb up the hill no one at all. The rain had softened a little and it was dry under the thick trees.

Nearing the top, at Hammer's raised hand they slowed, and before coming out into the open completed a circuit of the crown of the hill. When he was sure they were alone Hammer left the cover of the trees and walked around the statue, gazing up at the vastness of it. The figure of a woman, who looked down on the city with an olive branch in one hand and a book in the other.

"Glory of Georgia. Peace," said Koba.

"What's the book?"

Koba shrugged.

Hammer surveyed the ground. "OK. We wait. Probably they'll come up the way we did, so you should be in the trees on the other side, over there. Keep your ears open and if you hear someone coming toward you move quietly away. It's important they don't know you're here."

Koba tilted his head and gave Hammer an insulted look.

"It needs to be right. Usually I'd have six men on this."

"I do not think you should give them money."

"It's the price I pay for finding out who they are. That's all."

Hammer took a deep breath and had a final look around. The steps stretching out beneath him were broken and overgrown with weeds, the lamps lining them, despite the growing darkness, still unlit.

"So. I talk to them, give them the money. What next?"

"I follow. Not close."

"And what do we want?"

"Car license or house number."

Koba's expression was somehow impatient but resigned, like a child who has heard the same admonition dozens of times.

"I should be more close. They might hurt you."

"They won't hurt me. They'll want more of my money."

Koba raised an eyebrow and stumped off into the trees.

Hammer sat on the top step of the hundred or more running down the hill and took in the gray, wet sweep of the city, the red roofs and the coned towers and the dull green river threaded through it all. Apart from the patter of raindrops on his coat all was quiet; apart from the odd figure coming through the gates in the distance nothing moved in the scene. Once, he thought he heard a voice in the woods but when he listened closely there was nothing above the sound of the rain.

His mind, besides, was not on this tedious distraction but on what would happen next: find somewhere to stay that night, get some rest, and head for the mountains, to follow the first real trace of Ben's footsteps. Take Natela with him. It was the obvious course. Provided they weren't followed out of the city, she would be safe there. And the alternatives were too complicated: how could she cross a border, if she was being tracked? Anticipating her reluctance, he began to prepare his arguments.

Four days left. Four days to find Ben and get back to London. The deadline seemed increasingly unreal, irrelevant. What would he do on that last day if he hadn't found him? Give up and go back to Sander? Leave Natela unprotected? The idea was absurd. This quest had its own shape, and now he was committed to it. It was genuine; everything else was paste.

At least now there was a destination. He felt it like a release. There was only one road to Tusheti, and Koba was happy to drive it. Insistent, in fact: of course his wife would not mind, and there was no way Isaac should attempt it himself. It was a motherfucker road. He had driven people up it before and would of course go again. That was his job.

Was it cold? Hammer had asked. Now, not bad, but getting colder. He would need some mountain things. At night, yes, it was cold. Very high. Who lived there? In the winter, which was nine months long, fifty crazy idiots to stop the sheep from freezing. In the summer their families joined them, but they would soon be leaving. Some hikers. The rangers in the national park. Otherwise it is big empty place, and if your friend has gone there, Isaac, he must be crazy, too.

He didn't hear it but some instinct told him there was movement behind him, and he turned to see the two men from the riot, the one who had held him and the one who had taken his passport. His reaction was curious. He had been expecting to feel fear, or nerves, but in their place there was only a slightly weary resentment that these idiots should be wasting his time, and a fresh irritation at the thought of their excitement. Probably they were more nervous than he was, giddy with the opportunity and the boldness of their scheme.

He stood, shook out his coat, and let them come to him at the top of the steps. From here Koba would have a clear view, no matter which way they went.

The younger and slighter of the two, cap and scrappy mustache still in place, stopped with his hands in his pockets, cocked his head, and stared into Hammer's eyes with the willed assurance of someone keen to make an impression. He wore a black leather bomber jacket, zipped up to the neck. His friend, in a neon blue tracksuit, chains hanging from his neck, stood a pace back, holding Hammer's briefcase at his side and in his other hand a compact silver gun. A pistol, an automatic. Hammer felt the weariness leave him. Almost certainly they had never done anything like this before. It would be remarkable if they made no mistakes.

"You have money?" said the leader.

"That's a good opening. I've heard it before but it's strong." The man looked baffled. "Yes, I have money."

"Please." He nodded, to indicate that he wanted to see it.

Hammer took the money half out of the pocket of his coat, thumbed the edge of the wad, and then put it back.

"Give money."

"We have other things to discuss."

The leader stepped forward and handed Hammer a piece of paper. On it, printed in a standard font, were the details of a Western Union office in Tbilisi. That's not bad, thought Hammer. They're not such schmucks. But they still had to pick up the money, and it would be easy enough to have someone waiting for them.

"Fifty thousand dollars. In one week."

"You see, this is what we need to discuss. First of all, fifty thousand dollars is too high. I made a mistake, probably I deserve to pay for it, but it's a ten-thousand-dollar mistake, not fifty. So in one week you get ten thousand dollars, which is more money than you idiots know what to do with in any case. That'll keep you in girls and chacha for a good while, impress your friends. Wait. I haven't finished. Second, I need you to understand something. It's important, so tell me if you don't."

He had him now.

"I'm an investigator. I investigate things. Like a private policeman, yes? Like I say, I made a mistake, but ten is all you get. Forever. You ever try to get more from me and I will find you, and I will make your life very, very difficult. You get it? Same goes if you try to use any of the information you've found. Understand that I am much, much better than you at this, and you won't win. Tell me if this isn't clear."

The leader's cocksure stare had slipped into a frown.

"Fifty thousand," he said. "One time."

Hammer smiled.

"I thought you had it. Let's go through it again. Here's how it works. I give you this thousand bucks. You give me my things and get ten thousand next week. Ten. And I come after you the first time you try to get more out of me or anyone else. That's as good as it's going to get."

The man turned to his friend and talked to him in a hushed voice. Hammer could imagine what was being said: we take the cash now, take the ten thousand next week, figure out a way to get more later. There'll be a way. But the friend bristled, looked away, started shaking his head, and then, dropping the case, walked abruptly toward Hammer with his right hand out and his arm crooked and the gun pointing at Hammer's head. Hammer backed away with his hands out, trying to pacify him, but the big man grabbed him by the lapel and pushed the stubby barrel of the gun against his temple. Hammer could feel the skin moving under the cold metal.

The big man said something in Georgian, and Hammer could imagine roughly what it meant.

"It's OK. It's OK. You're going to get what you want. Let's just take our time." As he spoke, hardly conscious of his words, Hammer imagined the bullet at the top of the magazine, saw it waiting there, stable and ready, the powder waiting for the blow of the pin.

Reason suggested he would be fine. He couldn't pay them if he was dead. But he didn't want to rely on this man's sense of logic. As Hammer talked, the gun screwed harder into the thin flesh over the bone and the man's eyes grew wider and crazier. Where was Koba? Probably it was better that he stay away. The situation was volatile enough.

Hammer looked to the leader, if he was the leader. "Tell your friend that we can negotiate. He needn't worry. You'll get what you want."

The sound of twigs breaking came from somewhere to his left, and he wondered at Koba's clumsiness. The two men looked to the source of it and each took a step backward, scanning the area behind them, as a policeman in black, a helmet on his head and a machine gun slung across his chest, came out of the trees behind Hammer. The leader turned to run, but stopped when he met another policeman walking steadily from the other side. His friend, behind Hammer now, still pressing the gun to his head, twisted round and began to back away from the police.

Hammer heard movement behind him, and a short flat roar that seemed to pitch him forward with great force, and then he was on the ground, his face pressed into the wet stone by the heavy arm of the big man, who had fallen at the same time and now lay half across him. He was conscious of a fiery, metallic smell, and pain in his neck, and a strange warmth in the rain on his cheek. Without knowing why, he wanted it gone. Using his legs against the weight, he pushed the man's arm aside to wipe away the water, and stared for a moment at the red wash on his palm.

In panic, his body wild with revulsion, he scrabbled at the stone, crawled out from under the body, and rolled away. The big man was sprawled on his front beside him, his eye and cheekbone smashed and black with thick blood.

The rest of his face was pale and wet and bright in the growing dark. He made no sound. His remaining eye had lost focus on the stone, and the light had gone from it.

The fiery smell came through the rain. From the trees two more policemen emerged, the stocks of their guns braced against their shoulders, still training their sights on the dead man and ignoring Hammer and the leader, who had his hands raised in front of him and a look of bewilderment in his eyes. No one said anything; but for the burst of the gun, the scene played out in silence. Hammer, a shrill tone in his ears and nothing but noise in his head, turned away to look elsewhere, to make sense of what he had seen. Another man was now in front of him, the detective from the police station who had interviewed him on the first night. He held the briefcase in one hand. What are you doing here? Hammer wanted to ask, but simply watched as the detective closed a pair of handcuffs over his wrists.

TWENTY-FOUR

The sight of Vekua in the doorway made no sense to him. His mind was still in the park, reeling from the noise of the gun, collapsing under the weight of the corpse. All the questions he would have coolly addressed on another's behalf had barely been framed: how the police had found him, why they had fired the shot, for whose benefit the whole thing had taken place. How his simple task had come to be so deadly, and so crazed.

Find a man. That's all he had to do. Quickly and quietly, without anyone noticing. For someone who had found fortunes and secrets in darker corners than this it should have been straightforward. But he had blundered through it, and his thoughts could gain no purchase on the chaos he had created. His shirt was cold and damp on his skin, with blood or rain he didn't know; on his hands the blood had dried, and now he held them open on the table, the fingers separated so that no part of him would touch another.

And in the storm of his thoughts, one kept returning to torment him. They had taken his things. His phones, his wallet. And in the wallet was Luka's address.

When Vekua opened the door she was carrying his briefcase, and his first instinctive thought was that she had again come to let him go. She dismissed the guard with a single wag of her finger and waited for him to close the door before speaking. Her eyes stayed on Hammer throughout.

"Your reputation is not accurate, Isaac."

Hammer stared at the angular face, impossible to read, and felt only a deep impatience with the game.

"For once, just tell me what you fucking mean."

"Your file says you are honest man. If you make a promise you keep it."

"For fuck's sake—just tell me."

"You interfered. Now it is serious. I can't help you."

The disappointment in her face seemed constructed, an artifice. At her unknowability, Hammer felt rage well up in him.

"Now it's serious. Now it is. Before, it was just a bomb and seventeen dead Georgians and a few riots. Now I've interfered, the whole fucking thing has tipped into chaos."

"I have been trying to help."

Hammer stood up, shaking his head, not prepared to reason.

"You know what, I need to wash my hands. They have a dead man's blood on them, and I've been sitting with them out like this for the past hour. So now, I wash my hands, and then maybe I'll listen to you."

"You must listen."

"I won't hear a thing, I won't say a fucking thing, until these hands are clean."

Vekua looked at him, understood, and opened the door.

"Come."

She led him down corridors to a pair of doors marked with signs for men and women, and held open the women's door.

"I'm not going in there."

Vekua continued to hold the door as Hammer pushed against the men's with his shoulder and went in. Vekua followed.

A Georgian policeman in uniform was drying his hands under an air blower. He saw Hammer, saw Vekua, thought better of saying something, and left. Hammer went to the row of sinks, ran the water until it was hot, and held his hands under them for as long as he could stand it, watching the grime and the brown blood rinse reluctantly away.

"You need soap," said Vekua. "Here."

He cupped his hands and she worked the dispenser for him. Awkwardly against the handcuffs he rubbed the soap between his fingers, underneath his nails, into every wrinkle and crease. When he was satisfied, he kept his hands under the water for another minute until they were red and tender from the heat. New and old at once, they looked, the skin on his knuckles gathered and loose.

Throughout, Vekua had stood silent and watched.

"I am sorry," she said at last, when the noise of the dryer had stopped.

"There was no need to shoot him. He was just scared."

"And you were not?"

"He wasn't going to hurt me."

"The police were not so confident."

Hammer shook his head, resigned. He would never know whether that was why they had taken the shot.

"Why were they there? How did they know?"

"Come. I will drive you."

"Where?"

"Come."

As before, Vekua sat upright and correct behind the driver, Hammer next to her; as before, they drove along the river, but now they went east, away from the old town. Beside the driver was another policeman, or spy, both plainclothes, both with guns that they had wanted Hammer to see. The briefcase lay on her lap.

"Where are we going?" said Hammer.

"Tell me. Why did you go to Gori?"

"Why does anyone go to Gori? To see the Stalin museum."

"You went to the apartments. You talked to the soldiers."

She must have interviewed Koba. Hammer hoped he was all right. He would be fine. Koba was one person he didn't need to worry about.

"I did."

"Your briefcase is full of documents about the bomb. So is your computer. All Karlo Toreli's articles, translated and in sequence."

"How did you get in?"

"We are a government. We have ways."

"Then you'll know that all that stuff was from the Internet. Google translated. My researchers put together a pack for me before I left."

"You broke our agreement."

"I was looking for my friend. Nothing more. Can you please tell me where we're going?"

"Who is paying you?"

"For the last time, no one is fucking paying me."

"Who is paying your friend?"

"Where are we going, and when are you going to give me that case?"

"To the airport. You are leaving Georgia."

He had been expecting it but wasn't prepared. Something like panic started in him. He saw Ben in some mountain prison. Saw Natela innocently waiting for the people who wanted her dead as they headed straight for her with his slip of paper in their hand.

"No. No, I'm not. Since I saw you I've done exactly what I said I'd do. I went to Batumi. I stopped off in Gori because Ben had been there, he had lunch there. I went to see the apartments because I was curious. We investigators are curious. You, you're only interested in what you're told to be interested in. I'm different. I like to know things. After Batumi I came back here and tried to get my briefcase back. That's it. Our agreement stands."

"Why did you come back?"

Ever since meeting Vekua he had asked himself whether he could trust her, and no answer had come. She was clever, and she was involved. If she was the one who had arranged the trail to Batumi, he needed her to think that he was convinced by it. If she wasn't, he needed her help. It was a simple choice, and in a sense he had already made it: why was he so keen to stay in Georgia if he believed Ben was safely in Istanbul living it up with his Russian?

"Because he wasn't there."

"Batumi is a big city."

"Someone wanted me to think he was there. But they made mistakes."

"You said he sent his wife a card."

"I lied. Listen, I'll level with you. I think you're right. I think Ben started looking into Karlo's death and someone didn't like it. So I have a suggestion for you. We try to find him together. Your country's not easy. I've been in difficult places and some dark places but for sheer confusion, this takes it.

I have no idea what you're all doing. Who you all are. What you want. Who's pulling the strings. But you do. So how's this? I know my friend. You know your country, you know the case. We find him together, and if he's done something wrong, fine, you throw the book at him. I may enjoy watching you throw it. Along the way maybe you find whatever it is you need. I just need to tell his wife if he's alive. Or if he's not."

He didn't mean the offer, didn't know how on earth it would work, hadn't considered what it meant for Natela, but it was all he had. Vekua didn't move; not a flicker of the eye or a parting of the lips. The studied engagement had gone, and as she stared at him Hammer couldn't tell whether she was assessing the proposition, or letting him sweat, or working out how to continue her manipulation of him.

"It is too late for you to trade."

"No it isn't. It makes sense for everyone. You'd be with me. I couldn't do anything you didn't want me to do. We find my friend, you kick us both out. The problem's gone."

"Your friend is not a problem to us. You are the problem."

Hammer wasn't used to feeling powerless. He saw himself back in London, answering Sander's questions while two thousand miles away Ben and Natela perished without him. He couldn't go home. He belonged here.

The driver's handgun was on his right hip under his jacket, and for a moment he let himself imagine what would happen if he grabbed it, held it to Vekua's neck, issued his demands. The gun was power. If he was a different kind of American he might have lived by that creed, but as it was the thing was alien to him. The last time he had held one was in Iraq, where a stringer for *The Times* had got himself a handgun for protection and was flashing it round the hotel bar.

Maybe it was simple enough. Grab it, stick it into her side—more comfortable—tell her to order her men to stop the car, open the door with his free hand, and edge out backward into the night, keeping the gun trained on the three of them. It was crazy, the stuff of movies, but maybe that stuff worked. Shit like this happened. He was just never there to see it.

Don't press it against her, though. You need space between her and the gun.

The car was on the freeway now and smoothly racing forward. He watched the blank suburban landscape pass, gaging the distance to the driver's hip with the corner of his eye and shaking his head, apparently beaten, for Vekua's benefit.

With as much spring as he could manage he reached out and snatched at the gun. His hand was under the jacket, felt the hard, textured grip, and pulled at it. It wouldn't come. As he fumbled with the leather clasp on the holster the car veered sharply and then Vekua's hand was at his throat, grabbing his collar and pushing him back into his seat.

"Enough!"

Her voice was hard and straight. He pushed back at her but knew that it was over. They tussled for a moment and then in her free hand there was a gun, smaller than the one that he had tried to take but a solid fact nevertheless. He let go of her, and she let go of him. The driver corrected the car.

"Enough."

Vekua stretched her neck, and then calmly smoothed out her suit. Her face was composed but she was breathing hard and her eyes were fierce.

"Your file said you were clever."

"I have to stay."

"You are gone, Isaac."

TWENTY-FIVE

She had timed it all, he realized, so that from the moment she appeared at the police station he would have no opportunity to wriggle. From the cell to the car to the airport, with the minimum of bumps, his bag recovered from Koba's car and now in the trunk, his passport and tickets in Vekua's hand. As she walked him into the check-in hall, one hand on his arm, he saw that the Lufthansa flight to Munich left in thirty minutes.

For him there was no check-in, no passport control, no lines. Straight through, with agonizing simplicity. There was nothing to take advantage of. They arrived at the gate to find perhaps twenty passengers standing in line ready to board.

"These are yours." Vekua handed him his wallet and his English phone, its battery dead. He checked his cards, the cash, the note of Luka's address. They were all still there.

"My other phones?"

"There were no other phones."

The way she said it, he almost believed her. For a moment they looked at each other.

"You needn't wait," said Hammer.

"We will go when you are on the plane," said Vekua.

"That was more of a joke."

"Your jokes are better in London, I think."

The driver put his bag down, and they stood a little distance away from the queue.

"I want to change my clothes."

"On the plane."

"I have the man's blood on me."

"You can change on the plane."

He had one last idea. It was basic, and cheap, and though he held out little hope for it, it had worked before.

"One thing I need you to do." Hammer took his wallet from his back pocket. They had taken none of his cash. "My driver. I never paid him."

Vekua nodded.

"Give him this. It's not much. I have more. Much more."

"I am not interested in your money."

Of course she wasn't. It would be easier to corrupt a nun.

Vekua's charm had all gone. She was the efficient servant of the state. Hammer looked at her and wished he knew what weakness to exploit, what final card to play. But she was all straight lines and smooth, hard surface. He could find no hold.

Whose side was she on? If he knew, he could work on her. If she was who she said she was, he could enlist her to protect Natela. And if she was the one who had wanted him gone from Georgia all along, if she'd spent all that time soft-soaping him, well, he was going, wasn't he? She'd got what she wanted. He might convince her that Natela was the irrelevance she so clearly was. Except that Vekua had never seemed one for convincing.

The last stragglers were having their boarding cards checked. Hammer hesitated for a moment before walking to the desk, watching people disembark from a plane out on the tarmac. The driver handed him his suitcase.

Hammer held out his hand for his briefcase.

"Your case was not recovered, Mr. Hammer."

Vekua brought the case round in front of her and clasped the handle in both hands.

"National security."

"You're a piece of work, you know that?"

Hammer looked at her one last time, calculating. Perhaps it didn't matter what side she was on.

"Natela Toreli," he said.

"Yes."

"I don't know whether you're good or bad, Elene, but she's in trouble, and she needs help. Someone's trying to kill her. Maybe that's you, I don't know. This place, it's beaten me. I can't figure it out. Some investigator." He held her eye but it gave nothing out; she was blank. "If it's someone else, protect her for me. She's a good woman and she needs it. And if it's you, drop it. She's not a part of this. She doesn't know anything. Not a thing. She and her husband barely spoke."

Vekua nodded, her expression unchanged, and Hammer was left wondering what he had achieved.

"Go," was all she said.

What a way to end it. One friend almost certainly dead and another about to be. All those years of work, all that expertise, and he had fucked up the only job that had ever really mattered.

A woman took his ticket, checked it against his passport, waved him through. Thank you, Mr. Hammer. With those friendly, cheerless words he was back in that reassuring world where his money accomplished things effortlessly and his name was magically known. He had no appetite for it. Tomorrow he would briefly be a somebody again; in London, in his perfect little house, sleeping between sheets freshly washed and pressed by a housekeeper who anticipated every tiny thing he might need. He could barely accept the thought, it seemed so ludicrous.

Well, it might not be for long. He was due to see Sander in five days' time.

Row twenty-seven. Way back, past twenty-six rows of faces looking up at the last man to board and finding him fascinating, in his crumpled clothes with the bloodstains at his neck. His seat was on the aisle, next to a serious teenager in glasses who was already intently studying his book. In Russian, a hardback. Hammer sat down, settled into his tiny space, took his phone from his pocket, and vainly pressed the power button. The screen stayed black.

Natela. He could barely bring himself to think of her. His sense of powerlessness was complete.

He leaned forward and looked across for the last time at Georgia. Three days he had lasted. Three days was a humiliation; he should have entrusted the job to someone who knew this world well enough not to stomp all over it. Moscow. That was it. He would go to Moscow, enlist the help of Mr. V. He could be persuaded. Probably he knew people here who could help Natela, find Ben.

Cabin crew busied themselves. Hammer twisted in his seat and vainly imagined rushing for the rear exit, overpowering a steward, opening the door, and dropping to the tarmac. Who was he kidding? He was fifty-eight, and exhausted. His body was a dead loss, and his brain had failed him.

At the other end of the plane a man in a fluorescent yellow jacket came on board with the flight manifest and took it into the cockpit. When he was done, he would leave and the doors would close and that would be that. Hammer closed his eyes and tried to accept the finality. Opened them again and tried to imagine spending the next four hours motionless in this seat.

Then the woman who had checked his ticket appeared in the doorway and caught the attention of a steward. The steward called over a stewardess, and the three conferred, looking up at the passengers from time to time, before finally the stewardess made her way down the aisle. An overbooking, Hammer assumed, or some problem with the luggage. But she didn't stop until she reached him.

"Mr. Hammer," she said, squatting down and talking quietly, confidentially, in the most discreet of German accents. "I must tell you that, if you wish, you may leave the plane."

"If I wish."

"If you wish."

"I wish."

He unbuckled his safety belt, got his things together, and, before she changed her mind, walked as fast as he could back down the aisle, conscious of all the eyes on his back. The crew, uncertain what to do, wished him a pleasant evening.

By the gate were Vekua and the policeman. Her arms were crossed, her lips tightly pressed into a line, and she watched him with a burning look. At first Hammer didn't recognize the two men standing opposite them, one burly, the other scruffy and pale, but then it came to him: the big one was Iosava's man. The goon who had driven him to Iosava's house.

No one in either group seemed to want to speak, least of all to each other.

"What's going on?"

The goon looked at Vekua, who looked at Hammer.

"So you have no client," she said, with a final glare, and walked away.

"Outside," said the big man.

TWENTY-SIX

Hammer's new chaperone guided him firmly through the airport, back the way he had come to the passport barrier, where a grunted conversation in Georgian was all it took to release him again into the city. In the departures concourse Hammer shrugged his arm free of the man's grip and came to a stop.

"Where are we going?"

Iosava's man just looked down at him and held out a great thick arm to usher him toward the door. To Iosava, no question, with a new set of crazed demands.

"I need to make a call," said Hammer. "Give me some money."

Still he held his arm out.

"Coins. I need coins." Hammer rubbed his fingers together, "Look, you great fucking galoot."

He set off across the concourse toward a bank of phones, pulling the bigger man after him by the lapel.

"I need to make a fucking call. OK? Now."

He barely noticed that Iosava's man didn't resist, but even in his desperation had a dim sense that they cut a peculiar figure, the little bald man dragging the giant meekly behind him. Stopping by the phones he rubbed his fingers in the man's face.

"Coins. Change. Money."

Pointing emphatically at the slot he pulled out his notebook and leafed through the pages. There they were, under Thomas North, her initials reversed: her number and the number of the phone he had given her. Iosava's man patted the pockets of his trousers, then of his jacket, and shook his head. Strangely he seemed now to be in Hammer's power.

"Well, fucking find some."

Three phones down a young man with long, matted, mousy hair leaned against the wall, the receiver pressed to his ear, his back to Hammer. A backpack rested by his feet. Iosava's man walked over to him, spun him round by the shoulder, and saying something in Georgian held out his hand. He was a kid, all of twenty, and he didn't seem to understand.

"Dollars," said the goon. "For phone."

Scared, the kid muttered something into the phone in what sounded like German and reached into his pockets. He came out with an assortment of stuff, and from his open palm Iosava's man picked out three coins.

"Gamarjobat," said Hammer, but the kid had turned his back again and gone back to his call, shaking his head.

Hammer fed the coins into the slot and dialed her cell phone. It rang—once, then again, then again. Six rings in all, and then a constant tone. He tried again, and again it rang out. The third time he dialed the untraceable cell he had given her, and listened despairingly to the dead tone that instantly filled his ear.

He replaced the receiver, let the coins tumble down, and walked over to hand them back to their owner.

"Thanks," he said. "Sorry about that."

Iosava's car was a sleek, long German thing parked illegally and all on its own directly in front of the terminal. It couldn't have belonged to anyone else. But Hammer had no room for Iosava and his grandness, his pomposity. His head was occupied by one question alone.

The goon put Hammer's suitcase in the trunk, opened a door, and steered him into the backseat.

"You try to leave."

The door shut, and as the lamps dimmed Hammer saw Iosava's grotesque image fading back into the amber half-light.

"Excuse me?"

"We have contract. You try to leave."

Despite everything, Hammer laughed, and shook his head.

"You people are fucking crazy."

Iosava, who had been looking straight ahead, turned to face Hammer.

"I am only man in Georgia who can keep you in Georgia. And you laugh?"

"She wants to throw me out because of what I know, and you want to keep me here. What's funny is, I don't know anything. Nothing. There are stray dogs in Tbilisi who know as much as I do. I don't even know what you really want."

"She is nobody."

"Everyone's nobody to you."

By now the goon had joined the driver in the front. Iosava said something in Georgian to them, the engine started with the gentlest rumble, and the car pulled away.

"Where are we going?"

"Where you want. Is your job."

"Take me here." From his wallet he slid a piece of paper and passed it to the driver. "Quickly. Fast. And I need to charge this phone."

Iosava said something in Georgian and the car made a controlled surge forward.

"What is here?" said Iosava, as the driver passed the slip back to him.

"None of your business."

"We still have contract."

Hammer buckled his seat belt and took a deep breath. "Mr. Iosava, I don't make contracts with people like you. Your idea of a contract is my idea of an order, and I don't take orders. You got me off that plane, great. It suits me, but it suits you, too, otherwise you wouldn't have done it. I have no reason to be grateful to you and no reason to do what you say."

Iosava shut his eyes for a moment, in impatience or contemplation. As he did, what little light there was in his face went out, and all that was left was a lifeless canker.

"You are clever man but you see me and you judge. It makes you go wrong, think wrong. No trust, OK. But you and me, we want same thing. Find your friend, finish president. Is same thing. Understand? I work, you work. We work together."

Hammer took a long, slow breath. If he could have trusted this man at all, there was truth in this.

"So. You tell me. Your friend is here?" He flicked the piece of paper with a stubby finger.

"I don't know where my friend is."

Iosava screwed the paper into a tight ball and threw it, hard, at Hammer, who raised a hand to parry it.

"You do not tell me, my men will cut your face. Like this." With his finger he slit his mouth from one corner up to his ear. "One second it take."

Hammer ran through his choices. Two things he knew. If Iosava had wanted him killed, it would have happened by now. And if he'd killed Ben, they wouldn't be going through all this. He plunged in.

"What's in Tusheti?"

"Where?"

"Tusheti. Is that how you say it?"

"Nothing. Mountains. Sheep."

"No connection to anything? To the bomb."

"Sure. Truck was in Tusheti."

"I don't know what that means."

"The bombers. Truck was found, hidden. In Diklo. On border, next to Dagestan."

"That wasn't in the press."

"Press prints what I want. Police were there."

"Diklo?"

"Diklo, Tusheti."

"What else should you tell me?"

Iosava shrugged. They were well clear of the airport now, driving with speed through the light traffic heading into the city.

"What is this?"

He retrieved the ball of paper from the seat between them.

"Something I have to do."

Iosava rolled the ball between his fingertips, crushing it down.

"My men take you."

"I told you. I work alone."

"You need driver."

"I have a driver."

Iosava blinked slowly in quiet frustration.

"Mountains not safe."

"And this place is?"

Luka opened the door like a man disturbed from his sleep for the third time that night, and even before he threw his arms up and muttered something in angry Georgian, Hammer knew she wasn't there. Where is she, he asked; did she go alone? But Luka just shrugged and muttered some more. How could he be expected to know? He hadn't seen the woman for five years and now he was her keeper? If this wasn't what he said it was something like it. Hammer asked for pen and paper and once Luka had grumpily returned with them wrote down his phone number, pressing it into the man's reluctant hand with enough urgency to make the message clear.

There was some comfort. Recluse he might be, but even Luka would have behaved differently if Natela had been dragged away by secret service men. He wasn't alarmed, merely cross.

It had been five hours since he left her here. Of course, she hadn't just sat and meekly waited. At a guess, she had gone home to pack some things, anticipating a spell in hiding; or she had gone to her brother's, because a mere attempt on her life wasn't going to upset her routine.

Parked up on the pavement, the Mercedes was laughably conspicuous, the very last thing for discreet intelligence work. But the time for discretion was past. Once he had found her he could figure out how to hide her again.

"What is here?" said Iosava, not for the first time, as Hammer got back into the car.

"I have to talk to someone."

"OK. Good. We go home. Tomorrow you go to mountains."

"She wasn't here. We need to go to 23 Gudauri Street. And on the way I need you to find out the name of Natela Toreli's brother. Or brothers."

Iosava laughed, a dry gurgle.

"Of course. You have to talk."

Hammer shook his head. How could he be in league with this piece of shit?

"Just take me there."

"She has new man quick, yes? One week since funeral? Karlo deserve better."

"You say one more word about her and I will fuck you up. Goons or no fucking goons."

Even as the words came out he knew he should have kept them to himself. She could protect her own honor, no doubt. But at that moment all he wanted to do was throttle all the ugliness out of the man.

Iosava cocked his head to the side, put his hand on Hammer's thigh, and squeezed, strong fingers locking deep into the muscle. There was only deadness behind his eyes, an expanse of black.

"You make threat, I kill you. Myself. Here." Hammer tried to raise his hand up but it was stuck fast. "We have agreement. For this, I let you live."

He held his grip for a moment then let go.

"Out."

Hammer smoothed his trousers down, keeping his eyes on Iosava's. A week earlier this episode would have shocked him; now it barely registered.

"My experience, men who want to do things do them. The rest is talk. And for such a big man I think you're a big talker, too. OK? So let's cut all the posturing, and let's try to tolerate each other like a pair of fucking grown-ups. Yes?"

Iosava said nothing.

"Good. Half an hour ago you offered me a driver. You can start by driving me to Gudauri Street."

Iosava continued to stare at him with those blank eyes, so empty of anything human. Then, without looking away, he said something to his driver, and the car raced away down the narrow street.

Natela wasn't at her apartment—or if she was, she wasn't coming to the door or answering her phone, or responding to Hammer's shouts from the street.

She had two brothers, but only one in Tbilisi, and he lived in the old town, in a rare well-kept house. His wife answered the door, letting the sounds of laughter and boisterous conversation out into the street. Blankly shaking her head at Hammer's question, she fetched her husband, and in a broken exchange he managed to explain that Natela hadn't been there— and no, no phone calls either. Why, he wanted to know, but Hammer just thanked him and went back to the car.

"Maybe there is third man," said Iosava when he saw Hammer's face.

But Hammer was now too anxious to fight him.

"Take me to my hotel."

Iosava said something in Georgian to his driver and the car pulled away.

"You think your friend is in mountains?"

Barely hearing him, Hammer looked across.

"I think that's where he was going."

"Why does he go? What is there?"

"You tell me."

Iosava kept his gaze on Hammer, then reached across and pulled down an armrest from the seat between them. In the space it left was a small wooden cabinet with a glass door, and inside a neat row of cigars, each in its individual slot. He took one, took a clipper from the cabinet, trimmed one end, and then spent thirty seconds lighting it from a single long match. Hammer opened his window and watched as it began to suck the smoke from the car.

"Is good place to hide a man," said Iosava, when he was done. "Or to kill him."

PART
THREE

ONE

In the morning it rained hard, and on the slick, newly wet roads that wound into the mountains Koba's big arms had to work hard to keep the Toyota from sliding into the shoulder. But still he drove fast, swinging round long corners, racing up behind ancient army trucks, overtaking on the shortest clear stretch, and finding fewer and fewer checks on his speed as the traffic gradually thinned. Hammer, keen to get on, discovered a handle above the window and gripping it firmly did his best to concentrate on the world outside. Dark, twisting tunnels of oaks gave way to gently rising plains, and through the gloom he could just make out shadowy peaks ahead. Grasses and wildflowers everywhere grew uncontained.

"The road's not too bad," Hammer said, after a long period of silence.

Koba threw back his head and laughed one of his tremendous, grand laughs.

"This is not road," he said.

"That's great," said Hammer, and watched the landscape change around him. He wasn't sure how to say what he wanted to say.

"Koba," he said at last. "Last night. You OK?"

Koba looked across at him, frowning.

"Ya," he said, with emphasis. "Why not?"

"I didn't expect that to happen."

"Isaac, is best thing. Motherfuckers die. So? They are motherfuckers. Is OK."

It seemed to have made no more impression on him than the car in the ditch the day before. Hammer envied his robustness. Georgians had to be tough, he guessed.

"Did they talk to you? The police?"

"Ya, is normal."

"Did they mention my friend?"

"No. Only you."

That was interesting. Heaven knew what it meant.

Before leaving town Hammer had called each of the two numbers he had for Natela three times before giving up. Finally, he had sent her a text, and tried to consign her to the back of his thoughts, where she had no intention of remaining.

He had slept patchily, and woken without appetite—either for a run, which would have helped him, or for breakfast, which he forced down in any case. He couldn't leave, but couldn't stay. What would he tell Elsa, that he'd ignored his only lead to wait for a phone call that might never come?

The truth was, of course, that he had no power over Natela's life. She could be dead, or in danger, or she might simply never want to see him again. He would never know, and in each case there was little he could do. So he had called Koba, and once they had driven round enough to be sure that no one was following them—to Koba's great enjoyment—they had stopped only to buy phones, boots, and a winter coat before heading out on the road east to the mountains.

"You are quiet, Isaac," Koba had said, half an hour in.

"I'm sorry, Koba. I didn't sleep so well."

"Mountain air. You will be good."

Now, after an hour's climb, still in trees, the way began to level out and then slowly descend. Through gaps in the green Hammer thought he could see a great plain below them, and wondered when they would start to climb again.

"Is this Tusheti?"

Koba turned to look at him, gripped his shoulder with a sturdy hand, and beamed.

"This is Kakheti. Tusheti like this." He raised his hand to the roof.

"I thought these were the mountains?"

"No," he said, stretching out the syllable on one low note.

"This isn't the road, and these aren't the mountains. OK. How long to the real mountains?"

"One hour. Two. First we stop and eat, buy food. Wait for end of rain."

It took Hammer a moment to register this.

"We don't have time to wait."

"Road not possible in rain. Too much danger."

"Koba, we have no choice. I need to get up there."

"Only way in rain is fly."

"Fly?"

"Helicopter. From Tbilisi." He looked at Hammer. "It's OK. Rain will stop."

Hammer checked his watch. It was noon, and the city was already more than an hour behind them. Their route was set—and besides, this was the way that Ben would have come. There was only one road up.

Soon they were down on the flat, at the edge of a wide plain that was checkered with fields and bounded in the distance by an immense wall of mountains that rose sheer out of nothing and disappeared into dull clouds. So straight was this wall across the horizon, so abrupt and complete, that it was little effort to imagine a just god setting it down to protect the blessed land of Georgia—less a part of the land than a fortification. Down here the world was human; there were vines and crumbling square houses and tractors left abandoned at the side of the road, and every so often the distinctive conical tower of a church, but it was all made tiny by the mass of black rock behind, where men and women were surely never meant to live.

"Caucasus," said Koba, with pride and respect. "We must cross."

In a town called Telavi, which was set a little above the plain and had a jumbled, Alpine air, they stopped and bought provisions. How long would they be gone, Koba wanted to know, and when he found that Hammer wasn't sure—two days, four—bought enough for a week, on the grounds that there was nothing to eat where they were going but milk and cheese. He had been once before, and yes, it was beautiful, but for him he preferred to look at the mountains than sit on top of them with a lot of crazy sheep people (or shepherds, as Hammer slowly realized he meant). Still, they needn't suffer; they would eat well. As he got out of the car Koba held his hand out, looked up at the sky, and announced that the rain would stop in twenty minutes.

The supermarket first, for rice, pasta, tea, beer, wine, crackers, biscuits, oil, butter, salt. Then to the covered market, where an old man sliced them huge cuts of lamb and old ladies sold heavy bags of the freshest tomatoes, aubergines, potatoes, parsley, apricots, cherries, the dirt still on some of it and bloom on the rest. Koba went about his business with the pointed confidence of a city dweller among hicks and Hammer, to compensate, supplied unlooked-for smiles and gamarjobats as he followed. When they came out, the rain had indeed stopped, and the sky had started to lighten from the south. Their last job was to fill up the Toyota and its reserve tank—when Hammer saw the plastic barrel in the trunk he felt sure that Ben had done the same, on his way here—and after that Koba declared that they were ready. Or would be, just as soon as they had had lunch.

"Koba, we have enough food for a platoon. We need to go."

Turning down the corners of his mouth and shaking his head, Koba pointed north to the mountains, where black clouds still sat on the peaks.

"We wait. Best thing we wait for tomorrow, dry road, but you cannot. OK. I drive good, it's OK. Now have lunch, my friend's hotel, very good, we can see, we watch the . . ." He gestured upward, not knowing the word.

"Clouds," said Hammer.

"We watch the clouds. One hour, maybe two."

Hammer saw the resolve in his broad face and realized that arguing wouldn't work.

Two hours, in the end, which was enough for Koba to have his fill of trustworthy food. Hammer ate a little, said less, and tried to stop checking his phone by forcing his mind up into the mountains and keeping his eyes on the sky. When he was done he went outside, took his phone from his pocket, and dialed.

"Ike?"

The line was bad and the connection slow, but he could still hear a world of fear and hope in that one word.

"Elsa. I'm so sorry. I should have called."

"Are you OK?"

Extraordinary, that she could spare a thought for him.

"I'm fine. Fine. Yesterday just got away from me."

"How—how is it?"

What to tell her? Did he give her hope or prepare her for the moment it might die?

"I'm getting there. He feels closer."

"You don't know where he is?"

"I think I do. I think he's in the mountains."

He heard her sigh, and for the first time realized that his quest must be beginning to look very much like one of her husband's. In and out, he had told her. A quick result. Then, he had been happy to play the savior, the wise man, the sane alternative to Ben's madness. Now, all that felt foolish, and cheap. Not so noble, those first intentions.

"Ike, it's been days."

"I know."

"How long . . ."

She couldn't frame the question, but he knew what it was. How long before the odds lengthened into impossibility?

He told her about Natela, and her conversation with Ben, and everything else that had set him on this course.

"This is the closest I've been."

"She might have told you sooner."

She was afraid, he wanted to say but he didn't want to explain why.

"We'll get there," was all he said, and somehow he still meant it. "I'll call when I can, but it's wilderness up there."

He hung up. Inside, Koba was pushing his plate away, finally satisfied.

Slowly the sky lightened, the lower peaks began to show themselves, and by the time Koba was drinking his second coffee and smoking his third cigarette the whole range could be seen: damp, forbidding, but no longer inundated. In Telavi the sun had begun to shine.

"I make call," said Koba, "then we go. My wife." He wandered into the parking lot to make it.

TWO

The good roads were behind them now. For a while there was rough tarmac, and then the tarmac began to break up, and as they drew near the foothills they were on a wide track lined with trees, even enough but muddy after the rain and scattered with stones and potholes. Civilization began to slip away. They passed overgrown farmsteads, wild horses grazing under wet oaks, herds of bony cattle ambling about. From time to time the sun broke through and lit some part of the scene with glistening light, causing Hammer to forget his mission, forget the trials of the last four days, and wonder at the innocent perfection of the place, the magic of its simple elements.

"It's beautiful here," he said, more to himself than to Koba, and tried to remember the last time he had been in nature like this, with the world he knew unimaginable and forgotten.

"Ya," said Koba, unengaged.

The road settled alongside a fast-flowing river and started to climb.

Soon the river was far below them and the road had narrowed to a single rocky track, a foot wider than the car, that clung to the rocky hillside. Grass gave way to sinewy trees that still dripped after the rain, and hardy bushes sprouted over the cliff face. Every so often wooden posts set back in little clusters marked their progress. If Hammer looked down to his right all he saw was an abrupt and growing drop and a shoulder that just crumbled into space, but Koba charged on unaffected, taking corners at the same speed as the straights and letting the car veer wide in the mud as he fished in his top pocket for his cigarettes and rummaged in the glove box for his lighter. They might be in a hurry, Hammer told him at one point, but there was no need to rush on his account—as long as they arrived today. But Koba insisted he was taking it slowly, they'd be OK, and bristled, if anything, at the implied slight on his driving. Entrusting himself to the god of the road, Hammer held on. As long as they arrived.

Perhaps because of the recent rain they saw few other cars going their way, and those they did see were soon compelled to stop on one of the rare stretches that were wide enough to let them by. The drop now was sheer, and already hundreds of feet. As Koba crept past them, no more than an inch away, Hammer forced himself to look ahead so that he couldn't see how close the wheels beneath him were to the edge. At every moment he expected to feel them start to slip and then give.

As a cursing Koba maneuvered around a Lada that was barely coping with the steeper stretches, Hammer got to inspect the wooden marker posts by the side of the road. There were three together, in the form of crosses, carefully made, and at each intersection was a faded portrait.

"I guess they didn't make it."

Koba, concentrating on the Lada, merely grunted.

"The posts," said Hammer.

Koba glanced across. His mood seemed to be declining as they left his world behind. Hammer suspected that he was finding the driving more taxing than he let on. "Idiots. They drink, fall from mountain. You will see. All this people are idiots."

With a final curse he was free of the other car.

"Should we help them?" said Hammer, looking back. "They're never going to get up."

"I tell you. Idiots!"

For all Koba's dispatch, progress was slow. In a straight line it was only twelve miles to Omalo, where they were headed, but the road snaked so tightly upward, hairpin after hairpin, that there were eighty to cover in all. After an hour the last straggling trees ran out and they emerged into sunshine; when he looked down, Hammer could see glimpses of the way they had come, the track winding in and out of sight hundreds of feet below, and beyond, already unimaginably remote, the distant plain. Above and around them were sublime peaks and green ridges folded like cloth.

Another hour passed, his ears popped twice, the air grew cold, and still there seemed to be more mountain above them than there was below. Except to make the odd curse, Koba drove in silence now. Hammer's conversation had dried up.

"Fuck," Koba said, straining to look at the road above them. Hammer followed his gaze, and saw, a hundred feet up, three vehicles in convoy, two of them the old army trucks he had grown used to seeing everywhere, and in between them a smaller white van.

Within ten minutes they had caught up with the second truck as it waited for the first to pull the van through a particularly steep hairpin, its huge wheels laboring and slipping on the rocky ground. Somehow it managed it, whereupon both stopped, the rope was released, and they all set off lumbering toward the next turn. Koba looked at Hammer and slowly shook his head.

"All way up," he said. "You see. No way past. All way up."

This corner the van tried to take on its own, but it failed and the procedure was repeated. Koba turned off the engine and lit another cigarette, watching the group climbing at the slowest possible speed up one leg, then another, and another. Shadows began to appear on the eastern slopes. Hammer's watch showed four.

"Must be in Omalo before night," said Koba.

"There's plenty of time." He didn't mean it. It was the hardest part of this whole thing, racing against time and having no idea how much was left.

"Is dark early, the other side."

"Of course."

"Not good in dark."

For almost another hour they hung back, caught up, hung back, Koba occasionally trying to find a way around, frustrated now beyond measure. Dead pylons bent by winter snowfalls loomed over the road. Then, rounding a long corner, they found the first truck stopped in a crook of the track where it crossed a shallow stream, from which the driver and another man were filling a collection of plastic bottles. Koba saw his opportunity and moved sharply to the left to go past.

"Stop!" shouted Hammer. What Koba had seen as a dip in the road was in fact the shoulder. There was no road, just space.

Hammer felt the wheel underneath him lose grip and begin to slip away. There was nothing to check their fall but scree and scrub. By the stream the two men were shouting, their arms up in warning and disbelief.

Koba braked hard, and the car's three wheels scrabbled to a stop on the loose grit. Hammer, fear coursing through every part of him, looked across at Koba with astonishment and reproach, but Koba just stared straight ahead, his big face white and furious. Even in that moment Hammer felt a certain awe at the extent of the man's pride.

Koba put the car in reverse, checked twice that he had the right gear, and slowly took them back. Outside, the Georgians were incredulous and let Koba know it. Through the open window he shouted back.

Hammer breathed deeply, but his pulse still raced. "I think I'd like a smoke," he said.

Still staring straight ahead, Koba removed the pack from his shirt pocket, took one for himself, and offered the rest to Hammer, who found the lighter in the glove box and lit first Koba's, then his own. This cigarette was different from last night's. Calming, yes, but not comforting. Two thoughts occupied him as he smoked: that if he and Koba had tumbled down the cliff, there was no one who might come for him as he had come for Ben; and that the only memorial he might leave behind was a cross at the side of this fucking road.

"That was close," he said, already thinking about Koba's fury and the rest of the journey. "You did good."

But Koba either didn't believe him or was still too angry—with himself, with the other drivers, with the mountains—to speak.

"For a moment I thought you and I were going to have a nice little spot on the road, here, with a couple of crosses." He gave Koba a chance to respond in kind. "We could have been together forever. People would have taken us for brothers."

Koba flicked his half-finished cigarette out of the window.

"Idiots. Up here, like this." His jaw jutted out as he shook his head. "Motherfuckers."

THREE

They had to wait until the summit to pass the convoy, and the far side of the range was already in deep shadow. All the way Hammer had thought that every peak would be the last, but here it was finally clear that they had made it: behind and giddily far below them was the plain, and ahead a long green ridge curved down toward a high plateau, taking the road with it and drawing his eye to the distance, where, just emerging from the retreating band of dark clouds, were the real mountains, immense, snow-capped, unrelentingly endless, range upon range stretching into Russia.

"Tell me we don't have to go up there," he said as they began to descend.

"That is Caucasus," said Koba, his first words since the incident besides great Georgian oaths.

"To keep the Russians out."

"Russians not so bad. Better than mountain motherfuckers."

Miles above the world, and much further from his own, Hammer felt a simplicity settle on him, as if everything he had learned, everything he knew, had slipped away. How he wished Natela was with him.

Slowly, they reconnected with the land. It was as if they'd been flying; the sense of potential collapse was the same. As the road slowly sank down, and the drop beside him diminished, and normal things began to appear—a river, a bridge, the first trees—he felt a great joy in seeing them that went beyond relief. Here again were the elements of things, which for years he hadn't seen.

Circled by mountains, Tusheti was a place of great quiet. The wind, fierce in the last stages of their ascent, had dropped to nothing, and the pines that bunched together on the gentle hills didn't stir. Rough fences divided up the pasture where cows and horses grazed together; set back from the road were houses made of wood and piled slate. In the thinning twilight it felt like a place for fairy tales. There was no logic to it—he had no idea where it came from—but after the chaos and rage of the city and the trials of the last few days Hammer felt that this place was benign, and that he might be safe here. If Ben had come to harm here it was despite Tusheti, not because of it.

They reached Omalo just as night was falling—too late for work but in time for dinner. On a hill above the road he could make out perhaps twenty wooden houses, only three of them lit up. By the first of these Koba pulled over, muttered something that Hammer didn't catch, and stumped his way up some steps and along a balcony to the front door. Within a minute he was back.

"This is place."

Hammer got out of the car, stretched his arms above his head, and breathed the sweet air, which was cool now and smelled of damp grass. His neck ached with the day's tension. He wanted a bath, and a drink, and some time away from Koba.

There was unloading to be done, and hosts to be greeted, and rooms to be chosen, but his first thought was to ask whether there was any signal in the village. There was, a thread, if you walked up to the top of the hill behind the house, and through it he picked up a single message, a voice mail from Hibbert, sounding less worried now than alarmed, to tell him that they had just a week left to prepare, and that a normal person would have been busy preparing. It wasn't a reality Hammer could contemplate. When he was done, Koba wandered up after him and spent five minutes tapping out texts to his wife.

The house was Henrikh and Irine's, the Omalo Guesthouse, as it said on a hand-painted sign above the door, where for thirty lari, which Hammer insisted on paying in advance, travelers and hikers could spend the night in a simple, wood-lined room and be fed whatever it was they ate in Tusheti. Tonight Hammer would not find out, because Koba was not ready for local food after the day he had had and insisted on taking over the kitchen to cook his own. Irine seemed not to mind, and provided him with knives for him to cut up his lamb, and skewers to run the pieces through. These he placed on the open fire, once he had seen to it that the coals were burned down and hot, and while they cooked he went to one of his bags and produced three old plastic water bottles full of brown liquid. Irine began to chop the vegetables they had brought, and Henrikh left them all to it.

"Tonight, need chacha," said Koba.

Hammer saw no reason to argue. Koba poured two glasses—this was clearly not an honor to be conferred on mountain folk—and passed one to Hammer, who waited politely for his first proper Georgian toast. It was warm in here, and the air was beginning to fill with smoke from the lamb fat dripping onto the fire. With his elbow high, Koba held up his glass and looked Hammer in the eye.

"Georgia is beautiful country. Very beautiful. Old country. Old as mountains." Hammer doubted this, but kept quiet. Koba had the air of someone who was not to be interrupted. "People try, hurt Georgia. Muslims from Turkey, Iran, Genghis Khan—all people. Now, people hurt Georgia from inside. President, politicians. No jobs, people hungry. Young people not marry. Tbilisi full of . . . how you say? Men who like men?"

Hammer closed his eyes. This was a new side of Koba that he didn't relish coming to know. Next it would be the Jews.

"We say gay. Gay men."

"Ya, gay. Tbilisi full of gays. Women wear nothing, in church wear nothing. But. But." He punctuated this turning point with his glass. "Georgia survive. Always it survives. We get new president, will be new times, more like old times. So. Toast. New day for Georgia."

He raised his glass another inch, touched it against Hammer's, shouted "Gaumarjos!" and downed the chacha in a gulp, keeping his eyes on Hammer's throughout. When he was done he wiped his mouth with the back of his hand and beamed. "Come. Drink!"

Hammer hesitated. Koba, he was beginning to understand, was an angry man, and by drinking he would be complicit in his anger. But not to drink would be the deepest insult, and really he had no cause. He had drunk with worse people, after all. And he wanted the drink.

He knocked it back. It was rougher than the chacha Natela had given him, and scorched the back of his throat on its way down.

"Ha!" said Koba. "Good, ya? One more."

He poured again, slightly less carefully than before.

"Here. Take." They raised their glasses. Koba leaned forward across the table, took Hammer's glass from his left hand, and transferred it to his right. Then, not quite happy, he gripped Hammer's elbow and lifted it until it was level with the glass. Feeling like a marionette, Hammer let himself be manipulated.

"Now. Is good." Adopting a serious expression, Koba resumed. "You are good friend. First time in Georgia. Good man. You look for your friend. This is honor. You are man of honor. Your friend, maybe not. But you, yes. I hope you find your friend. Here, I think, we will not find him, but somewhere, yes. So, toast. To friendship." He brought the glass to his lips, then "Gaumarjos!" and down it went.

"Gaumarjos," said Hammer, and drank. The day began slowly to slip from him.

Koba drew his sleeve across his mouth. "Your friend, he is like you?"

"What am I?"

"Good man." Koba clenched his fist and held it to his breast, filling their glasses with his other hand. "True friend."

Before Hammer could answer, the third toast was made, to God, plain and simple, and the third glass drained.

"All friends let us down sometimes, Koba. No one's completely true."

"Bullshit. Good friend is good friend. Always."

"No one ever let you down?"

"Let me down?"

"Sure. Kept the money you loaned them. Stole your girl. Lied to you. Shared a secret you didn't want shared."

Koba frowned a lopsided frown, somewhere between suspicious and confused. "Such person no friend."

"You don't do forgiveness?"

"I forgive, I am weak."

It was all about perspective, Hammer thought, and one's surroundings. Come as far as he had and it felt petty to blame Ben for anything, but that could change, if the two of them ever made it home.

By the time they were ready to eat, Irine had gone to bed, the room was full of smoking lamb fat, and they were on their sixth toast, which Hammer resolved should be the last. They would start early in the morning and he wanted to be alert. After a lengthy speech about his father, and his grandfather, and the great heroes of Georgia, Koba stood, with immense solemnity, and as Hammer did the same they toasted the dead.

He could cook, Hammer had to concede. The lamb came with raw onions and salad and everything was good. By now they were drinking wine, and Hammer could tell that another toast was coming, and when Koba moved to fill his glass he put his hand over the top of it and, smiling, shook his head.

"Koba, thank you, you're very kind, but that's enough for me. I need my wits tomorrow." Koba frowned. "I need to be fresh, in the morning. You drink, go ahead."

"No. Must drink."

"When we find my friend, then I drink. But for now, no more."

"You sleep well. Mountain air."

"I hope so."

Koba was beginning to be drunk, and his face made an exaggerated display of puzzlement, dismay, resignation. "OK. Is best for you, OK. We drink later. But now, one more. Important toast."

Drunk enough himself, Hammer couldn't find the will to resist. He took his hand away.

"Very important toast. For you. We are men. We make work. We fight. We drink chacha. But," Koba took his voice down low, "each man, he has mother. Yes? With no woman, he is nothing. They are mothers and wives and daughters. They are brave like ten men. And beauty. In Georgia, women are most beautiful in world. I think you know this, yes?" He winked at Hammer, who, even through the creeping haze, wondered what he meant by it. "Men come to Georgia, they never leave. Stay forever with Georgian woman. You should do same, yes?" Another wink. "So. Drink, please. To mothers and wives. To women. Gaumarjos!"

Hammer woke in the middle of the night to the noise of Koba's snores coming through his closed door. They had a growling quality, like a wild animal disturbed. He fumbled on the floor for his phone and checked the time. Almost two. His head hurt, and his limbs still felt as if someone had pulled taut all the tendons inside. He brought the heavy sheets and blankets up round his ears against the cold.

His first memory was of the road, and the drop beside it; his second, of Koba's great red face winking at him over the chacha. It had meant something, he was sure, but perhaps nothing more than a leering guess that Hammer's frequent walks had masked some sexual escapade.

A bare bulb was shining on the landing and he squinted past it as he shuffled quickly to the bathroom in the cold. On his way back, he went to close Koba's door, in the faint hope that it might cut out some of the noise, and for a moment watched him sleeping, the big sprawled frame vibrating noticeably with every breath. The room was already a mess: his clothes were on the floor where he had stepped out of them, the contents of his plastic bags emptied against the wall, his wallet and phones by the foot of the bed.

Two phones. The notion struck Hammer as odd, as the winking had struck him as odd. He looked at the phones, then at Koba, who appeared to be in the deepest imaginable sleep, and after briefly consulting his conscience stole inside.

A minute later he was back in the bathroom, examining his haul—ready to act if the snoring stopped but not sure what he would do. The phones were locked. Both were simple models, but to judge by their condition one had been used for a long time and one was almost new. The wallet was similarly anonymous. It was well made and well worn, and at one point must have held more than it currently did, because the leather sagged around its contents: nine hundred lari in cash, which was something like five hundred dollars—a large amount, especially given that he had refused to take any of Hammer's money until the end of the job; and two receipts, one from the supermarket and one for the gas that Hammer had paid for that day. That was all. No credit cards, no driver's license, no loyalty cards, no notes, photographs, or tickets. Nothing that might identify him. Perhaps this was what a normal Georgian wallet looked like. Perhaps, when he traveled to the mountains, Koba kept things light and emptied his wallet of anything he didn't truly need.

From the next room the snores still came. Hammer crept in, left Koba's things as he had found them, gently closed the door, and almost tiptoed back to bed. As far as he knew, Koba hadn't stirred, but that made it no easier to get to sleep, and for a while he lay in the dark, wandering round this strange new world and trying to force it against its will to take on any kind of shape.

FOUR

The next time he woke, the night was over and a cheerful light was coming through the flimsy checked curtain in his room. He splashed cold water on his face in the bathroom, skipped shaving for the first time in perhaps ten years, dressed quickly, and went downstairs, seeing on the way that Koba was still out cold, on his front now and making less noise.

Irine was busying herself with breakfast in the one big room where food was cooked and eaten, which smelled faintly of sour milk and last night's smoke. She had a round face and the wind-browned look of a sailor. Three large nylon bags were lined up on the floor, and she had filled them with pans and plates and bowls, the contents of a tall dresser by the window. Hammer greeted her, exchanged smiles, and headed outside into the cold sun of the morning.

No messages, so with no great purpose beyond needing to wake up, Hammer walked. Irine's was one of the neater houses: some looked spruce, some shabby, some uninhabited and standing on the verge of ruin. In between them, any ground that hadn't been trodden into a path was thick with grass and wildflowers. He met cows grazing and a sheep tied up, saw horses in the pasture in the distance and a 4 x 4 speeding by on the road, wandered down the hill to a meadow where the bones of two rusted jeeps sat neatly in a corner, all their parts plucked for further use.

But there were no people. On his way back up, feeling the extra exertion in the thin air, he peered through the window of an abandoned house and saw inside a blackened room where a cloth still covered the kitchen table and empty bottles, perhaps from one last celebration, lined up neatly against one of the walls, covered in dust. The road had been built only thirty years earlier, Koba had told him, and before that the only way down to the plain had been on horseback. Already it seemed to have taken many people with it.

"It's quiet out there," he said to Irine on his return. But she didn't understand him, and rather than try to explain he smiled and let her serve him his breakfast of fried eggs and tea and slices of an enormous, pitted cheese that tasted of farmyards. Hammer's appetite surprised him, and he was on his third egg when Koba made his entrance, slow and bear-headed, and took his place at the table with a heavy sort of grunt. The sour smell about him announced that he'd already smoked a cigarette in his room. Irine gave him tea, which he acknowledged with the smallest nod.

"Morning, Koba," said Hammer, his tone warm enough but firm. He needed his driver alert up here. "How you doing?"

Koba's eyes were red and a little swollen. He nodded a greeting.

"In mountains feel not so good," he said. "Air is . . ." He rubbed his thumb and forefingers together, as if testing its quality.

"Thin," said Hammer.

"Ya. Thin," said Koba, rolling his head from side to side to stretch out some discomfort in his neck and failing to meet Hammer's eye.

"It sure is. But we have an easy day. We drive round, ask some questions. That's it. No mountains to climb."

Koba raised one eyebrow as he sipped at his tea.

Irine brought Koba his eggs and cheese, and without thanking her he started forking one of the eggs round the plate.

"Tell her breakfast was delicious. And ask her why there are so few people in the village. Please."

With another raised eyebrow Koba put the question to Irine, who turned from the sink and gave a nod and with it a short answer.

"All people left," said Koba, fixing another piece of egg with his fork. He seemed to be leaving the cheese. "Summer ended. In week, two weeks, first snow fall, road closed. No way down."

"Does everyone go?"

Koba asked.

"All go, except sheep people. Crazy people."

Irine said something and for a moment she and Koba went back and forth in Georgian. Hammer wanted to apologize for the brusqueness of his interpreter's manner, but she seemed not to mind.

"She goes today," said Koba.

"Today?"

"Is smart. Smart for us also."

"Is there anywhere else we can stay?"

"No."

Hammer didn't pursue it. Unless there was a miracle there was no way he could leave today.

"Ask her if there have been many visitors in the past week. Since last Tuesday. Foreigners."

Irine shook her head.

"She says none," said Koba. "Wrong time. Is too late."

Hammer thought for a moment, hesitating to ask his next question. Two days ago he would have been happy for Koba to hear it but now something gave him pause. He asked another instead.

"Where is Diklo?"

"Diklo?" said Koba. "What is Diklo?"

"Just ask her, please."

Irine knew it; she illustrated her directions with her hands.

"She say is six miles. That way. First Shenako, then Diklo. Is on Russian border. Right next."

"Only one road?"

Koba nodded.

"The road is good?"

"Good road."

"Then that's where we'll go."

Koba looked crestfallen.

"Koba, it's fine. If you don't want to stay up here just drive me to Diklo and get back down the mountain. I don't want to stop you."

Koba coughed and shook his head, without conviction.

"Is OK. We go. I tell my wife." He pulled a phone—the older of the two—from his top pocket, and asked something of Irine, who pointed out of the window, up the hill. Muttering about the terrible signal, Koba left the room.

They saw no one before Shenako, a rough, pretty village that sat on two spurs of land—at the end of one, a grand house, at the end of the other a weathered church, both built from slate. Here, too, there was a sense of quiet, of emptiness. Mountains stared down on the place. Two men repairing a roof with old pieces of rust-red corrugated iron were the only people in the scene. The city, all that noise and scheming, seemed impossibly far away.

Hammer told Koba to stop and for once Koba did not object. He hadn't been able to make his call earlier—"fucking mountains"—and was becoming restless about it, checking his phone for a signal every two minutes. As they drew up he checked it again, and Hammer told him he should get out, stretch his legs, find a place to make the call, and get it out of the way, and as he did so thought he'd take the opportunity to see how far he'd get on his own. They wandered over to the men on the low roof, who directed Koba to a piece of high ground beyond the church. Hammer watched him go, and when he was out of earshot gave the roofers one of his best gamarjobats. He smiled up at them, and they stopped work to look down at him with faces that were neither friendly, nor unfriendly, nor curious.

"Gamarjobat," he said again. "Beautiful day. Forgive me, but I'm wondering whether you gentlemen might have seen this man." He passed up his phone. "He's a friend. I'm looking for him."

The first man studied the face and handed the phone to his friend, who after a minute reached down to return it to Hammer. Neither said a word, or showed any response. It was hopeless. Hammer smiled at them, thanked them in Georgian, and looked around him. In among the three dozen houses smoke was coming from two of the chimneys. Colorful washing blew on a line. A hundred yards from the village Koba was struggling up a steep slope with his phone in his hand. This is it, Hammer thought. There's me, my angry driver, and a small collection of people who don't speak my language or have any reason to care what I say.

Clouds had crept in from the east and now moved across the sun, bringing a new chill to the air. Hammer rubbed his hands together, raised a hand in good-bye to the men on the roof, and walked up to the church, keeping one eye on Koba and his call. When he was finished they would try the two houses that seemed inhabited, and then move on to Diklo.

He was peering in through one of the church's tiny windows when a voice addressed him, deep and startling.

"Gamarjobat," it said, and as Hammer turned to greet it he saw a man in a simple black robe with a chain across his chest and a domed black cap on his head. He was tall, young behind the mass of blond beard, and his eyes were an innocent, serious blue. There was something of the explorer about his face.

Hammer gave a respectful bow of his head in reply, and the priest asked him something in Georgian.

"Sorry," said Hammer. "I'm American. English. I can't speak Georgian."

The priest gave a little nod himself, and when he spoke again it was in good English and a European accent that Hammer couldn't immediately place. He didn't smile, but his face was mild.

"Welcome," he said. "I am sorry that the church is locked."

"That's no problem, Father. Is Father OK?"

"If you like."

"I'm Isaac Hammer."

The priest shook the hand that Hammer offered, but didn't give his name.

"I was just having a look around. I'm on my way to Diklo."

"You seem to be going the wrong way."

Hammer looked confused. "I thought it was up the valley."

"I meant that everyone else is leaving."

"Aren't they just. I think I am the tourism industry right now." Now the priest smiled. "You're a little out of place yourself, Father, if I may say."

"Sometimes I feel that. There are not so many German priests here."

"German?"

"I came with a group from my seminary and stayed. Here it is like the Early Church."

Hammer nodded. This was not so hard to imagine.

"So what do they do for priests up here when it snows?"

"They manage without. Possibly they could manage without in the summer, too."

Hammer grinned. Over the priest's shoulder he could see Koba beginning a slippery descent from his perch, phone still in hand.

"Say, Father, do you know of anywhere round here I could spend the night? Here or Diklo."

"You're staying?"

"Just a day or two. The thing is, I'm looking for a friend."

Hammer described his mission, not the full version. His friend had been traveling in Georgia and hadn't been heard from for days. The trail had led here, to this unlikely place.

The priest had not seen anyone up here, nor heard of anyone, but then he had been busy preparing for his own departure to the low ground. Such a person would almost certainly be noticed, especially now, at the end of the season—Tusheti was a huge place, but a small one—and he knew who would know, if anyone did.

"Vano and Eka. They live in Diklo. Vano is the head man in the village. Their son is a ranger in the national park. Everyone knows them. Tell them I sent you. For money, they may help."

"Can they put me up?"

"Maybe. You can ask."

"They speak English?"

The priest shook his head. Behind him Koba was scrambling down the last of the bank.

"Too bad. I don't suppose you want to introduce us? I'd make a big contribution to your church." The priest smiled. "I'm serious."

"I will be there later. After lunch. You can say that I sent you."

"Thank you, Father. That's kind. Listen." Koba would soon be with them. "One last thing. Do you happen to know where they found that truck? The one that was involved in the bomb in Gori?"

The priest looked at him with a new kind of concern.

"My friend's a journalist. I think he was chasing a story."

"Then your friend was chasing trouble." Before, the priest had been welcoming, in an august, almost ceremonial way; now he was wary. He looked at Hammer as if evaluating a changed proposition. "Are you a journalist also?"

"Not anymore."

"These people are innocent. The world doesn't come here. They don't need stories."

"No story, Father. I just want to find my friend and go. Quietly as I can."

The priest breathed out slowly, with the air of a man considering an offer he doesn't trust, and for a moment kept his eyes steadily on Hammer's.

"Are you here to make trouble, Mr. Hammer?"

"I think it may be here already."

"What happened to your nose?"

Hammer brought his hand up to the plaster that now ran across its bridge. It no longer needed a bandage.

"This? I wandered into a riot. It wasn't my idea."

The priest didn't smile, but he seemed to finish his appraisal.

"You seem a good man."

He did. He seemed it. But a good man would be here to rescue Ben, not to save himself by dragging him back home. A good man would do it without thought of being proved right.

"I don't feel like one, Father."

"No good man does."

Koba was by them now. He stopped with his legs planted and his arms crossed, blankly eyeing the priest, who nodded to both men and then touched Hammer on the arm.

"Do not make trouble for my friends."

And with a final look into Hammer's eyes he walked away.

FIVE

To Diklo, at the end of the road. Two miles short of Russia. For a moment, Hammer saw himself as a pinprick on the globe, slowly heading for its remotest corner, beyond it miles of mountains and thousands of miles of steppe and desert, with only the Caspian and a few lonely, dusty cities for relief. As if to emphasize the point, a flatbed truck piled high with assorted possessions—suitcases, a mattress, two wooden chairs tied back-to-back—passed them on its way out.

Here the landscape flattened out, but ahead the mountains seemed to grow in number and in size. Hammer wondered whether this was a psychological effect, and whether Ben had had the chance to register it, too. Without doubt it was wilder here. On the way, Koba had to stop to let a herd of horses cross in front of them, and Hammer could see hawks, or what looked like hawks, circling in the sky above. By now the dark forests that edged closer to the road were surely full of wolves, and bears, and heaven knew what. As they arrived at the edge of the village a huge white dog barked madly at them from its wooden pen.

The priest was right. The first person that Koba asked was able to direct them to Vano's house, which was notably more substantial than its neighbors. There was an air of tidiness and activity and general upkeep that was missing elsewhere: chickens strutted about, herbs and flowers hung drying, pans and pails sat ready for fresh milk, firewood lay stacked and dry.

Koba knocked on the door, waited a while, knocked hard again, and, after another half a minute, just as they were turning away, it opened. This was Vano. There was no doubt even before he confirmed it. Like the landscape in which he lived, he gave the impression of wildness more or less tamed, and of peace won only with great vigilance. He was utterly calm and utterly watchful at once. Though he might have been ten years out, Hammer put his age at sixty: there were decades of healthy work in that face, but whether they had aged it or kept it young was hard to say. Regardless, it was handsome, and narrow, in a way that wasn't like other Georgians, and his skin was the color of oiled oak, made deeper by the white of his hair—all of which, Hammer noted with a certain envy, he still had. He wore an old black anorak and black trousers and a cap pushed up at the peak.

Hammer talked and Koba translated while Vano listened without saying a word. When they were done, he moved inside the house and they followed, Koba giving Hammer a glance that said these mountain people are crazy. Hammer wasn't so sure.

The back of the house opened into a neat yard where more chickens roamed and muslin bags full of curds dripped into buckets. Vano gestured for them to sit at a table in the middle of a large, low room whose walls were lined with dark wood, and finally, when they were all seated, he spoke in short, contained sentences. Koba fished a cigarette from his pocket and lit it.

"He no see your friend. Irodi, his son, he can help."

Hammer looked at Vano and nodded his thanks.

"Tell him that would be great. I'll pay him well. Ask him if there's anywhere for me to stay."

There was; twenty dollars a night. They would feed him. But there was room only for one. Vano glanced at Koba with a fixed sternness as he said it, and Hammer heard him with a sort of relief.

"OK," he said, glancing at Koba. "We'll sort something out. When can we start?"

His son would be back at lunchtime.

Hammer checked his watch. It was eleven. He thanked Vano and asked Koba if he would talk to him outside. Head hung, he came, like a dog in disgrace, cigarette in hand.

"Koba," said Hammer, his expression as sincere as he could make it, "I want to thank you for everything you've done for me. Really. You've been great."

"I find different place. To stay."

"You should get down the mountain, before the snow. To your wife. It's not fair to keep you here."

"How you get out?"

"Push comes to shove I'll get a helicopter."

Koba shook his head. "No. Not right, leave you with this idiots. I stay. I cook."

Hammer took his wallet from his back pocket. "I'm going to pay you through Thursday. We had an agreement for that. You take the food."

"Who say to you what they say, in English?"

"The priest."

"The priest leave."

"Not straightaway."

Koba took his cigarettes from the pocket of his shirt and lit one.

"Look," said Hammer. "I feel bad about this. Probably this whole trip is for nothing, and I don't want to risk you and your car getting stuck up here because of my wild-goose chase." Koba frowned at the phrase. "Mrs. Koba would never forgive me. Also, anything happens here I'm going to need someone in Tbilisi to help. OK? That's you. I don't have anyone else."

Koba nodded and Hammer, thinking he was about to relent, felt an unacknowledged weight lift.

"I stay. I find room. Is not safe for you, with this people. Quiet, yes. Safe, no."

Koba stubbed his cigarette out on the ground with a determined finality, and clasped Hammer by the shoulder.

"Money later. These people, they look simple. But they are not."

On his way to find lodgings Koba dropped Hammer at the only spot with a signal anywhere nearby, halfway along the road back to Shenako, and with a great resolve told Isaac that he would see him later, for sure. By wandering around with his arm stretched up Hammer eventually found a little patch where his phone worked long enough to show him there was no word. He tried Natela's number but the line was dead. With his thoughts half in the city and half on his afternoon's work—half desperate, half hopeful—he walked back to his new hosts.

While he waited for Irodi he watched his mother make lunch and busy herself in the kitchen, and as he did so he slowly became enchanted by the spareness of the house and the sureness of her touch around it. Eka seemed sanctified, somehow, whether by the air or the work he couldn't say, and when she looked up occasionally to smile at him he felt his heart lighten, as if it had received a blessing. This lifted him, but there was regret in it, too. How natural were her routines, and how artificial his own. Everything he had ever accomplished had been communication—finding stories, checking them, telling them. Words upon words, endlessly; here in the mountains, next to Eka's quiet activity, they felt like not much more than noise.

They ate in silence together, or near silence; Hammer couldn't prevent himself from thanking her, in Georgian, or telling her as best he could that the food was good. Her hair was thick and fair, her skin an even brown from the sun and the wind, and she served the food with rough, calloused hands. When Hammer was done she offered him chacha and he declined.

Irodi came shortly afterward and greeted the stranger in his house with a noncommittal nod that was again neither friendly nor unfriendly. Eka's short explanation drew another nod as he sat down to eat. Like all the villagers Hammer had met he was dressed in well-worn Western clothes—a sweatshirt and baggy trousers—and throughout his lunch he kept an old white sun hat on his head. Under it were the sharp eyes of his father and the softer face of his mother and the golden brown skin of them both. There was no hurry about him. He ate and drank with appetite but no haste, and from time to time his eyes rested on Hammer as they might on a bird or a dog or some other beast under his charge: calmly, with the curiosity one creature might show another. Twenty-five, Hammer guessed, not much older, but despite the round face and the patchy stubble and the boyish clothes there was little of the boy left in him.

Hammer checked his impatience—here it would get him nowhere—until eventually the priest came, and the three men agreed to a plan. This afternoon Irodi would take Hammer around the eastern side of Tusheti.

Where they saw people, Irodi would ask them if they had seen a foreigner who matched Webster's description, or a car of the kind he had been using. Along the way they would stop at the place where the truck had been left by the bombers, a prospect that seemed to alarm Irodi much less than it did the priest, who argued with Irodi about it in Georgian but eventually held his hands up in concession. This would take all afternoon, probably longer. The light would fail before six.

Because it was detective work and not tourism, Hammer agreed to pay double Irodi's usual rate. Irodi signaled their departure by simply getting up and walking outside, where he told Hammer to wait. Hammer looked to the priest for an explanation but received none, and for a while they stood by the house, warm in the sunshine, not saying anything.

"You are in good hands," said the priest, after a time.

"I won't abuse it, Father. Your trust."

The priest looked up at the sun and then back along the road.

"Here is your friend."

Hammer followed his gaze and saw the distinctive white shirt and heavy urban tread of Koba just rounding a house at the end of the village. Twenty yards off, he raised his hand and bellowed a greeting.

"Isaac! I find room. In Shenako. Old man, he has place, not so good, but one night, two nights, is OK."

He was pleased with himself, but not happy. With a cigarette burning in his fingers and his arms crossed he came and stood next to the priest, reasserting his primacy.

"So. Now we look."

Irodi and Koba would not get on well. That was clear, and would make at best for a tedious afternoon and at worst a pointless one. What was less straightforward was why Koba insisted on staying. The more time Hammer spent with him, the less he knew this man.

"That's great, Koba. Now we look." Hammer managed a stiff smile, failing to come up with an idea that might get rid of him.

At that moment Irodi returned, sitting on a horse and leading another by a rope. Both were chestnuts and compact, with slightly bandy legs that seemed shaped by the mountain slopes, and Irodi rode his slightly askew in the saddle, like a cap set at a jaunty angle. He had an old rifle slung across his back. Laughing at the alarm he saw in Hammer's face, he said something to the priest and jumped down.

"He says it is the only way. By car you will not see anything. He needs to look."

Hammer's first thought was that it would take weeks to cover this vast landscape on these two. Neither looked quick.

"Really?"

"He knows this country," said the priest.

Koba said something in Georgian, in the blunt tone he used to address his countrymen, and for a minute he and Irodi argued.

"There are only two horses," said the priest to Hammer while they went at it.

"Thank heaven for that."

Koba, realizing that his opponent was at least as stubborn as he was, with great reluctance was backing down.

"I no ride horse," he said, drawing firmly on his cigarette. "Dangerous. You go on this, Isaac?"

Hammer tried to look resolute and said yes, he was.

"Be careful. Cannot know what horse will do. Has own mind. Like these people."

"I'll be careful. What I need you to do is go back to Omalo, and then take the road west from there. In case Ben went that way. Can you do that for me? Ask people, sniff around."

Koba let his cigarette drop to the ground and rubbed his mustache.

"It would be very helpful to me," said Hammer.

With a slow, churlish nod Koba agreed, and turned away.

Hammer hadn't ridden for twenty years, and then only once, but without allowing himself to voice his countless objections he stepped forward, took the reins of the horse, put his foot in the stirrup as Irodi showed him, and hoisted himself into the saddle. Irodi made sure he was holding the reins properly and then gave Hammer his briefing: kick the heels to go, hold the reins firmly but not tight, pull them back to slow and stop.

"He says you will be fine," said the priest, smiling at Hammer's attempts to settle. "She is called Shakari. There are two rules. Be firm with her . . . And if you see dogs, stop."

"What's wrong with the dogs?"

"They are sheepdogs. Bred to kill wolves. Or men who come to steal."

Before getting back onto his horse Irodi collected four good stones, each the size of a baseball, and put them in his pockets.

"For the dogs," said the priest.

Hammer patted his coat. "What if you don't have stones?"

"Then you lie down and submit. Show you are not a threat."

Hammer raised an eyebrow and waited for the priest to smile.

"You're serious?"

"Vano does this. I have seen him."

"I like the stones better."

The priest patted Shakari's flank and reached up to shake Hammer's hand.

"Thank you, Father. Will I see you again?"

"Eka has asked me to eat this evening. The last time before the winter. I will bless the house."

"I'm delighted to hear it."

"Do you think your friend will attend?"

Hammer smiled. "I'll think of something. Don't worry."

SIX

All Hammer could remember from his first ride—on a ranch in Texas, covering a story about migrants—was that it was important that the horse knew who was in charge. Now, as then, it was all too clearly the horse.

They set off at a slow walk, back the way Hammer had come that morning. In the fields outside the village they met the dog that had barked at them earlier, a grand creature with thick fur and a wolf's face that stood and watched them approach like a king suffering travelers to enter his kingdom. When they were close, Irodi dismounted, holding up a hand to tell Hammer to stay where he was, and crouched down to pat its head and stroke the fur under its chin. Rather you than me, thought Hammer.

"Vano," said Irodi, pointing. "Vano dzaghli." Vano's dog. Of course it was. They had the same bearing, the same stateliness.

Soon they left the road for a track that headed upward to their left through densely planted pines. Rolling in the saddle, Hammer did his best to keep his balance correct but found himself always slightly out of kilter on one side or the other, something that seemed to annoy Shakari, who from time to time would snort and come to a stop. Irodi, who was soon a good fifty yards ahead, continued to ride at a casual lean without his horse making any complaint.

They crested a hill, and came out into the light again in a gentle valley where the grass was thick with wildflowers. The track had run out, and Shakari made her own mind up about which route to take, sometimes more or less following Irodi and sometimes going entirely her own way. The first time this happened, Hammer, as he failed to bring her back in line, imagined with a sense of powerlessness and growing alarm a night spent lost in the mountains with only this obstinate creature for company. But he soon realized that she wasn't wayward but merely independent: if she was going to suffer a fool on her back she was going to do so on her own terms. Within a little while they were getting on pretty well, in a state of mutual understanding if not respect. Talking to her seemed to help, so Hammer did.

Their way went slowly down, through meadows and birch, and after half an hour they came out at a crossroads of two rough tracks, one of which rose steeply into a dark pine wood. Irodi took this, and for once Shakari was happy simply to do the same. Tightly packed, their lower branches brittle and gray, the trees kept out all but a dim light, and the air between them was still and cool.

Irodi was going more slowly now and closely watching the ground. At a bend in the track he stopped, peered into the darkness to his right and then turned, slowly guiding his horse through the trees, which were set slightly further apart here and allowed a barely perceptible path between them, per-haps eight feet wide. Hammer crouched down to avoid the dry branches that began to scratch and pull at his head. Thirty yards away he could just make out a solid shape, and as they drew closer he saw that it was a truck, battered and olive green and looking like a relic of some long-forgotten war.

Irodi got down from his horse and squatted to inspect the floor, which was covered in cones and needles, and dry despite the recent rain. His eyes scanned the area around the truck and the route they had come along the path.

"It's still here," said Hammer, swinging his leg over the saddle and pat-ting Shakari's flank.

In this truck the two Dagestanis had crossed the border, on the other side of Tusheti where the one road ran into Russia. They had driven here, perhaps thirty miles across the wilderness, and then taken another vehicle down the mountain and on to Gori; the tracks were still clear. It seemed extraordinary that it hadn't been taken away to be examined, and stranger still that this place showed no sign of disruption. It looked as if no one had been here for fifty years.

The truck was really a jeep with a canvas canopy, Russian-made and ancient. Hammer got inside, ran his hand under the plastic seats, felt under the instruments and along the seal of the roof, checked the back, and found nothing at all. He even lay down and looked underneath, but whoever had found it had taken anything loose.

In the absence of evidence, he tried to engage his imagination. Two men had driven into these woods, left their vehicle, and then somehow, somewhere between here and Gori, taken delivery of a 4 x 4 full of explosives. The quietest place for that to happen would have been here, no question, and the easiest, too, in the dark of the forest with not a soul to witness anything. If this had been the place, how had it worked? Was the truck waiting for them, or had a Georgian been here to hand it over, and to seal this double betrayal—of the seventeen dead of Gori, and of the men persuaded to kill them?

Irodi was walking back along the path with his eyes set on the ground. Twenty yards back along the way they had come he stopped, straightened up, shaking his head, and turned round. When he reached Hammer he shook his head again and said something in Georgian, which might have been that no one had been here recently or that it was impossible to know if they had. Whatever his conclusion, there was no speculation about it; as with everything Irodi seemed to do, it had certainty.

He jumped onto his horse, springing up in a single motion, and set off, not waiting for Hammer to struggle with the stirrups and haul himself back on. At the crossroads beyond the woods he turned left, which, if Hammer's bearings were at all correct, took them away from the border and eventually to the road that would take them back to the plain, and for a while they rode uphill, the track so steep in parts that Hammer felt himself slipping off the saddle as Shakari charged up the sharper inclines. Lean forward going up and back coming down. Was it that way round?

Clouds were settling on the peaks ahead of them and a brisk wind was beginning to gust. Hammer had explained earlier that when his friend came over the mountains he would have headed this way, his intention to speak to local people about the truck—when it had been found, who had found it, what they had seen, what they knew—and now he guessed that Irodi was taking them back along Webster's route to see who they might come across. His fear was that he was five days too late, and that anyone who knew anything had probably already left for the winter. That was, of course, if Ben had made it over the mountains at all.

Houses here tended to cluster together, but after a little while they came across one that was set back and up from the road, on its own shelf of land that gave a view of the whole valley behind them, lit up as if from within by the afternoon sun shining out from behind dark clouds. A wooden fence at a little over waist height, screened with chicken wire, enclosed a large space around it, and sitting by the gate in the last of the sun were two dogs which, as Irodi turned off the main track, began to bark, loudly and with grim enthusiasm. Halfway up the path he dismounted, held up a hand for Hammer to stop, and walked the last twenty feet, keeping a decent distance between him and the fence, against which the dogs were now jumping, their paws scrabbling on the wire. Both were huge, with thick white coats. Even from a distance Hammer could see the red of their jaws and the white of their teeth, and he noticed that for the first time Irodi's gait wasn't its usual easy roll.

The door of the house opened, and from it came a tall, bearded man in a striped jumper and a blue cap, stooping a little and walking without hurry toward Irodi, who was standing a few feet short of the gate. In an improbably loud voice he shouted something, twice, and the dogs relaxed, stopped barking, and withdrew, deflated. Irodi thanked him, and for a while they talked, leaning on the fence, the tall man occasionally glancing back down the hill at Hammer. They seemed to have found something to talk about, though for all Hammer knew it might have been the weather, or the winter, or the idiocy of the foreigner standing at the bottom of the drive. As he watched them and Shakari chewed the grass on the shoulder, he felt a spot of rain fall on his arm, then another on his forehead, and at the same moment the sun went behind clouds and the wind started to blow steadily from the east. Irodi looked up, toward the mountains, where the sky was now black, thanked the tall man, and jogged down the hill to his horse, gesturing to Hammer to turn his horse round.

"Interesting?" said Hammer, knowing that any explanation was hopeless. Irodi ignored him, leaped onto his horse, and rode off at a brisker pace than he'd set on the way out, but Shakari showed no signs of wanting to follow. Hammer kicked his heels, once and then again, while she carried on eating, not even bothering to snort her disapproval.

"Go, would you?" said Hammer, zipping his fleece up as the rain began to fall, big drops on his balding head. Still he wasn't used to those first few drops falling directly onto his skin. He kicked again, with no response. Irodi was now on the track, waiting; he shouted Shakari's name, in among a few Georgian words that had no effect.

Hammer leaned forward in the saddle until his face was close to the horse's ear and whispered, in the gentlest voice he could manage. "Shakari, you're a lovely horse and I appreciate that you've got a good thing going on there, but you're making me feel a little foolish and very soon we're both going to get very wet. So how's this. You quit eating and when we get back I will get you something sweet and delicious from my good friend Koba's secret store. How does that sound? Otherwise I may buy you from Irodi and have you turned into glue, which is not something I want to do, of course." He patted her neck. "What do you say?"

With an air of resignation, Shakari lifted her head, circled neatly, and set off after her master, who was holding his thumb up for Hammer to see.

The rain poured from the sky in one long, heavy burst, with such force that Hammer wondered whether here he was truly closer to the heavens. It roared down, turning the grand landscape into a sodden gray patch around him and his horse. Ahead he could just make out Irodi on the track, which was an inch underwater and spitting with mud. The cold had come, too, and he was grateful for the warmth coming from Shakari, who had picked up her pace to a trot. Irodi, he assumed, could have galloped home, but he hung back, occasionally glancing behind him to check on his solitary charge.

Where the road climbed outside the village an unfamiliar noise sounded from somewhere inside his saturated clothes. The ping of a text message. His phone must have found some slender signal. He sat up in the saddle, eased it from his back pocket, and looked at the screen, which was instantly obscured by the rain. Wiping it on his sleeve, he looked again, and saw that there were three messages there, two of them from Georgian numbers he didn't recognize. Although they were simple, it took him a moment to make out the words. The first was from Hibbert:

Where are you? Three days left, Ike. Call me TODAY.

Hammer just looked at the screen until the rain obscured the letters again. He should call Hibbert. He would call Hibbert. But how distant that world was, and how disconnected he felt from it. He'd been in the mountains only one day and already it was impossible to imagine being anywhere else. Hibbert, Sander, Katerina, his staff, his clients, all seemed to occupy a phantom world that no longer had substance, and the thought left him feeling at once liberated and rootless, like a man set adrift from the shore.

He wiped his phone again but the second message took a moment to absorb.

Two days no news. OI.

OI. Otar Iosava. Hammer had forgotten about Iosava and his persistence. How did he have the number? For a moment he let this puzzle him, but the third message cut him short.

Isaac. There is problem. I must leave Tbilisi. Where are you? Natela.

Shakari kept on going, but Hammer felt as if he had stopped dead. The number was not Natela's, at least not the one he had stored for her in his phone, and his first thought was that the thing was a trick, played by someone exploiting this new vulnerability in him. In the same instant he hoped that this was and was not true: nothing could be worse than harm coming to Natela, but to help her, to have that opportunity—well, he would rather it came to him than to anyone else.

"Irodi!" He pulled firmly on the reins. "Irodi!" He shouted again, louder, but Irodi was almost out of sight and couldn't hear over the sound of the rain. "Shakari. Stop." He continued to pull at the reins, and with a snort Shakari slowed and came to a halt. "Good girl."

The signal was thin indeed. He wiped the phone again, smearing the water over the screen, and dialed the number. It rang, and the tone in his ear was the strangest sound. A female voice answered.

"Natela? It's Ike."

The voice said something that he didn't understand, and for a moment it crossed his mind, illogically, that the whole thing was a mistake, a wrong number.

"Natela. Can you hear me?"

The line was quiet, and then he heard a voice that he did recognize, even above the din.

"Isaac. Where are you?"

"I'm in Tusheti. It's raining like hell."

"Tell me where. My friend will bring me."

"What's happened?" Hammer hunched over the phone in an attempt to keep it dry.

"I cannot talk. Tell me where."

"Natela, you can't drive. No way. We're underwater up here."

Through the deluge Irodi was coming back, watching him silently.

"I need safe place."

"I'm not sure this is it."

"There is nowhere else."

Hammer looked at Irodi and shrugged. Maybe it was safe here.

"OK. You need to fly. A woman will call you from London. Her name is Katerina. She's a friend of mine and she'll tell you what to do. I'll call her now."

"OK."

"You OK?"

Natela was quiet on the other end of the line.

"Come. Bring a coat."

SEVEN

ka had laid a fire, and handing Hammer a towel she sent him to have
a shower, in the same slightly stern way that his mother might have
welcomed him back from some boyhood escapade. The shower wasn't
altogether hot, and out of respect for his hosts he didn't stay under it for
long, but by the time he was done and had put on fresh clothes he felt revived and ready to resume the search.

Even without the priest to translate Irodi's few words, though, Hammer
knew that there would be no more tracking today. Too much rain; impossible to see a thing. Irodi left, and Hammer, frustrated but resigned, helped
prepare for the evening's feast. He peeled potatoes, chopped cabbages,
ground walnuts in a stone mortar, letting his technique be guided by Eka,
who was amused by his incompetence, and patient with it. Probably she
imagines I'm too much the patriarch to cook, he thought, but the truth is
that for ten years I've had someone to do it for me, and before that I didn't
care enough to learn.

The work did little to calm his thoughts, which darted between fear and
a strange, unearned hope. Anxiety was more or less unknown to him, but
powerlessness made him think too much, and to replace action with an almost obsessive concentration on the facts—and in the absence of facts, on
the competing claims of improbable theories.

For a week these had been about Ben; now they moved to Natela. Questions hummed about him, and one kept returning. If he wasn't the cause of
her troubles, it seemed likely that he hadn't helped. At best he had disturbed
something that had barely begun to settle, and now he was responsible for

her as well. When he wasn't wondering what might be bringing her here he let himself imagine how good, in better circumstances, that might have felt.

After a while Irodi returned, bringing with him the priest, who fell to helping as well. Irodi disappeared again into the rain. There was much to be done, and while the three of them worked they talked. Hammer was finally able to tell Eka that a friend of his was coming, that she was in some danger, and that he regretted bringing these problems into their home. If she would like, they could find a place to stay elsewhere.

Whenever Eka looked him in the eye, as she did now, he had the unnerving, comforting sense that she understood him—that she knew there were things he couldn't express and other things he couldn't say—and that without good cause she trusted him, too. In her place he would not have done so. His friend could have her daughter's room, next to her own. Ordinarily, they did not let it out, but Lida had been gone for a week and the situation was unusual. That was the word the priest used, at any rate; Hammer sensed that Eka had meant more by it.

A little before five, Irodi drove Hammer to the point where the phone worked, just beyond Shenako.

The rain still fell, but with less force, and in the south, where the plain ran out and the mountains rose up, Hammer thought he could see some brightness in the sky. Opening his window, he held his palm out and let it collect the drops.

His phone sounded in his hand. A message from London, from Katerina at Ikertu, to tell him that everything was set. Natela was with a friend at an airfield outside Tbilisi. She was there now, waiting for the weather over the mountains to clear; if it didn't, there was a hotel booked for her under another name and she would try again tomorrow.

By seven it would be dark, and too late to land without lights. Hammer's fingers continued to beat a tattoo on his leg, and again he cleared the window to peer out at the sky. Through the gloom he saw headlights, and recognized Koba's Toyota, heading back toward Diklo with heaven knows what news. Irodi looked at him as if to ask whether he should signal his friend to stop, and Hammer shook his head. An understanding passed between them.

For an hour more they stayed, even though Hammer knew that there was nothing for him to do and nothing more to learn. Yesterday he had found the utter separation of this place exhilarating, but now there was comfort to be had in being at the end of a telephone line, even if he knew there was nothing coming down it. He felt like the stationmaster of some isolated western town in the first days of the railroad, on hand to take important communications from the wire. But there were none, and as the time passed the odds lengthened and his thoughts turned to whether he could get down the mountain that night.

But he hadn't been wrong about the sky. The peaks to the south were showing now, and behind them glowed late afternoon sun. His mood began to lift, and the phone to weigh heavier in his hand.

Arriving in Diklo, Hammer felt like the oldest son returning home with his new bride. There was even a priest, in case a blessing was needed.

He had been anxious about offending the morals of his hosts, but they received Natela with concern and warmth, as if she, too, had been caught out in a storm. Vano nodded his welcome, with a gravity that suggested that she had his sympathy, and Eka took her bag and showed her to her room.

A fire was burning in the wide hearth and on the table in the kitchen plastic bowls had been set out, full of salad and bread and cheese, and next to them skewers of cubed lamb rested on a plate. Koba hovered by them, a bottle of his beer in his hand, proprietorial about his contribution, a guest uncertain of his welcome. Though he said nothing, and seemed to be on good behavior, Hammer knew that he was wondering why the invitation to Natela had not been extended to him.

He offered a bottle to Irodi, who took it with a nod. Watching him, Hammer realized that some of his hostility to the mountains was mere awkwardness; not to know things was to lose face, and here he knew almost nothing. But he did know how to cook meat, and Hammer hoped that would restore his pride enough to keep him in check. It looked as if he had donated all his precious store of food to their dinner, and that was a positive sign.

Was this Hammer's first Georgian feast? the priest wanted to know. He was sitting at the table, paring cucumbers with a small knife, and was still wearing his black cap, which against the dark walls and the firelight gave him and the whole scene a medieval air. He should have been applying gold to an icon, or reading an illuminated text.

My very first, said Hammer, unless you count the feast that Koba cooked for me last night. And the other feasts he's had me eating every night. This, the priest explained, would be different. This was a supra, a conscious coming together of friends, and on centuries of such humble gatherings rested the language and culture of Georgia—and even its survival, if you listened to some. It was a little more formal than Hammer might imagine, and at the same time more intimate. There would be toasts, and he would get drunk.

"Not again," said Hammer, and Koba gave an extravagant laugh.

"Last night was not drunk," he said, and laughed again.

Hammer smiled, but he didn't need a drink or, for that matter, a feast. He had to speak to Natela, and to know what Irodi had been told earlier, and to make a plan for the next day, for which he wanted above all else to be alert. Instinct told him that if tomorrow yielded nothing, his search would soon be over. He did his best to mask his restlessness.

"Koba," he said. "Tell me. Have you seen a little notebook of mine, about this big, black leather? I've mislaid it. I wondered if it might be in the car."

Koba pushed his lips out and frowned.

"No, Isaac. I do not think so."

"I think it may have slipped out of my back pocket on the road. Can I have the key? I'm going to take a look."

Koba held up his hands. "No, Isaac. I go."

Hammer feigned protest, and then relented. He knew that Koba would want to go himself, though whether to stop Hammer from searching the car, or to read the notebook if he found it, or simply to do a selfless deed, he still couldn't tell.

"Father," he said, once Koba had shut the door behind him, "would you apologize to our hosts for me? I seem to have brought more people with me than I would have liked."

The priest nodded, and said something to Eka, who by means of a nod let Hammer know that she was grateful for his words, and that under the strict rules of Georgian hospitality all were welcome under her roof.

Hammer thanked them both, and addressed the priest again. "Can you ask Irodi what his friend with the dogs said this afternoon? We were out, and they talked, and I have no way of knowing what about."

The priest looked up from his peeling. "You do not want to talk in front of your friend?"

"Nothing wrong with your instincts, Father."

"Or with yours. I would not trust him."

"Why do you say that?"

The priest breathed deeply and started again with his knife. "I would like to know what he did before the revolution. In the old Georgia."

"You think he's got a history?"

"He seems an angry man."

The priest put down his knife, and asked a question of Irodi.

"He says the man he spoke to is a shepherd. He will stay here for the winter, and look after many of the flocks, for many people. One of these men told him before he left that he had seen a car abandoned in a wood near Keselo, toward Omalo. He saw it there one day, and it was there again the next day. He did not recognize it."

"Does he know what it was? The color?"

The priest asked, and it was clear from Irodi's response that he didn't know.

"Does Irodi know where this wood is?"

"He does. He will take you there tomorrow."

Hammer and Irodi shared a look. "Gmadlobt."

Irodi nodded and said something to his father, and together they left, meeting Koba on his way back in and giving him plenty of room to pass. The exchange was polite enough, but to Hammer at least it was clear that they'd prefer him not to be in their house.

Koba came into the room, shrugging.

"Nothing, Isaac. No book."

"You check under the seat?"

"Ya. Everyplace. Is not there."

"Then I'm sorry to have wasted your time, Koba. What are you cooking for us?"

"Shashlik. Very good." As Koba began to explain how he had marinated the meat and just how good it would be, Natela came down the stairs, followed by Eka. She was smiling, but her face was drawn, her eyes tired, and she had the look of someone who might prefer to be alone. Hammer had warned her that there would be dinner but hadn't expected a feast.

"How you doing?" he said.

"OK." She held her smile.

"Koba, this is Natela. She's a friend of mine from Tbilisi."

Koba nodded and held out his hand, and while he shook Natela's turned to grin at Hammer. "Gamarjobat," he said, and a few other words of Georgian. Natela thanked him and looked to Hammer.

"I need cigarette."

"Let's go," he said, and ushered her outside.

It was almost cold now. The sun had set and fresh clouds had covered the sky, but a pale light lingered. The slate of the houses, the grass they stood on, the dark woods beyond the village: everything was gray except Natela's face as she lit her cigarette from the flame of a match. She took a deep drag and let the smoke out into the breeze.

"Better here?"

She inhaled again and nodded, but with no certainty.

"It's going to be OK. Tomorrow, I look for Ben. You can stay here with Vano and Eka. They're good people. No one knows you're here. Then, when we're done, I'll figure out a way for you to be safe."

"What about him?"

"Koba? He leaves tomorrow. I'll make sure of it." He held her eye to show that he meant it. "What did he say to you?"

"That he was sorry for me and I would be safe up here."

How did he know to be sorry for her? Eka must have told him, Hammer thought. Or Koba had asked her. He let it go.

"So what happened? Where did you go?"

She closed her eyes and drew on the cigarette.

"You leave Luka's. I waited for hour, maybe two. It made me crazy, and I need cigarettes, so I leave, go to shop. One hour I walk, I have air, I go back to Luka's and two men are there, in door on street, they come out talking. Two big men. I stop, they go to car and sit. So I go."

"Why didn't you call me?"

"I did not want."

"Why not?"

"I tell you before. Your world, I do not want it."

"It's not my world. And I'm afraid we're both in it."

She nodded slowly, as if she had always known it.

"So, where did you go?"

"My friend. Marta. In Rustavi, out of Tbilisi. She is good friend. I think I stay one week, they forget, the police. I go back. But the police, they come there, today, they say to Marta, where am I? How they know? Where I am. How?"

Hammer had been wondering the same thing. "Maybe they didn't. Maybe they were checking everybody you know."

Natela's chin jutted out and she gave a brisk shake of her head in suppressed fury.

"They stayed. In car, outside, as before. Made me crazy. Crazy with it. Then I think, God, what can I do? I cannot leave, I cannot stay. So then I think, I am in your world. And I call you."

"How did you get out?"

"Through window, at back. Marta lives on fourth floor but knows someone on first floor. They drove me out in the . . . how you say where bag goes?"

"The trunk?"

"The trunk."

Natela flicked her cigarette away, took the pack from her pocket, and lit another. She smoked too much, Hammer thought.

"So. You. You find your friend?"

He shook his head.

"I think we found his car. I know he was here."

"You find him, maybe we stop all this crazy shit. Maybe they stop."

"Is that why you're here? To tell me that?"

"What else can I do?"

The look she gave him was full of understanding and challenge. I know this is not your fault, but you have to end it. It can't go on. Her trust was a spur and a weight at once, but he didn't remember being so glad of anything.

"I'm close. We'll be safe here."

Then Natela took a step toward him and hugged him, holding him close, and he couldn't tell whether she was taking succor or giving it. Perhaps it was just the closing of the deal between them. In any event, he didn't mind. He felt her cheek against his, smelled that already familiar smell of perfume and fresh smoke, and closed his eyes for a moment.

"It'll be OK."

She pulled away, took another drag, and smiled.

"How you find these people?"

"This is how I make friends. I force my way into people's lives."

The smile stayed.

"Come on," he said. "It's dinner. I need your help."

"I finish this."

"How many packs you bring? How long can we last up here?"

EIGHT

They were seven for the supra, three on each side of the kitchen table and Vano at the head. In front of him lay a curled, polished ram's horn; everyone else had a small glass, which Eka and Irodi filled from two jugs of dark white wine, but these remained untouched until Vano, without his cap and wearing a fresh checked shirt, rose and made his speech, looking deliberately from face to face as he spoke and lending his voice a rolling, melodic quality that suggested he knew precisely what he was going to say and had said it many times before. Hammer was struck by his manner, which was welcoming but stern and seemed to suggest that, while their coming together might be pleasant, the tradition they now embodied was grave, and of the greatest significance. Next to him Natela had bowed her head a little, as one might at the dispensing of a sacrament, while Koba, in the opposite corner and less controllable than Hammer would have liked, sat up straight and crossed his arms over his belly. The only light in the room came from three candles on the table, and from the fire burning quietly in the hearth.

All this Hammer took in without the benefit of knowing what was being said. Vano talked for a long time, perhaps two minutes, and then with a nod signaled that the priest might translate. This he did in summary, with one eye on Vano, who was clearly keen to begin the feast. It was an honor to have guests in their home; an opportunity to discharge the ancient Georgian obligation of hospitality, and to make new friends in the process; the food they were about to eat and the wine they would drink were a blessing from God and part of the great bounty of their dear country. Hammer thanked the priest and went to raise his glass.

But the toast had not yet come. Vano checked him with a look and resumed, taking up the horn and holding it out for Eka to fill from a jug. At his words everyone stood, and the priest just had time to tell Hammer that they were drinking to the heroic dead of Diklo before Vano shouted "Gaumarjos!" and they all tossed back their first tumbler of wine. Hammer kept his elbow high, and watched with a certain awe as Vano, the chieftain, drained the horn.

The taste was familiar by now, but this was sharper than the stuff he'd had last night, and though it brought a pleasant flush of warmth he was grateful that before dinner he'd persuaded Eka, who had clearly thought him crazy, to give him a glass of sheep's milk. Filthy stuff, which was not quite cool and tasted of hay and animal, but he had got it down with a smile and could feel it now, doing its work, softening the blow a little.

Then they sat, and they ate. Hammer tried to take as much bread and potato as he decently could to soak up the alcohol that was to come. He was a pretty good drinker, and for his weight no slouch, but these people were likely to be in a different class. They had had a lifetime of training.

"Meat, Isaac," shouted Koba from the other end of the table. "Eat meat and you will not be drunk, yes?"

Hammer had heard this theory of Koba's before, and trusted it as little as he trusted his other one, that if you ate a little after each toast you would have no hangover. The problem came when you ate like an American, one big dish of food all at once. Then you would suffer the next day.

Conversation was slow. Hammer didn't know whether it was supposed to be, or whether people were holding back because it would be rude to speak Georgian and daunting to speak anything else. Unable to leave a silence unfilled, he filled it.

"Does every village have dead heroes, Father?" he said, smiling across the table.

The priest chewed deliberately before he spoke. "All Georgia toasts its dead, but in the towns it is . . . it is not so real, perhaps. Here it is real, and every village in the mountains. . . . " He stopped to let his hosts know what he was talking about, and to ask Vano's consent to continue—which was given with a nod.

"Over the ridge here, into Russia, is barren country. Not like this. It is all stone and ice. The people who live there are hard, like their world. They once had a leader, Shamil, who fought the Russians when they first came to this part of the world." At the mention of his name Vano crossed his arms, and seemed to grow more rigid still. "He fought them bravely, viciously, but he fought the Georgians, too. They were all Christians, he saw no difference.

"One day, two hundred years ago, Shamil's men crossed the border and attacked the fortress here. Everyone from the village was inside. Sixteen men held out for eighteen days, but not for longer. All were killed. Men and women and children. One man killed his wife and sister so that they would not be taken. They requested it."

"Gutiso," said Vano, with a deep nod of respect.

"That is the man," said the priest.

Hammer had no adequate response. Koba, sitting next to the priest, let out a little puff of air that might have expressed consternation or derision.

"It's not so long ago, I guess," said Hammer at last.

"For these people it is yesterday," said the priest.

"It is terrible story," said Koba, as he speared a piece of meat and put it in his mouth.

The next toast was to family, the great bond of life without which none of them would have been present. This prompted some questioning of the three visitors. When it came to Hammer, his stock answer seemed inadequate; this was not a place to hold back the truth. So he told them that he had been in love once, and that it had ended badly, and that he had never found love again. The words were strange to him, but there was comfort in hearing them said. Only Eka responded, speaking directly to him.

"She says that you have a good heart," said the priest, "and that a good heart will find its reward in the world."

"Thank you," said Hammer, strangely affected by the wine, and the soft light, and the quiet, and by the simplicity of Eka's words, which she spoke with warmth and as fact. He expected the silence that followed to be broken by Koba, but even he seemed briefly under the spell of the feast.

Glass after glass was filled; glass after glass knocked back. After family came friends, and then Georgia, and children, and after that a suite of others, all proposed by Vano with great weight and eloquence, among them a solemn plea for the health of their guest's missing friend, whose misfortune had brought them all together.

When Vano wasn't making toasts he said little, watched his guests, and somehow managed, despite the quantities of wine they had all now drunk, to remain dignified and upright, prompting Hammer, whose thoughts were sliding about, and whose tongue was beginning to slip, to wonder whether there was perhaps some magic trick to the horn—a tube attached to the leg of the chair and down into the ground. His own battle was lost, in any case. The alcohol had won, and he was glad of it. No; delighted, comfortable, unexpectedly happy. Everything glowed; everybody glowed. What a good, simple thing it sometimes was to be human, and what a talent these people had for it. How strange to find something that felt like home in the furthest corner of the world.

And he was fairly sure, after all, that even Vano was looking a little less stern, a shade more approachable. When everyone laughed, as they often did, the corners of his mouth would crease, and he would allow himself a gentle nod. The rest of the table had settled happily. Irodi, who had said only a dozen words all day, revealed himself as a wry storyteller, full of tales of the cunning of the Chechens, the ruthlessness of the Dagestanis, and the stupidity of tourists. Natela and the priest translated what they could and summarized the rest. Koba—his arms still crossed, but now in what appeared to be contentment—ate his fill and between toasts helped himself to wine from the jug.

Just as Hammer thought they must have left no toasts unsaid, Vano touched him on the arm and with some words of Georgian and a gracious gesture invited him to make one of his own. This was a great honor, he knew, and the hush that came over the table confirmed it. Natela put an encouraging hand on his arm and though he welcomed it, it didn't help. Ideas floated about just beyond his grasp. No word would come. The one thought in his head was that he couldn't bear to fail his hosts, or Natela; and behind that there lay a dim sense that he wasn't as good in these situations as he had once been, and had lost the art of being drunk. He looked around at the faces waiting for him, and then remembered where he was.

"It's a long time since I was in the mountains. I make it thirty years. I live in a city, and I've always lived in cities. But my house is next to a park, a very beautiful park, and every day I'm in it. Every day. It's where I go to find peace, because in London there's a lot of noise."

He paused to allow the priest to translate.

"So it's this quiet place surrounded by cars and buildings and millions of people, all running around in a frenzy all the time. But the park needs the city. Without it, it's not a park, and not as beautiful, I always thought. It's just a piece of country, like anywhere else."

The priest gave him a slightly wondering look, as if he wasn't sure that what he was saying conformed to etiquette, but relayed Hammer's words just the same.

"But the beauty I find here? Boy. This is some park you have. All of Georgia seems blessed, but I think God saved his best work for you. Really. I don't know what it's like when you live here, but for me, someone who's always running, running all over, doing a lot, achieving not so much, for me coming here, it's like the park. Everything is that much more lovely because it's set inside a world that's loud, and busy, and violent sometimes. You have nasty things going on just over your border, some terrible fighting between some pretty ugly people, but here, it's paradise. I don't mean it's easy, but it's perfect. It's how it's meant to be. Sorry, Father."

He let the priest catch up.

"Listen. I'm talking too much. I talk too much. That may be why I feel so comfortable here. Let me get to the point. My toast is to the mountains. They're what keep you apart. They're what keep you safe. Long may they stand to protect you and your people."

He raised his glass, and when the priest was done, said in the steadiest voice he could manage, "To the mountains. Gaumarjos!" and downed the wine. Then, wiping his mouth with the back of his hand, he set his glass on the table uncertainly, collected his swaying thoughts, and looked to Vano for his judgment.

Still holding the sheep's horn in one hand, Vano fixed him with a clear and level eye, leaned forward to grip his arm, and said something in Georgian, in great earnest. Across the table Eka beamed.

"He says you are Tushetian now," said the priest, and Hammer felt a great wave of pride go through him. He thanked Vano, who with a deep nod sat back in his chair.

Natela leaned in confidentially. "This means you must stay, forever."

"I can think of worse things," he said.

What no one had told him, though, was how a newly ennobled Tushetian might leave a supra. It seemed wrong just to stand up and retire, since that would divide the group, and was surely only done on Vano's say-so. But really, any more wine and he would need to be carried, and some distant voice told him that his new reputation might not survive that. It was all he could do not to slump onto the table. God, these people could drink. With the exception of the priest, who had his head propped heavily on his hand, they all looked, if not quite unaffected, then at least in control. Even Natela looked as if she might go on all night. He was just considering going to the bathroom and not returning when he became aware of Koba's voice, which was louder than it had been and growing strident.

Leaning forward in his chair, Koba wore that sneering, contemptuous look that seemed to come on him when he was considering the claims of people he deemed inferior; he was jabbing a thick finger at Irodi opposite, who was listening with his head on one side, calm enough but clearly irritated. The priest's tired face registered concern. Hammer waited a moment, expecting Vano to intervene, but he just sat and observed, a slight frown on his face. Natela had stiffened in her seat.

"Koba," said Hammer, doing his best to compose himself. "I don't think our friends want an argument."

Koba finished his point, jabbed the finger one last time, and sat back in his chair, like a man who has said his piece. Irodi simply glared at him, his eyes narrowed under heavy lids.

"Koba, let's you and I have a smoke," said Hammer, pushing his chair back and preparing for the challenge of standing.

"Isaac, you know, maybe this is not issue for you," said Koba, reaching into his pocket for his cigarettes nevertheless.

"You're upsetting these good people. I brought us here, so it is my issue. Now, let's get some air."

But Koba wasn't going anywhere. Irodi continued to stare at him, with hostile indifference, and Koba, when he wasn't engaging with Hammer, stared back.

"This not your country, Isaac." His voice had a sharp quality that Hammer hadn't heard before. "You like our mountains, yes, you like our women, I think, but tomorrow or day after you go home and be here no more. You see good things. I live here. I see bad. These people, you love so much, they live like old days, ya? House of wood, and sheep, and no water, no phone. No light." He raised his hands and looked up at the ceiling. "Where are lights? We sit in dark. This place, is like Georgia. We all sit in dark. We go nowhere."

"Koba. We're leaving." Hammer stood, pushing himself up and holding on to the table for balance.

"All people is going. This place, ten years, will be no people here. Is dying. But is OK. Georgia is free. These motherfuckers are free. They have no light. No future. But is free. How good is this, Isaac? You still like this place?"

Hammer squeezed past Natela's chair and walked round the table to Koba's seat, concentrating on every step.

Koba looked up at him and laughed an ugly, leering laugh.

"You take me home? Where is home? Here with your Georgian woman? Maybe I stay with her."

Hammer closed his eyes for a moment, fought with some effort to control his anger, and put his hand on Koba's shoulder, solid and hot under his white shirt.

"You're leaving."

"Ya, to my bed, with motherfucker sheep." He looked down drunkenly at Hammer's hand, slow to register it.

"No one asked you to stay, Koba."

With lazy, threatening eyes Koba leered up at him, stood with surprising deftness, and said something in Georgian as a parting shot to the table. Even before he had finished, Irodi was on his feet, ready to finally challenge him; but Vano barked a reprimand at him, and with great reluctance he sat again, never for a moment taking his eyes off Koba, who, having said his piece, raised a dismissive hand and with a stagger made for the door. Halfway there he checked himself and turned to Hammer.

"This people took your friend. Ya. This is what happened. I stay, make you safe but you don't want. OK. OK."

He turned again, and with his heavy tread disappeared into the blackness of the passage. Hammer heard the sound of the front door opening, and then Koba's voice before he slammed it shut.

"You love mountains, but this mountains kill. Kill your friend. Kill you, Isaac."

NINE

The next morning, Hammer was full of apology, and his head full of jagged stones. He woke with the first light, which came unchecked through the thin curtains of his little room, and his first thoughts were a mortified recollection, one by one, of the words and events of the night before. God, it was bright. And cold on his face. His brain, shrunken and rattling about, cried out for water, and for air, and for the chance to say sorry to Eka for letting that ogre into her home. So with resolution, and some pain, he got up.

Eka was already downstairs, and though she didn't understand a word of his short speech, seemed to know precisely what he meant. Smiling in a slightly harassed way, she told him, as far as he could tell, not to worry about it in the least, and carried on her work with a concentration that belied the amount Hammer had seen her drink in that same room not eight hours earlier. She was busy with something particular, Hammer sensed, and she brought him tea and bread and cheese with a distracted air. As he sat down, wanting very much not to eat, he finally looked out of the little windows and saw what might account for it.

In the night, some time after his last cigarette with Natela, it had begun to snow. Real snow, which now lay four inches thick on the corrugated iron roofs and had already been trodden into slush in the yard outside. Two chickens strutted about in it, unconcerned.

The world was changed, as it always was when it snowed, but here the change was practical, and complete. The road would be closed. The helicopter had gone, and might not be persuaded to come back. Koba would not be able to leave. Worst of all, Ben's trail would be covered. The one thread that might have led to him had surely just been cut, even if Irodi, whose priorities were presumably now rather different, were still able to help. Mortification about the previous night gave way to a frustrated imagining of the day ahead. He drank his tea and, because it was necessary, ate two slices of the dark bread.

Plates and bowls and glasses from the night before were draining beside the sink, but three plates and mugs that had not yet been washed up told Hammer that Vano and Irodi were already out and working. He knew nothing of their lives, but this must throw out all their plans, too. Perhaps he could help them, in order to give Irodi the chance to help him. Perhaps, crude though it was, he could simply pay him more money. Maybe he still needed Koba.

No. That was out. An easy decision, which was just as well, because he was tired of trying to decide what Koba was. Regardless of whether he could be trusted, there was now good reason to have had enough of him. Let him find his own way down to the plain. It was over, or would be once he had been paid, and with a moment's irritation Hammer realized that meant seeing the bastard once more. If he had made it back to his room, that is, and hadn't frozen to death on the road.

While Hammer was calculating, or failing to calculate, Natela came down the stairs behind him, and so immersed was he that he only noticed her when he felt her hand on his back. She wore no makeup, and though her face was tired some of the strain had gone from it. She was wearing jeans and sneakers and a soft red sweater.

"Now we have to stay," she said as he stood.

"I guess so." He smiled. "How's your head?"

"Better than yours, I think."

"You got that right."

He pulled out a chair for her and went to pour her tea from the pot, raising a hand to Eka to let her know that it was fine, he could do this himself. She and Natela exchanged greetings.

"I need to smoke," said Natela.

"Are you kidding? You just got up."

"Exactly."

Hammer laughed. "OK. You want company?"

Natela didn't understand.

"Shall I come with you?"

She nodded, and he went to get their coats.

Outside, all the color of Tusheti had become the flat brilliance of snow and the wet gray of damp wood. Fresh footprints neatly marked the path between the houses of Diklo, beyond them the pine forests were black touched with white and the whole scene was softened by the fat flakes that still fell. To the east, the mountains of Russia were lost behind settled clouds.

Natela lit her cigarette and pulled her coat tightly about her.

"Where is your driver?" she said.

"Up here somewhere, I guess. Unless he drove off the mountain last night."

"I am sorry."

"What for?"

"Some Georgians are like him. Angry. They think always about what they do not have. What they have not done."

"Not just Georgians."

For a moment he watched her smoke, and the snowflakes lighting on her hair.

"What did he say, anyway? Just before he left."

Natela shook her head, her eyebrows raised.

"He said that the Tusheti people will finish what Shamil started."

Hammer didn't understand.

"They will stop being. He said, in twenty years, only thing here is dead sheep."

Hammer took a deep breath in the hope that it would clear his head. Around him the houses looked cold and hollow, and half of them were broken. Smoke came only from Eka's chimney and one other. Maybe Koba wasn't a thug but a seer, his blunt truths unpopular but correct.

"He's not very charming, is he?"

"Where did you find him?" said Natela.

"My hotel." Natela raised an eyebrow. "I know, I've wondered myself."

"Did they offer him?"

"No. I asked them to find me a driver, and he was the only one. When I first arrived, there was another guy but then there was the riot," he touched his nose, where the plaster was beginning to feel a little loose, "and he couldn't do it, so they got me this one."

Natela just looked at him.

"I didn't have much choice. And for the first day, to Batumi, he was fine. A little hungry, but fine. I didn't mind who knew what I was up to at that point, and in the meantime I kept an eye on him. He didn't do anything strange. Really. Just kept wanting to eat and show me the sights. Even, he even . . . it's hard to explain but he did things that you wouldn't do if you were spying on someone. Not unless you were an idiot." He paused. "He could be an idiot, he could be something worse. But whatever he is, he's not a rich guy, and if he's bad, he's working for someone else. I'm going to find out who."

Natela raised her eyebrow again and flicked the end of her cigarette into the snow.

"He is not idiot," she said, and went back inside.

When Irodi returned, not long afterward, he dusted the snow off his jacket, greeted everyone with his usual bow, and asked Hammer if he was ready to get going. As far as he was concerned there was no change. He had been helping his father get some of the sheep under shelter, but most of them were too far away to move now, so until the weather cleared, as it surely would, there wasn't very much to be done.

Relieved, and eager, Hammer found his coat and passed Natela hers, but Irodi stopped them and explained that they would be on horseback again today. Horses were better, especially in the snow—they could go everywhere, and 4 x 4s only some places. He could saddle up another if Natela wished, or she could stay with Eka and Vano, who would be back shortly and for most of the day. Natela was no rider, and in any case they wouldn't be long: they would follow the lead to the abandoned 4 x 4, and be back within two hours.

"I thought you only had two horses," said Hammer, and as Natela translated Irodi grinned.

Shakari was more subdued today. For half an hour they trotted quietly along, to the sound of hooves crunching on the snow, seeing no one and saying nothing. A seductive peace fell on Hammer. It occurred to him that, however briefly, his head was empty of all thoughts of London, and Hibbert, and Sander. Usually it swarmed with ideas and plans and risks to be avoided and conversations that needed to be had, but here there was nothing but air, and light, and the troubles of two people who were dear to him.

When they reached the right spot, Hammer sent a message to Koba telling him to come to Diklo at three o'clock that afternoon to get his money. And in Shenako they looked for him, asking at the house where he had stayed. But he had gone in the night, the old man said, and in words to Irodi and gestures to Hammer, let them know that he had already driven off, toward Omalo and the road down the mountain. Perhaps he had decided to brave it, unable to tolerate these people and their simple ways a moment longer, and for an instant Hammer had a vision of Koba's face fading on a rude cross by the wayside.

Past Shenako they rode for a mile or two along the road before taking a steep track on the right side of the valley that led to a wide stretch of pine woods on the crest of a hill. Here the terrain was less forgiving than any they had ridden yesterday, and Hammer, after his gentle warm-up, had to concentrate to stay in the saddle. If Shakari's hooves slipped a little on the snow, as they sometimes did, she would stop, give a snort of determination, and try again, until together they made steady progress up the slope.

Over his breathing and her panting he heard a noise that he struggled to place. He pulled back on the reins and for once Shakari responded immediately, as if she shared his curiosity. A rhythmic murmur, growing louder and more distinct. Fifty yards ahead Irodi had stopped and was scanning the sky to the south. Hammer couldn't tell where the sound was coming from but followed Irodi's gaze and after a moment the white nose of a helicopter emerged above woods on a hill to their right and flew above them, perhaps a hundred feet up. It was a small, commercial model, and as it passed them and banked away he thought he could see two men inside, one at the controls and one alongside him. Hammer directed an exaggerated shrug at Irodi, who watched the thing until it was gone and then resumed his course without comment.

Hammer had begun to think that perhaps he had been left to get on with his search alone—that no one cared, finally, about a missing Englishman and the little American who had come to find him.

Soon they were in among the pine trees again, where the ground leveled off and the floor was dry. If it was peaceful outside it was sepulchral in here.

Irodi went more slowly now, carefully inspecting the ground, Hammer as carefully watching him. This was the most elemental detective work of all; how much more delicate it was than surveillance, that bluntest of tools. He was envious of the skill. To track someone as they went along was one thing, to do it days afterward a more magical proposition by far. Nature recorded movement in ways that the city would not. Hammer had been doing the same thing, to an extent, but here the signs were not credit card bills but broken pine needles, not telephone records but marks left in the mud.

After four or five hundred yards, where the light had dimmed to a perpetual dusk, the track split, one fork going sharply left and the other curving round to the right. There was a tiny clearing here, a patch of brightness where some snow had fallen, and on the white ground, extending for just five yards but plain enough, what looked like three sets of tire marks. Irodi got down from his horse and squatted by them, carefully brushing the surface snow with the finger of his glove. Even to Hammer it was clear that not all three sets headed in the same direction, but in what sequence they had been made was far beyond his expertise.

Irodi spent a good minute examining the scene before standing up with great decisiveness and pointing further into the forest, down the right-hand fork. From here he walked, leading his horse by the reins and keeping it off the middle of the track, his eyes not leaving the ground until he stopped again, at a point where the shoulder was a little thicker and pushed its way into the trees. There was no snow here, just needles and earth, and so little light that Hammer couldn't begin to see what had drawn Irodi's attention.

Without saying anything, or turning to look at him, Irodi beckoned him down from his horse and together they sat on their haunches in the gloom. Irodi pointed to two slight depressions at the edge of the track, and then to two more a few feet further in. Hammer ran his hand over one of them; it sank an inch or more into the dry ground. A car had stood here for some time. Around the depressions the pine needles seemed to have been recently disturbed.

Irodi said something in Georgian and pointed at the ground. Then he wandered a few yards further up the track, leaped into his saddle, turned around, and trotted off back down the track the way they had come. Hammer dusted his hands and with less grace did the same.

At the fork in the track Irodi hesitated for a moment, checking his calculations on the ground, then circled his horse and waited for Hammer to catch up. He held up one finger, and pointed into the forest; held up a second, brought his hand back, and pointed down the fork in the track where they had not yet been; then set off along it, at a decent walk. There was an alertness about him now. He had the scent.

One car had come in here. Two had come out, along this new path—to judge by the snow that had fallen in the clearing a few hours earlier, perhaps at first light. Hammer felt his heart quicken.

For perhaps a mile or more they went slowly so that every now and then Irodi might stop to check the trail, and then abruptly the trees stopped and the tire tracks ran clearly in the snow, staying close to the woods and taking them up onto higher ground.

TEN

This was harder work still. Hammer grew hot in his coat, and Shakari began to steam. Snowflakes dotted her mane but melted on her flanks. The trees alongside ran out, and the wind quickened, and the air became colder. Eventually, the road rose sharply to a ridge, and then down to a handful of ruined buildings, the remains of a village. A grand village once, by the look of it, now a jagged collection of collapsed slate. Orange lichen grew on it, giving it the color of flame, and wild flowers poked through the snow. There had been a tower here, four stories high, but its windows were gone and its heavy walls leaned in on each other for support, balanced against all probability.

Hammer thought this might be their destination, but the road and the tracks skirted the village and ran down the other side of the ridge. There, half a mile away, in a little hollow with its back to the hillside, sat a lone house. Even in this distant place it was remote. Only its front was visible, and that only through the pines that grew around it, but it was possible to see that it was not as ruined as the rest; its walls hadn't crumbled, and part of its roof was in place. There was no sign that it was occupied, but the tire tracks stopped at its door.

Irodi pulled his horse up and turned back to the shelter of ruins, Hammer clumsily following. When they were both out of sight, Irodi looked Hammer in the eye, silently asking him what he wanted to do. It was difficult to know. From the little they could see there appeared to be no cars outside the house, but that didn't mean no one was inside, and there was no way of approaching along the road without being seen.

Hammer assessed the terrain. The ridge they had just crossed curved slowly round behind the house, which was perhaps a hundred feet from the top. The only way to come at it unseen was to follow the ridge and then make a steepish descent down the bare slope to the back door. They would still be exposed, but so unlikely was the approach, and so snugly did the house sit against the hill, that there seemed a reasonable chance no one would be watching. Pointing and signing, he managed to convey his idea to Irodi, who nodded his head from side to side, as if to say it could just about be done, and got down to tie up his horse. Hammer was glad to get back on his feet, and Shakari could use the rest.

Up on the ridge, Hammer turned his face away from the wind, which swept the falling snow across them, and concentrated on putting his feet where Irodi put his. They kept to the windward side, where they were out of sight of the valley and where the snow was already beginning to form an icy crust. The going was easy enough but the snow was deep here and the air thin and Hammer's chest burned with the effort. Irodi seemed to glide over the surface, his rolling gait unchanged.

Soon they were above the house and looking down at it from the top of the slope, which from the valley had seemed steep and now seemed sheer. A sparse line of pines ringed the place, but otherwise there was nothing between them and the back wall of the house. Slip, and you would gather speed until you hit it.

Irodi turned to Hammer, motioned for him to follow his steps as closely as he could, and set off, bending his knees and keeping his feet parallel with the line of the ridge. With each step he tested the snow to make sure it would hold his weight, but before long he seemed satisfied and began to move down more quickly in a shallow zigzag. The two men were the same weight, more or less, and Hammer found the footholds that had been made for him stable enough, and with every yard began to feel a little more secure. The wind fell, and the drop diminished, and fear of the descent gave way to apprehension at what they might find when they reached the bottom.

With twenty yards still to go Hammer was changing direction to start another tack across when he felt loose stuff under his foot, shingle or scree, and his balance getting away from him. With no chance to correct himself his grip went. He slid the first five yards, hit a slight rise in the ground, and was thrown down the rest of the slope, tumbling over, his arms round his head, snow driving its way into his face and down his neck. At the back of the house he hit a drift with enough force to knock the breath from him.

There was a booming in his head, and pain in his shoulder, but his first thought was that he had made enough noise to rouse the deafest of guards. Lifting his face from the cold, he saw Irodi scrambling down and the next moment landing next to him in the soft snow. He touched Hammer's arm.

"OK?" he whispered, and it was only when he spoke that Hammer realized how quiet it was. He pushed himself up, nodded without conviction, wiped the snow from his face, and together they listened, expecting shouts and footsteps and hearing nothing but the faint breath of the wind in the trees above. Exchanging a glance, they stood, Hammer warily trying his arm, and stole toward the end of the wall, where Irodi stopped, peered round, and gave the all-clear.

There was one window in the side of the house, nearer the road, and once they had ducked under it Hammer, with his face up to the wall and ever so slowly, took a look inside. Three of the four panes were missing and the frame was cracked, and he had a clear view of a dark, dusty, bare room that ran the width of the house. A table was pushed up against the far wall beside a fireplace, and around it sat three decrepit chairs, but otherwise it was empty. The walls were black with soot, and on one of them, incongruous, hung a bunch of colorless dried flowers.

Irodi had taken the rifle off his back and was now waiting for instructions. Hammer looked to the front of the house. The tire tracks did stop here; cars had turned, and he could make out sets of footprints. He felt sure that the place was empty but didn't want to risk walking through the front door, particularly as Irodi would insist on going first. He squatted down and picked up a large piece of slate that had been dislodged from the wall, and with a glance of understanding from Irodi, lobbed it through the window and into the room, where it landed with a great clatter. Irodi moved beyond the corner and trained his gun on the front of the house. After the noise came silence. Nothing. Ducking past the next window, Irodi waited by the door while Hammer checked again that there was no movement inside.

With a crack, Irodi kicked the door open, and Hammer followed him into the house. Two doors led from the main room, one into a storeroom, the other into what must once have been a bedroom. There was no one in either, nor anything that might suggest anyone had recently left. Hammer felt his hope slip away once more. This was where Ben had been held, he was sure, but now he began to imagine all the other stories that might account for the tracks in the snow. While Irodi went to check outside, Hammer began to look for signs that someone had been kept here.

A dank cold smell had settled in the place. In one corner a pool of water had collected under a hole in the roof. There were ashes in the grate, but they were cold and compacted by time and seemed not to have been disturbed. The table was covered with a scattering of dirt. He checked under it for traces of food and saw none. In the bedroom he ran his hand over the floor, which was compacted earth, looking for a hair or any other sign that someone had been here, but all he found was soil and grit.

By the light of his phone he scoured the storeroom; nothing. He scanned the ceiling, stood on a chair, and felt around in the rafters, looked up the chimney. Hopeless, he watched Irodi crouching down to inspect the tire marks outside and wondered what they would do next. If this house had never held Ben, the trail was as cold as it had always been. As he thought, he ran his finger through the dust on the sill of the window, rubbed it off with his thumb, and felt a familiar thrill go through him.

Sitting in a chair, from as close as he could manage, he looked afresh at the top of the table. It was grubby, like everything else, but not with dust. Reaching down, he rubbed the ground hard, pinched a quantity of earth between his fingers, and crumbled it onto the table from a height. The result was of a piece with the rest. With great care he blew some of the dirt off the surface. There was no dust beneath. Someone had wiped the table clean and then done their best to disguise that it had been used.

"Irodi!" he shouted, and when he came demonstrated what he had just discovered. Irodi grinned, put his hand on Hammer's back, in appreciation of his talents, and took him outside, where he managed to explain that two cars had been here, that morning. He set off at a run back to the deserted village and Hammer, no longer feeling the exertion, followed.

ELEVEN

From the village they took a new road to the south, following the twin sets of tire tracks showing clearly under the fresh snow. Irodi rode more quickly now and the road obliged, descending gently and threading through a string of hills. The snow kept coming at a steady rate, and Hammer did his best to ignore the pain in his shoulder, which was stiffening up in the cold. Whenever he took a hand off the reins to work it round Shakari would turn her head and snort.

It was afternoon now, and at the back of his mind was the thought that he must return to Natela soon. Had he been able, he'd have asked Irodi where this road led and how long it might take to get there, but as it was he had no choice but to ride in silence, and anticipation.

They rode into a dark forest, and abruptly the road became steeper, snaking down an ever narrowing valley. Everything was perfectly still, and the faint smell of pine was in the air. From time to time the road would split, but each time Irodi, after careful thought, continued on the downward fork. Over the noise of the needles underfoot and Shakari's breathing, Hammer could hear water running, indistinctly at first and then with growing clarity. Through the trees came glimpses of the river, flowing fast over rocks on a broad bed.

Eventually, the road leveled out and for half a mile it wound alongside the water, still in dense trees. Irodi slowed and sat upright in the saddle. At a curve in the river the road left the wood and simply came to an end, running out in a broad pebbled beach which was covered in snow.

Hammer pulled on the reins and brought Shakari to a halt, with an odd sense that though there was nothing to see they had found what they were looking for.

He scanned the scene. On every side rose thick green forest, overhung by immense stony peaks to the east. But in among the trees, fifty yards higher up, a fleck of red caught his eye. He shouted to Irodi, dismounted, and set off up the bank. There it was: a silver 4 x 4, with snow on its roof and no one inside. A Mitsubishi Pajero, its license plates removed. Ben's car, no question. At the sight of it Hammer felt exhilaration and fear start in his chest, for the journey that had brought him here and the journey that still lay ahead.

The car's doors were locked. From the flat ground by the river he found the largest rock he could, brought it up to the car, and with both hands brought it down on the driver's window, which shattered and bowed inward but didn't give. For a moment he was back in the riot that had started all this, and he had a sense of how far he had come. At the third strike the whole pane fell in, and he was able to open the door from the inside. The car was empty. No papers, no belongings. On the driver's seat he found a gray hair, short, as Ben kept his. It meant nothing but confirmed his hope.

Outside, he looked around for a trail through the woods, but there was none, and to his inexpert eye the forest floor revealed nothing. Irodi was clambering up behind, and as Hammer turned he noticed, through the trees and at the far end of the beach, a line of footprints in the snow to the water's edge.

Up close it looked as if there were two sets, perhaps three, but in places they had been disturbed, as if whoever had left them had dragged a heavy weight behind them, and in a patch by the river all the snow had been trodden into slush. A single set went back toward the trees. Hammer and Irodi stood and watched the water flowing by.

"Where?" said Hammer, nodding downstream to the mountains. "Where does it go?"

Irodi understood him, and Hammer understood his reply.

"Ruseti," he said, his face grave. "Russki."

Russia. Vast and unassailable, like the mountains that protected it. An ancient swallower of secrets. And lives.

Shakari was a sturdy horse, and strong with it, but by the end of the climb she was tired, and the decent thing to do would have been to let her rest. But Hammer had to press on and Irodi, at least, understood. Until this moment the silence between them had been expectant; now it was anxious and flat at once. As they rode, Hammer tried to make sense of what they had just seen, and to separate what was likely from what he wanted to believe.

A sequence began to piece itself together in his mind. Sometime after renting his car Ben had been kidnapped, by at least two men, who had taken him to a house in the most remote part of this most remote place, and kept him there, for what reasons only they knew. Today, they had gone, into Russia, taking their charge somewhere even less accessible. Hammer felt like a sap chasing a dollar bill on a string, but for the first time he felt sure that there was something to be chased. That Ben was alive. That it had not yet proved imperative, or convenient, to kill him.

He should phone Elsa, but there simply wasn't the time. One thought forced all others aside: that he hadn't yet found the second car. If someone had taken Ben into Russia, someone had stayed behind.

As soon as the road began to level out Hammer clamped his legs tighter, willing Shakari to find some speed, talking to her all the while, half in encouragement and half in apology. She took it, and together they trotted at a decent pace. The snow eased and then stopped, and the sky began to lighten. But for Hammer this stretch of his journey was the longest. He needed to get back.

From a mile or so outside Diklo he thought he could make out Koba's car, parked on the shoulder of the road where the houses started, and as they drew closer his fears were confirmed. All the doubts of the past two days coalesced into a single question: where had he been that morning?

Hammer brought Shakari to a halt by the car and jumped down, barely noticing how easily he now did so. He squatted behind the Toyota and brought up on his phone the photographs he had taken that morning. Comparing those tracks with what he saw now on the ground he felt certain, even before Irodi, without the benefit of pictures, made up his mind, and gave a somber nod. Hammer photographed the scene.

Footsteps led from the car but Hammer didn't need to follow them to know where Koba was. He and Irodi walked their horses the last hundred yards and tied them outside the house, and before they went in, Hammer raised a finger to his lips and made sure Irodi understood. For the first time in this whole affair, he knew something, and he didn't mean to squander the advantage, scant though it might be.

The fire was lit and the kitchen smelled of smoke and cabbage. Koba was alone, standing over a pot, stirring it with a wooden spoon.

"Isaac! Is good see you. I think maybe you are lost. Your friend, she think bad things has happened." He grinned at Hammer and nodded at Irodi, who went out into the yard with the two guns.

Hammer smiled as best he could. "We got stuck in a little snow. Nothing serious."

"Good, good. You find your friend?"

"No. No, we didn't. We thought we'd found his car but it had gone."

"Is bad news. I am sorry."

Hammer watched him stir the soup. Since the snow had started falling, Koba had put on two worn fleeces, one red, one black. Underneath, at the collar, was his trusty white shirt. Through the lamb and cabbage Hammer thought he could smell his sweat, fresh and acrid. He was all geniality, but Hammer no longer believed it.

"Where is Natela?"

Koba pointed upward. "She is quiet lady." The words were innocent enough but Hammer, on edge, found something sinister in them. He started up the stairs.

"What about Vano?" he said.

Koba shrugged.

In the dark corridor above, Hammer stopped for a moment, felt the urgent beating of his heart, and knocked.

"Diakh?"

"It's Isaac."

Two footsteps, and the door opened.

"You are here," she said. Her hair was tangled where she had been lying down.

"When did Koba come?"

"An hour. He wanted to talk. I did not."

"Where's Vano?"

"I thought he was here."

"OK. Can I come in?"

Puzzled by his seriousness, she took a step backward and let him into the room.

"Close the door," said Hammer, crossing to the window. It looked out over the yard, and across white rooftops. Irodi was talking to his mother down below.

Natela came and stood by him.

"You found something."

"I know more than I did," said Hammer, keeping his voice low. "Ben has been here. They've taken him into Russia. He," he pointed at the floor, "has something to do with it."

He told her about the tracks, and the house, and the river, and when he was done she thought for a while.

"And for sure they take him there? It is not a lie?"

"I have to accept what I saw. Otherwise, I don't have anything."

"And Koba?"

"I buy him. He's been waiting for this opportunity his whole life."

Natela said nothing, and Hammer read her quietness as doubt.

"Whatever this is, he's not in charge. He's taking orders from someone."

She shook her head.

"If he is in this now, when did he begin?"

Hammer didn't understand.

"You give money to him, you give money to people who killed Karlo."

Her eyes were dark and set on his.

"OK." He reached out and touched her arm. "OK. First, we don't know that but yes, probably you're right. The important thing is, I pay him money, I can find out who he is. Where he is. He can't take that money without me seeing him take it."

"Always it is money."

"I don't have much else. I can't shoot him, because then I'm in the dark again. Also, I'm not a big shooter. I'm a little rusty in that area. This is the only way. Money, and a trick or two. It's all I've got."

Natela continued to look at him, not ready to yield.

"I need your help with this," he said. "I need you to tell Irodi what to do."

"He will suffer?"

"If he's guilty, he'll suffer."

TWELVE

Koba had gone outside for a cigarette. The soup blipped occasionally at the side of the hearth and Hammer, while he waited, gave it a stir. Either the riding, the mountain air, or the deep uncertainty had given him a hunger. Natela took a seat at the table. Neither spoke.

When he returned, Koba grinned, looking his most satisfied, and took the spoon from Hammer.

"You need food, Isaac. We eat."

Hammer sat next to Natela and watched the big man taste the soup.

"Is OK. Where is salt?" Koba started searching on the low table by the fire, his back to Hammer.

"Koba, how are you planning on getting down the mountain?"

Koba, continuing to look, made a deep humming noise, signifying a weary resignation. "Snow will melt. Is October. Very early."

"What if it doesn't?"

Koba shrugged. "Ah! Here is salt."

"Because I was wondering if something else had kept you in Tusheti. If you had other business here."

Koba pinched salt between his fingers and scattered it into the soup.

"How you mean, Isaac?"

"I think I'm not your only client."

He turned to Natela, frowning. "What is 'client?'"

"Koba, it's just us talking here. No one can hear us, OK? I'm not recording what we say. But if you try anything, Irodi and Vano are outside with their guns and while I'm sure you're good, probably you're not that good.

Besides which, it will make no sense for you to kill me before you've heard what I have to say."

Koba rested the spoon on the table and looked at Hammer.

"This is last night, yes? What I say. I say bad things to your friend." He appealed to Natela, whose eyes didn't leave his.

Hammer shook his head. You had to admire his technique.

"Forget it. You spent all morning camouflaging 4 x 4s and tidying up your little hiding place. Every five minutes you've been disappearing off to phone your boss, whoever he is. Yes? You've got an extra phone just for that. My guess, your job is to keep an eye on me and stop me getting too close. Is that right? Or have you got plans for me like you've got for Ben?"

Koba shrugged and held his hands out, a final attempt to convince.

"Isaac, I think you are hungry, maybe. The mountains, they—"

"Enough. I have an offer for you. I think you'll like it. I don't know who you are—are you really called Koba, by the way?"

Koba just watched him.

"Let's stick with Koba. So. I don't know who you are, but I know this world and I'm guessing either you're a policeman or a spy, or you were once and now you're working for yourself. Any event, probably you're being paid OK by Georgian standards, right? If you're private, maybe what, five hundred bucks a day? At the top end, I should say. You're taking some major risks, but in this business I should say five hundred was generous. So this year, give or take, you've got some quiet periods, the most you're going to be taking home is sixty, seventy thousand, after tax. Am I right?"

Koba put his hands in his pockets and tilted his head to the side. Casual, but listening.

"Now, here's what I've got. I can get Irodi in here and have him shoot you in the leg. Nothing dangerous, just something that's going to stop you running around for a little bit. OK? He'd like to do it, I think, even if it isn't exactly Georgian hospitality. Then we figure out what you've been doing and try and get my friend back. This isn't great for either of us, but hey. If it's necessary.

"That's up to you. The other way, I pay you lots of money and you give us everything, nice and direct. Did they tell you I was rich? No? Well, I am, and I can pay you a lot more than whoever's paying you now. What I had in mind was twenty-five thousand straightaway, show I'm serious, then seventy-five thousand when you've brought me my friend and explained what in hell's name is going on here. What it's all about. The bomb, Ben, everything. You tell me everything you know and I won't tell anyone where I got it. You'll be free to spend the money. That's a lot of cash. Give me an account, I can make a call, wire the twenty-five right now."

Hammer glanced at Natela and then watched Koba, who had stopped listening and was now thinking. "That much money, you could give up this line of work. Cultivate your bees with Mrs. Koba."

"I no have wife."

"No kidding. So just you and the bees."

Koba's face was set now. It was the face he had worn when kicking the drunk in Batumi: professional, resolute, unhurried. He took in a deep, deliberate breath through his nose, stood, picked up a bowl from the side, and used it to scoop up a helping of soup straight from the pot. It dripped as he brought it back to the table, where he ate with his face low over the bowl. After three mouthfuls he looked up at Natela and then Hammer, who were both watching him with something between awe and dread.

"I know you. Ya." He pointed with his spoon. "I know much. You are Isaac Joel Hammer. You live in London. You are detective. Is right word? Detective. Well done, Isaac Hammer. You are good detective, but not now."

He bent his head again and returned to his soup. Hammer thought he understood.

"Why not?"

"My job, it was to keep you living. Stop you seeing things. You not find anything, is OK. You live. Now, is not good. You find something."

A string of cabbage hung on his lip; with a slurp he sucked it in.

"So you have to kill me?" said Hammer, a little daunted by the man's composure.

"Me, or other man. When time will be good. Like your friend."

"My friend is dead?"

"No. Time is not good."

Hammer wished he could believe him. Koba took another deliberate mouthful and chewed, his eyes cold, and as Hammer watched him he felt an increasing repugnance. *Imagine the things this man has done.*

"Koba, you're in trouble. Even if you manage to get out of here, you can't get down the mountain. Thank you for protecting me, really, but your job's over. My offer is good."

Koba swallowed his soup and laughed. "When sky is clear, I call for helicopter. Yes?" He laughed again. "This mountains are not fortress. Not now."

Hammer looked at Natela, and if his own face was full of perplexity hers was full of disgust. With her chin up, she spat a short volley of Georgian words at him, and his response was to raise his eyes to look at her with black eyes full of a cold violence. Hammer felt fury run through him like ice.

"Fuck this," he said, and stood. Koba looked up, for the first time engaged. "Irodi!"

"What are you doing?" said Natela.

Irodi appeared from the passage, his rifle held across his body.

"I'm going to shoot him in the leg. I'm sick of his bullshit."

Hammer moved round the table and motioned to Irodi to lend him the gun. Concerned but calm, Irodi handed it to him. Koba, still chewing, looked at them as a bored man might a pair of flies fussing in the heat.

It had been a long time since Hammer had had a gun in his hands. Not for the first time he wondered how old it was, and when it had last been fired. It felt like a remnant of some mythical Georgian last stand. He cocked it, and holding it low pointed it at Koba's thigh.

Koba sat up straight, put his spoon down beside the bowl, and held Hammer's eye. He barely blinked. For a moment the room was still, and then Koba spoke.

"Two million dollars. One now, one when finished. For your friend."

He reached inside a trouser pocket. Hammer's finger tensed around the trigger, but all Koba pulled out was a phone. He pressed some keys, and put it on the table. From it came a voice that Hammer knew, thin and faint.

"This is Ben Webster. I think this is Wednesday, the third of October. It snowed last night. I'm being held by three men. They've taken me . . ."

The recording stopped.

"Two million dollars," said Koba.

Hammer released his grip.

"I don't have two million dollars."

Koba scraped his spoon round the bowl for the last of the soup.

"Yes," he said, without looking up. "You have. Four million in Fidelity, in New York. In London, three million and half pounds with Barclays, two million with Moore Capital. You have house in London, house in New York. There is more." He looked up. "You have no family, Isaac. How much is life of friend to you?"

Hammer held the gun as firmly as he could while his thoughts reeled. Who was this man?

"One million."

"Two. This is not meat market."

"What's your boss going to say about this?"

"I am boss," said Koba.

THIRTEEN

Webster was in Russia. Or so Koba said—there was no real reason to trust him one way or the other. The whole deal rested squarely on his greed.

That night they would meet on the path to the east of the village, at the fork that led to the fortress. There, at the edge of the woods, Hammer would find a shrine built of rocks and Koba waiting for him. Both men would come alone.

Before he left, Koba told them little. The rendezvous; three account numbers, all in Russia; that he would check shortly that the first part of the payment had been made, and only then radio his men with his instructions; that the money was for Webster, and nothing else. Despite Hammer's pressing, he would reveal nothing about the job he had been doing.

Then he went, driving off, no one knew where.

For an hour, Hammer was busy. He drove Irodi's car until he picked up a signal, and stopped to make two calls. To his bank, who needed some persuading that the transaction was genuine, and to Elsa, to tell her that he had heard her husband's voice and was going to see him that evening, all being well. The last went to voice mail. He tried hard not to make promises. For a moment he imagined how distant she must feel, and how scared, and compared it with his own sense of powerlessness.

He returned resolute. This would not go wrong.

Then came the wait. They would leave at seven, and it was now only two. For Hammer, inactivity was a foreign state, especially when he might have been doing so many things. Follow Koba, for instance; find a radio and monitor his communications with his men; start checking on those accounts. None was sensible. Hammer might not like not knowing, but here knowledge wouldn't help. The deal was delicate, but balanced. Nothing could be allowed to upset it.

He found his new friends finishing lunch, and with some aversion but greater appetite accepted the last bowl of Koba's soup. Through Natela, he thanked his hosts for their hospitality, which had gone far beyond their duty, and promised that he would find some way to show his gratitude before the affair was done. Vano heard his speech with his usual gravity, and then declared that it was no burden to protect a good man against thieves, and that they expected no reward for it. The honest people of the world must defend each other, and it had always been this way.

Then Natela and Hammer were alone. For a while they talked, but there seemed an unstated understanding between them that to talk about the exchange would be bad luck, and about anything else impossible, so at Hammer's suggestion, they agreed to walk, for the air and for their sanity.

The sun shone full now, and the dull, close world of the morning was transformed into glistening monochrome. A thin crust was forming on the snow, and wherever they looked, they had to squint against the light. The little village of Diklo seemed pristine and tiny among the white slopes and the black forests and the great peaks that circled them all.

"Chances are I won't see this place again," said Hammer.

"You sound sad."

"Part of me could stay here," he said, and wondered if that were really true, and how much of it had to do with the company he had been keeping.

They walked up the main street, if you could call it that, past the houses all closed for the winter, past the one other house still occupied and out along the path that led to the fortress, stopping to read the sign that commemorated the siege. "Sixteen fearless heroes live on in vivid memories to this day," it read, and Hammer wondered how long his own shabby episode might be remembered.

After a while they began to talk, about all manner of things. The lives led by these people, and their fading culture. The relationship between the mountain Georgians and their neighbors on the plain. How precious wilderness was, and how vulnerable. Natela's children, and their father's death.

London, and Hammer's solitary life there. Soon they were out of sight of the village, and alone in the hills. They seemed to slip briefly out of time, until Hammer was barely conscious of what was set to happen that night, somewhere further along that same path.

Rounding a corner, they saw three dogs on a ledge of land across a shallow gorge, just below the trail, all lying in the snow, apparently asleep. They were all too familiar to Hammer. He touched Natela on the arm.

"We should go back."

She looked at her watch. "We have long time."

Hammer pointed to the dogs, talking quietly. "We don't want to disturb them."

"You are scared? Of dogs?"

"Not even Irodi messes with these dogs. They're sheepdogs. I guess they're bred to fight."

"If you want. They look OK."

"More excitement I don't need. Really."

Natela shrugged. Across the way, one of the dogs had woken and was lazily lifting its head. It barked, once, got to its feet, and started barking furiously, an almighty noise in the silence. Its two friends roused themselves and joined in.

"OK," said Natela, more concerned now, but as they turned Hammer heard a scrambling in the snow above them, and then another burst of noise. A fourth dog had been waiting on the slope above and now stopped on the path, immense, its mouth wide, blocking their way back. It was wilder than the others; its fur was matted with mud, its eyes enraged. Hammer pulled Natela back so that she was standing behind him.

"Don't move," he said. "Don't run."

Squatting down, he ran a hand under the snow in search of a rock. Nothing but stones, and none bigger than the end of his thumb. He considered his options. They could walk away, but even if the dog accepted their retreat they would still have to negotiate its friends, who were now making their way up the shallow bank to the path. They could try to climb over this little spur and go around the dog, but that was its territory, and perhaps the worst place they could go. Or they could stand still until it got bored or decided to act.

Oh God, thought Hammer, as he realized what he had to do.

"If it attacks me," he said, over his shoulder, "get out of here." He pointed up the slope. "Fast as you can."

The dog was close, and he dared not advance too far. With his hand behind him he motioned to Natela to back up, and moved forward, setting his foot slowly onto the snow. He had never been so conscious of a single step. The dog's barking slowed. He watched it carefully, avoiding its eye, ready for the sign of a muscle flexing, of the first hint of a spring. A second step gently down, and a third.

Crouching, he stretched a hand out onto the ground, lowered himself as steadily as he could until he was on his side, and relaxed onto his back. How blue the sky was, and not a cloud in it. He twisted his head a little to see Natela, who was standing utterly still. A breeze he hadn't known was there brushed his face, and cold bit the back of his head.

The dog was quiet now but he heard its breath, a lazy panting, and its paws on the snow. He kept his eyes open. A foot away from him it stopped, so that he could see the underside of its snout and the U-shaped bone of its jaw and the two long teeth that poked sharply out of its wet mouth; stopped and paused, looking about it at Natela and the dogs across the gorge. Dipping its head to Hammer's waist, it sniffed, rubbing its nose against his jacket. Inside, his whole body was rigid, like a man long dead, but his heart beat wildly against his ribs. The dog sniffed his belly, and his chest, and then it was nuzzling his neck, its nose cold on his exposed skin, its breath a warm fug that stank of old meat, warm drool swinging from its muzzle. He closed his eyes, so that all he knew was the panting and its wet touch. The dog spent so long at his throat that Hammer, beyond thought, found himself imagining what was inside: the veins, the larynx, the gullet, all the soft flesh. All waiting, still, while every instinct told him to bolt.

But the dog was done. With a low grumble it lifted its head and in one movement turned away down the bank toward its friends. Before he opened his eyes Hammer felt the sky lighten and the air clear, and a strange elation spread through him that was not all relief. He had submitted, and yet he had won.

Natela was by him, helping him up and clasping his hand. They watched the dog trudge down the slope until it was clear it wouldn't return, and then set off back to the village as quietly as they could.

Neither spoke the whole way, but where the path broadened Natela again took Hammer's hand in hers.

The fire was out when they returned, and a chill was settling on the kitchen. Natela called for Eka, and, receiving no response, started up the stairs, turning to look at Hammer.

"You need to rest," she said, and he followed.

She led the way, past her room to his. Inside, she closed the curtains, went to the bed, and pulled back the cover, waiting for him to come. Hammer was still dazed, a little, and his instincts slow after years of sleep, and for a moment he thought, with a great dip of regret—grief, almost—that she was planning to see that he was comfortable and leave. But that wouldn't do, and couldn't be. He drew him to her, and she to him, and their eyes joined before they kissed. She smelled of perfume and skin and the cigarette smoke that was a part of her.

"Are you . . ."

"No words," she said, and kissed him again.

FOURTEEN

When Hammer woke, roused by some foreign sound in the distance, the room was cast in the last silver light that bounced off the snow. Natela lay pressed up against him on the narrow bed; they breathed together, in time, with nothing to separate them; and for a while he simply watched her, the lock of hair across her eye, the proud nose, the lines in her forehead, the rise and fall of her breast. He felt a deep peace, and at its limits a new and encroaching fear.

It must be after six. He should get dressed, and eat, and prepare. Collect any messages he might have been left. Show solidarity with Irodi, the staunchest of guides, and respect for Eka and Vano, whose home he had just defiled. In the dark he smiled, a teenager once more in a strange house. He wanted to go nowhere.

Slowly, he left the bed, lifting Natela's arm and sliding out, and began to dress as quietly as he could. Thick socks, long johns, a thermal shirt.

"You are going?" Her voice was warm with sleep.

"Not yet. Soon."

"Lie with me."

"I look like a prospector."

She didn't reply, and he got in beside her, his clothes against her skin.

"You have to come back."

"I'll come back."

"I hope your friend is worth this."

"So do I."

"Does he know you look for him?"

"No. We fell out. We haven't spoken in months."

"Why?"

"One of those things that doesn't matter."

For a minute they lay together, not talking.

"Who would look for you?" said Natela at last.

"That's a good question. Ben would, if he knew."

"But in London, you are alone?"

Hammer turned on his side and pulled himself closer into her back, feeling the warm skin of her neck against his cheek.

"I'm alone in London. Alone everywhere."

"Why?"

"How do you mean, why?"

"This is the woman you loved?"

She rolled over to face him, and in the near dark he could see her eyes intently on his. He let out a long breath and thought how best to say it. He had been asked the question often enough, but never before had he needed to give an honest answer, though he knew it so well.

"I guess."

"That was the last time?"

"The last time what?"

"You loved someone."

"That was the last time I did a lot of things."

"How she died?"

In the icy half-light, safe in the warm dark of the bed, Hammer told her, and the telling alone was like a great release.

"We were in Mexico. Do you know Mexico?"

Natela shook her head.

"It's a hell of a place. I used to go all the time, get out of New York. This time we went trekking in the mountains, a place I knew, and we were a day away from anywhere and Tanya got sick. Really sick, so she couldn't walk. Horrible. There were no phones and I was terrified. We couldn't stay but she couldn't walk. So I carried her, as best I could. I had her on my back, and

I walked almost through the night, didn't see a soul. We got back to town, I found a doctor, woke him up. She died in a car on the way to the city."

Natela said nothing but reached up and held her hand to his cheek.

"That kind of shut me down, for a while."

For a minute they lay together, Natela gently stroking the hair behind his ear.

"I hated to tell that story. I got back to New York, and people knew, and all the time I wanted it to go away but every face I saw, there it was. It was my idea to go, my place, my plan. I took her there." He paused for a moment, let out a slow sigh. "It was a tick. You know a tick? Like a little bug, tiny. Like this. I checked for them when she got sick but it was up in her hair and I didn't find it. Doctors said it had probably been there for days. The smallest thing. This tiny stupid thing. Anyway. I went home. Got her home. And I just couldn't be there. So I went to London. Got asked by this guy I hardly knew to do some work for him. That was my first case."

Natela smoothed the hair on the side of his head and held his cheek in her hand, as if she had something to say that he must hear.

"It made you sick also, I think."

"Maybe."

Natela kissed him, and in the rich silence that followed there came a soft knock at the door.

"Diakh?" said Natela, frowning at Hammer in mock alarm.

It was Irodi. Hanging back, he opened the door a crack and said something in Georgian.

"OK," said Natela, and the door closed. There was worry in her voice. "Someone is here. For you."

"Koba?"

"Not Koba."

That was crazy. No one could be here. All Hammer's anxieties about the plan, the trek to the border, and the chances of success returned.

"Fuck."

"Who is it?"

"No one good."

There were voices below, in intense conversation: Vano's and another, which Hammer didn't recognize at first. Vano glanced up with a look of annoyance and carried on remonstrating with the stranger, whose back was to Hammer and who carried on talking in firm, calm tones. As Eka tried to pacify her husband the stranger turned.

"Good evening, Mr. Hammer. You are still on the tourist trail."

Vekua was there, dressed in a thick black ski jacket and smiling a cold, straight smile. There was something icy in it even by the light of the fire, and it settled in his stomach like a deadweight.

"Elene. Good to see you."

"Mr. Sukhishvili says there have been enough of my kind in his house. But I am here to help."

Next to Eka she seemed more than ever pale and lean, a frozen creature finally in her habitat.

"That's very kind of you. Help who?" said Hammer.

"You."

"How did you know where I was?"

"I didn't. Not exactly. The priest in Shenako told me you were here."

"So how . . ."

"I have come to find your friend."

Hammer sized her up, wondering what had really brought her here and whether she bought for a moment his shtick. Whether he bought hers.

He prayed that Natela would have the sense to stay upstairs.

"You have? Well, that's great. I could do with some help."

"Let us give these people some peace."

Hammer glanced at Eka, who told him with her eyes that she wanted him to stay. He pulled a chair out. "It's OK. It's warm in here. Take a seat." Vano, when he realized that his home was still not his own, grunted and walked out, leaving a frost behind.

"He says he has had enough of strangers in his house," said Vekua. "It takes a lot for a Georgian to say this. Who else has been here?"

"Do you know, I don't know. There was a big party here last night."

She smiled, in a way that suggested that the pleasantries were over.

"So," she said. "Why did you come here?"

Hammer couldn't remember finding anyone so hard to read. His fingers tapped softly on the table. She could be doing her job or preparing to kill him. Perhaps it didn't matter: if she was genuine, he should tell her everything, and if she wasn't, she almost certainly knew it all in any case. Except the deal. Whoever she was, she couldn't be that good.

"I got a lead. He told someone he was coming here."

"Who was that?"

"I'd rather not say."

Vekua raised an eyebrow. "They were correct."

"Really?"

"He was here. Now he is in Russia."

Despite himself, Hammer felt a kick of hope and something else—a tiredness, a sense of tension releasing after days of tightening. He tried not to show it.

Footsteps sounded softly on the stairs, and although Hammer kept his eyes on Vekua she twisted in her chair to look.

Natela had brushed her hair and put on fresh lipstick. She greeted Eka and waited for Hammer to introduce her. Vekua did the same, but Hammer, for once, couldn't find the words.

"Another guest?" said Vekua.

"This is a friend of mine."

"I know who you are. I am Elene Vekua." She half rose from the table to shake hands, and as she did so said something in Georgian that prompted a wary nod from Natela. She turned to Hammer: "I am familiar with Mrs. Toreli's case. Of course."

Natela held cigarettes and a lighter in her hand and put them on the table as she sat. Eka came to the table with a jug of water and another of wine.

"But I didn't know you knew each other. You came here together?"

"More or less," said Hammer.

There was silence while Vekua poured water into three glasses.

"We do not need wine this evening," she said, looking frankly at Hammer and Natela in turn. Her gaze was untiring. "It is good I find you here. I can ask you both." But the question was to Hammer. "Do you know a man called Dima Zoidze?"

Hammer shook his head. "I don't think so. No, I don't."

From the floor by her side she brought up onto her lap a neat black briefcase, unzipped it, took from a clear plastic folder a small sheaf of photographs, and slid them across the table.

"This man."

The pictures were of him and Koba: one outside the hotel in Batumi, one in Gori by the bombed flats, another of them leaving Tbilisi two days earlier, all taken from a distance with a good lens. He passed them to Natela, and wondered where this would lead and what it meant. Either he had just gained an ally or the whole thing was about to become complicated. In either case, he feigned more surprise than he felt.

"Koba?"

"His name is not Koba."

"He drove me here. What's he done?"

"How do you know him?"

"I asked the hotel for a driver and that's who they gave me."

"He is not a driver."

"Then what is he?"

Vekua waited for Natela to finish and replaced the photographs in the folder, keeping one back.

"He is a colleague. A former colleague. He would not know me. He left the service ten years ago. Now he runs a security company. He provides bodyguards, solves his clients' problems, finds compromising material on their enemies."

"Sounds like a competitor."

"He is not of your caliber, Mr. Hammer. And he does not have your morals. He is not a good man."

"I've had my doubts."

"We think he did this." She propped the last photo up on its edge. It showed Koba talking to a soldier while Hammer shielded his eyes against the sun and peered at the destroyed apartment building in Gori.

"He did what?"

"We think he built the bomb, from materials stolen from my service. Then he gave it to rebels from Dagestan. Here. A few miles from this village."

Hammer thought he was good at spotting a lie but with Vekua it was pointless. Her voice was calm, her thin lips composed. She might have been giving him directions or telling him the time.

"Why?"

"For a client. There are rich men in Georgia who do not want to see the president change. They do not want to lose what they have."

"Rich men or a rich man?"

"I cannot say."

Hammer sat back, still shaking his head, wondering whether to mention Iosava.

"When did you find out?"

"I could not tell you. You can see that. I tried to help."

"How do you know all this?"

"We have been following him for some time. He has made some mistakes. Your friend saw them. So did Toreli."

Natela shifted on her chair, and Vekua went on.

"When your friend came here, to the mountains, Zoidze's men followed him and took him. Zoidze called his client on the day it happened to say that he had found the dog that went missing—these were his words—and he would keep it safely."

"Why not kill him?"

Vekua smiled, in her cool way. "It is not good to kill Englishmen. Or Americans. Russians, OK. Georgians, yes. But if you kill an Englishman, people notice, and foreign police come, and media. You would have come. The situation was too delicate. Too dangerous. So he took him, and made a false trail so no one would look for him."

"He's going to let him go?"

"He will not. Probably he planned to kill him when the time will be good. When no one will be watching. In three months, six months it will not look like anything. A body somewhere, a story for it, there is no connection. But now that you are searching for him, he has changed his plan.

Today he moved him. Across the border, where no body will be found and no murder can be investigated. Zoidze called his client this morning at ten o'clock to say that the dog was on its way to Makhachkala to be put down. Makhachkala is capital of Dagestan."

"Then he's long gone."

Vekua shook her head, a quick, precise motion.

"No. They are using radio to communicate. Two transmissions have been made from the same place in the last four hours. It is three miles past the border."

"He might be dead already."

"He might. They may be waiting for final instruction." She paused. "It is a good place for them. No one lives there now. Just mountains."

Three miles across the border. If Vekua was right, Ben was five miles away. But there were so many other possibilities. She was lying. Koba was lying. They were lying together. Not for the first time Hammer felt that he was jumping from one patch of quicksand to another, and sinking slowly all the while.

"And Karlo?" said Natela, sharply, as if the primary question had been unaddressed.

Vekua blinked slowly and turned to her. "We think this man killed your husband as well."

Hammer felt Natela go tense next to him. "How? He killed himself. You all say it."

"Maybe he did not make the cut. Maybe someone forced him to make it."

Natela clasped her hands together on the table until the skin on her knuckles went white.

"It's all right," said Hammer, but when he touched her arm she jerked it away. She closed her eyes, her jaw set.

"And you give money to this man," she said.

Hammer liked his deal with Koba. It was balanced, and there was something to be said for that. A transaction: money for value. He understood it, and his instinct told him that Koba did, too. Everyone might be lying, and the deal could still hold.

In desperation he clung on.

"Well, I was going to. Hundred bucks a day. He wouldn't take anything off me yet."

Hammer willed Natela to take the hint, but she just shook her head, furious.

"He kills, he kills again, and you make him rich man."

It was his fault, after all. He should have briefed her.

"It's only a hundred bucks."

But Vekua was looking at him, her straight brow creased, waiting for his explanation. He didn't know who she was, or what she wanted, and it made her impossible to play against. All he could do was try to keep control.

"All right."

He took a deep breath, scrambling to work out what new plan might work to his advantage.

"I figured out something wasn't right with him. With Koba. Whatever his name is. He'd been running around making calls, going missing, leaving and coming back. I confronted him, and he told me where Ben is. No, that's not true, he told me where he would be. Tonight."

"You have paid for his release?"

"Something like that."

"And you meet tonight?"

"We meet tonight. He and I. No one else. Look," he said, leaning in to Vekua. "All I want is Ben out of there, OK? I don't care how much it costs or who I pay. You want Koba, right? Zoidze. We each have our prize. So tonight we let my plan play out, and then you can have yours."

"I will come with you."

"No, you won't. I'm going alone."

"Tell me. Why do you go with him, into Russia? He can call his men, they will bring Webster here."

"Because, what he told me, they can't use the radio in Russia."

"But they are using it. I told you this."

She had. He had failed to register it.

"Mr. Hammer, you go with him, he will kill you. He is clever, perhaps he will make it seem that you killed your friend, then yourself. In Georgia we say that with one stone you kill two birds."

"No kidding. We say that, too. He needs me alive to pay the second half of his money."

Vekua smiled. "Consider. He has one-half money, and happy client. Perfect conclusion."

FIFTEEN

For a while they argued. Vekua wanted to take Hammer's place, and force Koba to take her to Ben; Hammer wanted to stick with his original plan—if he was in danger he would go armed and alert. In the end they found a compromise: Hammer would meet Koba as agreed, and Vekua would follow them at a distance, ready to help as required. In truth, Hammer liked none of the variations, and the last perhaps least of all—better to be out in the mountains with one person you didn't trust than with two—but as Vekua had reminded him, he had no authority here. It had briefly been his show, but no longer.

Hammer finished dressing, as warmly as possible, checked his flashlight, and laced his boots. Then he went to find Natela outside.

She was hopping from foot to foot in the cold; he took his coat off and draped it over her shoulders. Twenty yards away, standing rigid like a soldier with his back to the neighboring house, was a man in a thick black ski jacket, woolen cap, and heavy black boots. In and out of clouds the half-moon cast a weak light, and a small window by the door threw uncertain shadows on the snow. For the first time since Vekua's arrival Natela looked him full in the eye, and he felt half the fear he had been feeling disappear. She was wounded, but not by him.

She drew on the cigarette and turned her head to send the smoke into the night.

"If you go you will not come back."

"I have to go."

"You trust her?"

Hammer took the half-smoked cigarette from her fingers and drew on it. Strange, how it made him closer to her.

"I want to. But no."

"Take a gun."

"There are two guns. I want Vano and Irodi here with them, watching over you."

He walked a few paces and with his boot cleared the snow away from a section of the path outside the house. At first he didn't find what he was looking for, but a yard or two further on he stopped and picked up three good-sized stones.

"I'm more worried about the dogs," he said, and put them in his pocket.

Natela threw her cigarette down and followed him inside. Eka was making dinner and paying no attention to Vekua, who was checking her bag and taking inventory of the items on the table: a flashlight, a compass, a knife, water, a map in a waterproof case.

"Give me a minute with my hosts," Hammer said. "With these people."

"There is not time."

"I need a minute."

Vekua hesitated, then gathered up her things and stood.

"Of course. But not long."

Hammer waited until she had left.

"Eka, where is Vano?"

Natela translated, and Eka went out into the yard. A minute later she came back with her husband and her son. They stood together in a line with their backs to the sink, Vano grave, Eka concerned, Irodi impassive.

"Natela, I want you to tell them what I'm saying. It's important, so if you don't understand something let me know. OK? I'll go slow. OK." He turned to Vano, who held his hands clasped in front of him. "Sir, I'm grateful to you for inviting me into your home, and more sorry than I can say that I've invited trouble in return." He paused to make sure that Natela had understood, and nodded that she should translate. "I didn't expect to, and I didn't mean to, but there are some bad people in your country, like there are in every country, as you know better than me, I'm sure. Now, what I would love to do, for your good and mine, is to leave here this minute with Natela and go a long way away until we were safe and you were safe, too. But I can't do that. I have a duty to you, and a duty to her, but also to my friend, who's somewhere across the border, heaven knows where, and I guess I have this last chance to find him and bring him back. And I have to take this chance. It's a question of honor as much as anything else. I can't run." As Natela translated this part, Vano gave a nod.

Though part of me would like to run. Away, with Natela, to some other paradise where the world would not intrude.

"So, I'm going across the border tonight, with that woman who was just here. She works for your government, but like everyone down on the plain I can't work out whether she's a good person or a bad one. She could be either or both. The reason I'm telling you this is that you four, you and Natela, are the only people I can trust, and I need you all to help each other. It's possible I won't come back. It's possible the man outside will try to hurt you, and particularly," he hesitated to say it, "particularly you, Natela." He addressed Vano now, directly. "I have no right to ask this, sir, but I think I know what kind of man you are. If you could protect this woman here, who is very dear to me, for the next few hours while I'm away, I shall be always in your debt. Always. And if I don't return, see that these people don't harm her, and that she gets down the mountain. I have no right to ask it, but I hope you'll do it."

Throughout Hammer's speech and Natela's halting translation Vano had listened with respect, as one elder should listen to another. His eyes were stern and gray and seemed to contain all the wisdom of his land, and when he spoke he kept them on Hammer. Two short sentences were all it took.

"He says that last night you became a Tusheti man and you are still a Tusheti man. He will protect your family like his own."

Hammer bowed deeply, and a huge sense of gratitude and relief came over him. Somehow it was unimaginable that this man would let him down. Or Natela.

"Thank you," he said. "I cannot thank you enough."

He shook Vano's hand, and Eka's, and made to leave. Eka stopped him, and quickly gathered some food into a plastic bag: some bread, a hunk of cheese, two apples, some plain biscuits. Hammer bowed again.

To Natela he gave a card, which he had ready in his pocket.

"If there's any trouble, and you get out of this place, call this number and ask for Katerina."

Natela held the card in both hands, unable to take her eyes from it, and then without looking up tore it in two and handed the pieces back to him.

"I want you. I do not want your world."

SIXTEEN

At first he knew the path: out of the village, past the sign remembering Diklo's dead, through the gate and into sheepdog country, following the hillside as it wound toward the fortress. The silver slopes magnified the half-light of the moon and made the way clear ahead; no wind blew, and with each step he heard the creak of his boots on the frosting snow. Vekua had started after him, and though he listened for her and from time to time looked back he couldn't make her out.

There was only one way across the border, or at least only one that made sense. Leading down from the fortress was a path which wound steeply through forest and then followed the water as it flowed toward Russia. Half a mile further on, high up on a shoulder of land that ended in a sheer cliff, a border post overlooked both the narrow chasm and the old rising trail cut into the opposite hillside that had once carried trade between villages. At night it would be possible to take this trail unobserved.

Hammer was used to the terrain now, and refreshed to be out in the cold air. His heart beat fast from the exertion, and his nerves strained against his skin. He counted the uncertainties: his mercenary guide ahead, his unknowable guard behind, the sense of closing on his treacherous goal. As he went he scanned the path for dark shapes, resting his hand on the rocks in his pocket.

Soon he passed the point that he had reached with Natela just a few hours before, and after another half a mile he dimly made out a split in the path and by it a mound of rocks four or five feet high. As he drew closer a brief flare showed Koba's red face as he lit a cigarette.

He said nothing as Hammer approached, and little when he arrived.

"We go."

"You lead the way," said Hammer, and saw that the shrine was made not of rocks but of rams' skulls, their horns twisting and writhing together in the moonlight.

Some journey this was. Walking into the icy wastes of Dagestan with two people he couldn't trust. With every step he felt less safe.

Koba set off at a pace that belied his age and his bulk, and for a while Hammer had to concentrate on keeping up. The only noise was the crunching of boots and the gruff seesawing of Koba's breath. Before long, they came off the path onto a high, wide spur of land that fell away into darkness on either side, where the snow was deep and the going heavier, and loosely spaced trees began to cut out some of the light. Hammer got closer to Koba, until he was on his shoulder and could begin to talk. Talking might help. It might tell him something.

"You check your account?"

Koba looked over his shoulder but said nothing.

"I was just wondering," said Hammer, breathing hard himself, "whether you had a chance to check your account. The money should be there."

"Money is fine."

"You ever had a payout like that before, Koba? I'm going to keep calling you Koba, save me having to learn your real name."

Koba trudged on.

"How much you being paid by your boss, Koba? Roughly. You don't want to say, OK. Because I would love to know who that is. You want more money, just tell me who he is and what he wants."

Koba took another few steps, then stopped and turned, his face dark with exertion.

"Less talk. Yes? We have deal. Is all."

"Sorry. I like to talk."

Koba set off again.

"Another five hundred, you tell me who he is."

Koba simply raised a hand and carried on walking.

Hammer left it for a while, then tried again, talking between breaths.

"Koba, tell me. What was the plan for me? For my friend? You going to kill us both or what?"

Nothing.

"Come on. You can tell me that much. No one's going to hear."

"No talk."

"It's just, it's kind of personal. I'm curious."

"No talk."

Hammer hadn't expected a reply to any of this, but he sensed he was getting the response he wanted. The new Koba might be different from the old but he still had a temper.

"OK. I'm sorry. Just one last thing. Your guys, do they know we're coming?"

"No radios. Cannot know."

"That's right. You said. So how are they going to know it's us? What's to stop them shooting us?"

"I make signal."

"That's good."

Hammer took the next few steps in silence, to give Koba the impression he was thinking.

"That's good. A signal. So how d'you communicate with your guys?"

"We have plan."

"What if the plan changes?"

But Koba was standing still and alert, and his hand was up for him to be quiet. Hammer peered ahead but there was nothing to see; just dark trees and lighter patches of snow and one small clearing where the moon reached. Then he saw them: two gray shapes on the ground, twenty yards away, not moving. Koba pointed up the slope and set off carefully, keeping his eye on the spot. Hammer's hand hovered by his jacket pocket.

Up they went, but after ten steps Koba again went rigid. In the clearing a shape stirred and let out a bark that split the night. It waited for its companion to stand before approaching steadily, barking all the while.

Hammer stepped forward, a rock ready in his hand, and saw a gun in Koba's. He touched his sleeve.

"I can handle this."

"Mountain motherfuckers," said Koba, and raised the pistol.

"Koba, there's no need."

To Hammer it seemed that the sound came before the white flash in the dark. There was no echo, just a blunt report, immense and instantly gone, and then another noise immediately, the same but more distant. Hammer brought his hands to his ears, saw the dog crumple to its left, heard a roar from Koba, who clutched at his cheek and wheeled round as if someone had spun him. A third shot broke his cries and sent him sprawling silent onto the snow.

"Koba!" shouted Hammer, and kneeled by him, not understanding. His gun must have misfired. His face was pushed into the snow, which was suffused with black.

"Leave him," said a voice behind him. "Back."

Hammer turned to her.

"What the fuck have you done? What the fuck?"

Vekua ignored him and walked up to the body, kneeling by it and taking off a glove to check the pulse in his neck, her pistol still in her hand. Her fingers came away covered in Koba's blood. She cleaned it off in the snow, dried her hand on her coat, and put her glove back on; then walked a few paces to where his gun lay, picked it up, and put a gun in each pocket.

Shocked, the shots still playing in his ears, hardly believing what he had seen, Hammer sat back on the ground. Bile rose in his throat.

"What the fuck did you do?"

"He took out his gun. I shot."

"He shot the dog. He shot the fucking dog."

"I saw no dog. Now it is simple. Come."

Returning to Koba, Vekua went through his coat and pulled out a flashlight, a compass, two packets of cigarettes, a lighter, and a bottle of water. No radio. The dog's companion loped away through the clearing.

"What are you doing?"

Vekua glanced up at him. In the half-light he couldn't make out whether her expression was shocked, exhilarated, or triumphant, but her poise was still evident. She was in control.

"Investigating," she said, pocketing the flashlight and leaving the rest. "Come."

Hammer watched her set off and pass the dead heap of the dog, stepping lightly and steadily, as if she had just encountered nothing more than an everyday obstacle. The sight of her chilled him more than the cold that had begun to settle in his limbs as soon as they had stopped.

"How the fuck are we going to find the way?"

"I know the way."

How did she know? Hammer followed, doing his best to breathe, to think, to quieten the noise in his head. Before, he had known he was walking into trouble; now he was more sure than ever that what lay in wait for him was a trap.

He paused for a moment by the dog's corpse. In the near dark he couldn't tell for certain, but it looked like his dog, the one that had released him earlier, and this upset him further. It was an innocent. Alone of all these bastards it had honored their contract.

By the time he caught up with her they were scrambling up a bank of snow and scree at the end of the ridge to the ruined fortress, whose jagged walls cut the sky. This was the highest point until the mountains that lined the border, and from it cliffs dropped a thousand feet to the winding river below. Hammer saw miles of peaks and forests, endless and empty, and had the odd sensation that this really was all theirs; that there was no one else to lay claim to it. Behind them, the two or three tiny dim lights of Diklo were the only sign in the whole world that they weren't altogether alone. He wondered whether Natela had heard the shots, and what she would now be thinking.

At the fortress Vekua stopped and surveyed the scene, waiting for him to catch up.

"And what happens when we get there?" said Hammer. "Who does the exchange?"

"Understand. At some point, in Russia, he would shoot you and then kill your friend. There was no exchange. Now we are two people, and he has two men. We are equal."

Hammer shook his head, his breath showing thickly in the cold. How does she know there are two men?

"And you think we're getting across the border, after all that noise."

Vekua laughed, for once as if she meant it.

"Russian border police. There will be two of them. By now they have drunk half a bottle of vodka each and are beginning to fight. In a half hour they will be friends again. They will not look outside until long after dawn."

"Not even when some crazy's shooting outside their door?"

"Georgia is like America. Everyone shoots guns. Come."

Vekua headed carefully down toward a dark line of trees and Hammer followed, wondering with every step what grounds he had to entrust his fate to this woman. Of the various outcomes that filed through his thoughts, few were good, and those that were depended utterly on her honesty. She had all the power, and both of the guns. His only comfort was an absence of choice.

Then, far behind them, with a flat report and an echo that rang round the mountains, sounded a shot. It was distant but unmistakable, and it was followed quickly by another, and a third. All fired behind them; all fired, as far as he could tell, from the same gun.

Hammer's calculations ceased; every thought but one left his head.

"What was that?"

Vekua had stopped and was dead still, listening, like prey suspecting the presence of a hunter.

"Shots."

"From the village."

"I think so."

"We have to go back."

"We cannot go back."

"We'll go quickly."

"If we do not go now, we will be too late. Koba's men are expecting him."

"But I have to know those people are safe."

"Then you have a decision. You can return. But I will go on."

Her white face seemed to shine with certainty. Out here in the half-light, Hammer found himself hating its symmetry, its disengagement.

"Your man," he said. "What orders did you give him?"

"To protect the village."

"From what?"

"From Zoidze and his men, of course."

"How many men does he have?"

"I do not know. That is why I left a guard. And in case I do not return, he can fly your friend to Tbilisi."

Hammer looked into her black eyes and saw nothing there that might help him. She might be telling the truth, or she might have given an instruction that as soon as he heard her own shot her man was to shoot Vano, Irodi, and Natela. To go back was to give up on Ben. To go ahead was to fail Natela.

"We go," said Vekua.

Hammer didn't answer her. How to make the choice? It was part of his personal legend that he was good at decisions. Have a client throw the world's most complicated situation at him and after a little while he would know what to do. But clients were easy, because their problems were abstract. This was real, and in its simplicity impossible. The woman he was coming to love might be beyond help, and the man he loved like a son might in any case stand no chance. Underneath the two cups there might be two balls, or none; lift one, and the other ball might disappear.

Vano and Irodi. He could do no more than they would to protect her.

Vekua had set off again. She stopped now and turned.

"Time is going. Your friends are protected. Your duty is here."

Hammer willed himself to abandon logic and surrender himself to this place, to its rules. He would trust his new friends and go on. And with each step he would doubt his choice.

SEVENTEEN

Now they went steeply down, and where the trees thickened Vekua produced her flashlight, keeping the beam trained on the ground. In places the trees were so tight that the path was free of snow, and they made good time until the river appeared a little way below them and before long they came out on the pebble beach where Koba's men had dragged Ben onto their boat. It was too dark to see whether the 4 x 4 was still in the woods, and he didn't mention it.

At the water they turned left, threading in and out of the trees along the bank.

"It is easy now until we reach the border," said Vekua.

Hammer wondered what she meant by easy.

The river ran directly beneath the border station under sheer cliffs of rock on the opposite bank, and from this point the path was treeless and open to the night. If anyone had been watching they would have seen two figures, slightly blacker than the ground they walked on, both small, both precise, moving swiftly and silently along the exposed stretch like escaping prisoners waiting for the searchlight to pick them out against a great, bare wall. But it never came, and soon Hammer's shoulders relaxed and the feeling receded that eyes were on his back. Clouds thickened round the moon and after a while Vekua clicked on her flashlight.

"We are in Russia," she said, in a voice that seemed to suggest that now she was in her element. Land of spies and deception, of devious conflicts played out on its edges, and here they were in its blackest corner, where law did not exist and light would never be shone. What happened here would stay here. Hammer felt tiny and alone, as if he had crept through a narrow crack into the furthest corner of some vast enemy fortress.

The country changed as they climbed. The trees ran out, until there was just snow and scree and stone. The angles became sheerer, the ground more rocky, and the path rose nervelessly up until it was a narrow strip on a vertiginous slope. Cliffs above them, cliffs below, and three feet of flat ground in between. Hammer kept as far from the edge as he could manage, and took some comfort from not being able to see the drop.

At one point the path leveled a little and then split, one half carrying straight on and up, the other turning sharply down to their right. At the junction footsteps appeared in the snow.

"The river is below. This is how they came," said Vekua, staying left.

Hammer thought he had acclimatized to the altitude, but up here his lungs burned afresh and his head reeled. The colonel showed no signs of slowing. Whatever she was planning, she wanted it done quickly. Hammer watched the silhouette of her back in the flashlight's beam and carefully assessed the odds, as he had done a thousand times, in situations much safer and less vexed.

Stop her now and he might never find the place at all; stay with her till the end and there was a strong chance that he and Ben would be shot. Delay his move too long and he might discover that her only intention in bringing him here was to turn, any moment, and throw him to his death. Timing. As so often, it all seemed to come down to timing.

He sensed that they were nearing the top of their ascent; the path began to flatten and the slope above him to level out. Vekua stopped here, and Hammer, his hand going to the rocks in his pocket, wondered whether the time had come, but she turned and beckoned him to look. Where she was standing, the path had collapsed, resuming on the other side of a decent gap. A long jumper might have cleared it, but Hammer was no athlete. Below, the earth and stones from the landslide had collected on a ledge ten feet down.

Vekua shone her flashlight all over the spot, and eventually reached the same conclusion as Hammer—that the only way round was to do what the party ahead of them had done, and traverse the slope above. It wasn't sheer, but it was by no means flat.

"You go first," said Hammer, as it crossed his mind that if she wanted to be rid of him this was a perfect opportunity. The same was true for him, of course, but in this she had the march on him. No jumper, and no killer.

Starting a foot or two back from the edge and clasping the flashlight in her mouth, Vekua took her first, hesitant steps upward, keeping her body close to the ground and using her hands for balance. Testing her grip with each movement, she began to head across, and with great reluctance he followed, the memory of his earlier fall playing out in his mind.

Twelve sideways steps, he calculated, were all that was needed. It wasn't so much. If he hadn't been a thousand feet up, with no ropes, on wind-frozen snow, it wouldn't have merited a thought—not, for instance, the notion that his smashed body might not be found for months, and then only if it escaped the notice of the wolves. Already parched from the effort of the climb, his mouth dried up and filled with something that he imagined was the taste of fear.

Another step, taken slowly and with immense care. As a distraction he calculated his chances, and then wished he hadn't. If each step carried a one in ten chance of a fall, the chances of his reaching the other side were only thirty percent. But Vekua was making progress, and in the available light he followed her closely and tried to put his feet where she had put hers.

As he had the thought he felt his boot scratch at the ice and fail to find a grip. With his other foot he dug in harder but under the extra weight it gave and began to slip.

"Fuck."

Slowly but with growing momentum he started to slide over the ice. Terror surged in his chest. He clutched in vain at the crumbling snow.

"Elene."

He stuck out a hand. No more than three feet away, she only had to reach down and take it, but all she did was watch; didn't move, not so much as a twitch, her eyes steady in the flashlight's beam. Watched him go.

With a last desperate stretch he grabbed her boot, felt his pace checked, and then she was sliding, flashlight too. She took the torch from her mouth and dug it in to slow her, but it didn't catch. Down they both went, slipping helplessly to the edge.

Together they dropped, for an instant, until with a dead thud Hammer hit the rubble a little way below and rolled toward the lip of the tiny ledge. Instinctively he grabbed, at anything, and his clumsy stupid gloves closed on Vekua's sleeve and slowed him just enough to stop his body following his legs into space. There was silence, and the silence told him that he had come to rest. Just above him, Vekua didn't move. Clawing at her clothes, scrabbling for purchase with his knees in the loose stones and earth, he pulled himself up and sat beside her, panting and terrified.

"Sweet God," he said to the night, feeling the great support of the earth beneath him. There was no light; her flashlight had tumbled over the edge. Ahead of him all was black.

But Vekua didn't answer. Gingerly, he shrugged off his pack and felt in it for his flashlight. She was unconscious, but breathing; he could see her breath in the cold, and the dark blood beginning to show in the snow beneath her head. Some instinct made him reach out and touch it, and he felt that she was resting on jagged rock.

For a minute he collected himself, and then he went to work. Her pack was lying awkwardly under her, but he managed to pull from it the knife, the map, and the compass. He took both guns from her coat and put them in his own. As carefully as he could, he went through her other pockets, but found only a set of keys, a phone, a radio receiver, a lighter, and, incongruously, a lipstick. He left her the keys and the lipstick, and nothing else.

Training the light above him, he tried to plot a route out. The way up was vertical, more or less, and made up of loose stones and dry clay. Standing with one foot on either side of Vekua's prone body, he took off his gloves, stuffed them in his pockets, and tried his hands in the frozen earth, pushing his fingers in to get a grip. It was denser than he had realized, and there was some moisture in it, and it held. He did the same with one foot, working it in, and then the other, and slowly, with great effort and care, pulled himself up.

He never imagined that the path could feel so solid. He walked for twenty yards, then stopped to rest, exhausted by the effort and the constant, persistent fear. For a minute he stared into the darkness, did his best not to imagine the way down and breathed as deeply as he could. The air was palpably thinner here than it had been down by the river, and his lungs burned from the work and the cold. Then he took the map from his pack and tried to get his bearings. There were no markings on it to indicate their destination, but after studying it for a while he convinced himself that at least he knew where he was. In about half a mile, if he was right, there was an old hamlet, or some kind of settlement, indicated by six tiny rectangles and a name in Russian that he couldn't read.

The path climbed, skirted the summit, and then descended slowly onto a saddle of land between two peaks. From the highest point he saw light. Two golden squares glowing in a shapeless world of blacks and grays.

EIGHTEEN

It took longer than he had imagined—coming down, if anything, was harder than going up—but in another half an hour he was there, on flat ground, softly approaching the deserted settlement by the light of the moon, his flashlight off and his heart going at a steady gallop. He smelled woodsmoke on the air. The houses were barely houses anymore; even in the overwhelming dark he could see that their walls had collapsed and their roofs had fallen in. Tall weeds grew in the snow around them and swayed in the gathering wind. If there was a lonelier place in the world, he didn't know it; a more desolate journey to be ending here, he couldn't imagine it.

Two rough rows of three houses stretched ahead of him, arranged along a central track, and now, pulling a gun from his pocket, he crept toward the furthest on the left. It was little more than a shack. One room, he guessed, with two small windows on each long side. By their light he could see that its walls were in a better state than its neighbors', and that someone had stretched a tarpaulin tight over one corner to complete the roof. Its windows were almost intact, and a mess of footprints ran up to the door from the other direction.

The snow softened his tread, and in silence he crouched down by the window and slowly brought his eyes up to the level of the glass. The tarpaulin flapped gently above his head. The first thing he saw was a fire burned almost to ashes in the grate, and on the wall next to it two large rucksacks, full, with sleeping bags and bedrolls hanging off them. Two pairs of legs stretched out on the floor, in black combat trousers and walking boots. Sitting with their backs against the black slate were two men, both dark, both unshaven, both big, playing dice by the light of a single candle. Hammer didn't stop to watch them, but saw in their faces something of the discipline of soldiers and the brutishness of mercenaries.

There was no sign of Ben, but the walls were too thick and the windows too small for him to see the far end of the room, so he moved carefully across the door and checked the second window. In the opposite corner there were a stack of three plastic plates, two enamel mugs and two plastic bags, each neatly tied. That was all. At the thought that there was no one else here he felt sweat start on his brow and sickness in his stomach. That the whole business had been an elaborate ruse to bring him up here to his death. He crossed to the back of the house and from the window there saw, at last, the friend he had come to find: on his side, on the floor, his feet bound at the ankle, his hands tied behind his back, and a blindfold over his eyes, but it was Ben, no question, under the matted hair and the silver of his new beard. Deathly still he lay; Hammer would have given all he had to see him twitch, or shift, or struggle.

What to do? He had two guns and little choice but to use them. Koba's was in his hand, improbably smooth, and heavy, and almost laughably powerful. He had no idea who had made it, but he was glad of their crafts-manship, of the time and care spent engineering the thing. Here, on a mountaintop in the wilderness, this rather slight figure was about to take on two professionals in a contest of strength, and because he had surprise on his side, and a gun, his odds weren't as bad as they should have been.

Still he barely knew how to proceed. He had the gun but no desire to use it. With gloves on, in the ring, he could hurt someone, with some sort of mutual consent. But simply to move your finger half an inch and watch the soul rip from the flesh . . . It was not what he did. He thought his way through.

No amount of thought would help. If there was only one guard he might tempt him outside, by some distraction, and knock him out with a roof joist from a ruined house. But by the time he'd done this to one, the other would have a gun to Ben's head. There seemed no middle way. He'd have to shoot them both and allow no time in between, and through these tiny windows there was hardly the freedom or the angle, even for an accom-plished shot with the stomach for such a thing. Shivering with cold and apprehension, he stood with his back to the wall and ran every scenario through in his mind. None ended well.

The two guards talked intermittently in low voices. Hammer moved to another window to get a better view, and saw the broader of the two stand and stretch extravagantly, his hands clasped at the back of his neck. He said something to his friend, and the friend grunted in response. The big man checked his watch, said something else, and walked to the other end of the room, out of Hammer's sight. He came back with a cigarette in his mouth, took the lighter that his friend offered, and lit it.

From his pocket Hammer pulled Vekua's lighter, and tiptoed through the weeds back to the front of the house. He clicked the wheel and held the flame up to the edge of the tarpaulin, willing the thing to take. There was no snow on it, at least—it must have been fixed earlier that day, once the worst had fallen—and soon the blue plastic began to melt and burn, with a livid orange flame that crept up the wall. As soon as he was sure that it had caught, Hammer positioned himself five yards away from the house, Koba's gun trained on the door. He held it in both hands to keep it from shaking.

A toxic smell and a crackling sound drifted on the air. Hammer waited for the noise, and soon it came, a Georgian bellow that filled the night. Then more shouting from behind the ancient door. Through the window Hammer could see the light from the flames playing on the far wall of the hut.

The door opened and one of the Georgians was there, half turning to inspect the roof as he came, a gun in his hand. His friend was directly behind him. Neither would have seen Hammer in the darkness.

He let them take another few steps, until they were just clear of the building.

"Stop!" Hammer shouted. "Stop right fucking there!"

Even as he began to say it he saw the second man bringing a gun up from beside his hip, and without thought pulled the trigger of his own. Noise burst from the gun and filled his head, ringing on in the silence as he watched the man reel away and blood splash from his shoulder. Nausea coursed up in him. Be ready straightaway for the next shot, Hammer had told himself. You will be shocked, but you cannot be.

The guard clutched his shoulder as he fell, the barrel of his gun flashed, and Hammer fired again, hardly aiming, hitting him in the cheek. In the wavering light of the flames he saw the man's head snap backward, saw his face crack and sheer, and knew that he had killed him. Sickened, confusion like a flood in his head, Hammer had only one clear thought: that he had never been so aware of the size of a man, of the substance of him, of all that flesh that held the spirit.

"Fucking stop!"

The first man had turned to face Hammer, and was reaching behind him to his waist.

"Stop!"

God, how he meant it. Please stop. Make this easy now.

The guard's hand hung in the air, and for a moment he and Hammer stared at each other, their breath rising against the blazing house. Then he nodded once and slowly raised both arms.

"Turn round." Hammer gestured with his free hand. The man turned and with his eyes fixed on him, aware of every step, Hammer approached and took the pistol from his waistband. He threw it behind him, as far as he could. The dead man had slid down the wall and was slumped awkwardly, hanging on his knees, his head flopped on his shoulder, his face half gone, his mouth gaping in a grim leer. Hammer saw this at a glance and looked away. Acid burned his throat. Thoughts came, and he shut them out.

"Inside."

He motioned with the gun, and his captive moved warily toward the door. The fire had spread to the beams and filled the room with black smoke that forced them to duck as they entered.

"Free him," said Hammer, bringing his sleeve to his throat to keep out the acrid, chemical fumes, and indicating with his foot the ropes binding Webster. With no expression the guard looked mechanically from Hammer to Webster and back to Hammer, taking his time, waiting for the amateur to make a mistake. He had a low brow and eyes that seemed to shine brightly in the guttering light.

"Do it," said Hammer, raising the gun and pointing it at the guard's face. With a final insolent look the guard squatted by Webster and began to pull halfheartedly at the knots that bound him. There were three, at his ankles, knees, and wrists, which were behind his back. Webster twisted his body into position, and Hammer crouched down out of the smoke.

"Quickly."

From above him came a wrenching, tearing noise, and he looked up to see a length of beam, about two feet, snap free and fall, still burning, between him and the guard. In that instant of distraction the guard turned and struck out at Hammer's hands, connecting hard and sending the gun rattling across the floor. Hammer lost his balance, and as he tried to right himself felt the guard's fist like a metal weight drive into his cheek, cracking bone and throwing him onto his back, gasping at the toxic air, thoughts disordered, pain uppermost. The roof of the house was all flame. Somehow in his bewilderment he held on to one idea: that while he was struggling to compose himself the guard was scrambling across the floor toward the dropped gun. He didn't see it but he knew it.

His left hand reached almost automatically for his pocket and found there the strange, cold, heavy form of Vekua's gun. He gripped the barrel, pulled it out, wrestled with it as it snagged against the loose material, then brought it out into the air, hearing the guard sliding for the gun just beyond him, perhaps three yards away, praying for time. His right hand took the pistol from his left, and raising his head he found his target; saw the guard spinning round with Koba's gun in his hand; and fired.

Two shots sounded, and for a second the two gunmen looked at each other, like duelists waiting to see a spreading patch of crimson on their white shirts, before the guard's look turned inward, in pain and dismay, and with an odd steadiness he settled back onto the earth, feeling with an outstretched hand for balance. Hammer kept his head lifted and his gun up, watching.

But the guard had nothing left. His last action was to hold a hand to his side, and there it rested, helpless against the flow of blood that pulsed through his fingers. The pulsing stopped. The man lay still. Smuts of dead plastic floated in the air.

Hammer closed his eyes, dwelled briefly on the images he found there, and got to his feet. Without relish, he stood over this second body and made sure that it was dead. By the light of the burning roof, he inspected the still bulk of the guard. The bullet had gone right through him, and blood leaked from a small exit wound in his back.

A corpse. It was a dishonest word—cold and final, but also remote. Distancing. These weren't two corpses. They were men that had lived and now were dead.

NINETEEN

A deep quiet filled the place, like soft rain after a long peal of thunder. The tarpaulin had burned out, and beyond the wrinkled iron roof the night looked down. In the darkness, Hammer heard a muffled cry. Taking his flashlight and his knife he knelt down and with delicacy cut the cloth by Webster's hair. It was indescribably comforting to see his face. An old bruise covered one eye.

"You hurt?" said Hammer. He took his knife and began cutting at the three strands of rope.

"Ike. What the fuck?"

"Elsa called. I said I'd find you."

"Jesus Christ."

"Are you hurt?"

"My leg. Is it just you?"

"Just me."

"Jesus, Ike."

Hammer had ripped Webster's trousers and was inspecting his calf. A bullet had sliced through the muscle, cutting an inch into the flesh. It was pouring blood.

"How did you . . ."

"Wait," said Hammer. Crossing to a window, he opened one of the guards' rucksacks, rummaged about in it, and pulled out a T-shirt, which he proceeded to rip with the knife. Then he tore Webster's trouser leg until the wound was exposed, and tied the strip of material tightly just below the knee.

"Are you hungry?" From his pack, which, absurdly, had been on his back throughout, he started to retrieve the food that Eka had given him.

"Ike. Jesus. How are you here?"

Hammer closed his eyes and sighed. He couldn't look his friend in the eye.

"I can't stop. Not yet." He paused. "Are you all right?"

"I'm fine."

"We need to get you fed."

"I'm not hungry. How's Elsa?"

"It's one hell of a walk."

Hammer helped Webster to sit up.

"Elsa's fine. Fucking worried. Furious with you. So am I. Here." Hammer passed him an apple. "You'll need it."

Still he carried on. In the guard's rucksack he found a pair of trousers and flapped them out to gage their size. There was a large bag of food in there, too, and he spread out its contents on the ground.

"Pass me that bottle," said Webster.

Automatically, Hammer did.

"Here. Have some," said Webster. "It's chacha."

"Theirs?"

"You need it. You're in shock."

Hammer shook his head. "It's not good, in the cold."

"Would you stop? Just a slug."

He took the bottle, an old water bottle two-thirds full of amber liquid, and sniffed it. Medicine from his victims; but he drank it nevertheless, and felt part of himself return as the liquid burned his throat and spread warmth through his chest. For half a minute he sat, Webster watching him, as a tremendous tiredness came, a chemical dryness in his limbs, a tiredness of the last minutes and hours, weeks and years.

"Better?"

At first Hammer didn't reply. In his mind a hundred images were present, held under tension, a crazed richness, as if his life had occupied a single moment in time. He felt them all, and focused on none: the good, the sweet, the humdrum, the shameful, all there, a dense compression of colors and shapes. He drank again and let them settle, his eyes closed. Elsa was there. And Sander. And Natela, willing him back.

He opened his eyes and tried a smile.

"Better."

"You will be," said Webster.

Hammer had no idea how that could be.

Webster began to eat with the cautious appetite of someone who had been half starved, and as Hammer watched him in the simple act he wondered how things had become so complicated between them. Everything that had pulled them apart seemed so distant—a London problem. A privileged problem. It was good to see him, in this desolate place.

"You want some of this?" said Webster, as he began to revive.

"Not with them here."

"Drink something, at least."

Hammer took the bottle of water from him and sat cross-legged on the ground. For a while neither spoke. Hammer crossed his arms tight against the cold.

"I didn't think I'd see you again," said Webster.

"Or anyone."

"I don't mean that. I mean before. I thought we were through."

"So did I."

Webster looked gaunt, stretched around the cheeks and eyes. A blackening bruise spread into his hairline from his temple.

"I'm sorry," he said.

"Really?"

But Hammer knew Ben didn't apologize unless he meant it.

"I should have found a better way to leave."

"It had been brewing."

Webster acknowledged the point with a nod.

"We have work to do when we get back," said Hammer.

Webster glanced up.

"Do you never stop thinking about work?"

"Just this last week." He paused, uncertain whether to go on. "This can wait."

"What is it?"

He weighed it up. It felt petty, and irrelevant.

"We can talk later."

"Ike."

"It's nothing. The police want to talk to us."

"I bet they do."

"Not here. In London."

"To me?"

"So you didn't know?"

"I have no idea what you're talking about."

"Two days before I came here fifteen police paid me a visit. All at once."

Webster was frowning, clearly confused.

"What did they want?"

"Every scrap of paper they could find on Pearl."

"You're kidding me."

"Every file. Your old computer."

"For what? What did we do?"

"Hacking. Among other things."

Webster shook his head, indignant.

"That's bullshit. I never did a thing."

Hammer wiped dust off his trousers and made to stand.

"We can talk about it later."

"Is that why you came here? To bring me back for trial?"

"To begin with."

Webster put down the bread in his hand and didn't respond.

Let it out, thought Hammer. You didn't come all this way to say nothing.

"I came here in a rage. I thought it was going to kill the company."

"And that it was all down to me."

"They'd been talking to Saber. You'd signed off on their work. But that wasn't what the rage was about."

"There was nothing dodgy."

"I came here to show you my way was better than your way. OK? Show you what happens when you charge off with an idea in your head and no thought for anyone else."

"Ike, really. Pearl was completely clean."

"It wasn't about Pearl."

Webster had the sense to wait for the rest.

"What you said, when you left, it cut me. You took the one thing I had and killed it."

"Jesus, Ike! I didn't mean . . ."

"If I hadn't known it all already I wouldn't have been upset. You were right. OK? That's why it hurt."

"I hated myself for saying it."

"So did I."

Smiling a weak smile, Hammer looked around the room at the chaos and the dead man, then up through the ragged roof at the black clouded sky.

"I needed to wake up," he said. "I think this may have done it."

On Webster's face now was a look only of concern.

"Ike, you're a good man. Think of everything you've done."

"I'd swap it all for something to care about."

Hammer stood, nodding, the words a refrain in his head.

"All of it."

Hammer made preparations for their return. He forced himself to eat some of the food, and wrapped what was left; emptied out both the men's rucksacks and took from them a rope, two ice picks, and a headlamp, which he immediately strapped on. He looked for painkillers—for Ben, though his own cheek and nose could use some—but found none. Finally, with an abhorrence that he knew he had to overcome, he searched the dead men. It was gruesome, but something about its ruthless practicality helped. It might not dispel the horror, but it brought clarity to the moral case.

Their effects were almost identical to Koba's: phones, cigarettes, a pair of lighters, some cash—Russian and Georgian—and no identification at all.

Two radios. Condoms and a compass, a hunting knife with a serrated edge. One set of what looked like house keys. And their two pistols, of course, with ammunition for both.

As he worked he asked Webster questions, willing himself to be practical.

"So why did you come?"

"I never could resist a trip."

"Or a cause."

"Karlo called me a week before he died. With a name for me to check."

"I know."

"This time he was beside himself, even for him. He was scared. The source for the story, he'd found out who she was."

"She?"

"She. He gave me her name, nothing else."

"I think I know it," said Hammer.

"Go on."

"How did he find out?"

"He wouldn't tell me over the phone. Tell me the name."

"Elene Vekua."

"Damn you're good. Who is she?"

"A colonel in the Georgian intelligence service. She just tried to kill me."

"Up here?"

"She's still out there. Which is why we should go."

Hammer could see him fitting the pieces together. He had missed these conversations.

"Quite an asset. No wonder Mr. V was nervous."

"You think she's a spy?"

"Why else would he tell us nothing?"

Hammer sighed. It helped to talk about this but he was finding it hard to concentrate. Echoes of recent events kept interrupting.

"So the story Karlo published was bullshit."

"What have you always said? The best lie sits next to the truth. Most of what she told him was completely true. A Georgian spy did engineer that bomb. It just happened to be her. And she wasn't doing it for any Georgian."

For a while Hammer simply thought, letting everything he knew settle.

Probably she had always meant to kill Karlo. Probably Koba had been working for her.

"So who's he?" said Webster, as Hammer went through the dead man's pockets.

"He's a blank. But I think he probably worked for my driver." He looked at Webster, who frowned, not understanding. "This country is nuts. Let's go home."

Webster stood, steady enough on his feet but clearly in pain.

"Here."

Hammer handed him the pistol and a box of bullets. Webster looked at them, raised an eyebrow, and put them in his pockets.

"Those your only shoes?" Hammer said.

Webster looked down at the exhausted sneakers on his feet.

"I was driving. Everything was in my bag."

"What size are you?"

"No. Forget it. I'll be fine."

"It's like climbing the fucking Eiger out there. These look OK?"

Hammer knelt down by the dead Georgian and started untying the laces. The calf was still warm as he pried off the boot.

He helped Webster out of his ripped trousers, checked the pockets, and threw them in a corner, giving him the spare pair from the man's rucksack. Then he looked around the hut. Every part of him needed to be gone.

"What will happen here?" he said.

"No one will be here till spring. Probably for years. And if they do come, they won't do anything. This is Dagestan. There are dead fighters everywhere."

Webster started for the door, but Hammer hesitated, still staring at the floor of the place.

"Let's burn it."

"There's no need."

"I don't want to be thinking about them here."

Together they dragged the second body inside and laid the two together.

From their rucksacks Hammer took the men's spare clothes and spread them out in two long piles. Then he found the chacha bottle and sprinkled its contents over each.

"Give me a hand."

They hoisted the bigger of the two and straightened out the smaller, swinging him onto the makeshift bier. Hammer sparked the lighter and touched it to one pile and then the next until the small blue flames grew and turned orange and licked at the limbs of the dead men.

"Forgive me," said Hammer, and turned to go.

TWENTY

It made a fine, grim sight, the burning house in the empty mountains, touching the snow with fire and lighting up one tiny patch of the blackness all around.

"Very Norse," said Webster, but Hammer didn't reply. He had forced his mind to consider the snow, now falling again, and their way ahead, a thin line through the wilderness. There was no other route round the landslide, and he had no idea how they would both cross it, or what he would find when they arrived. If Vekua was still there, she was a problem; if she had gone, she was again a threat.

Through the night they walked, in the deepening cold. The fresh snow was easier underfoot, and before they left Hammer had found two good sticks to give them balance, so that despite Webster's obvious pain they went, if not quickly, then at a decent pace, stopping from time to time to rest.

It took an hour to reach the landslide, and Hammer approached it with growing unease and a quickening pulse. When he finally made it out in the darkness he motioned silently to Webster to stay where he was, crept quietly to the point where the ground fell away, and listened. Just stillness. Turning on his flashlight, he peered over the edge. No one. Just a platform of earth and stone and snow. He shone the flashlight at his feet and tried to separate the footprints, but there were too many for him to make sense of them.

"She's not here."

"Is that good?"

Webster sat while Hammer tried to work out how best to cross the gap. He had rope now, but nowhere to tie it—no boulders, no trees, no roots— and his weight wouldn't take Webster's, not in the snow. From his bag he took the ice ax, examined its twin blades, and then swung the longer into the ground, where it sank in up to the handle. Tying the rope tightly round the protruding blade, he pulled against it, jerked it, leaned back from it, and watched it hold fast.

"Here. This is the worst of it. It's ten feet down and ten feet up the other side."

He passed the rope to Webster and stood on the handle of the ax to anchor it.

"What will you do?"

"I'll be fine. I've done it before. At speed."

They made it easily across. Once Webster was down, Hammer wrenched the ax out of the ground, half climbed, half slid down the steep clay face, and then scrambled up the other side to fix the rope for his friend. At the top Webster lay, panting, on the path.

"I think my muscles have wasted away."

"It's the altitude. It's hard."

They drank water and sat for a few minutes, not saying anything. As Hammer stood, brushing snow off him, Webster finally spoke.

"Thanks, Ike."

"Hey."

"I thought I wasn't coming down again."

"We're a long way from down."

Light he may have been, but Hammer found himself half walking, half slipping on the steeper stretches of the path, and thanking God every time a wary slide came to a stop. Webster had the ice pick, and instructions to drive it into the ground the moment he felt his weight getting away from him. The moon was out again to give them some help, but otherwise the mountain was making it clear they had no business being there.

Defiant, stubborn, they went on, until their descent became gentler, and they passed the fork in the path, and at last they saw below them the black shine of the river cutting through the valley and above it, still a way off, the two blue lights of the border station. Hammer pointed them out.

"Get past that and we're halfway home."

Webster didn't answer. He sat down, with his back to the slope and his legs bent across the path, and even in the glow from the flashlight Hammer could see that he was pale.

"Sorry. I just need a minute."

"Take your time. No rush."

But for the last half hour Hammer's thoughts had been squarely on Vekua, and where she was, and what she was planning for them, and what might happen if she made it back to Diklo. All his imaginings were red with violence. Rummaging in his bag, he found the water and biscuits and squatted by his friend.

"Here. This'll help."

In the quiet he could hear the river running below them and the wind in the trees across the valley, and for the first time since leaving Diklo felt again the beauty of the place, like a taunt.

"What about Iosava?" he said.

"My God. Iosava. You've met him?"

"Oh yes."

"I bet it was a pleasure."

"Some client to have."

"He wasn't my client."

"So what was he?"

Webster drank and passed the bottle to Hammer.

"After the funeral there was a big black Merc waiting outside my hotel and a bodyguard asking me did I want to see Mr. Iosava."

"You were asked?"

"Not exactly. So I go to his house."

"You meet the bear?"

"You, too? We need to free that poor fucking bear. So I went, and he gave me all this guff about Karlo being a great man cut down before he could finish his biggest story, and in his honor we had to finish his work, which was to pin the bombing on the president."

"And you said yes."

"No. I told him I'd investigate what happened to Karlo and if he wanted to pay me to tell him what I found that was fine by me. It didn't feel good, believe me."

Webster's breaths were short and he took a moment to collect himself.

"I needed the money."

"The money helps."

"Doesn't it? Anyway, that was it. Tbilisi was a nightmare. I couldn't get in anywhere. I met this guy two years ago on a case, he's like the president's right-hand man, and I called him to see if he could pull some strings. Nothing."

But Hammer, alert, held up a hand. From the ground a deep noise seemed to be coming, right beneath them, a vibration at first and then an alien low drone that didn't belong here and set his nerves instantly on alert.

"What is that?" he said.

Webster listened and the noise became more distinct. "Helicopter. It's coming from the north."

The north was Russia.

"Fuck," said Hammer. "She made it back."

"Really?"

"No one saw us cross the border."

"Your fire may not have helped."

"It's her. They wouldn't care about a fire." He stood up and scanned the sky, but could see nothing. "She's desperate now. We need to get down to the tree line."

Up here they were completely exposed, two alien shapes on a field of white waiting to be picked out, with no cover for another quarter of a mile at least. Hammer helped Webster up and they set off, forcing a fast pace, the sound growing louder and clearer until they could hear the purr of blades from beyond the ridge above them.

From time to time Hammer turned to check on Webster, who was now limping heavily and grimacing with every step.

"Not far now," he said, but to Webster the trees must have seemed a mile off.

In an instant the throbbing opened up into a roar and they found them-selves looking up at the helicopter as it flew over the ridge, heading away from them toward the border, oblivious to the startled figures below. Blue and red lights flashed and lit up the markings on its belly.

"Switch off your flashlight," said Hammer.

"That's Russian."

"So is she."

Hammer thought it was going to cross the border but it stayed close to the ridge, scanning the hillside with a powerful beam, before turning over the valley in a full loop until it was heading right for them.

"Fuck," said Hammer, and flattened himself on the path, waiting for the light to play over his back. Webster, more slowly, did the same. Seconds passed, and then the buzz of the blades changed timbre, and Hammer lifted his head to see the helicopter settling slowly toward the river about half a mile ahead.

He got up into a crouch and watched as it came to land on a small patch of level ground by the water. The engine noise died and the blades whirred down, and by the light reflected off the snow Hammer saw four men get out, and with them two dogs.

"We have to go," he said, turning and giving his hand to Webster.

"Go where?"

"Back. Down to the river. We just passed the turning. The way you came."

Behind them, not so far away, flashlights flashed on the snow and orders were shouted into the night. Even Hammer knew that they were Russian.

"What are they saying?"

"Shoot anyone you see," said Webster, with fear in his voice, and a new energy.

TWENTY-ONE

Rushing now, silent, going only by the light of the moon and no longer worrying about the drop or even conscious of it, they went back up the hill until they came to the split in the path and took the left fork, turning back on themselves down toward the river. Their tracks would give them away but then so would their scent, and their only hope was to get to the water before the men behind them. They loped on, and no matter how hard Webster pushed himself they both knew that their lead was narrowing.

"Do you have a plan?" said Webster, breathing hard.

"I have an idea."

"Then go ahead and see if it works."

Hammer hesitated, and then realized there was sense in this.

"You got your gun?"

Webster nodded.

"They shoot, or they get within thirty yards, shoot back. Otherwise let's be quiet."

They exchanged a look.

"And keep going, for fuck's sake. We're close."

But he had no idea how close they were; how long until he reached the water; whether what he hoped to find there would be there. He went with great reluctance, wondering whether, far from rescuing his friend, he had merely brought him to a different place to die.

He ran now, glanced behind him continually, risked his footing at every turn of the path. The men behind were gaining on Webster, no question, and he felt a horrible sickness at the inevitability of the pursuit. He wavered: should he have stayed and shot it out? No. These men, whoever they were, were professionals, and he was a reluctant novice. All he could do was go on.

The river rose slowly beside him, and after five minutes he was close enough to see it rippling over pebbles in the shallows. He shone his flashlight along the bank but saw nothing useful and kept going. Behind him, Webster and the Russians were out of sight, concealed by a collar of land, and Hammer waited with dread for the sound of the first shot.

Then there it was, pulled up onto a little beach that was like a widening of the path. A flat-bottomed boat, hull uppermost, covered in a thin layer of snow. He ran to it and turned it over. It was roughly made of wood and along every joint painted lavishly with tar to compensate for the workmanship; underneath there were two wooden paddles, crossed on the stones.

Hammer dragged it the few feet to the water, leaving it as close as he could without fear of it floating away, threw the paddles inside, and went back to smooth the snow where the boat had been sitting. Then he ran back toward Webster, hardly conscious of his pounding heart, barely wanting to know what he would find round each corner.

From somewhere beyond him he heard Webster's voice in a cry of pain, followed immediately by shouts a little further off. He ran faster still, struggling for purchase on the cold ground, seeing just enough in the dark, willing each turn in the path to be the last. Finally, he found him, trying to stand by pulling himself up on an outcrop of rock. Two flashlights flickered against the blackness behind him, much nearer than before. Hammer put his arm round his shoulder and whispered.

"You OK?"

"My leg. I can't . . ."

"It's OK. Lean on me."

Webster was almost a head taller, but Hammer was strong, and his blood was flowing, and there was no other way. With their three good legs they set off, Webster against the slope, Hammer by the diminishing drop, a strange lopsided creature hobbling at speed through the night. Webster's weight bore down on him and somehow he held it up. There was no more looking back; but he felt the men behind him, could almost hear the dogs sniffing and straining. Webster's breath was quick and shallow in his ear.

"Ike, you go on."

"Bullshit."

The path widened by the river and Hammer went faster still, using all the strength he could call on, until he was almost carrying his burden, and at last they were by the little boat. He looked behind him and saw the faint glare of flashlights in the sky above the final turn in the path.

"Get in. Stay low." He pushed the boat into the water.

With Hammer's help, Webster climbed into the boat and lay down weakly on the bare wood. Bending down with his hands on the stern, Hammer ran the boat through the first shallows, and when the freezing water was up to his knees jumped in, rocking the thing violently and ending up kneeling beside Webster. He turned to look, and saw no light; the Russians must be hard by the last turn; at any minute they would appear. He moved to the front of the boat, where it narrowed, and paddled as hard as he could, two strokes one side, two the other, guiding them into the middle of the river, checking over his shoulder all the while.

The waters here were still, and the boat hardly swift, and no matter how hard he worked the brisk escape that Hammer had imagined seemed becalmed. He contemplated jumping out and pushing them into the main channel, where the river raced, but after a few firm strokes the two Russians appeared, one flashlight trained on the ground, the other tracking the path ahead and the river below them. Hammer stopped paddling, crouched down, and let the boat drift. From his pocket he took his gun.

Along the path the two Russians went, quickly but paying thorough attention to the ground, until they were barely twenty yards away, and above the soft babble of the river he could hear them talking. Like the Georgians who had held Webster, they appeared military but wore standard winter clothes: woolen hats, bulky jackets. Where the path widened they stopped to inspect the ground where the boat had been left, and where the footprints they had been following ran out. One shone his flashlight up the slope above, and the other began to sweep his across the river in the direction of the boat.

Lying as low as he could, Hammer looked over the side, raised his gun, and wondered whether he had any chance of hitting a man at this distance, in the dark, while moving. Hardly moving; but then he felt the boat's front end swing round, and the rippling of the water grow louder. The current was taking them; the boat settled into it, gaining speed, and Hammer ducked down out of sight.

The flashlight swept over and past them, lighting up the trees on the far bank, and Hammer briefly thought that their low craft had been mistaken for a piece of driftwood, or not seen at all. But the light swung back and came to rest on them, in the same moment that a voice shouted from the bank and a shot ripped through the air above their heads. Before Hammer could collect himself the wood by his ear splintered and tore, and a third shot followed it, hitting the boat below the waterline. Hammer recoiled from the noise and the shock of it; Webster held his hands behind his head, his forearms over his ears. Icy water started pouring in.

"Motherfucker," said Hammer.

They had distance on their side, and the advantage was growing, but the boat gave no protection and a single decent shot might do for either of them. He raised his head, aimed, not carefully, and fired twice before dropping back down. The men were running along the bank, failing to stay level but still close enough. Three more shots came and one hit the boat, passing straight through an inch above Webster's thigh.

"Jesus!" said Webster. "We need to shoot the fuckers."

Not a chance, thought Hammer, though he didn't say it. But he peeked again, and fired twice at the source of the light that still held them. A different sort of shouting followed.

"They didn't like that," said Webster, leaning up on his arm and firing twice, waywardly. Water was streaming into the boat, which was now sitting dangerously low. Two shots whistled by, so close Hammer could imagine their flight through the air.

"Do that again," said Hammer, as Webster sank back beside him. "I need a second."

Webster collected himself, then raised himself up and shot, twice again.

In that instant Hammer shone his flashlight downstream and in a flash lit up the bank. They were near to it now, a mere ten yards, but the current was speeding them along and drawing them no closer. He clicked off the flashlight.

"And once more, when I say."

A second passed, and another. Hammer could hear the men running on the far bank, cursing and slipping.

"Now. Hold on."

Webster lifted his head and fired. Hammer stuck his paddle deep into the water and the boat, swinging around it, headed under the trees on the bank. The fear Hammer felt was physical. It was in his arms and his legs, in his exposed back as he raised himself up and grabbed for one of the low branches that overhung the water. He found one and, while the boat carried on its course beneath, held on somehow, losing and then righting his balance and bringing the boat in to the shore before it could get away from him. A bullet splashed with strange softness into the shallow water.

In one movement he jumped out, pulled the boat under the cover of the trees, and beached it, scraping it onto pebbles.

"Come on."

Webster, still lying down, fired a final shot and at an awkward crouch followed his friend.

"Up," he whispered. "Quickly."

Hammer took him by the arm and guided him up the slope. The Russians seemed to have lost sight of them; the flashlight beam flitted along the bank, back and forth.

"Keep going."

The wood was dense here, and soon there was no light from the moon. Hammer felt his way, bringing Webster after him. When they were sure that they were hidden, they stopped and sat.

"You're a genius," said Webster, with the last of his breath. His voice was thin, pained.

"If your friends had hidden their boat I'd be a dead genius."

They were silent for a while. Hammer's trousers stuck to him, and whenever he moved were freshly cold. The white light searched the trees then stopped for a moment some way beneath them. A shot sounded. The light moved on, further away upstream. Another shot.

"What now?" whispered Webster, picking up pine needles and letting them drop through his fingers onto the ground. Their eyes grew a little used to the dark.

"We walk," said Hammer.

TWENTY-TWO

They didn't walk so much as slip, scramble, grope from one tree to the next.

Before, they had been within half a mile of the border, but they had just gone at least a mile in the wrong direction. A mile and a half, thought Hammer, was really nothing—he ran three times as far each morning, even on a gentle day—but he didn't run with an injured companion, in almost full darkness, along a steep slope through a stiff mesh of dry branches, and after half an hour he was scratched and exhausted. The only benefit of it was that Webster, beside him, could stagger from tree to tree without falling.

After a while it felt safe. The Russians fired three more shots into the woods, each one far away and speculative. When they stopped and listened, Hammer and Webster could hear their pursuers talking, discussing what to do next, and eventually saw them by the light of their flashlights making their way back in the direction of the helicopter.

Hammer checked his watch. Half past twelve. Six hours since he had left Diklo, and heaven knows how many more until his return. He wondered whether he might leave Webster here and come back for him later when everything was calmer, but dismissed the thought. It was rash, illogical. Things would not get calmer. His lot was set.

To mark their progress, and to give Webster hope, he devised a schedule. They would walk for twenty minutes and rest for five. They still had some food left, and a little water. If they ran out, he could always drop down to the river and fill their bottle. They would be OK. There was no hurry.

That was one of the lies he told Webster; he kept to himself his visions of Vekua's return to the village, his calculation that it would make sense for her to keep Natela alive, his fear that his ability to figure these things out had long ago deserted him. While they made their slow way through the brush every part of him was straining to be with her, but he didn't let it show. When it had been Webster at risk he had felt fear, but not like this. This started in his chest and spread up into his throat and down through his body; it consumed him.

His other lie was about their journey, and how far they had to go. Perhaps it was a mile and a half to the border, but it was another mile at least up to Diklo and he had no idea how far they would have to go before they could cross the river back to the other side. He knew of no more boats.

Two lies, then, and one unspoken subject. Very plainly, the Russians had come to kill them. For a while it hadn't been convenient, or appropriate, but now their time had come. Something had changed, and as they went Hammer did his best to make sense of it.

Across the river on the opposite bank were the four Russians—three, perhaps, if one had been hit. By now, if they had any sense, they would have alerted the soldiers in the border station high up above this point, and they would be coming down through the trees to block the way. It was a long way down, but unless they were as drunk as Vekua had made out, which he doubted, they would make good time.

There wasn't long. Hammer kept pushing forward, quietly encouraging Webster, supporting him when he could. Their only advantages, as far as he could see, were the darkness and the density of the trees. Little else.

Now he kept one eye on the ground above him, and scanned the darkness for any sign of light. Each time he looked there was just blackness. Not ahead, not above, not below, except when a glint of moonlight reflected from the water found its way through the trees.

And then there was something. The merest glow on the hill, a faint flickering movement up the slope some way ahead. Hammer stopped for a moment, pleading fatigue, and watched it carefully. It was coming down and toward them, not quickly but with a steady inevitability.

"We have to go," he whispered.

"What is it?"

"Look up there."

The glow was hardening into two distinct lights.

"Fuck. Which way?"

"Ahead. There's nowhere else. Quick and quiet as you can."

Twigs crunched under their feet and sometimes Webster struggled to contain a stifled cry of pain. Whoever was coming for them was making easier work of the terrain, and before long it became clear to Hammer that unless he had underestimated the remaining distance; they were about to be cut off. To go back was hopeless: there was no shelter there, nowhere to hide, just hundreds of miles of mountain and wilderness. They could try to cross the river again, but he had no idea how, or how to get past the Russians on the other side. And above them was a climb steeper than Webster could attempt, even if they'd known where it led. No. Their only chance was to go on, to push through, to pray that somehow they made it across. And with each minute, no matter how hard he willed it, he saw the odds lengthen irrevocably.

There was no resting now, but when he was certain that they would be blocked he stopped and waited for Webster to catch up. The flashlights were close, perhaps fifty yards up the slope and another hundred ahead. They had five minutes, at most.

"How many bullets have you got left?" said Hammer.

"I have the box."

Webster was gasping for breath and the words barely came out. In the deep night his face was as pale and insubstantial as the moonlight on the river.

"We can't get past them. I'm going to climb for a bit, get above them, then take them out."

Webster said nothing.

"It's OK. They can't see us and I can see them. Give me your gun. You have this one."

Webster felt in his pocket and handed the gun to Hammer, who took it with that same thrill of repugnance and excitement.

"Stay right here," he said, but before he could set off up the hill he heard a sound, a hiss, somewhere close below them.

"Was that you?"

The sound came again, closer, oddly human in this bleak place. Hammer's finger found its way inside the trigger guard of the gun, and he squinted down to the river. There was a shape there, a solid blackness against the general dark, and it was moving. Beside him, Webster stiffened. Hammer gripped the gun.

"Ike." The hiss had become the quietest whisper, and Hammer took a moment to realize who it had to be.

"Come on," he said, and took Webster's arm.

Irodi waited for them to reach him, and then without a word set off down the hill, skipping noiselessly over the ground and sliding between the trees. After a minute he stopped and waited for them, pointing toward the border. He said something softly in Georgian, and Hammer realized that they were standing on a path that went wide and clear and level about twenty yards above the river. Somehow, in their rush up from the river, they had missed it.

"Oh good," said Hammer, and checked Irodi on the arm as he was about to set off. More light reached them here, and drawing Webster to him he showed Irodi his injured leg.

"OK," said Irodi, understanding at once, and without hesitating squatted down and gestured for Webster to come to him. As he approached, Irodi pushed his shoulder into Webster's groin and stood, lifting him off the ground as a father might a child. Over his other shoulder was slung his antique rifle.

"OK," he whispered, and started walking, so fast it was almost a run. Hammer jogged just behind him and watched the hill for the flashlights, which were now so close he could see the branches they picked out as they swept the wood.

When it seemed only a matter of moments before they must be discovered, Irodi slowed, and held up his free hand to caution Hammer. Carefully he let down Webster, motioned with a flat hand and some emphatic pointing that the two of them should wait here and then continue, and darted up into the woods. Hammer and Webster watched the two soldiers descending inevitably. For an instant, one appeared in the flashlight beam of the other, and Hammer saw olive green combat trousers and a thick green military jacket. When they drew level, they would scan the path, and when that happened the only thing preventing their discovery would be the trees they were crouching behind. Taking only shallow breaths, guns in hand, they waited.

From somewhere above them came a noise like a dry branch snapping; it took Hammer a moment to realize that it was a shot. The two soldiers, briefly panicked, stopped and turned, frozen, half expecting a second shot that didn't come. One extinguished his flashlight and shouted at the other to do the same, and they disappeared. From the other side of the river voices shouted in Russian and the two dogs started to bark.

For half a minute all was still. Then the beam of a single flashlight streaked across the wood and went out again. Hammer could hear whispering, urgent voices. There was movement, and again the thin band of light flashed over the trees, from a different point, and another shot sounded, fuller and louder than the first. It was met with a third from deep in the woods, and this time the two soldiers both fired, without aiming, up the slope.

Hammer tapped Webster on the arm and together they set off, Hammer in his own exhaustion supporting his friend as best he could. From the darkness above them came scraps of scared conversation and the familiar sound of twigs breaking underfoot, then more shots. They kept going, quietly and steadily, hardly daring to look anywhere but ahead, and to Hammer it felt like crossing the landslide: that each step might be the last. On the opposite bank they could see men milling uncertainly round the helicopter, looking in their direction, evidently trying to decide what to do.

But step followed step, until at last they were well beyond the guards, and the confusion in the woods was behind them. The two Russian guards had begun by moving cautiously toward the sound of the gun, but now they seemed fixed to the spot, as lost and helpless as Hammer and Webster had been only minutes before. Shots still rang through the trees but the answering fire was less intense. They went on, yard by yard, a good distance, until a silent presence came running through the trees to their left and dropped onto the path beside them.

"Sakartvelo," said Irodi, putting his hand on Hammer's shoulder.

"Thank Christ for that," said Webster, letting Irodi take over from Hammer in supporting him.

"What did he say?"

"Georgia. This is Georgia."

"Ask him for me," said Hammer. "How's Natela?"

TWENTY-THREE

Half a mile further on was Vano's 4 x 4, parked on a spit of pebble and sand above the river, which was shallow enough here to be forded, and as he drove Irodi explained in broken Russian that on hearing the helicopter he had come down to see if he might help, and at first had meant to pick off a Russian or two from the woods; but when he heard the American crashing about in the trees and saw the border guards heading toward him he had changed his plan. Probably the Russians would not follow; the only ones who came into Georgia were Dagestanis, and these were white Russians, military, and keen to keep their operation contained. To see such people here was rare.

"Ask him about Natela," said Hammer. "There were shots."

Natela was OK. They had heard gunfire and it scared her. She had gone outside to see where it had come from; Irodi had gone to follow her and found her arguing with the guard Vekua had stationed there. He wanted her to go back in the house, and when she refused and carried on walking he had fired his rifle in the air and made it clear she was going nowhere. After that no one was to leave. She was fine. Angry but fine.

"So who's there now?"

Vano was there.

"How did you get away?"

The guard was a city boy. He didn't have a clue.

In the stiff front seat, which even over these rough tracks felt unimaginably comfortable, Hammer fought sleep. His body had had enough, and his mind was so full of colliding images that thought was hard; but he forced himself, and continued to quiz Irodi. Communicating through the exhausted Webster as best he could, Hammer explained what had happened on the mountainside. Yes, Vekua could make it, Irodi said, without a flashlight, perhaps. It was not icy yet and there had been a little moon. But up there you must be a goat; one slip was the end.

Hammer told Irodi to hurry. She was in Diklo now, he was sure.

He had no plan. If they found Natela safe he would take her away and somehow arrange for a helicopter to take them down from the mountains. Then throw himself on the protection of the embassy, perhaps, or have Iosava find them a safe passage out. That was the extent of his thinking. If she wasn't safe, he didn't know what he would do.

How quiet Diklo was under its coat of snow, and how Hammer longed to fall into that tiny warm bed with Natela and sleep until spring; but the moment he stepped down from the car the cold air brought him to himself and forced him awake. After a brief, whispered conversation the three of them agreed that Hammer and Webster would stay put while Irodi went the back way to the house and found out what was going on inside. If Vekua wasn't there, they would take Natela and go. If she was, they would talk again.

Irodi left, moving without effort or sound into the blackness of the houses.

"How much are you paying him?" said Webster.

"Nothing like enough."

"You should hire him."

Webster still had the stick Hammer had found for him in the woods and by leaning on it now rested his injured leg.

"He won't be long," said Hammer.

"I'm fine."

It should have taken him three minutes at the most, four if he was going a long way round. After five, Hammer began to be concerned.

"I'm not sure this is good."

As he said it a voice broke the quiet, cutting clear through the night.

"Mr. Hammer! You can come now. All your friends are here."

Hammer considered his options and found them wanting.

"That her?" said Webster.

"That's her. Any ideas?"

"Improvise."

Hammer gave him his arm for support and together they walked to Vano's house.

The guard was still there, shifting his weight from foot to foot to keep out the cold. As Hammer and Webster came within sight he pointed his gun at them and said something in Georgian.

"He wants weapons," said Webster.

"I imagine he does," said Hammer, and fished one of the two guns from his pockets. Webster handed his own over and the guard patted him down before moving on to Hammer, stopping when he reached his waist.

"My memory's going," said Hammer, as the guard pulled out the second pistol. Finally happy, he followed them inside the house.

At the head of the table was Vano, stiff with dignified rage, and by him Eka and Natela. Irodi was sitting at the foot, and gave Hammer a look of apology as he came in. Vekua was standing beyond the table by the sink, pistol in hand. Next to her were the two rifles.

"Sit, please," said Vekua.

Hammer shook his head. "You want to tell me why you're holding these good people? What did they do?"

Vekua smiled. It was the same simple smile that she had used to charm him when they had first met, but behind it now there were signs of real agitation—the muscles were tight in her jaw, and her lips pressed firmly together. She spoke deliberately, but without conviction.

"I am not holding anyone. I have asked everyone to remain here and I have taken their guns, which I am entitled to do. As an officer of the law. Please, sit."

Hammer looked at Webster and they sat down opposite each other.

"You OK?" said Hammer, taking off his gloves and putting his hand on Natela's thigh. She nodded, but said nothing.

"I'm sorry about this," said Hammer, looking from Vano to Eka. Vano responded with a taut nod.

"So you have your friend," said Vekua. "He exists."

"You knew he existed."

"What happened after you tried to kill me?"

"Excuse me?"

"You tried to drag me off the mountain. Then you left me to die."

"You seem OK."

Vekua steadily held his eye, the smile gone.

"He was where I thought?"

"More or less."

"What did you do with the guards?"

"I did what I do. I bought the guards."

"You bought them?"

"I paid them, more than you were paying them, and now they're mine. They'll say anything I want, but the truth'll do. That they were working for Koba and that he was working for you. How they set the bomb off. Killed Karlo. The whole thing."

Vekua nodded several times, as if something finally made sense.

"OK. Enough. This is bullshit, of course. What happened to your leg?"

Blood was showing through the cloth. Without looking up, Webster said, "I slipped coming down. Hit a rock."

She turned back to Hammer. "You and your friend, I will take you to Tbilisi, and you will be questioned about your part in the Gori bombing."

Hammer let out a long sigh and shook his head.

"You know, Elene, maybe you have the energy for it but I'm too tired to lie. Too tired. I didn't pay the guards. We had to shoot them. I had to shoot them. I didn't want to but there was no other way. I hope they weren't dear to you. But it's OK because I reckon we have enough already, and we're not the only ones who know it."

Vekua was frowning now. Before he went on, Hammer turned and exchanged a look with Natela; he wanted to tell her that this would all be all right, he was going to look after her, but the next two minutes would be difficult. Trust me, in short.

"No one's coming with you. I trusted my life to you once already today and that's enough. I'm going to explain where we stand, you and I, but first it's important you hear something. Most important thing you ever heard. Everything I tell you, I've already dictated to a woman in my company in London, and she wrote it down, and if anything happens to me she's going to send it to the editor of the *Tribune* and a few other influential people. And she'll post it online somewhere for good measure. You understand the lay of the land?"

"There is nowhere for you to call."

"No. There is. There's a nice little spot about two miles west of here and we just came that way. How d'you think I got Natela up here?"

Vekua considered it, and tried one last way round.

"You are a bold man. In Russia you killed two men. You tried to kill me. This in return for my help. I should arrest you, leave you in a Georgian jail for ten years. But the country does not need this disturbance. I will take you to Tbilisi, and you will fly home."

"How did you know there were two of them?"

To her credit, she held his eye.

"Come." Vekua picked up the rifles. "We go."

"You're not there yet, are you? OK. Your world is falling apart. It was always going to. That's what happens to people like you."

"Get up."

"I'm not finished. I have a proposal for you. You'll want to hear it, because it's the only way you can get out of this mess."

Vekua was still now, all her attention on Hammer.

"For this to work," he said, "I need to know what you've done. Some pretty bad things, I imagine. I think you killed all those people in Gori. I saw you kill Koba tonight. He was yours, right? All the way through?"

Vekua said nothing.

"And Karlo?"

Hammer stared at her, wanting her to acknowledge part of this, to show the smallest crack.

"My point is, there's no going back, Elene. Your future's across the border."

So focused was he on Vekua, so absorbed in the contest, that he had forgotten Natela. He sensed movement at the corner of his eye, saw her stand
up from the bench and lunge at Vekua. In her hand she had a heavy earth-
enware jug that had been on the table, and as she moved past Vano she
swung it hard at Vekua's head, shouting in Georgian.

Vekua was no more prepared for it than Hammer, but reacted quickly
enough to raise an arm, so that her thick coat took the force of the blow.

"Natela, no!" shouted Hammer.

She didn't hear him. With her free hand she reached for Vekua's throat,
and as they struggled Hammer saw Vekua bring her pistol up into Natela's
side. He stood, expecting each moment the dead echoless noise he had
heard too many times that night. Vano was on his feet, his carved face helpless. The guard moved his gun from one to the other, shouting in Georgian.

No noise came. Just Vekua's voice, less certain than it had ever sounded.
Something in Georgian, then English.

"I will shoot if she does not stop."

Vano was next to them, and now he put one hand on Natela's shoulder
and with the other tried to pull her gently away. In the silence he spoke
softly, until her grip on Vekua's neck relaxed and he was able to separate
them.

Warily, they moved apart; they stared at each other for a moment, Natela
still taut and ready to attack, Vekua filled with adrenaline and menace.
Vano said something more to Natela, and after a long, final look at her adversary she began to turn away. Hammer saw something in Vekua's expression change: menace gave way to viciousness, and with the pistol still in her
hand she hooked her fist into the side of Natela's head. Vano watched her
reel away, then turned to Vekua, and Hammer thought his ancient instincts
of hospitality and fight were going to get the better of him; but Vekua waved
the pistol in his face, and motioned for him to sit down, and after several
long moments, he did.

Hammer had his arm round Natela now and guided her back to the
table. Blood had started on a bad cut at the base of her ear. Ignoring
Vekua, Eka stood and left the room, returning with a clean white hand-

kerchief, which she passed to Hammer. Hammer thanked her, and glared at Vekua.

"You should have kicked her off the mountain," said Webster.

"I wasn't sure then."

"Enough," said Vekua, her pistol out in front and her composure partly restored. "We go. All of you."

TWENTY-FOUR

Out of the village they marched, all six of them, with the guns leveled at their backs and Vekua's flashlight playing over the ground at their feet. Hammer walked beside Natela, who lit a cigarette and drew deeply on it in the cold; Irodi helped Webster along, and behind them came Vano and Eka. Vano looked back over his shoulder from time to time to let Vekua know he hadn't forgotten her. The sky was clear, and under the moon the snow shone with unnatural brightness, picking out each figure in monochrome.

Hammer fell into thought, but every idea stumbled on an objection. Something had to be done before they reached the helicopter, because as soon as they were in it Vekua's control would be complete. She could do anything with them. If he only knew what she was planning. If he could be sure that her henchman was an unwitting part of it all. If he'd had the sense to hide his gun.

"You get the chance," he whispered to Natela, "I want you to tell the pilot that his boss is a traitor. Convince him. I'll try to keep her attention elsewhere. Tell him she's the one who killed the people in Gori."

Natela looked at him and understood.

After a hundred yards they turned off the road through a line of trees into a flat field where the snow was deeper, and Hammer saw a little way off the awkward, drooping shape of an old military helicopter.

"Keep going," said Vekua, in Georgian and English, her voice stony in both.

She couldn't shoot them all here. Too much to clear up. And if the pilot was not one of hers, she'd have to shoot him, too. Hammer's guess was that she would take the pressing problems away to deal with on her own terms, and when she had better resources and more time come back for the villagers. They wouldn't be going anywhere, after all.

But this was logical, and he wondered whether Vekua was still operating according to logic. Her tight little plan had come loose, and she like Hammer was now making it up.

Still some way short of the helicopter he stopped and turned, planting his feet in the snow.

"I want to talk to you alone."

Everyone came to a stop.

"Keep going," said Vekua.

"Not until you and I have talked."

Vekua held the gun at arm's length and pointed it at Hammer's head.

"Go."

"You know who I am. You know what I can do for you. But I can only discuss it alone."

As he said the words, he became conscious of movement and sound behind her, a faint disturbance in the darkness. Vekua turned and stepped slightly aside, and past her Hammer saw something bounding through the deep powder at an unlikely speed.

Vano shouted at his dog. Hammer could see its distinctly wolfish look and its bared teeth. Vano shouted again; he could have been telling it to stop or to charge. The dog barked as it came, a terrifying noise against the silence. Off balance, Vekua stumbled backward, her boots caught in the snow, and as she fell the dog sprang for her from a great distance, its jaws open and ready. Another movement, to Hammer's left; he barely caught it but he heard the gunshot, registered the flash from the barrel of the pilot's pistol, and saw the dog stunned in its flight as the bullet passed through its neck.

It landed heavily on Vekua; Irodi ran to it as she struggled to pull herself clear. The pilot shouted at him to step back but Irodi ignored him, holding the dog's head and talking to it softly. Vekua stood by and stared as if in shock. Then he looked up at her and issued a command, in a cold hard voice Hammer hadn't heard him use before, and she raised her gun. Irodi said some final words, stroked the dog's ear, and stood, stepping back. He nodded to Vekua and she pulled the trigger.

For an instant, no one moved and no one spoke. Then it was over, and Vekua's gun was up once more.

"Go. You three, move." And then to Irodi, who went to stand by his mother: "Sad aris is? Where is the old man?"

Hammer looked around. Vano was gone.

Vekua had the pilot stay with Eka and Irodi, and marched the others the last fifty yards to the helicopter. Hammer watched her calculating: forget the old man. Get out of here before he can do any damage.

"You need to listen to me, Elene. You could do well out of this."

She waved her gun at Webster, who was struggling to get into the helicopter. "In. Now."

"His leg's hurt."

"I will shoot the other if he does not get in."

Hammer did his best to help Webster in through the sliding door, but he had left his gloves on the table in the house, and the metal was icy on his skin. Scanning the field, he could see no trace of Vano, not even his footsteps in the snow.

She shouted something in Georgian, and the pilot slowly walked away from Irodi, backward at first, then looking over his shoulder, then purposefully ahead to the cockpit.

"Now you." Vekua gestured to Natela, who hesitated.

"The thing is, Elene," said Hammer, leaning in to her and not quite whispering, "if it's money you like, I can make you rich. If it's something else, that same money could accomplish a lot."

She smiled, relaxing a touch, and then her face started at a sudden noise and she turned at the same time as Hammer to see the pilot sprawled in the snow not ten yards from them, and Vano barely visible against the outline of the village with a rifle at his shoulder. Irodi swept his mother to the ground, shielding her body; Hammer tried to get himself between Vekua and Natela, but Vekua had her, gripped by the sleeve, the pistol at her throat.

"Vano! Don't shoot!" screamed Hammer, and prayed he'd be understood.

Vekua looked about her, began to back away, shouted something behind her.

"Tell them. I will shoot."

"Niet!" shouted Hammer, waving his hands. "Ara! Don't shoot!"

Vekua walked backward now, away from the helicopter and toward the road, her gun still pressed into Natela's neck. More helpless than he had ever felt, Hammer watched them go in the eerie light. He had nothing left.

"What do I do?"

Webster shook his head. "Follow at a distance. That's all you can do."

"She'll shoot."

"No she won't. Not until she's sure she can get away."

"You have faith in her sense of logic."

"What else have we got?"

Irodi had his arm round his mother; Vekua passed them and continued steadily on.

"When?" said Hammer.

"When they get to the road."

Moving as one creature, Vekua and Natela passed through the trees that lined the road and turned toward the village. At a wary jog Hammer set off, and when he reached Irodi, beckoned for him to follow. Irodi looked at his mother and Eka waved him on.

He felt better with Irodi. A little. Together they went swiftly to the road and then slowed to Vekua's pace, creeping as softly as they could in the snow, waiting for her to turn and sweep the flashlight behind her. But her mind was on the village, and escape, and she kept it shining ahead.

Irodi's 4 x 4 was parked by the first house. Vekua went straight to it, let go of Natela, and opened the door. With the flashlight in one hand and the gun pointing as best she could back at Natela, she searched, sending the beam flashing about the dark cabin. Hammer felt Irodi's hand on his arm and looked up to see him holding the key.

Even at that distance Hammer could sense Vekua's anger when she eventually stepped out, and it sent fresh cold through him. He didn't want her desperate. She raised her gun hand at the car, shot one of the tires, and disappeared with Natela into the blackness between the houses.

Irodi began to run and Hammer followed him, feeling slow and old and out of ideas. Where they should have been there was only the sound of his boots going clumsily in the snow and the burn of his lungs as they struggled to take in enough of the frozen air.

Between the houses of the village there was barely any light, so Hammer followed the sound and sense of Irodi, just making out his form, which now stopped still to listen. Above the sound of his breath and his heart Hammer heard a rhythm that he recognized but couldn't place. It grew louder, until Irodi's hand pulled him sharply from the middle of the track and the dark weight of a horse thudded past them, already going at speed.

Irodi shouted at him, pressed something into his hand, and slapped him with urgency on the shoulder. Go. Hammer went, back the way he had come, slipping and staggering toward the car, yanking the door open, and scrambling in. Fumbling, he found the ignition, turned the key, found the lights, and drove in a wide arc away from Diklo and out onto the road, the beams picking out Vano as he helped Eka back across the great field of white.

On the snow, with one tire out, the car was wayward, tugging first right then left, and Hammer worked hard to respond. Carefully, he picked up speed and watched the furthest point of the headlights' reach for any sign, concentrating so hard that when Irodi's horse moved past him it made him start. He hadn't seen him ride like this, pressed forward in the saddle, head down, improbably fast. A rifle was slung across his back.

Hammer did his best to keep up but Irodi's horse pulled away. So sure it was on the road. And then he saw them: at the limits of the light, a strange dark shape.

They moved closer; Hammer could see Natela's green coat and her hair in the wind. As Irodi drew near he left the road and started to flank the other horse, heading out wide up an incline until he was riding level and higher. Vekua turned to look at him, waved her gun but kept riding. Now that Hammer could see her, she looked less than steady in the saddle.

Slowly, Irodi came down the bank, keeping slightly ahead now, so that the other horse was forced left, off the road, and across the field that sloped gradually away into darkness. Hammer's mouth was dry again as he followed, acrid with fear.

"What the fuck is he doing?"

The pace slowed in the deeper snow. Irodi continued to push the horse from the right, and signaled now for Hammer to move up on the other side. Where was this leading? He must have something in mind. Surely. As he drew nearer he saw that the horse Vekua had taken was Shakari.

Abruptly, she slowed, turned to her left, and pulled up, her breath pluming in the headlights. Vekua drove her heels into her flanks but she had had enough. Angrily, she threw her head back and neighed, a mournful sound.

Behind her the snow finished in a stark line, and beyond there was only black. Hammer knew where they were: at the top of a long ridge that curved round back to the village and fell away in a scrubby drop of fifty feet at least, not quite sheer.

Vekua looked down, looked back at Irodi and the car. She had nowhere to go.

Hammer turned off the engine, breathed steadily to compose himself, and opened the door. This was his time. He could make this work.

Shielding her eyes from the headlights, Vekua pulled her gun from the pocket of her coat, twisted around, and pushed it into Natela, who looked to Hammer with fearful eyes. The horse had no saddle, and seemed too small to support the two of them.

Irodi reached for the rifle on his back but Hammer raised a hand to tell him to leave it. All was silent except for the panting of the horse.

"Give me the key," shouted Vekua. "I will get down, you will stand back."

"The key's in the ignition, Elene. It's all yours. You go. You leave Natela here."

"I need her."

Hammer took two steps toward them, his palms up, ever so slowly.

"You don't need her. Take the car. The road down there, it leads to the river, and from there you can walk to the border. Cross the border, Elene. That's the country you serve. They'll look after you."

He took another step. Vekua swung the pistol away from Natela, who turned in the saddle and grabbed at it, knocking Vekua's hands away and sending the shot off over Hammer's head into the night. The loud dead crack sounded through the night; Shakari shied and backed away, swinging her head from side to side, her hooves scrabbling at the snow and then at air. She sank first, then slipped away, and with a single scream Natela and Vekua went with her.

Hammer saw the empty space and felt that he was tumbling, that he had fallen with them.

Before he could move, Irodi had jumped from his horse and was running to the edge. Hammer went to him, barely conscious of his movements, and together they stood hopelessly searching the blackness.

"Light," said Hammer. "We need light."

Irodi understood and left him.

"Natela!" In his mind he heard her voice, so clearly. The shape of it. It was the shape of her. It couldn't be gone. It wasn't finished. "Natela!"

Irodi was by his side again, flashlight in hand. He put a hand on Hammer's back and played the beam over the bone gray of the wiry trees and brush that covered the sheer slope. Where the horse had fallen the snow had been disturbed, and at the bottom by the road Hammer thought he could make out three dark shapes lying still.

"Oh God."

There was hardly enough light to see. He took the flashlight from Irodi and searched every foot, forcing himself to be systematic as the thundering grew louder in his head.

A noise. A rustling. Close, something settling. Irodi heard it, too, and guided the flashlight toward it. In among the gray and the white of the scrub was a patch of green, about twenty feet down, almost obscured.

As Hammer called Natela's name, he heard the sound of the car's engine and then Irodi was there, crouching down in the headlights with a rope in his hands. He looped it through the bumper and made to tie one end round his waist but Hammer stopped him. He had to be the first to know. Either way, he had to be the first.

Irodi tied the knot for him, checked that it would hold, and with a grave nod of respect and hope stepped back, bracing himself and paying out the rope as Hammer took his first step backward into space.

At first the slope was clear and he hung against Irodi's weight, and then he was in thick brush, and it was as if the world had been flipped on its side and he was climbing backward through the woods he had left just an hour before. The dry wood gave and cracked as he went down. Wedging his feet against a sturdier trunk, he took the flashlight from his pocket and turned to shine it below. He could see her now, suspended in a tangle of branches denser than the rest, as if they had come together to catch her as she fell.

"Natela," he said. She was so close. Her face was turned away from him, her head pushed into her body at an angle that caused the fear to start in him afresh. "Natela, it's OK."

But she didn't answer, and, putting the flashlight in his mouth, Hammer leaned against the rope once more and took the last few steps down, until finally he was beside her, searching for a hold, his breath blooming in the shaking light. He watched it, his heart beating hard, and wished it was hers.

"Natela."

She was so still. The branches that had caught her now seemed to claim her.

He shone the flashlight full on her face, which was pale but for a gauze of thin scratches. The light found no breath; not a wisp. A great emptiness took hold of him, as if the world had just changed.

"Natela," he said once more, in a different tone, and reached out to brush her hair from her cheek. For a moment he held his hand there, feeling the warmth of her, willing it to hold.

And then he knew that it would. Even before she opened her eyes he knew that there was life in her.

Tears came to his eyes, and in his joy he cried out to Irodi.

TWENTY-FIVE

The rain was still falling in Tbilisi, but this was a different kind, mild and fertile, a spring rain in autumn. The woods above Iosava's house had begun to turn, and their fading green and burned orange glowed calmly in the wet.

The guard knew Hammer, and returned after only a minute to take him into the house and up to the first floor, where Iosava was standing at the window looking down at the square, a gray-looking man at his side. He dismissed him with an irascible wave of the hand as Hammer approached; his anger, always an undercurrent, felt present and intense.

"Sit." He continued to stare at some papers spread out in front of him.

"Bad news?"

Iosava looked up, his black eyes burning.

"My news not your business."

"But mine is yours." Hammer pulled a chair out, set it at an angle to the table, and sat down.

"I hear nothing. Four days, nothing."

"I figured you might be getting updates from someone else."

Iosava didn't understand. His eyes challenged Hammer's.

"I've come to tell you that I've failed. I haven't found what you needed."

This he understood. His chin jutted forward. "Bullshit."

"You wanted proof the president killed his own people to get elected. It doesn't exist. OK? He didn't do it."

"Bullshit."

"He didn't do it."

"Who?"

"I have a feeling you know who, but maybe I'm wrong." He took his phone from his pocket and passed it to Iosava. "Do you know who this is?"

On it was a photograph of Vekua, lying dead at the bottom of the cliff, her severe face ashen against the snow in the light of the flash.

Iosava studied it, and Hammer studied him. In a normal face something would have registered, but in his there was nothing. No recognition, not even blankness.

"You do," said Hammer. "She was at the airport."

"No," he said, and passed it back.

"She was Karlo's source. She planned the bomb. She also killed Karlo."

"She work for president."

Hammer leaned in and lowered his voice.

"Mr. Iosava, I don't know whether that's what you want to believe or what you're pretending to believe. But she had one client, and that was the Russians."

Iosava's dark eyes studied him, and not for the first time Hammer felt glad that he hadn't seen what they had seen.

"Bullshit. You talk bullshit."

Hammer smiled.

"Hey, maybe you didn't know. Maybe they don't trust you with the important stuff. Keep their assets separate. Anyway, she didn't make it. Seems she went to the mountains to tie up a loose end, shot a colleague of hers, and when the locals chased her she fell off a cliff. That's the story I want in your newspaper. OK? That's the story I want the police to believe. Nice and simple. Yes? I don't want to be involved and I don't think you do either."

Iosava sniffed, drummed his fingers on the table, and said nothing.

"I'm sure that suits you, but you come after anybody who had anything to do with this and someone's going to start having a good deep look at you. Understand? You're such a great buddy of the Russians, we'll find it. If you're not, we'll find something else. OK? Leave the story alone, and we can all live in peace."

"Webster. My money."

"I paid you back this morning. You're a hundred grand better off. Enjoy it. Buy yourself some soup."

Hammer stood. Iosava sat back, crossed his legs, and watched him with the air of a man who's been threatened before.

"You leave Georgia. Today."

"Oh, I'm leaving. With regret. This country doesn't deserve people like you. I'm going to come back when the place has calmed down."

"Will never happen," said Iosava, with a final glare.

Outside, Hammer crossed to the car with his face up to the sky, relishing the rain. Almost over.

He climbed in beside Natela; she opened the window wide and flicked her cigarette out, waving the last smoke away.

"Sorry."

"Don't be silly."

"OK?"

"OK," he said. "I think it's OK."

"Did he know?"

"Impossible to tell. It doesn't matter."

Under the stares of the drivers and the bodyguards he started the engine, reversed, and swung the 4 x 4 out of the square into the narrow street that led down the hill to the river.

"Forgive me," he said, and took his phone from his pocket. "One last call."

The line rang three times.

"It's me. How's the leg?"

"Working. Just."

"And your passport?"

"Easy. I told them I'd had a hiking accident and my old one was at the bottom of a ravine. They were very concerned."

"I'm amazed."

"They need to review their procedures." Webster paused. "So. How long before we get arrested?"

"I think we're fine. Everyone wants us gone. Listen, do me a favor, OK? Your friend the president's friend? Give him a call."

"Really?"

"Really. Tell him if one of their colonels should happen to die any time around now they should look closely at her connections with the Russians. Very closely."

"I'm not sure I get it."

"It's time for them to do some work. I'm tired of being involved."

"Of course you are. You hate being involved." Webster laughed. "I'll see you at the airport."

"You won't."

"Ike, I'm sure you've got everything sewn up, but you need to leave."

"I bought a car. We're going to Turkey."

"What's in Turkey?"

"The slow road home. I'm not ready for London."

"But you need to be. The interview."

"It's different now. You can give them the answers."

Webster said OK, in a way that suggested he wasn't sure. Hammer scarcely cared.

He glanced across at Natela, but she wasn't listening. Her eyes seemed to be on the furthest point of the road. Before, he might have wondered what she was thinking, but now he felt no need. He knew and he didn't know, and that was good.

"When you get back, soon as you've seen your family and they've decided if they still want you, go see Hibbert. He's expecting you. Figure out between you how we get the police on the right track. They need to be looking for whoever really gave Saber their instructions."

"I have some ideas."

"I'll be back in a few days in any case. Send my love to your wife and try not to fuck anything up on your way home."

"No more fucking up."

"Of course not."

Hammer hung up. They were by the river now, just one of a stream of cars heading out of the city.

"How is Ben?" said Natela.

"Same old."

"I like him."

"He could be worse."

For a while they drove in silence, Hammer watching the road and doing his best with the other drivers and occasionally looking over at Natela, her hair rippling in the wind from the open window.

"She really hit you, huh?"

She didn't understand.

"With the gun. Here." He pointed to her cheekbone, where a bruise had spread up around her eye. "Does it hurt?"

"It is better now that she is gone."

"It sure is," said Hammer. "It sure is."

The city began to fall behind them. Trucks appeared by the side of the road selling vegetables and honey. Soon they were out on the green plain, with the mountains just visible in the distance on either side.

"You want to stop in Batumi? I know a good place for dinner."

Natela shook her head. "Stop when we are out of Georgia."

TWENTY-SIX

The road felt like Koba's road. They passed the corner where he had refused to help the car in the ditch, passed Gori, passed the point where the motherfuckers had made their first call. Hammer wondered where his computer was now, and what had happened to the boy who had lived.

A hundred dollars a day for the versatile Koba; some bargain that had been. He should have been wary of his presence from the start, the confidence, all that purposeful jollity that had felt so reassuring. Still, he owed the man his life, in a sense, and this opportunity: if Koba had been less greedy, if he'd played it straight with Vekua, the two of them could have done as they pleased with their two captives and there would have been no return journey to make.

The thought troubled Hammer, though he wasn't sure why, and to take his mind from it he asked Natela for a cigarette, which she gave him with a look of pleased bemusement, and for a long time as the road slipped by they talked, about things of consequence and others of no consequence at all. The rain cleared and the sun began to cut across them through the clouds, and when they finally reached the sea they turned to the south, so that the light was glaring off the wet tarmac and Hammer, doing his best with the unruly traffic around them, had to squint hard to see. He didn't mind. He was exhausted but not drained, full of some deeper energy that he hadn't felt for some time.

The road ran parallel to the coast now, sometimes through thickly wooded hills and sometimes by the water. Ten miles beyond Batumi the traffic slowed and they came to a stop in a queue of cars high above a strip of beach that gave onto the calm gray and green of the Black Sea. Just ahead of them the road curved round the side of a hill, so that Hammer couldn't see the cause of the delay.

"Border," said Natela. "Will take time."

This was predictable, of course, but until now the way had been so clear that Hammer felt a faint stab of anxiety prick his mood, like an echo of the fears that had first brought him here. Scenes from the riot and that first traffic jam flashed across his mind. He wanted to be gone, he realized, in a place that had no hold over either of them. Free. Nothing more than that.

Natela smoked continuously, and from time to time he joined her. The comfort lay in the companionship, he told himself, but the truth was his nerves needed it. As the queue slowly shortened he watched the surf and the handful of people who played in the waves, did his best to enjoy the faint breeze that did little to soften the heat pressing against the car. He wondered aloud what could be taking so long, and she told him that there were two sets of border guards, one Georgian, one Turkish, and that the only power they had in the world was to make people wait.

Hammer drove up to the barrier, one of a dozen in a low, modern building that stretched across a huge forecourt right to the beach. He cut the engine. Two Georgian border guards in green uniforms and peaked caps came to his window, and he handed over the two passports. The first guard, a round man with bad skin and broken veins across his cheeks, gave Natela's to his colleague, who walked round the front of the car, asked Natela to wind her window fully down, and then stared at her hard for a full ten seconds before leafing deliberately through every page.

Hammer watched him closely, resenting the bullying manner, the petty exercise of a petty power. He was skinny and sharp, and his jacket and shirt hung loosely off his frame, as if he was filling in for a larger man. Then he spoke, a command, and opened Natela's door. She looked at Hammer, and her face had lost its habitual calm. Whatever the guard had said, he repeated it.

"What does he want?"

"He says there is problem."

"What problem?"

"I don't know."

Natela turned to the guard and asked him, Hammer guessed, to elaborate. He grunted something in response.

"He says my passport is wrong. Too old."

"Is it?"

"No. No, it is OK."

There was no one left who had any interest in keeping them here. The story was over. Controlling his fear and his anger, Hammer leaned forward in his seat and looked across at the guard, who again told Natela to get out. Hammer hated every gaunt bit of him.

"How much does he want?"

Natela frowned, with that seriousness he loved in her, but behind her disapproval he could tell she was scared.

"Isaac."

"Either we're his bonus for the day or someone's telling him to do this. So he has his price."

"Always the answer is money."

"That's his choice. Not mine."

The first guard banged on the top of his car with an open hand; the second shouted, a single syllable. As Natela got down from the cab Hammer made to open his door but his guard held it shut.

"I'm with her," he said. "Let me out." But the guard kept his hand against the metal and told him in Georgian that he wasn't going anywhere. The unease Hammer had been feeling now built to something like panic.

"Natela, listen. This needs to come from me. Tell him you're translating what I say. Tell him when I came into the country I failed to declare some goods, and I'm feeling bad about it, and I'd like to pay the extra now."

Natela looked back at him, and with his eyes he tried to tell her that he wasn't a bad man, and that she must know this. That he understood this world.

"Just tell him."

Her eyes challenged his but eventually she nodded, turned, and spoke to the guard, slowly and coolly—how much greater she was than the little men who held power over her, Hammer thought. How much he loved her for it. The guard glanced at Hammer, and at first his expression suggested that everything would be all right, that a simple transaction was going to be enough. But then his face grew dark, and shaking his head he shut the car door and began to walk away, motioning for Natela to follow.

"Isaac?" This time it was a question, but he had nothing for her—no understanding, no ideas. If they weren't on the take, these two were following instructions, and the instructions were specific. Who benefited from this? Who even knew that he and Natela were here?

"Hold on. Hold on." He turned to the guard at his window, somehow still managing to keep his voice and his temper under control.

"Wait. Wait, OK? Telephone. OK?"

The guard simply looked at him, his expression between a sneer and a smile. Shouting something over the roof of the 4 x 4 he made some signal with his free hand, and the barrier opened.

The skinny guard had Natela by the sleeve now and was starting to lead her away from the car. Hammer shouted across.

"Tell him to wait. Tell him I'm calling his boss."

Natela said it, and the guard hesitated. The mood changed, just a fraction.

"I'm going to straighten this out."

He found the number and dialed. On the third ring came a croaked yes, in English, the voice low and cracked.

"OK. Listen to me. I'm at the border and I'm having some problems. I'm hoping you can make them go away."

"Like this you ask for help."

"They're stopping a friend of mine leaving the country. There's no reason for it, and I thought of you."

Natela watched him, her eyes no longer scared. There was a sadness in them that he had seen before.

"I let you leave." Iosava's voice was the same dry rumble.

"She's leaving with me."

"You cannot have all you want. No one can have."

"That's what this is? The last laugh?"

"Georgian problem stay in Georgia. Give phone to guard."

Hammer hesitated. He looked at Natela, whose dark eyes seemed to contain some deep understanding, as if she had always known that their paths could not run together. Her hair was tied back and loose strands at the nape of her neck waved in the wind. The guard still had his hand on her arm, and the sight of it crystallized Hammer's fury, and his helplessness.

"No tricks," he said to Iosava, and passed the phone through the window.

The guard listened for a moment, the smile gone, stood slightly more erect, nodded deeply, and said three or four words in Georgian. Then he hung up with a fat, clumsy thumb, put the phone in his trouser pocket, took two steps back from the car, and pulled out the gun from its holster on his waist.

"Go." He nodded at the Turkish border. "Tsavidet. Go."

Hammer shook his head and breathed deeply, in search of some final piece of inspiration that he knew would not come. Natela was trying to shrug off her guard, but his hold was strong and he was pulling her away now, making her stumble on the tarmac.

"I'll come for you," Hammer shouted, his voice loud and powerless. All there was in her eyes was good-bye, and it terrified him.

"They will not allow."

Gun up, his legs set apart, the other guard bellowed at him again to go.

"There's a way."

There was always a way. There had to be.

Natela held her eyes on his until she had no choice but to turn.